DOC SIDHE

AARON ALLSTON

Doc Sidhe

A Baen Books Original

Baen Publishing Enterprises
P.O. Box 1403
Riverdale, NY 10471

ISBN: 0-671-87662-7

Cover art by David Mattingly

First printing, May 1995

Distributed by Simon & Schuster
1230 Avenue of the Americas
New York, NY 10020

Typeset by Windhaven Press, Auburn, NH
Printed in the United States of America

Acknowledgements

Thanks go to Randy Greer, Ray Greer, Steven Long, Beth Loubet, Denis Loubet, Steve Peterson, Luray Richmond, Allen Varney, and Toni Weisskopf for research and advice.

Mistakes in this novel remain only in spite of the contributions of these people.

Dedication

To Lester Dent and Walter B. Gibson, who left before I could say thanks; and to Tom Allston and Rose Boehm, who didn't. Thanks, guys.

CHAPTER ONE

The Smile mocked him.

It was Sonny Walters' smile, sweat-dewed in the middle of the man's hardwood-brown face. It wasn't a friendly smile. It promised pain.

Harris Greene advanced anyway, his gloved hands high, his body constantly moving. Walters, with the longer reach, could afford to stand back and fight at distance; Harris had to play the aggressor, constantly closing.

Harris started the round with a snapkick to Walters' ribcage. Walters brought his left arm down to take the shot just above the elbow. Harris stepped in close, threw a right jab at the same ribs, then spun around counter-clockwise.

Harris Greene's patented Spinning Backfist. He should have come out of the spin with his left fist slamming into Walters' blocking forearm or, better yet, his unprotected head. But instead he unloaded the blow into empty air, the Smile somehow magically transported just beyond his reach. The exertion kept Harris spinning a fraction of a turn too far, leaving him out of position.

Walters' right hook came up out of nowhere and took Harris on the point of his jaw. The blow rocked his head and he staggered a half-step back.

It didn't really hurt, but bright little lights appeared

in his vision, tiny fireflies dancing in front of him; he ignored them and kept moving backwards, buying time to recover.

But his feet wouldn't cooperate. His back and head slammed into the canvas before he ever felt off balance. The crowd roared its approval.

They hadn't yelled for Harris once during the match. He could smell the stink of their sweat, stronger than his own odor or Walters', and for a moment he hated them—beer-chugging, screaming, sweating, cousin-fondling morons who should have been at home with their families but instead came to cheer while Harris Greene took a beating.

Already they counted him a loser. They were just waiting for him to prove them right.

Harris rolled up to a kneeling position and waited. The dancing stars began to fade. When the referee's count reached seven, he stood. He forced his features back into his war-face, all glowering eyes and sullen expression, just as he'd practiced a hundred times for the mirror, but he was no longer sure who he was doing it for. The referee got out from between the two men and signaled for them to resume.

Harris forced himself to move forward again, straight for the Smile.

Miles away, on Manhattan, Carlo Salvanelli sat in a cardboard box.

It was a good box. Twelve weeks ago it had held a brand-new Whirlpool refrigerator, Model #ED25DQ, almond-colored with water and ice dispensers right there in the freezer door. It had stood resolutely upright after the work-men unloaded it; as soon as the workmen had turned their backs, Carlo had grabbed the box from just inside the delivery dock and made off with it.

Carlo didn't know how far past seventy years old he was, but he was in good shape: lean, with all his own teeth, still graceful, health good in spite of the way he lived. He was certainly sound enough to run off with a refrigerator box and be safely away before the workmen came back.

Now the box sat lengthwise up against the alley wall. The alley was an even bigger stroke of luck than the box; the manager of the apartments behind him let him stay there, even gave him the combination to the gate that blocked the alley mouth, just for hauling a little trash and mopping a few floors.

Between the new box and the sheltered alley, this had been a better winter than the last one. Maybe the new year would give him a job, a real home.

Someone rapped on the end of the box.

Carlo jolted in surprise. His hearing was keen. Had Mr. Montague come out through the alley door of his building, had someone come in through the creaking gate at the alley end, Carlo would have heard it. But there had been no sound.

At a loss, he called, "Come in."

The visitor pulled open the box flaps and probed around with a flashlight beam that caught and blinded Carlo. Then the visitor turned the light on himself.

He was a silver-haired man, Carlo's age. That was the only similarity between them; in contrast to Carlo's tattered, unwashed jeans and flannel shirt, this man wore an elegant silk suit, a long coat of lined black leather, a red scarf, a new fedora—nobody wore fedoras anymore. No one but old men.

The visitor smiled reassuringly at Carlo. "May I come in?"

"I—of course." Carlo squirmed. He'd never had a visitor to a box that served him as home, and the visitor's elegance reminded him pointedly of the shabbiness of his clothes, of his few belongings. He knew he smelled bad, and he was suddenly embarrassed.

The visitor slid in and sat, like Carlo, tinker-style with his back to the side of the box against the alley wall. He took a moment to pull the box flaps closed. "I apologize for visiting you under these circumstances. But I'm used to seizing opportunities where I find them." His pronunciation was precise, his accent a little odd; German, perhaps. Carlo couldn't tell; his own speech was still heavily flavored, and English was sometimes hard for him. "I'm looking for some men to do some work for me. Special men. I think you're one of them. Tell me, are you currently employed?"

Carlo shook his head and waved a hand at the sleeping bag and backpack that made up his possessions. "I am between employments."

"Good. I mean, that's good for me. Tell me, uh—"

"Carlo. Carlo Salvanelli."

"One of the Salvanelli. Of course. Tell me, Carlo, do you like the outdoors? Forests, trees?"

Carlo beamed. "Yes, very much. I am a city boy, but I love the country."

"And do you remember much about the old country?"

Carlo hesitated. "I came to America very young."

"Not too young. Your accent is very pronounced." The visitor leaned forward and his voice became low, conspiratorial. "And we're not talking about Italy, either. Are we?"

Carlo looked at his visitor, at the man's eager, encouraging expression, and hesitated before shaking his head. "Italy, no."

"Symaithia, I'd say, to judge from your accent."

Carlo's eyes widened. "Yes, Symaithia. But the doctors, they said it was all imagination, that I should stop thinking about it. How you know about Symaithia?"

"The doctors were wrong. Poor Carlo. I imagine no one took you seriously. It must have been impossible to keep a job, to make friends." The visitor shifted, drawing even closer. "Tell me, Carlo, this is very important. Have you ever met anyone like yourself? From the old country? Not just Symaithia. Anywhere."

"Oh, no. Never." Carlo started as a tear dropped from his cheek onto his hand; shamed, he reached up to dry his eyes. "All my life, I think that the doctors are right.

That I must have been in an accident, hurt my head, dreamed everything about the old country. You are real? You are not some new dream?" He looked up again into his visitor's sympathetic eyes.

"I'm no dream." The visitor reached into one of his coat pockets and brought out something dark and glinting. "Carlo, I think you're just exactly the man I want, but I need to know one more thing. Can you handle one of these?"

Carlo looked down at the gleaming metal object in his visitor's hands. "A gun? Yes, of course. I fought for America in World War Two. I need gloves. Why will I need to use a gun?"

The visitor smiled again. "Come to think of it, you won't." He aimed and pulled the trigger.

The blast hammered Carlo's ears and fire tore through his chest.

For a moment he could not move. He just stared uncomprehendingly at his visitor. Then he looked down at the hole over his heart.

Blood pooled slowly out of the hole. A hole in his best shirt . . . it was so hard to get bloodstains out of clothes, and there would be the hole to sew up. And another in the back of the shirt, where he felt more wetness and pain.

He looked at the man with the gun. "Why you do this?"

"Hush." The visitor brought the barrel of the automatic to within an inch of Carlo's forehead and fired again.

The old man looked down at the body of Carlo Salvanelli. Satisfied that no life remained, he wriggled back out of the box and stood.

His two men waited a few yards off. Phipps, the small one, a mere four inches above six feet, stood in the alley's patch of moonlight. The big one kept back in the shadows.

Phipps stepped forward, looming solicitously over the old man. "You okay?"

"Of course. I enjoy doing this sort of thing from time

to time. Good for the constitution." The elderly gentleman pocketed his gun, then reached up to straighten Phipps' collar. "Though we should leave now. You just can't count on the police not to come. Now, you're sure about this other one?"

The small one nodded. "I had the meter out and on her for four or five minutes. She's a good, strong signal. But as far as I've been able to determine, she really was born here."

"Then I don't think she'll join poor Carlo right away. I may need to send her home for study first."

The three moved away down the alley, leaving Carlo Salvanelli alone in the box that served him as home.

Harris Greene sat on the stool in his corner and concentrated on keeping his war-face on. It wasn't easy; dizziness and weariness tugged at him, and Zeb was talking. Talking and talking.

"Dammit, Harris, you're being too predictable. The same combinations over and over. Mix it up more. He's onto your backfist; forget about it. Work on his gut. I think he's still hurting from the Helberson fight. And watch out when you close with him. When you make the transition between your range and his, in or out, that's when he's nailing you."

Harris accepted a mouthful of water from the trainer's bottle, then swallowed it instead of spitting. He stared for a long moment at the PKC banner on the auditorium wall, at the crowd that had shouted for his blood just a few minutes ago, and he turned to look at Zeb. "I'm going to lose," he said.

Zeb Watson stared back at him, hard-eyed. Black, bearded, intense, he'd once been a fighter and could still project the attitude. His gaze was like a knife raking at Harris' face. "No, you're not. You can take him. You have more than he does. Just do what I say and *stop thinking* so much!"

The warning whistle sounded. Zeb cursed, slipped the

plastic guard back into Harris' mouth, and slipped out of the ring. Harris rose. The bell sounded, announcing the fifth round.

Harris got underway, resumed his erratic up-and-down, right-and-left motion, and headed toward the Smile again.

It took only a few moments. Walters switched tactics, went on the offensive, drove Harris into a corner. Harris blocked the blows coming in at his ribs, saw an opening, and automatically threw his backfist again. He felt Walters draw away from him.

Walters, still in retreat, caught the backfist on his left glove, then kicked high. His foot slammed into Harris' temple, a blast of pain as sharp and distinct as a cymbal crash from a symphony, and Harris watched through gray fog as the canvas rose up to slap him.

Cheers rolled over him. The crowd loved it. Damn them.

He got up. It took a while. The referee talked to him, and Harris didn't understand his words. Maybe it wasn't English. Maybe he was just concentrating too hard on staying upright to make sense of his speech. Then the referee went away and the crowd roared again.

Harris saw Sonny Walters dancing around, his arms high. The Smile had won. The Smile had been right all along. Harris headed for his corner. The faces there weren't smiling.

It took Harris a long time to tie his shoe. There didn't seem to be any reason to do it faster. And this way he didn't have to look up, to stare into disappointed faces.

Zeb sat on the locker-room bench in front of him and cleared his throat. "Harris, I think we're done."

"Okay. I'll see you Monday." *Good. Just leave. Don't make me look at you.*

"No, that's not what I mean. I think you and I are done. I can't work with you anymore."

Finally Harris did look up, into Zeb's sympathetic, set expression. "What do you mean?"

"Harris, why did you get into kick-boxing?"

"Same reason you did."

"No, tell me."

Harris thought back. "Two Olympics on the tae kwon do team. I didn't take any medals, but hey, I was a kid for the first one. Everybody seemed to think I could go all the way. Be a champion. That's what it was. I wanted to be a champ."

"Wanted."

"Want. I still want it."

"I don't think so." Zeb sighed. "Harris, you *are* a champion . . . in practice. In training, nobody can match you. You've got more speed and power than anyone your size. But when it turns into a competition, when the fight becomes real, you just fold up."

Harris felt a lump form in his throat as he realized Zeb meant it. "You're really cutting me loose, aren't you?"

"As a fighter, yeah. That's business. I need to manage fighters who are going to have careers. That's not you. But I'm not cutting you loose as a friend."

"Thanks." Harris looked back at his shoe. He pulled the knot out and began tying it again.

"Are you seeing Gaby tonight?"

"Yeah. We're having dinner." Great. He'd have to tell her, too. *Gaby, you know how I don't exactly have a job? Well, I just got fired anyway.*

"Are you two serious?"

"Yeah."

"You going to marry her?"

"Yeah."

"Good."

Harris heard the silence stretch out, felt the awkwardness grow between them. He ignored it, not letting Zeb off the hook. By millimeters, he adjusted the size of the bow in his shoelace.

Finally, Zeb held his hand out.

Harris looked at it a moment, then took it. "Okay, Zeb."

"You going to be all right?"

"Sure."

"You might think about teaching. Lotta schools out there would be happy to have you."

"Sure."

"Give me a call." Zeb left, looking nearly as gloomy as Harris felt.

Two Olympic appearances down the toilet.

What the hell. His life wasn't over. He had a great girlfriend and a pair of well-tied shoes.

Gaby was waiting for him on the sidewalk outside the Chinese restaurant. He spotted her from the corner across the street and took an extra minute just to watch her, as he always did when he had the chance.

She was an Aztec princess by way of *Elle* magazine. With her high cheekbones and blacker-than-night hair, she took after her Mexican mother more than her Irish-American father. She wore jeans and a simple red silk blouse with confidence enough to suggest that she surpassed the dress code of the island's trendiest club. At this distance, he couldn't see her eyes, but he knew the way they looked at everything, focusing on this and dismissing that with intensity and razory speed.

Then she spotted him. He expected her broad, welcoming smile, but all she did was wave. He crossed the street and joined her.

She looked at his battered face and winced, then stretched up on tiptoe to give him a quick kiss. "How'd it go?"

"Well, you'd know if you'd been there."

"Yes, I know. I'm sorry. Let's go in, I'm starved."

He held the door open for her. "So, what were you up to today?"

"Tell you later."

He ordered shrimp fried rice; she just asked for a cup of wonton soup. When the waitress left, he said, "I thought you were starving."

"I am. Well, sort of starving." She looked uncomfortable and shut up.

He let the silence hang between them for a moment. "Well, I've got some news," he said, just as she said, "I need to talk about something."

They both smiled at the awkwardness.

Harris didn't feel like smiling. Maybe she wanted to move in together. He didn't think he was ready for that. Maybe she even wanted to set a date. Oh, God; maybe, in spite of their precautions, she was pregnant. "You go first," he said.

"No, you."

"No, you."

"Okay." She took a deep breath. "Harris, I think maybe we . . . ought to kind of go our separate ways."

He put his head down on the table.

"Harris?"

"What?"

"Did you understand me?"

"I don't think so." He straightened up. Maybe she was speaking the same language as the referee earlier tonight. Taken apart, the words were English; put together, they made no sense.

"Harris, it's not working."

"What's not working?"

"*We're* not working. Out. Working out."

"The hell we're not. How are we not working out? We hardly ever fight."

"I know we don't. You're one of the *nicest* men I've ever met."

"Am I lousing up your career? Did your parents forget to tell me that they hate me?"

"Nothing like that."

"Is there another guy?"

"No."

"Another *girl*?"

She almost smiled. "Harris."

"Look, if it's *my* career choice, let me tell you, I just went through a big change."

"No."

"Gaby, I love you." There they were, the magic words. He'd never had any problem saying them. He meant them.

He waited, but this time she didn't say them back. She just gave him a look full of hurtful sympathy.

"Oh, Jesus." He slumped back in his chair. "When did this happen?"

"Harris." She closed her eyes for a moment. When she opened them again, he knew she'd found the words. "I think the world of you. I don't want to lose you as a friend. But . . . well, this is *my* fault. I keep expecting you to be something you're not."

"Which is what? Just where exactly do I fall short?" He searched her face for a clue.

She moved like a butterfly impaled on a pin, struggling with words that didn't seem to want to come out. "I don't think I can describe it."

"Try." His voice fell to a whisper. "I can change."

It was the wrong thing to say. He'd never known he could sound so pathetic. Suddenly he knew why she was doing this. He'd become a neighborhood dog and she was the woman he'd followed home.

He wouldn't want a dog, either.

Her next words were the rocks thrown to drive him off. "I think I need my keys back." She set down his own apartment key beside his silverware, then wiped at the tear that threatened to roll down her cheek.

He looked at the key. She didn't even want to come out to his doghouse anymore. He almost laughed.

He pulled out his keychain and wrestled her building and apartment keys off the metal coil. He set them down in front of her.

She put them in her fanny pack and zipped it up. Her voice was low, pained. "Good-bye, Harris." And she left.

Harris watched the door swing closed behind her. "Zeb should've put you in the ring tonight," he said. "You would've pounded Sonny flat."

The waitress set Gaby's soup down in front of him.

What the hell. His life wasn't over. He had a great bowl of wonton soup and a pair of well-tied shoes.

CHAPTER TWO

Phipps looked up as Gaby come out of the restaurant.

An interesting change. Before, she'd been alert. Now she walked with her head down, hands stuffed into her jeans pockets. A more likely target for a mugger. Phipps might actually have to protect her. The irony amused him.

The guy in the jeans jacket, the one who'd met her at the door, didn't come out with her. Phipps liked that. One less complication, assuming that she didn't hook up with him again later.

He glanced at his watch. Three hours until midnight. All he had to do was keep near her for a couple more hours and everything would be all right. He gathered up his newspaper and blended in with the sidewalk traffic as he followed her.

There was still some of the Stolichnaya in his cabinet. Harris uncapped it and carried it to his sagging couch. Gaby would be annoyed with him for treating the expensive vodka like common booze. He looked forward to that.

On the end table was the file full of newspaper clippings his mother had sent him over the years. He groaned when he saw it. That's a call he didn't want to make. *Hi, Mom, Dad. You know all that money you spent to support*

*me while I beat people up in New York? Uncle Charlie
was right: you wasted it.*

He picked up the folder and shuffled through the clippings.

Some of it was college paper stuff about the theater
productions he'd been involved with: a picture of him
onstage in *Death of a Salesman*, another of him back-
stage doing his own makeup for *Ethan Frome*. But the
majority of stories were about tae kwon do.

So many tournaments, competitions, demonstrations.
His home-town newspaper had glowingly reported his
Olympic career. It even made his first-round loss in Seoul
sound like a moral victory. It wasn't; he'd just gone out
there and gotten clobbered.

Harris looked at the pictures of the happy, cocky, eager
kid he used to be. Dark hair, features that looked brooding
even when he was happy. "A soap opera hero face," Gaby
had said a long time ago. "You ought to go over to NBC
and try out for a part. Put that theater major to some
good use for once."

He tipped the bottle up and took a pull on it, felt the
liquor burn down his throat. Maybe he'd do that now.
They'd hire him to be the next bare-chested hunk. Gaby
would be channel-surfing and would spot him licking the
tonsils of some soap opera sweetheart. She'd drop her
teeth.

The thought warmed him. Or maybe that was the
vodka. He took another swallow.

Later, when the bottle barely sloshed as he set it down,
it occurred to Harris that it was time to talk some sense
into her. He needed to get out of the apartment anyway; ever since it had started rocking he'd felt seasick.
Fresh air would help.

Down on the sidewalk, he tried to take another drink,
but lifted a wad of newsprint to his mouth.

He stared accusingly at his hand. It had brought the
wrong stuff. It failed him even when he wasn't throwing a backfist with it.

He smoothed out the wad of paper and smiled down at the expectation and hope he saw in his own younger face.

Then, with meticulous care, he tore the first article's headline free and let it flutter to the sidewalk. That felt good. Half a dozen words he no longer had to live up to.

Walking toward Gaby's home, he ripped loose another strip of words.

Gaby got her apartment door closed and threw the three deadbolts on it.

Her feet hurt. She must have walked for two hours after she left Harris.

And she still hadn't eaten. Small wonder. That talk had killed her appetite. She wondered if she'd be hungry again before summer.

Someone knocked on the front door, startling her. Her visitor must have come up the stairs right behind her. Gaby put her eye to the peephole.

Her visitor was an old man, elegantly dressed, his face merry—the perfect grandfather, obviously rich and good-natured. It had to be one of the other tenants; she hadn't buzzed anyone into the building. She'd never seen him before. "Who is it?" she asked.

"Miss, ah, Gabriela Donohue?"

"That's right." She waited patiently; no need to unlock the door, no matter how innocuous he looked, until he satisfied her that she had a reason to.

"Thank you," he said. Then he stepped away from the door, out of sight.

Someone moved in to take his place. It was a man in a dark overcoat, so tall that she could not see above the knot of his gray necktie, so wide that he seemed to match the door in breadth. Gaby took an involuntary step back.

There was a sharp *bang!* and the door crashed down, its locks and hinges shattered; it fell against Gaby and staggered her. Beyond, the huge man was striding forward, and the old man and another intruder came close behind. . . .

Gaby felt icy terror grip her stomach. She turned and ran. She had to reach her bedroom, the fire escape outside her window—

The huge man caught up to her before she reached the door to her room. He hit her like someone might swat a puppy. The blow took her on the hip and spun her to the floor, sent her rolling into the corner with her TV.

She stared up at him and got a good look at what served him as a face.

The sight froze the breath in her lungs. She sat unmoving as he came at her.

Harris dropped the last piece of the last article and watched it float off into the darkness.

There. A paper trail led from his apartment to Gaby's Greenwich Village brownstone. She could find her way back to him now.

From the corner, he looked up at her fourth-story window, saw that it was still lit. She was awake, obviously waiting for him.

The main entrance's outer door was unlocked. Not so with the inner door. He stood there fiddling with his keychain for a couple of minutes before he remembered that she'd taken his key.

Dammit. He'd have to climb the fire escape. On the other hand, she used to like that.

Would that make him a stalker? He frowned over that one. Maybe he'd follow her around until she got scared and got a restraining order and he did something stupid and they made a TV-movie about him. The thought bothered him.

He went around to the 11th Street side of the building and looked up at the fire escape. It seemed higher than usual. There was a car, actually a stretch limo, illegally parked near it, and he debated trying a jump from its roof, but decided that was impolite.

It took him three jumps to catch the bottom of the fire escape, and a greater effort than usual to haul himself up onto its bottom level. He must have gained weight, too, because his exertion set this whole part of the world rocking just like his apartment. He lay there resting while he waited for the world to steady itself.

Below him, three men in dressy long coats came around the corner and headed for the limo. One was an old man, but the second was big like a football player. The third one, the one with the hat worn low and the big, lumpy duffel bag over his shoulder, was so tall that Harris could have reached down and plucked his hat off, so broad that bodybuilders could have bitten small pieces off him for a steroid fix. It was probably a good thing that Harris hadn't left footprints all over their limo.

The old man was saying, "—plenty of time to get to the great lawn, but there's no sense in dilly-dallying." Then they were climbing into the limo, slamming doors, driving off.

Leaving Harris alone.

Resting was nice, but Gaby was still two stories up. He reluctantly rose and began climbing the narrow, shaky metal steps of the fire escape.

Gaby floated up into wakefulness. The side of her face still hurt where *he*—

She veered away from thinking about *him*. This wasn't hard. There was plenty to occupy her attention.

She was folded up in fetal position, wrapped in what felt like heavy linen. The air was so close and warm she found it hard to breathe. She was being jolted up and down, but was up against a hard surface: muscle over bone, someone's back, a very broad back.

His back. She was being carried.

She groped around as much as she could—not easy, as she was tightly pinned—and reached over her head. There was a small hole above her, drawn nearly closed by cords; she twisted and looked up through it, seeing nighttime clouds.

She was in a bag. They'd stuffed her into a duffel bag and were carrying her around like so much laundry.

Laundry. Fully awake and furious, she shoved up against the hole and shouted, "Hey! Call the police! I'm being kidnapped! Can anyone hear me?"

He didn't slacken his pace, but Gaby felt a sharp knock against the side of her head. It hurt. She stopped shoving; she rubbed where the blow had landed. "Hey!"

It was the old man's voice: "If you make any more noise, Miss Donohue, I'm going to have Adonis here let you out of the bag and punish you. It wants to punish you. It will enjoy doing so."

And she felt a rumbling from the back of the thing carrying her. It sounded like deep, quiet laughter.

Her stomach went cold. Adonis' face—God, what was he? She didn't want to look at that face again. She didn't want to see it turn angry. And she understood, with crystal certainty, that the moves she'd once learned in self-defense class were not going to impress *him*.

She sat still.

After another minute of walking, Adonis swung her down. She didn't hit the ground hard, but she landed on a sharp rock hard enough to bruise her rear.

The old man spoke again. "Just relax here for a few minutes and everything will be fine. We don't want to hurt you." His accent sounded strange—as though it were part German, part English.

She said, "Can I ask you something?"

"No. Be silent."

Fuming, she did as she was told.

Harris trotted along the tree-lined footpath and prayed to God he'd heard right. Prayed that Mr. Crenshaw had done as Harris had asked. But Harris had completed almost an entire circuit around Central Park's Great Lawn and had seen nothing but a pair of tough-looking kids who'd eyed him speculatively as he ran past.

When he'd reached Gaby's window on the fire escape,

he'd looked in and seen a man in a bathrobe—thin, balding Mr. Crenshaw, Gaby's neighbor—talking on the phone in Gaby's bedroom. Crenshaw looked alarmed as he talked, and hung up almost as soon as Harris spotted him.

Harris knocked on the window, and Crenshaw went from his usual sunless color to nearly true white. Then the man recognized Harris. He threw open the window and started babbling.

"Someone took her, a really huge son of a bitch. Her door's all over the living room. Thank God they didn't see me. I've called the police . . ."

Something like an electrical current jolted Harris. All of a sudden he had a hard time breathing. On the other hand, he didn't feel drunk anymore.

He told Mr. Crenshaw what he'd heard the old man say. "Call the police again, tell them what I saw." Then he ran back down the fire escape.

Now, as he reached the footpath opposite the Met, the point where he'd started his circuit of the Great Lawn, he had no illusions that he wasn't drunk. Keeping his balance while he ran was an interesting effort, and whenever he stood still, his surroundings spun slowly counterclockwise. At least he was alert.

No sign of the three guys or Gaby. Maybe the old man was talking about the really great lawn he had in front of his house in Queens or something. Harris cursed and turned off the footpath, crossing through a fringe of trees onto the grass of the Great Lawn itself. It spread out before him, a featureless plain of darkness.

Please, God, let him find Gaby. And if he couldn't find her right away, please give him a mugger. Someone he could beat and beat in order to release the howling fear and rage he felt building inside him.

As he was making his second crossing of the lawn he saw them. Three reverse silhouettes off in the darkness, given away by their tan coats. He turned their way and trotted as quietly as he could. In his jeans, jeans jacket, and dark shirt, he thought maybe he wouldn't be spotted too fast.

When he was a few yards away he was sure it was them, and he could see the duffel bag resting on the ground several yards from them. It lay on a line of white rocks twenty feet long.

He was confused. A second line crossed the first at right angles in the middle. The two lines were surrounded by a circle of more white rocks.

X Marks the Spot. Under other circumstances, he would have laughed.

The three men were huddled, talking, just outside the circle of stones, and still hadn't seen him. He picked up speed, saw the old man notice his presence and turn.

He came up off his jumping foot and brought the same leg up before him in extension—a flying side kick he could tell was picture-perfect. It took the biggest man in the side and the impact jarred Harris from foot to gut.

The huge man felt as though he were made of skin stretched over Jell-O, but he still fell over backwards, hissing out a gasp of air. Harris hit the ground hard but scrambled up instantly. "Gaby?"

The bag said, "Harris?" and her arm reached out of it.

The old man merely said, "Mine." He took a step toward Harris and reached under his coat.

Harris saw the glint of the gun's slide in the moonlight. He threw a hard block, cracking his forearm into the older man's wrist, and the pistol went flying into the darkness.

The old man stepped back, grabbing at his wrist and frowning. "Phipps, I need this young man removed. Adonis, get up."

"Gaby, get the hell out of here!"

The man with the football player's build stood his ground and pulled something out from under his armpit.

Harris felt fear clutching at him, but he charged and

side-kicked just as Phipps got his revolver out into the open. His kick connected, driving the man's arm hard into his chest, cracking something, knocking the man clean off his feet.

The gun dropped, but Phipps sat up and scrabbled around for it with his good arm. Harris stepped forward again and rotated through a spinning side kick, straight out of tournament demonstrations, and felt a satisfying crack as his foot connected. Phipps flopped back hard, his head banging on the ground.

Harris almost grinned. From the opening bell to the knockout, one point five seconds. Not bad for a drunk loser. He bent over, grabbed up Phipps' revolver, and swung it around to aim.

The huge man's gloved hand clamped on the barrel and yanked. The gun fired into nothingness and came out of Harris' grip, stinging his hand. The huge man flung it off into the darkness. With his free hand, he pulled his hat away from his head and looked down at Harris. Moonlight illuminated his face.

With his build, he couldn't be old. But his skin, cinnamon brown, hung in packed layers of wrinkles like earthworms laid lengthwise. No mouth or ears were discernible, but there were eyes, animal's eyes, deep in the mass of wrinkles. Harris took an involuntary step back, looking for the sign, the seam that proved this was a mask.

But the mouth opened. It was too large and wide to belong to any human. No man or woman possessed a forest of sharklike teeth like those. This was no mask. It twisted into a smile.

The Smile mocked him.

CHAPTER THREE

Gaby shoved her way out of the bag and looked around frantically. No one was paying her any attention.

Just yards away was the broad back of Adonis. The big . . . thing . . . was moving away from her. Toward Harris.

He looked scared. No wonder. He was looking right into Adonis' face. But he dropped into his tae kwon do stance and shouted, "Gaby, run!"

Gaby scrambled to her feet and hesitated. She couldn't just run out on Harris. But, no, if she could get over to the street, maybe she could flag down a cop. That's what everybody needed just now. She turned and bolted.

Right into the old man's arms.

He grabbed her almost tenderly, but he was a lot stronger than an elderly businessman should be. "You can't leave," he said, calmly, persuasively. "It's only half a minute until—"

"You *bastard*." She kneed him in the balls.

His testicles seemed to have been in good working order; he bent over with a grunt of surprise and pain, but he didn't let go. She kneed him again, then slammed the edge of her heel down across his ankle. This time he did let go, staggering to one side. She ran.

One last glance for Harris. He was still up, his body

angling back as he directed a kick against Adonis' knee. She heard the crack of the impact but wasn't surprised when Adonis didn't fall or react to the blow. Harris wobbled from the exertion but was still fast enough to elude Adonis' quick return blow.

Then Gaby got up to speed and raced toward the concealment of the trees.

Harris heard her go but kept his eye on his opponent. The thing called Adonis was big and fast, and the sharp bits on the ends of its wrinkled fingers looked suspiciously like *claws* . . . and Harris was still drunk. He had to stay focused, now more than in any match he'd ever fought.

Harris backed away, staying just outside the thing's easy range, and circled around his opponent. Adonis came at him again, swinging a paw as big as a tennis racquet; Harris danced backward, saw how his opponent's too-energetic swings were pulling him off balance. Another missed slash with those claws, and Harris darted in, planting a hard side kick into Adonis' gut. He scrambled back before Adonis could recover. Adonis' mockery of a face twisted in something like pain. So it *could* be hurt.

Movement in his peripheral vision: the old man was up, his face a mask of anger; he limped in the direction Gaby had fled. But he was moving so slowly there was little chance he'd catch her. At least he wasn't groping for his pistol.

Adonis slashed again, swinging wide. Harris stepped in, launching the same kick he'd succeeded with a second ago, and saw too late that the Adonis' maneuver was a feint; as Harris' heel connected hard with Adonis' gut, the big thing's left paw sliced across his kicking leg.

Harris felt fire flash across the back of his thigh, felt claws rip through his flesh as if through cloth. Almost blinded by the sudden pain, he staggered back, away from his opponent. He regained his balance and touched the injury with his hand.

His palm came away covered with blood. The gash

was long, maybe deep as well, and probably fatal if he stood around bleeding while he fought the thing that had made it.

As his vision cleared, he saw that he'd backed onto the circle of stones, and that his kick had actually taken Adonis off its feet again.

Then the world started to change.

Impossibly, the high-rise buildings on the far side of Central Park West began to grow, stretching taller but growing no thinner, curving like bowed legs. Harris gaped at the optical illusion, momentarily forgetting the clawed thing on the ground in front of him. The buildings rose as tall as the Empire State Building, and taller. The trees in the middle distance were growing, too, tall as redwoods.

Adonis stood up in front of him—and oh, God, the thing with the inhuman face was now twice the height of a man, now three times, still growing, and striding closer and closer to the circle of stones, looming over Harris, leering down at him.

Vertigo seized him. He swayed back from Adonis, struggling to keep his balance, tasting bile in his mouth—

Then the world popped.

It was as if he'd been in a giant soap-bubble that magnified the appearance of everything outside it, and suddenly the bubble burst. Harris' ears popped, his vision swam as everything in it swayed and changed, and he fell over backwards on sharp white rocks. They ground into his spine and shoulder blades.

Then he could see, swimming out of the blur, the tops of trees surrounding him. Normal-sized trees. But the nearest trees were only twenty feet from him, scores of yards too close—and they were now evergreens.

The trees were illuminated by old-fashioned oil lamps hung from their lower branches. And overhead, though a few thickening clouds promised rain to come, the sky was full of stars like a velvet carpet sewn with diamonds, when moments ago it had been hazy.

He didn't have time to wonder. A figure moved into his line of sight and stood over him.

This was a man, the most *beautiful* man Harris had ever seen. He was lean, with short, curly hair that was golden rather than blond. His eyes were the bright blue of the daytime sky. His face was a Greek ideal of sensitivity and youthful, masculine beauty, and shone as though lit by internal fires. He wore a dark suit, nearly black in the dim light, that looked years out of date, with its high waistline and too-broad lapels and tie, and yet didn't manage to detract from the startling impact of his physical presence. Harris thought, *When I'm a soap opera hunk, this guy can be my blond rival.*

He stood by Harris' knee, leaned over and asked, in a rich, controlled voice, "Where is Adonis?"

Harris grimaced, letting his confusion show. "Where the hell am I?"

The golden man's expression changed, losing its serenity, growing angry. "When I ask, you answer. It's time for your first lesson. I think I'll take your thumb." He reached the long, delicate fingers of his right hand into the sleeve of his left arm and extracted a knife—a long, thin, two-edged blade on a slim golden hilt. "Give me your hand, you bug."

Harris just looked up at him, amazed. Another maniac. He kicked out with his good leg, slamming his heel into the beautiful man's kneecap.

The golden man's face twisted and he fell beside Harris. Harris lashed out, cracking his fist and forearm into the man's temple once, twice, three times . . . and the golden man's eyes rolled up into his head. He was out for the moment.

Harris stood. The burning in his injured leg made it difficult. He took an uneasy look around. No, this sure as hell wasn't Central Park. He stood in a good-sized lawn filled with trees; the clearing in the center was barely large enough to accommodate the circle-and-X of white stones, similar to the one back in the park. He could see, in gaps between the trees, a wall, nine or ten feet tall, bounding the property on three sides. On the fourth side rose some sort of house, hard to make out in the darkness, but massive and taller than the trees.

Where was Gaby? And how had he gotten here? Had he passed out and been brought by Adonis and the crazy old man? No, that just wasn't right. There were no breaks in his memory from the time he arrived in the park. But even the *air* was different. He took a deep breath, and it was richer than he was used to, like the air of a greenhouse.

And now was no time to think about it. From the direction of the house came a voice, low and rumbling and thickly flavored with what he recognized as a Scottish accent: "Sir? Clock belled six. Did Adonis come?"

No time to stay around, either. As quietly as he could manage, he walked toward the wall and directly away from the source of the voice.

Within a couple of limping steps his thigh began to burn with pain. His leg trembled as he walked.

Not ten feet ahead on the ground was the duffel bag Adonis had used to carry Gaby. Hanging half-out of it was her fanny pack. Harris grabbed it, buckled it on, and continued.

The clearing narrowed into an earthen pathway between the trees. A few yards further, he reached the wall itself: ten feet high, made of beautifully dressed stone assembled without mortar. Expensive and classy. The gate to the outside was just as tall, heavy hardwood with metal hinges and edges—they looked liked tarnished brass—and closed with a wooden bar set into brackets. There were lights beyond.

Yards behind him, the Scottish voice sounded again: "Sir! Who did this? Where is he?" And Harris heard a faint reply; the golden man had to be conscious again. Grimacing, Harris put his shoulder to the bar and shoved it up out of the brackets. He juggled it but couldn't keep it from falling to the ground; the impact was loud.

He pushed against the heavy gate and it swung slowly outward; as fast as he could manage, he ran out onto the sidewalk beyond.

CHAPTER FOUR

Broad sidewalks with trees growing from them, wide streets with tree-filled medians, roadways made up of *brick* instead of asphalt, flickering streetlights set atop what looked like tall, narrow Greek columns—where the hell was he? He turned right and trotted, fast as the pain in his leg would allow, along the concrete sidewalk.

The first car that passed him was like something out of a classic car show, a golden-brown roadster so vast that its hood alone stretched as long as an entire compact car. The spare tire, the spokes and hub of its wire-wheel assembly painted incongruously white to match the other wheels, sat tucked firmly in a notch at the rear of the car's running board. The driver's seat was an enclosed, separate compartment of the car, with the steering wheel to the right, like a British auto; the driver, his lean face pale in the glow from the streetlights, was a liveried chauffeur all in black.

And the car was driving the wrong way down the street, left of the median. Harris fought down an urge to shout after the driver.

He stared a moment after the classic automobile, then stepped out to cross to the median—and immediately leaped back as a horn blared to his right. He stared as a second car drove by, also traveling on the wrong side of the

street. This was a narrower, boxier car, resembling a Model
T with its black body and high carriage. In the seat were
a young couple, he in a broad-lapelled suit jacket in glaring
red, she in a green, high-neckline dress like something
Harris had once seen in pictures of his grandmother. The
steering wheel on this one was also on the wrong side. The
woman, smiling at the driver, was oblivious to Harris. Both
of them were lean, delicate of appearance.

Then they were gone, taillights fading into the dark.
Harris shook his head after this parade of classic cars;
then he checked both directions for traffic before trotting to the median as fast as his bad leg would let him.

It wasn't fast enough.

"You, there!" The shout came from the way he'd come;
it was the Scottish accent. Harris spun around to look.

The man who stood at the gates looked like a wreck-
ing ball: short and squat and heavy. He couldn't have
been more than five feet tall. But he was built like an
inverted triangle, his shoulders huge, his body narrow-
ing down to his waist and incongruously lean legs. His
clothes were brown, baggy, and featureless, his leather
boots heavy and thick, like workmen's garments from
decades earlier, and were set off by his wiry gray mass
of hair and heavy beard. On his head he wore a bright
red beret.

As he shouted after Harris, his eyes seemed to glow
red in the streetlights' glow . . .

. . . and his teeth, long and white, were sharp. *Pointed*.

Harris felt a shudder across his shoulders. Of all the
strange and wrong things he'd seen this night, sharp,
pointed teeth on a squat man weren't the worst. But they
were his limit—one thing too many for him to accept.

"You, there!" the man called again. "You're dead!" And
the squat man with the beret bent over, dug his fingers
in the gap between two concrete paving blocks . . . and
pulled one block up, the effort breaking it away from
its neighbor. He hefted it one-handed as though it were
a paperback book.

Harris felt his world reel around him again. He heard
more automobile traffic driving the wrong way on the
street behind him, felt his injury burning along his thigh,
tasted the unaccustomed sweetness of the air, but all he
was aware of was the man in the beret and the huge block
of concrete he handled.

The man drew the massive concrete square back over
his shoulder. And threw it at him.

Harris dived behind the nearest tree, fetching up against
the rough bark, and saw a gray-white flash as the concrete sailed past. The slab flew across the median and
the street beyond. It smashed into a stone wall, the impact
sounding like the world's largest porcelain jar shattering,
and threw gravel-sized chips in all directions.

Wide-eyed, Harris looked back at the man who'd
thrown it. The stunted man was already in motion, running his way.

Harris bolted, running beside the median, cursing the
pain in his leg as it slowed him. There was no question
of him trying to defend himself against a man like that.
A glance over his shoulder showed the short man catching
up—damn, he ran fast. Like a sprinter, like an Olympic
gymnast charging toward the vaulting horse.

But just beyond the short man was a truck, passing
him by and headed Harris' way. It looked like an Army
truck, but dark crimson instead of green.

As it came abreast of Harris, he angled toward it, got his
hands on the tailgate, and hauled himself into the rear.

Dragging himself over the tailgate and dropping into
the truck bed sent fiery pain through his injured thigh.
A gold-and-red haze obscured his vision. He lay on his
back, gulping in air, waiting for the haze to fade.

He was either someplace very strange, or he was having
a psychotic episode. After all his recent disappointments
and all that vodka, he could believe the latter. But he
didn't; this was all too real.

After half a minute his vision returned to normal. He
could see wooden crates lashed down to the front half

of the truck bed. He sat up wearily and looked out over the tailgate.

The squat man was still there. About fifteen feet back, he was running hard and fast. And as he caught sight of Harris, his eyes gleamed redly again; he put on another burst of speed, gaining a couple of feet on the truck.

He'd lost his beret, sweat poured down his face and into his gray mustache and beard, his shirt was askew with its tails free of his pants, and he was still running faster than any man Harris had ever seen. Harris froze, shocked beyond thinking.

The truck bed beneath him vibrated and rumbled; Harris heard its gears shift. It slowed and the short man gained another half-dozen feet. Harris forced himself to rise to a half-crouch, ready for a futile fight against this unstoppable little man.

But the truck accelerated. The gap between two-legged pursuer and four-wheeled prey widened. Harris might have cheered, but all his air seemed to be going to fuel the pounding of his heart. The short man was twenty feet back, twenty-five and still running, then thirty . . . and at last Harris saw him give up the chase, stopping in the middle of the road, shaking a fist furiously after the truck and its passenger.

Then, finally, Harris felt he could slump back down behind the tailgate and get his heart under control.

The skyscraper loomed up fifty or more stories, but was round instead of square, with its upper floors shaped like the top of a medieval castle's tower. Electric light poured out of round-topped windows on each story. Stone gargoyles lurked on ledges every few stories, and their neon light eyes blinked on and off. The building stood between other skyscrapers equally tall, equally strange. Then the truck left the building behind and a slight bend in the road hid it from sight.

More neon blinked, advertising storefronts: "Pingel's Cafe," "Gwenllian's Beauty Salon," "Drakshire Opera

House." Many of these signs were tall vertical marquees extending from the faces and corners of buildings. Harris saw signs with neon lines twisted like Celtic knotwork to frame glowing, blinking words.

"The Tamlyn Club. Featuring Addison Trow and His New Castilians. Light, Dark, Dusky Welcome." Men in tuxedos and top hats, women in evening dresses and gloves reaching nearly to their shoulders, walked in and out of the club's double doors, admitted by uniformed doormen. These patrons seemed short and slight, with unlined faces, so that it looked like a parade of acne-free teenagers out for a night on the town.

The tuxedos weren't normal. Dark green, dark red, dark gray—no black. The women's dresses were more brightly varied in hue, some of them in lamé that caught the light and held it, shimmering with color.

A newsboy—work shirt, shorts with suspenders, beret—hawked newspapers on a street corner, mere feet from a cart laden with fruit; its hand-lettered sign read, "Apples 1p, Pomegranates 5p."

The buildings were all of stone or brick, many with ornately carved lintels or panels flanking the doorways. They bore no graffiti, no metal bars on the windows or across closed storefronts. Few buildings had windows on the first floor.

The cars, brightly colored blocky things with extended hoods and running boards, most with steering wheels on the right, all drove on the wrong side of the road.

Harris watched this parade of bewildering images whenever he could no longer resist, but most of his attention was focused on his injury. Bounced around by the motion of the truck, he managed to brace himself in the corner by the tailgate, then pulled off his shoes and pants to look at the wound.

There was a lot of blood, but the parallel slashes were not deep . . . just long. Swearing, he pulled off his denim jacket and shirt, then tore the latter into strips. As well as he was able, he bound his injury, cinching the impromptu bandages as tight as he dared. Then he pulled his clothes on again.

By now the street scenery had become monotonous: block after block of stone-faced residential buildings, curiously clean, the streets free of trash. Here, there were windows on the first floor, about eight feet off the ground, and Harris could see into the apartments. Occasionally he caught the smell of meat roasting.

The truck pulled over and parked. Harris scrambled up and over the tailgate as fast as his leg would allow him. But as his feet came down on the brick of the street more pain jolted through his wound and his head swam with dizziness. It was a moment before he could turn to the sidewalk. Once again, he wasn't fast enough.

From behind him: "Here, now!" A man's voice, clipped, deep.

Harris sighed and turned.

The truck's driver stood at the left rear quarter of the truck. He was a short man, no more than five and a half feet tall, but very broad shouldered. He wore a flannel shirt and dark pants but, incongruously, was barefoot. His gray hair, flowing long from beneath his fedora-type hat, suggested that he was an older man, but his face was ruddy and unlined. He held an elaborately curved pipe in one hand and an unlit match in the other as he looked gravely at Harris. "You steal anything, son?"

Harris shook his head. It was a stupid question; he couldn't have stuffed one of those wooden crates under his jacket.

"Imagine that," the man said. He lit his pipe, puffing a moment, and then tossed the match into the street. "Truck full of talk-boxes and you don't try to take a thing. Must be an honest man." He spoke without irony. There was a faint accent, an odd lilt to his words, but Harris couldn't place it. "You look like you're fresh off the boat. Looking for work? I have a fair of sisters' worth of deliveries left tonight. Could use a man to unload. I'll pay a dec."

Harris tried to follow the man's odd words, couldn't quite grasp all their meaning. "Uh, no, I can't. I—" He gestured vaguely at his leg. "I got hurt."

The barefoot man glanced, and his eyebrows rose. "You did. Lot o' red, son. You have any money?"

Harris shook his head.

The barefoot man fished around in one of his shirt pockets and drew out something that glinted silver in the streetlight; he pressed it into Harris' hand. "Get to a doctor before that cut fouls. I saw enough of that in the war, don't need to see it at home."

Harris stared stupidly at what the man had given him. It was a big coin, maybe two and a half inches in diameter, and heavy. On the face was the profile of a handsome, lean man with a prominent nose and a crown; on the back, a three-masted sailing ship. It looked like real silver.

"That's a full lib, son," the barefoot man continued. He unlatched and lowered the truck's tailgate. "That'll get you fixed up. When you're on your feet again, you can pay it back to Banwite's Talk-Boxes and Electrical Eccentricities. That's me, Brian Banwite." He scrambled up into the bed of the truck.

"Brian Banwite," Harris repeated dully. "Thanks." He slid the coin into his pants pocket and moved to the sidewalk, then turned back to the truck.

Banwite climbed back out of the bed, a large wooden crate over his shoulder. On its side were stenciled the words "Model 20, Double, Black."

"Uh, sir?"

"Yes, son."

"Where am I?"

"Cranshire." Brian pointed past Harris. "A few blocks that way you get to Binshire." He jerked a thumb over his shoulder, gesturing the other way. "North is Drakshire. That's my neighborhood, Drakshire." Then he pointed to Harris' right. "River's that way."

"No, I mean . . . what city?"

Banwite laughed. "You aren't just fresh off the boat, you stowed away on it. This is Neckerdam, son. You've reached the big city." He turned away and marched up the walk to the nearest house.

Harris wanted to say, *No, what I want to know is, where's Gaby?* But Brian Banwite wouldn't know. For lack of anything better to do, he slowly turned toward Binshire and moved that way.

The breeze was cool. The concrete was solid under his feet. Harris passed stoops leading up to building doorways a few feet above street level and could grip them, feel the reality of them. Feel the insistent burn of the slashes on his leg. Nothing that had happened since he woke up in Central Park made any sense, but it *had* happened.

And yet, in the half-dozen lit windows he peered up into, there were furnishings that looked like the ones they'd cleaned out of his late grandfather's house. Wooden chairs with carved, curved legs. Stiff, upright sofas. There was something that looked like a TV set, but with a round screen; it was not turned on. Most of these furnishings were new, in good shape.

And the people . . . One man in three wore a tie in the comfort of his own home. The women were in knee-length dresses, dated of style but bright of color. A happy young couple listened to a radio, which blared something that sounded like Irish dance music.

There were no old people. Well, no old people who looked really old. White hair framing young faces.

Then he caught sight of the woman working over her stove. The woman with pointed ears.

They weren't like those of Mr. Spock on TV, not rising to a devilish point at the rear. They were normal except for the slight, subtle point right in the middle of the curve at the top. Harris looked for pointed ears in the next dozen people whose windows he passed and saw them on three; the rest had ears he considered normal.

Dully, he shook his head. He didn't understand what was happening. It confused him. It had hurt him.

Therefore it was the enemy.

It wasn't enough that the whole world was his enemy. Now, it was a world he didn't even recognize.

When you didn't know what an opponent could do, you stood back, ducked and feinted, watched him work until you understood what you were up against.

That's what Harris would do. Then he would fight back.

His shoelaces flopped around as he walked; his shoes had come untied. Noticing that, he suddenly felt sad, but couldn't explain why.

CHAPTER FIVE

Harris looked out over what should have been the Brooklyn Bridge.

It stretched across a broad waterway that, lined with lights on both shores, seemed to follow the contours of the East River. But where both of the Brooklyn Bridge's stone support towers had two soaring arches, this bridge's towers had only one apiece . . . and yellow lights shone from windows at the top of each tower, as though the bridge's heights were occupied. Where the Brooklyn Bridge had its elevated pedestrian walkway along the center, between the outbound and inbound roadways, this bridge had two wooden walkways at road level along the sides, overlooking the water. And this bridge seemed darker and heavier than the one he was used to, its support pillars more massive.

It was the right river and the right place . . . but the wrong bridge. Harris limped along its walkway to see more.

The brisk north wind tugged at his clothes and chilled him. His leg ached worse than ever and his hands trembled from exhaustion when he didn't keep them jammed into his pockets. Maybe he should have done what Brian Banwite said—find a doctor, get it bandaged up. But with everything so wrong, he knew deep down that all the doctors had to be wrong, too. Instead, he kept moving. The strangeness of this place wouldn't get him if he kept moving.

An endless stream of antiquated cars roared by, always going the wrong direction on the road. Once there was a motorcycle with a sidecar attached, its helmetless driver not even glancing at Harris through his thick aviator-style goggles.

Harris caught sight of lights moving up in the sky; they floated over the skyline in far too slow, steady and stately a fashion to be an airplane or even a helicopter. He watched, puzzled, until portions of the aircraft were caught in a spotlight shining up from the city, and Harris recognized it as a zeppelin, drifting as serenely as a cloud.

He passed the first of the bridge's two support towers and walked underneath its enormous arch. Far overhead, small spotlights were carefully situated to illuminate the stone gargoyles leering down at him. He numbly shook his head and kept going.

Off to his left, there was no Manhattan Bridge to be seen. To his right, he could see the contours of Governor's Island—better, in fact, than he should have been able to see them at night. The whole island was brilliantly lit, and Harris could only stare at the island's giant wooden roller coaster and Ferris wheel, which had never been there before. Both were in motion, as were other amusement-park rides too distant to make out in detail. Beyond should be the glinting golden point of the Statue of Liberty's torch, but there was no such beacon.

As he reached the center of the bridge, exhaustion finally caught up with him. He sagged against the rail, shutting his eyes against the parade of lights lining the river, and tried to keep his legs from shaking.

And still the cars roared by, each one carrying someone who wasn't hurt, wasn't confused, wasn't totally out of place. Harris felt resentment stir in him. They'd probably enjoy seeing him slip and fall, like the crowd earlier tonight.

He concentrated on taking long, deep breaths; he tried to slip into a calmer, meditative state, the kind he once enjoyed while performing the exercise forms of tae kwon do.

A faint squeal of brakes—Harris heard one of the outbound cars slow to stop just behind him. A cop, had to be a cop; but when he sneaked a glance over his shoulder, it was nothing he could recognize as a police car. It was a beautiful, massive two-tone thing gleaming black and gold in the bridge lights; its passenger compartment was a four-door box, the engine compartment a lower rectangle just as long, its front grille capped by a hood ornament shaped like a dragon in flight.

The far door opened and the driver emerged. Tall for one of these Neckerdam people, he was Harris' height, though he had to weigh forty or fifty pounds less; he was thin-boned and lean-muscled. He was paler in the overhead lights than Harris; this contrasted starkly with his trim, black mustache and beard. His eyes were bright and alert, his features so mobile and full of sympathy that Harris decided he looked like a stand-up comedian who did psychotherapy on the side.

And his clothes—a full tuxedo in the brightest red imaginable, black shirt and white cummerbund, a combination that was eye-hurting even in the dim bridge lights. Harris felt a laugh bubble up inside of him, but managed to choke it before it emerged.

The newcomer walked around the car and up onto the walkway. His voice was a musical, melodious treat: "Son, don't do it."

"Don't do what?"

The tuxedoed man shook his head gravely. "Don't jump. I know things may seem hopeless now, but—"

The laugh Harris had restrained finally emerged, a high-pitched cackle that sounded crazy even to Harris' ears. "Don't *jump*? Mister, you've come to the wrong place. I wasn't going to jump."

The man took a cautious step forward. "You might not have known that you were. But the moon's full and there's a storm in your heart. You could have hit the water before you knew what you were doing. Come away with me."

Ah, so that was it. This guy wanted something. Was he a smooth-talking mugger or a stubborn homosexual who wouldn't take no for an answer? Harris didn't care; he waved the intruder away. "Scram."

"Is that your name? Scram? I am Jean-Pierre." The man took another careful step forward; he was now within half a dozen feet of Harris. "But if you're not going to jump, you can come away with me. I'll take you somewhere safe. Warm food. We can talk."

Harris gave the man his most knowing smile. "Yeah. Sure. I don't know what you want, man, but you're not getting it from me. And if you don't get in that freak show of a car and get out of my face, I'm going to have to break your head. You got that?"

The man with the French name paused and frowned over that. Then: "Yes. Yes, I do." He started to turn— and then made a sudden lunge for Harris, both hands outstretched.

A bad, clumsy move. Harris stepped sideways and fell into a back stance, keeping his weight mostly off his bad leg; he was surprised to feel himself go off balance from dizziness and he nearly fell over. But he still managed to use his left hand to sweep the man's arms out of line, a hard knifehand block, and brought his right up in a fast uppercut that cracked into Jean-Pierre's jaw. The man in the red tuxedo looked dazed and surprised, as though some six-year-old had walked up and broken a shovel across his face, and took an involuntary step backward.

Which set him up for a follow-through kick. Harris brought his injured leg up in a front straight kick that ended with the ball of his foot cracking into the man's jaw. Harris' extended leg seemed to scream as the move stretched his wound taut, but Jean-Pierre stiffened, spun partway around, and slammed down to the boards of the walkway.

Weakness washed over Harris again; he swayed and heard

a roaring in his ears. The exertion had come close to taking him out, too. But, tired and hurt as he was, he'd won.

He'd better leave before Mr. Fashion Disaster woke up, though.

He turned, and there she was.

Not Gaby. This woman was short, beautiful, and Asian. All he had time to register was her face, the somber expression it wore, and the stick she held.

The stick she rapped against his temple.

Suddenly the pain in his leg was gone.

Along with his eyesight. His hearing.

He never even felt the impact when he hit the walkway beside Jean-Pierre.

Sound returned first. Indistinct murmurings that became words: " . . . said he wasn't . . . off-guard . . . stop laughing . . . "

Then, sensation. Warmth. Uncomfortable, lumpy softness under his back. A little pain in his leg. The pain was actually comforting. It meant that the events he was starting to remember had actually occurred.

Light through his eyelids.

He opened his eyes, and for the second time in hours saw a face hovering over his.

It wasn't the beautiful blond man again. This was a large pug nose surrounded by a merry round face and eyes as green as jade; this man's skin and hair were nearly as brown as a pecan shell. He wore a stiff white shirt, undecorated and short-sleeved, and a large, bulky stethoscope around his neck. He glanced back over his shoulder, revealing his ear to be sharply pointed, and called, "Your *rescuee* is awake, my prince." His voice was surprisingly light, his accent cultivated and not quite American.

"You'll be healing yourself if you keep at me." The voice was Jean-Pierre's, and angry. Harris groggily turned his head to look.

He was in a big room, the size of a low-ceilinged gymnasium, crowded with dozens of large work tables. Some tables were piled high with books, others with burners and glass tubes and complicated glass-and-wood arrays Harris didn't recognize, still others with what looked like mason jars filled with jams and jellies. The walls were paneled in dark, rich wood, and the floor was wooden planking of a lighter tone.

Bright light, the color and warmth of noonday sunlight, glowed from banks of overhead lights that resembled fluorescent light fixtures. Along the far wall, a bank of tall windows looked out over a glittering vista of skyscrapers at night.

Harris found that he was lying on a long paisley sofa in a corner of the room; there was other living-room furniture arranged nearby, including a very large version of the round-screen TVs he'd seen earlier.

On a nearby stuffed chair sat Jean-Pierre, his tuxedo jacket off, a blue bruised spot on his jaw the souvenir of their meeting; he looked irritable. Nearby, curled up in a corner of a divan, sat the woman who'd clobbered Harris. From ten feet away, she seemed tiny, even more dainty than most of the women he'd seen earlier. She wore some sort of pantsuit cut from burgundy silk, the jacket sleeves full and flaring; her expression was serene. Next to Harris, the man with the nut-brown skin sat on a sturdy high-backed wooden chair.

Jean-Pierre rubbed his jaw and the bruise Harris had given him, then narrowed his eyes. "Awake, are we? Then it's time to answer a few questions."

Harris ignored him for the moment; he struggled to sit up and pulled himself back so that the high arm of the sofa supported him. Only then did he realize that under the blanket they'd thrown over his legs he wore only underwear; his pants and shoes were gone. "Hey!"

The moon-faced doctor grinned. "Sorry, son. Had to tend your wound. Your breeches were a loss, torn and bloody." He reached down behind his chair, where a pair of gray trousers lay folded across an old-fashioned doctor's bag. He handed the pants over to Harris. "Try these."

"Thanks." Harris hurriedly pulled the trousers on, barely glancing at the white bandage wrapped around his thigh. His injury wasn't giving him much trouble; the doctor must have given him something for the pain. "Okay. Where am I?"

"The Monarch Building, up ninety. I am Alastair Kornbock. I hear you have already met Jean-Pierre Lamignac and Noriko Nomura; formal introductions are probably moot."

Jean-Pierre picked up something from his lap, a wallet, which he flipped open. "Is your name Harris Greene?"

"Yeah. Hey, that's my wallet." Harris tried to stand, but weariness tugged at him and he thought better of it.

"Yes, it appears to be." Jean-Pierre flipped it shut and negligently tossed it to Harris. "I gather from the way you defended yourself that you really weren't trying to harm yourself on the bridge. So what injured you?"

Harris actually felt himself flinch away from the memory of Adonis. "You'd never believe it."

"Tell me anyway."

"No, you tell *me*. Tell me what the hell is going on. What all this crap is about Neckerdam. What happened to the Brooklyn Bridge. The streets. The cars, for Christ's sake. Barefoot truck drivers and dwarfs who've filed their teeth. Because, believe me, I was knocking down some pretty good vodka before all this started happening, and I don't want to waste time talking to you if you're just DTs." Harris glanced through his wallet to make sure everything was in place, then pocketed it.

The three of them looked blankly from one to the other before returning their attention to Harris. "So," said Jean-Pierre, his pleasant tone not quite concealing his irritation, "what injured you?"

"You know, that was just about the worst attempted tackle I ever saw. If that's the way you normally try to rescue people, I'd be amazed if most of them didn't make it into the water."

Jean-Pierre flushed red and stood. He grabbed at

something on his belt—something that wasn't there, but just where the handle of a hunting knife might protrude under other circumstances. In spite of his exhaustion, Harris stood up and readied himself for the attack he saw in the other man's face. The doctor merely scooted his chair back and got out from between them; he looked from one to the other with interest.

The Asian woman spoke; her speech bore a faint accent that was exotic and appealing to Harris' ears. "Jean-Pierre. Sit down. He is correct; the attack was clumsy. He has suffered more than you today." Harris didn't miss the extra stress she put on the last word, nor that she was communicating something else, but he couldn't read the extra meaning in her statement.

At least Jean-Pierre got himself under control. He sat and angrily drummed his fingers on the arms of the chair. Alastair assumed the same pose and drummed his fingers the same way, a cheerful mockery of Jean-Pierre's motion. Harris sat too, but did not relax.

"Now," Noriko said, "please. We don't know the answers to your questions. We don't even know what they mean. If you tell us the story of how you came to be on the Island Bridge, perhaps we can puzzle it out."

"That's . . . reasonable." For the briefest of moments, Harris saw himself through these peoples' eyes, as he sometimes saw himself from the perspective of his opponents; and this time he was an inexplicable creature, a wounded man who was too big and strange, possibly also dangerous and insane. He didn't like that image. "I guess it started at tonight's fight."

When Harris reached the encounter with the pointy-toothed dwarf in the street, Jean-Pierre jumped up again. Harris tensed, but the other man wasn't angry this time. Even paler than before, he stared in disbelief at Harris. "Angus Powrie," he said.

Alastair shook his head. "There are a lot of redcaps out there, Jean-Pierre. And a lot of hooligans from the Powrie clans."

"Maybe." Jean-Pierre dug around in a jacket pocket and brought out his own wallet. He flipped it open, pulled free a piece of cardstock and shoved it at Harris.

It was a black-and-white photograph, blurry and grainy; it looked like a police photo. The man in it was a little younger than the one who'd chased Harris earlier, but recognizable. Harris nodded. "That's him."

Jean-Pierre took the photograph back and looked numbly at it. "What have you been doing all these years, Angus?"

"Mind telling me why you carry his picture around?"

Jean-Pierre ignored the question. He retreated to his chair and sat, still looking dazed. He fingered the bruise on his jaw. "Kick-boxing, eh?"

"Yeah. It's the professional form of a whole bunch of martial arts."

"Well, I certainly feel as though I've been kick-boxed. Noriko, I know some of the people of Wo and their descendants in the New World fight like that."

Noriko nodded. "Not so much Wo, but Silla and Shanga. I do not think I have ever met a westerner trained in the arts."

Alastair said, "There's more to him than that. He's got an aura. All-asparkle. I see it with my good eye. But it's not like anything I've ever seen before. I'd love to test his Firbolg Valence."

Harris sighed. "It sounds to me like nothing I said means a thing to you. Jesus."

"To speak the truth, it doesn't," said Noriko. "Except one thing. Are you of the Carpenter Cult?"

"The what?"

"I have heard you invoke the Carpenter twice. Once just now."

"Who the hell is the Carpenter?" Then Harris had a sudden suspicion. "Wait a minute. Jesus Christ."

"Yes. Though his followers hesitate to name him as . . . freely as you do."

"Oh." Harris had to think about it. "No, I guess I'm

not. I'm not anything that way. My parents are, though. Of the 'Carpenter Cult'." He sat back frowning as it came home to him that one of the world's largest religions had suddenly been reduced to the status of cult. But there was a little comfort to that, as well. Noriko had heard of something he knew about. One lonely point in common.

The other three looked helplessly among themselves. Alastair said, "I think we need Doc."

"Who's Doc? I thought you were a doctor."

Alastair beamed. "I am. But I'm not Doc. Doc is Doc. And Doc is due . . . " He reached inelegantly under his shirt and pulled out a large pocket watch. "Two chimes ago. Late, as ever."

"So this Doc can get me figured out?"

Jean-Pierre shrugged. "If anyone can. He's a deviser, you know."

"Ah. Well, that explains everything, doesn't it?" Harris shook his head dubiously . . . and caught sight of what was tacked up on the wall behind him: a map. A map with the recognizable outlines of the continents.

He read some of the names printed there . . . and suddenly found himself standing on his sofa, both palms pressed against the map as he stared disbelievingly at it.

There was Manhattan, but the name Neckerdam was printed next to it, and some of the other boroughs were colored more like park than city. And New York State wasn't outlined with familiar borders. Its boundaries reaching about as far north as Albany should be, and much farther south, to the Philadelphia area ("Nyrax"); the whole area was labelled Novimagos.

Farther north, Nova Scotia and some of whatever province was next to it—New Brunswick? Harris couldn't remember—were labelled Acadia. To the south, much of Central America was labelled Mejicalia, a name that at least looked a little familiar, but few borders were drawn in that area of the map. Southeast of Mejicalia, what was Aluxia?

Things were no better in Europe. Most of central Spain

was taken up by Castilia, a name Harris thought he remembered from school. All of England and Ireland were labelled Cretanis. These nations were further broken up into hundreds more small territories with names he didn't know. So was all the rest of Europe.

There was no sign of Hawaii, or most of the islands of the South Pacific, just the words "Many Islands" and a picture of a sea serpent.

Harris turned away from the map, feeling faint and not entirely able to accept what he'd just seen. He sank back down to sit on the sofa, feeling the gaze of the others on him, and didn't bother to ask them if that thing on the wall were a joke.

Nearly a thousand feet below, a dozen men entered the lobby of the Monarch Building. They paid no attention to the doorman who admitted them, to the veined white marble walls and reflective black marble floor, to the bustle of people moving in and out of the building even at this late hour. With the nonchalance of office workers familiar with the building, they moved straight to the elevators and boarded the first available car.

But they weren't office workers. The green-uniformed elevator operator took a look at the large instrument cases they carried, at the cheap red suits they wore, and sighed. Musicians. Rowdy musicians with their bad tips. Still, he adjusted his cap and put on his most professional face, and as the band entered his car he said, "Floor, goodsirs."

The smallest of the musicians, the one who stood right by the door with the trumpet case in his hands, smiled winningly at him. "Roof."

"I'm sorry, this car only goes up eighty-nine. The remaining floors are private property."

The trumpeter frowned. "Private? We have an engagement on the roof. A wedding."

The elevator operator tried not to look as confused as he was. "I don't think so, sir. There's no place up there to have a wedding. A talk-box reception tower and some machinery, I think."

"Then what's that black thing on your uniform?"

The uniformed man looked down at his front and finally showed confusion. "Sir, there's nothing—"

He did not see the other musician wield the black-jack. He did feel blinding pain as the lead shot-filled weapon rapped down on his uniform cap, and that was the last he knew. His legs gave way and he thudded onto the carpeted floor of the elevator car.

The trumpeter tipped his hat at the unconscious elevator operator, then nodded at the sap-wielder. "Now. Take us up."

The big man pocketed the sap. He took the car's control handle. "He was telling the truth. You know whose building this is."

"Yes."

"So this car won't go up past up eighty-nine. You know he has to be higher than that."

"Yes. Take us up eighty-nine." The trumpeter smiled and patted his instrument case. "Everything we need is in here. Trust me. Trust *him*."

The big man grimaced, then set the car into motion.

CHAPTER SIX

Noriko tilted her head to the side, concentrating. "Rotorkite," she announced. "Doc is here."

The others listened. At first Harris could hear nothing but a constant, dull wash of noise—the faint remnants of street sound from a thousand feet below. Then he caught the sound that had alerted Noriko: a faint *thup-thup-thup* that began to grow louder. It sounded just like an incoming helicopter.

Noriko and Jean-Pierre were up in an instant, headed out through the nearest door in the wall; Harris and then Alastair followed. The door nearest the sofas opened into a dim, carpeted corridor, and Noriko and Jean-Pierre led the way to a nearby bank of elevators.

One elevator was already open. They piled into it, Jean-Pierre sliding shut first the gratelike outer door and then the matching inner door, pulling up on the handle that sent the elevator upward.

The elevator rose three stories into what had to be a hangar. It was enormous, taking up at least two building stories; the floor was concrete and splashed with oil. There were work-benches and tools, rolling carts, and what looked liked oversized car engines hanging from chains and pulleys. On one side of the big chamber was a strange carlike vehicle, a rounded lozenge forty feet long and ten wide; it rested on a series of struts with wheels at the bottom, and a large, irregular mass of what looked like tan sails lashed to the top.

Noriko headed over to a wall-mounted board of large mechanical switches and pushed one up.

There was an immediate grinding noise from overhead and the lights dimmed briefly. Then, slowly and ponderously, one large section of roof, directly over the flooring, began to open up. It was a huge door powered by mechanical hinges. Above it, Harris could see a widening stripe of nighttime sky, clouds reflecting the city lights below them. It had clouded up in the time since he was brought here. It was sprinkling, and a stray breeze tossed droplets of rain into their faces.

The *thup-thup-thup* grew louder. It took Harris a moment to spot its source: a vague, dark shape with tiny red and green lights glinting on its belly. It got bigger until light from the hangar bathed the underside.

It descended into the hangar, a diamond shape all in dark blue, with a helicopter-style rotor at either end. It was about as large as a Coast Guard rescue helicopter, but broader in the middle where the diamond shape was at its widest. It touched down on four wheels.

As the rotors spun down, Noriko returned the switch to its original position; the overhead door groaned and began to close again. On a narrow end of the helicopter—rotorkite? that's what Noriko had called it—a gullwing door opened. A man climbed out and dropped to the hangar floor.

He was tall—taller even than Harris, the first man Harris had seen here who didn't make him feel like some sort of Viking invader. He was broad-shouldered but otherwise built lean, and moved as gracefully as a dancer.

He wore loose-fitting dark slacks tucked into high leather boots, and was bundled into a waist-length coat of yellow leather worn over a white shirt with an elaborate frilled collar. As he turned toward Harris and the others, he tugged off a yellow leather helmet fitted with

archaic glass goggles; out tumbled shoulder-length hair.
Hair that was pure white, the precise white and softness
of thick clouds. Hair that didn't quite conceal the most
sharply pointed ears Harris had yet seen.

His features were young, of a man perhaps thirty, but
there was nothing youthful in his unsettling, pale blue
eyes.

He saw Harris and stopped. With a trace of curiosity
in his expression, he looked Harris over before turning
to the other three.

"A guest," Alastair said, gesturing at Harris. "You
remember *guests*, don't you? We used to have them from
time to time. Doc, this is Harris Greene, who wears blue
so we don't understand the name. Harris, this is your
host, Doc—Doctor Desmond MaqqRee, founder of the
Sidhe Foundation." He pronounced it "She Foundation."

Doc looked at Harris again, his lips moving a little; he
appeared to be working out a problem. Finally, in a surprisingly deep and rich voice, he said, "Grace upon you, Harris,
health and wealth, love and children, and on all your line."

"Hi," Harris said.

"High." Doc wasn't returning the greeting; he was puz-
zling it out. Alastair snickered at his obvious discomfi-
ture.

It took twenty minutes, as Doc and Jean-Pierre checked
the rotorkite from end to end, for Harris to repeat his
story. Doc had him back up and go over several points
and incidents; he paid special attention to Harris' descrip-
tions of the glorious blond man. They returned to the
laboratory before the story was done. Doc was remov-
ing his pilot's gear and settling on one of the sofas when
Harris described the dwarf who'd thrown the concrete
block. Doc looked over at Jean-Pierre.

The other man nodded grimly. "I've already shown him
the picture. It was Angus Powrie."

Doc returned his attention to Harris. "You mention a
thing called a pannyfack."

"Fanny pack." Harris looked around for it but didn't see it.

Jean-Pierre brought it up from behind his chair and tossed it to Doc. "It's all there. One pocketbook crowded with paper treasury notes and draft-notes I don't recognize, many cards all bearing the name of Gabriela Donohooey—"

"That's Donohue."

"Thank you, Harris, why don't you and your friends learn to spell more sensibly?—including one of the drover licenses like Harris had, some coins, a small gnarled canister of 'pepper spray,' seasonings I suppose, and miscellaneous items. I also put Harris' keys and clasp-knife in there." As Harris groped his pocket, belatedly realizing that his things wouldn't be in these pants anyway, Jean-Pierre smiled mockingly at him. "My apologies, Harris. I didn't know whether or not you would want to come after me with that knife. I couldn't risk it, once I noticed your knife's special trait."

Harris frowned at that. "What trait is that?"

Doc looked at him, then unzipped the main pocket of the fanny pack. He pulled out the lockback hunting knife Harris usually carried. He turned it over, looking at the wooden tang with its brass ends. "Unusual design, but I see nothing else strange about it." Then his thumb brushed the back of the blade.

Doc hissed and involuntarily dropped the knife back into the pack. He put the last joint of his thumb into his mouth and looked curiously at Harris. Then he blew on his injured thumb, on the blister Harris saw rising there, and asked, "You carry a knife with a *steel* blade, Harris?"

"Sure. Why not?"

"Odd question. Because it will make you sick. Noriko at least has the sense to keep her steel fully sheathed when she's not using it. You must touch that blade every time you put your hand in your pocket."

"So what?" Harris moved over to Doc, then reached

into the fanny pack and came up with his knife. He held it so that the closed blade touched his skin. Then, slowly and with exaggerated care, he opened it out and placed the blade across his palm.

He lifted the blade to show them there was no problem with his skin. The surprised reactions of the other four were very gratifying. Then, with malicious humor, he slowly drew the back of the blade across his tongue, and was rewarded with a startled hiss from Alastair.

Jean-Pierre stood and took a step away from Harris. "He's obviously insane, Doc. A high degree of immunity, surely. But mad anyway."

Doc also stood, looking troubled. "I don't think so. He shows no pain at all."

"Completely immune," Alastair said. "I've heard of such people, but never thought I'd live long enough to see one."

Harris folded and pocketed the knife. In spite of the fact he didn't know what any of this meant, he felt strangely superior. He rooted around in the pack, retrieved and pocketed his keys, and then took the fanny pack back to the sofa.

He told himself that all he wanted to do was make sure she hadn't lost anything. But after he determined that the pack still held Gaby's keychain and pocketbook, he kept looking.

On the chain was her canister of defensive pepper spray. Harris grinned at the thought of Jean-Pierre trying to hose down a salad with the stuff. Maybe he should let him try; that might be entertaining. But the canister was strangely twisted, as if exposed to great heat, and the plastic spray mechanism on top was melted and fused, obviously not usable. He'd seen it only two days ago, and it was normal then.

He looked in the fanny pack's other compartment; it still held things he didn't care to prowl through, like wadded facial tissues, bottles of nail polish, tampons.

The others murmured among themselves, excluding

him from their conversation. That was fine. He used the
opportunity to sneak a look through the contents of her
pocketbook. Maybe there he'd find some clue explaining why she'd left him. He had a right to know, didn't
he? He ignored the little voice that immediately whispered *No*.

Two credit cards, two gas cards, a New York driver's
license that gave her address on Waverly, an employee
identification card for the local UHF TV station she served
as program manager, her miniature address book, thirty
dollars plus change, her checkbook showing less than two
hundred dollars in the bank, miscellaneous other effects.

No photograph of some new guy who looked like he
belonged on a soap opera. No letter to her friend Elaine
explaining the situation. No checklist detailing the characteristics of her ideal man with notes on where Harris
fell short. No names in her address book that he didn't
recognize. Of course, it could be someone they both
already knew. Zeb? Nah.

A shadow fell across Harris; he started guiltily and
looked up at Doc, who'd appeared beside his couch without making a sound. "The Changeling," said Doc.

"Huh?"

"The blond man you describe sounds like the Changeling. I do not know his true name. He's a criminal. His
men rob treasuries, brew and sell glitter-bright, and try
to control rulers and industries. It's very bad to know
that an old-time strong-arm man like Angus Powrie is
working with him. I want you to take us where you saw
them."

"I'm not sure I can find it again. I wasn't looking at a
map when I was running away from the little son of a
bitch—"

Harris realized that Doc was no longer listening. The
white-haired man frowned, staring at the pocketbook in
Harris' hands, and reached down to pluck the driver's
license away. "This is Gabrielle."

"It's Gabriela. It's Spanish. She goes by Gaby."

Doc gave him a puzzled look. "This cameo is very bad, but it is definitely her. Gabrielle." He turned back to the others and showed them the license. "Have any of you seen her?"

Alastair shook his head. "Just you, Doc. She never talks in when we're around. We decided that she was either imaginary, or sweet on you."

Doc spun to face Harris again, his expression oddly intent. "And this is your lover, the woman you rescued."

"If you can call it a rescue, yeah. How do you know her?" His tone was more hostile than he intended. He reined in his emotions.

"We've never met in person; she has spoken to me a few times on the talk-box. Always when there is trouble brewing. Now it seems that trouble has found *her*. Now, it's even more important that we—"

He was interrupted by a loud pop from the large round-screened TV. A white dot appeared in the center of the screen, and expanded outward to resolve itself into a black-and-white picture.

Of Gabriela Donohue.

She didn't wear the clothes she had on at the park. Now she wore an elaborate dress, something with a scooped neckline lined with embroidery and flaring long sleeves that spread out over the tabletop they rested on. Her hair was longer than before, was twined into a single braid and brought over her shoulder to hang in front. It had to be a wig or hair extenders. She stared straight into the screen, her expression concerned. Behind her was a wall of large, irregular stones.

She looked great. Harris felt his heart trying to break out through his breastbone. "Gaby! Are you okay?"

She glanced at him with a curious expression, dismissed him instantly, looked at Doc. "They're coming to kill you, Doc. And some man you have here." Her American-heartland accent was gone; she spoke with the same mid-Atlantic accent he'd heard on Jean-Pierre, Alastair and Doc.

"Who is?" Doc asked.

"I don't know, but they are *close*. I've only just heard. Don't waste time talking to me. We'll talk later." She raised a hand as if to wave good-bye.

Harris found his voice: "Gaby, *wait*. Are you okay, honey?"

He would have said more, but she looked at him as though he were some stranger babbling at her on a street corner. She finished her motion, gesturing good-bye to Doc. The screen went blank, the image contracting down to a white dot. The TV set crackled with static electricity.

Harris found that he had to sit down again.

She couldn't even admit that he existed.

Harris glared up at Doc . . . and was startled to see that a gun had appeared in the man's grip. It was a monstrous automatic pistol, bigger than any he'd ever seen, and seemingly made of copper or bronze. Harris glanced nervously at the others, but they were in motion, moving across the room toward several wall cabinets.

A sudden *bang!* nearly deafened Harris and he felt a shock in the soles of his feet. Not twenty feet away, just in his peripheral vision, a black spike sprang up out of the floor, throwing splinters of wood up as it emerged.

Harris felt Doc's hand close on the collar of his jacket. Doc yanked him backwards and casually hurled him behind the big TV set. The impact didn't seem to hurt his leg. He scrambled up to kneel behind the set and could see that the spike in the floor was now pouring out black fluid, a steady stream in all directions like a lawn sprinkler.

And then they were there—men, appearing as suddenly as though they'd been there all along and he'd only just noticed them. There were a dozen of them, wearing dull red suits, holding big firearms that looked like tommy guns made of brass. Each man stood half a dozen feet from the spike in the floor, facing outward from that center point.

Doc shouted, "Surrender, or—"

They opened fire, short sprays of flame erupting from the muzzles of their weapons. All around Doc, things shattered and exploded: books blew off the tops of tables, colored glass beakers disintegrated in spectacular sprays of glittering debris, impacts rocked the case of the television Harris crouched behind. The roar of the weapons hammered at Harris' ears, deafening him. Harris crouched lower, hugging the wall, and looked around for a doorway out, a heavier piece of furniture to get behind, even something heavy to throw.

Doc sensed rather than saw the explosive lines of gunfire converging on him. He dived away—hurled his body under an adjacent table and past it, rolled beneath a third. The bullets sought him out, but he lashed out with a boot and toppled the table, making a shield of its top.

He saw the table shudder under the impact of gunfire. This was bad, very bad. His people had handguns, the enemy had autoguns, and the odds were more than two to one against him. He had to divert the invaders until Alastair and Jean-Pierre could get to their heavy artillery.

For speed, rely on simplicity. Was that a memory of his father's voice, or of his own voice when he taught? He didn't know. He set the gun down and found the small box of matches in his pocket. Out of his sight, men were shouting, firing, maybe advancing.

There was no time to figure out links of contagion; therefore, it had to be similarity. He struck the match. He breathed the smoke and felt the life of the fire beneath it; then he tossed the match over the shuddering tabletop, toward his enemies. *Go, little fire. Find your kin.*

For a brief moment, he was with the match as it flew, the fire atop it precariously alive. Hungry to feed, it sought out the food Doc had promised it. It flew past the startled face of a gunman, sensed the burner on the table beyond, and with the last of its vitality reached the simple scientific device.

The knob on the burner twisted and bright new fire a half-dozen feet high leaped into the air. The red-suited gunman nearest the table edged away from the sudden eruption of heat.

Doc struck another match. *Now, big fire, do as your little brother does.* He touched the flickering flame to the skin on his arm.

Harris saw the Bunsen burner on the table flare up in spontaneous combustion and saw Doc burn himself with the match. It made no sense.

But the flame from the burner bent as though it were hinged and struck one of the gunmen in the back, igniting his suit coat. The man yelled, spun around to confront his tormenter, and the wash of living fire struck him across his face; he screamed again as his hair and hat ignited.

It was a moment's distraction for the battery of men firing against Doc's associates; they glanced at their burning comrade, their faces angry, confused.

Doc popped up from behind his table and fired twice with that big pistol. One of the red-suited men jerked and fell, spraying more gunfire into the floor as he collapsed. Another staggered back, the deeper red of blood staining the arm of his coat. And all the while, the living fire reached out, hungrily straining to touch another of the red-suited men.

Harris spotted Alastair crouching beside one of the wall cabinets. The doctor had gotten it open; inside hung pistols, a sword that looked like an ornate fencing weapon, and a submachine gun much like the ones the red-suited men carried. Alastair, daring, reached up to grab the big gun. Bullets plowed into the case around him but he snatched the weapon down.

Jean-Pierre and Noriko were nowhere to be seen.

Then he saw the woman; on the far side of the attacking men, she popped up from behind a table like a lightning-fast jack-in-the-box. She held a sword in a two-handed grip, the blade back over her shoulder, and lunged at the nearest man, whose back was to her. She swung the blade at him, blindingly fast, but missed; she immediately ducked out of sight again.

No—she *didn't* miss. Harris saw a thin red line appear on the man's neck. The red-suited man fell over. Impossibly, horribly, his head separated from his body and the two parts seemed to fall in slow motion. Arterial spray from the neck hit the ceiling as if fired from a water-sprinkler, then tracked down the wall as the body hit the floor. The head hit, rolled a few yards, and fetched up against a stool.

Most of the men were fanning out and away from the aggressive burner flame but concentrating their fire on Doc, keeping him pinned down. Two were hosing down another, distant, toppled table, perhaps where Jean-Pierre was. But one, armed with a revolver instead of a submachine gun, seemed to be intent on an object he held in one hand; it looked like an old-fashioned volt-meter with a black plastic case. He waved it around, then pointed it more or less in Harris' direction . . . and looked straight at Harris. He smiled.

The man trotted toward him, ignoring the gunfire as though it were a light rain. Another gunman, this one carrying a submachine gun, followed.

Harris sank down and retreated, scooting on his stomach to slide back under the sofa he'd lain on a few minutes before.

Just in time. The two men skidded as they reached the television set. They opened fire on the space behind it before they even saw it. Harris saw bullets explode into the floor where he had crouched just a moment ago; he felt splinters tear at his face.

Harris bellowed his fear and anger. He heaved up on the sofa, shoved it at the two men, rising and uncoiling behind it. The heavy piece of furniture slammed into them, knocking the second man down and sending his submachine gun skidding away, driving the first man backwards an off-balance step. The sofa crashed down on the man who'd fallen.

Follow through. Throw combinations. Harris drove forward at the man who still stood. The impact with the sofa had driven the man's gun hand up; the brassy-colored revolver was pointed at the ceiling but starting to come down again.

Harris grabbed the gunman's wrist with his left hand and struck him with his right, a palm strike that smashed his nose. Harris followed through, continuing to crowd the gunman, slipping his right arm over his enemy's gun arm and folding his elbow across the man's joint, pinning the limb; then he rotated the man's wrist down and back, bending the arm in a direction it wasn't meant to go.

The cracking noise surprised him; adrenaline must have given him strength he hadn't counted on. He watched the man's elbow break and felt the forearm freewheel, no longer supported by bone. The man's pistol fell to the floorboards. The gunman followed it down, unconscious from the pain.

Harris spun and went after the submachine gunner. The man was still down but already scrambling toward his weapon. Harris' kick took him in the solar plexus and folded him double. Harris dropped, following him down, and used his momentum and an open-palm blow to drive the man's head into the floorboards. There was a sharp crack and this gunman went limp, too.

Leaving Harris out in the open. He stayed down and scuttled sideways to get under another table.

But no one was paying him any attention. In fact, fewer men were firing. One was Alastair, opening up with short, carefully measured bursts of gunfire. The attackers who weren't already down had taken cover. Harris saw one of them pop up from behind a table to spray the room—then he stiffened as the point of Noriko's sword emerged from his chest. He looked stupidly at the blade as it retracted. Then he collapsed out of sight.

A dozen yards away, Jean-Pierre rose so that he was partially exposed; he held a long-barrelled revolver in his right hand and what looked like a carved crystal paper-weight in his left hand. He heaved the paperweight behind another toppled table. As it hit, he shouted, "Stickbomb!"

The red-suited man behind the table didn't wait to see. He dove away from his cover. Jean-Pierre's shot took him in the side and he lay still. The crystal paperweight did not explode.

There was a brief lull in the gunfire. Doc, his tone dry, finished his statement: "— or my associates and I will be forced to defend ourselves."

No answer. Then one of the gunmen dropped his weapon over the side of his table and raised his hands in the air. A moment later two others did the same.

It was too late for the rest.

CHAPTER SEVEN

The shriek rang in Gaby's ears and she sat up, disoriented. In the dimness, nothing looked familiar, not the nightstand beside the bed, not the curtains on the windows; where were her bookshelves? And who screamed?

The door into the bedroom opened, spilling light over her, and Elaine hurried in, clutching her robe close. Blond, frowzy, busy Elaine; Gaby sighed her relief as she remembered where she was. Elaine's guest room, miles and state lines between her and all that craziness in the city.

Elaine sat on the bed beside her and brushed Gaby's bangs out of her eyes. "You okay, honey?"

"Yeah." Gaby shivered and tried to pull the blanket up around her shoulders. "I heard a noise. Like someone shouted."

"That was *you*, poor thing. You must have been dreaming. You were shouting something about they're coming, get out of there. You must have been remembering, you know, *them*. This evening."

"I suppose." Gaby frowned. The last faint tendrils of her dream were slipping away from her, but she didn't remember being fearful for herself. It was others she had worried about, others she couldn't remember now.

It must have been Harris. Concern for him ate at her again. "Has there been any word—"

"No, nothing. Still no answer at his apartment."

"Damn."

"Did you get anything figured out? Like why some old guy and his two creeps would . . . "

"Kidnap me? No. It doesn't make any sense." She lay back to stare up at Elaine's sympathetic, weary face. "I don't think they wanted to rape me. I think they wanted to find something out from me. God knows what. I don't *know* anything. Anything a program manager knows, they could hire a consultant to find out, right?"

"Well, you're safe here. We have a security system, Jim has his guns—"

"I want to learn to shoot."

Elaine looked startled. "You always hated guns."

"Still do. Guess what I hate more."

"Yeah. Okay, I'll tell Jim. He'll be glad to take you out to the range he uses."

"Thanks, Lainie."

Elaine hugged her, then rose and patted her hand. "You try to get some sleep. But if you can't, and you want to talk, knock on our door. Anytime. It's okay."

"I'll do that."

" 'Night, hon." Elaine left, shutting the door and closing out the hallway light, but Gaby was glad to see the faint glow around the edges of the door. Nice to know that light was only a few steps away, Elaine only a few steps beyond that.

But if she didn't get good news from the police soon, she'd have to leave all of it. Deep inside, she knew the old man and his two thugs, including the one she'd described as wearing a Halloween mask when she knew that wasn't the truth, would come looking for her again.

She knew because of the way the old man's face lit up when they caught her. Because of how happy he'd been to have her. He'd be back. She couldn't let Lainie and Jim get caught up in the old man's craziness. And she had to find Harris, make sure he was safe.

The thought kept her awake as she lay alone in the dark.

✿   ✿   ✿

Twelve men had appeared to attack them. Three surrendered unhurt. Four, including Harris' attackers, were alive but seriously injured. Five more were dead.

Alastair set his submachine gun aside, clucked over the dead and did what he could to bandage the wounded; Jean-Pierre bound the hands of the living and took their weapons away.

Doc gestured at the writhing flame atop the burner as if communicating with it; he frowned, clearly displeased, and closed his fist, a dramatic gesture. The fire snuffed out; the burner beneath continued to hiss until Doc walked up to twist the knob at its base.

Harris dully looked over the scene of carnage.

He'd never seen dead men before. Four of them lay in strange poses, blood slowly spreading from chests, heads, limbs. One of them was burned black in places. The last of them, whose head lay four yards from the rest of him, was worst. Harris felt his stomach lurch. He returned to the safe haven of the television corner, restored the sofa to its wall position, and sprawled on it.

Noriko sat on the sofa opposite, serenely cleaning her blade with a cloth. Her expression was as calm as if she were a statue made of jade. Her weapon—she must have gone straight for it after Gabriela's warning—was a little like the Japanese swords he'd once seen, but much straighter; the sheath lay beside her on the sofa. The sword went from blood-smeared to silvery clean in a couple of minutes, and Harris could see the care Noriko took not to touch its blade. Then she returned it to its sheath and gave him a calm stare. He looked away.

"You did very well," she said.

"I want to throw up."

"Reasonable." She gestured at a small door in the corner. "That is the water closet."

But he didn't really feel the need, not quite yet.

✿   ✿   ✿

Doc and Alastair came clattering in from the hallway. The doctor walked over to Harris and Noriko: "The room just downstairs, where they launched that device, is all clear. Smoke all over the room from the rocket. They sapped Leith in the elevator, but he'll recover."

"The thing that came through the floor was a rocket?" Harris asked.

"I fear so." Alastair looked disturbed. "Not an explosive one. But then, these floors have wards to protect us against explosive attacks from outside. They must have known that."

Doc knelt beside the spike in the floor, studying it without touching it, then moved off a few feet to examine what looked like streaks of black paint on the floor. He gave a whistle that sounded appreciative to Harris. "Very clever," he said. "Alastair, look at this."

The moon-faced doctor wandered over. Doc continued, "This projectile shoots paint out in all directions, very precisely. The paint is so carefully oriented that it forms a continuous circle."

Alastair looked up at him, startled. "A conjuring circle."

"Yes. See here, a few shunts sprayed other patches of paint in recognizable patterns. The required symbols of transference."

Alastair looked at the symbols, and Harris did, too. They appeared to be smeared blobs on the wood, meaningless paint-squiggles. Alastair said, "They're very sloppy, but correct in form. But you have all four floors warded against devisements of transference like that . . . "

Doc nodded, smiling, encouraging him to continue, and Alastair got it. "But they *fired the projectile through the wards*, got past them physically. I understand. Damned clever."

Doc's smile turned grim. "Which means *all* my wards are effectively useless. I wonder if they can adapt this device for longer-range attacks. Get through any set of wards. I'll have to prepare some new types. All of this means that whoever they are—I assume the Changeling— have a deviser working with them."

"Hey," said Harris. They all looked at him. "Don't you think it's about time you called the police?"

"The . . . police," Alastair echoed.

"You know. Whoever you call when people break into your house, try to kill you, and get killed. They come, they arrest people, there are trials . . . Police."

Doc nodded and stood. "I have a commission with the Novimagos Guard by special order of the King. By extension, so do my associates. So in a sense, we *are* the . . . police. Proper forms are being observed."

"That makes me feel *so* much better."

"Everyone, change for the street. Alastair, get Harris some appropriate clothes. We need to find the place where Harris arrived."

Alastair took Harris up two floors by back stairways to a small, bare bedroom. The room was dusty and had a fan mounted on a swivel bracket on the wall. The anonymity of the furnishings gave the place the feel of a hotel room. However, its closet was stuffed full of men's and women's garments in various sizes, and in a few minutes Alastair had found him an outfit to replace his torn, smoke-stained clothes.

Harris looked dubiously at the black leather shoes, long-sleeved white shirt, silk boxer shorts, and gray two-piece suit with a lace-edged handkerchief in the breast pocket. The clothing was dated, with the jacket's wide lapels and trousers' high waistline, but not too garish, if you overlooked the two-tone red-and-green suspenders and matching tie.

In the attached bathroom, Harris shucked the baggy brown pants they'd given him minutes ago, then stooped to pull on the new pair. He moved carefully; it wouldn't do to make his injury any worse.

Wait a second. He'd kicked the guts out of the man with the submachine gun and hadn't even felt the wound pull. Adrenaline and painkillers could only mask so much; he'd have felt additional injury after he started to wind down. Curious, he unwrapped Alastair's bandage from his thigh.

His wound was gone.

Where Adonis' claws had torn open his flesh, angry red marks remained, like scars left from an injury that had been healing for days. They hurt when he pressed hard on them, but gave him no trouble otherwise.

He sighed. It really was no use getting upset over strange things anymore, so he pulled on his new underwear and trousers. "Alastair?"

The doctor called through the door, "Yes?"

"What exactly did you do to me?"

Alastair's chuckle was faint but unmistakable. "Thatched you, of course. A good mending. You took to it well. Which reminds me, you'll be ravenous in a bell or two. How does it look?"

"Great. Like it's been weeks since I scrapped with something with teeth and claws."

"Good. Don't strain that leg for a few days unless you absolutely have to. Though if you decide you have to 'scrap' again with Jean-Pierre, I'll allow it . . . provided you let me watch. Oh, and something else."

"Yes?"

"Don't bring any silver against that wound. You'd hate to see it spring open again."

They returned to the lab just as brown-clothed workmen carried out the last of the dead assassins on a stretcher. The living attackers were already gone, and more men were at work with mops on the bloody patches of floor.

Doc stood in the center of the room, the lead assassin's volt-meter in his hand, and looked up as Harris and Alastair entered. He indicated the volt-meter. "Harris, it's you they wanted. This little device let me follow your movements to within a few paces."

"Oh, great. Does that mean I have a radio on me?" Seeing Doc's blank look, he explained, "Am I carrying some gizmo that this thing can trace?"

"No. It follows *you*. Probably the charge of energy

Alastair sees as an aura around you." He closed his right
eye and widened his left to look at Harris. "I can see it
a little, too. We'll have to subject you to some tests when
we return."

"How do you know Gaby?"

Doc hesitated. "I've actually never met her in the flesh.
A few years ago, she started calling me on the talk-box.
Always with hints and clues. News about what the crime
gangs were doing. Sometimes things they were planning
to do to me. She never told me how she learned them.
She's never told me about herself." He shrugged. "And
now you come with her cameo in your pack . . . and she
seems not to recognize you."

"I can't explain that part."

"We'll think on it later. For now, we need to begin our
search."

Noriko, a yellow topcoat thrown over her clothes,
straightened up from the television set. "Not so. Harris
appeared at Six Heinzlin Corners, Brambleton South."

Doc gave her a curious look. "How do you know?"

"I called to Civic Hall on the talk-box and asked if anyone had reported a damaged walkway in a good neighborhood."

Doc looked pained. "Angus Powrie's attack. If I had
been thinking . . . "

"They said there was. And that there was blood on the
walk not far away. Workmen will fix it all tomorrow."

"After we look at it."

Harris gave Noriko a disbelieving look. "Your city hall
is open at this hour?"

"Of course. Why not?"

"Because it would be too convenient?"

Doc's private elevator took them down to floor level
and below, to a spacious basement garage filled with cars.
All of them were the antiques Harris had come to expect,
but they were otherwise of every imaginable type and
color: a long, low two-seat roadster in an abusive glowing

orange, a slab-sided panel truck in a shade of drab green Harris was already thinking of as comparatively inconspicuous, a pair of matching black-and-silver motorcycles, a long red monstrosity of a car with a decadently comfortable-looking interior, perhaps a dozen more cars in all. They settled on Jean-Pierre's black-and-gold sedan, and the pale-faced, dark-haired mechanic on duty—Jean-Pierre introduced him as Fergus Bootblack—told them that it was fueled and ready.

Jean-Pierre drove them up the ramp out of the garage and onto the still-busy street with a disregard for traffic and the laws of physics that Harris found unsettling.

Ten minutes later, they were parked outside the walled estate Harris had fled earlier that night. There was the hole in the sidewalk made by Angus Powrie; there were the gates . . . hanging open.

And half an hour after that, as the sun began to send tentative shafts of light slanting between the tall buildings, Harris and the others prowled around the estate's mansion. They looked at furniture long stored under dusty sheets and moved through echoingly empty rooms.

"Hasn't been lived in for months," Alastair said. He and Harris, in the kitchen, peered into the empty walk-in pantry and saw nothing but memories of crumbs. "I wager your friends hired it from the homelord, or moved in when he wasn't looking. When you got away, they fled."

"So what's that ex-in-a-circle thing out on the front lawn?"

"A conjurer's circle."

"That's what you called the circle in your lab. The thing with the paint."

Alastair nodded. "Same principle. Same use. There are always two: one here, one there. What starts in one—"

"— ends up in the other. I get it. I *did* it." Harris paused, worrying briefly about how easy it was for him to speak the language of the impossible when he was confronted with it. "Alastair, the other one of the circle out there is where I'm from, and that's an awful long way away."

"You want to return."

"Right now. No offense. I have to find Gaby."

A smile tugged at Alastair's lip. "I doubt we can help you so soon. We have to know which rituals they used on this circle. But if anyone can help you find your way, it's Doc."

Harris asked, "Why?" Seeing Alastair's blank look, he continued: "Why would he want to help?"

Alastair thought about that for a moment. "I don't know too much about it. He's almost the last of his kind, and he'd like for them to be remembered kindly."

"Who is 'them'?"

"Purebloods from a long time ago." Alastair opened a floor-level cabinet and bent over to peer within it. "Amapershiat itifuwadda—"

"I can't hear you."

"Sorry." Alastair straightened, looking dubious. "I'd appreciate it if you wouldn't bandy this about. A lot of it is public record, but Doc doesn't care to have it discussed in his presence."

"Sure."

Alastair kept his attention on the door. "There was a bad one a while back. One of the Daoine Sidhe, like Doc. Did a lot of harm in the years leading up to the last war. Made their kind infamous. Doc fought him several times, but the people mostly remembered the bad that one did. If you said 'Daoine Sidhe' to the average man on the walk twenty years ago, he'd have bit his thumb and spat."

"Whatever that means."

"Well, it just means that Doc ended up being the heir to a very nasty legacy. That's why the Sidhe Foundation. It's all charities and philanthropies and fixing problems. Nowadays, you say Daoine Sidhe to the man on the walk, and he's just as likely to think of the Foundation. Which is a victory."

"I guess it'd kind of be like growing up with the name Hitler."

"Whatever that means."

The night had brought Gaby very little sleep, so she substituted caffeine for wakefulness and tried to keep her manner pleasant. She'd be dealing with people all day.

She called the police. There was no news about Harris or the old man.

She called work to tell them why she wouldn't be coming in that day, or for the next several. She didn't tell her boss where she'd be staying, and he said he understood. She hoped it was true. It would be monstrously unfair for her to be replaced for something that just wasn't her fault.

She called in the theft of her credit cards to all the issuers.

That afternoon, she went for her first shooting lesson with Elaine's husband Jim.

The directed explosions from the revolver rattled her nerves. Still, he complimented her on learning not to flinch with each pull of the trigger. Soon he was making approving noises at the way her wadcutter rounds punched holes in the paper silhouette of a target. "Not a bad grouping," he said. "And we're talking about self-defense here, not target shooting. That means closer range than this. You'll do just fine . . . if you don't let adrenaline mess up your reactions and your aim. You have to stay controlled."

"Controlled," she repeated, and flipped the switch on the booth to send the new target back on its mechanical rail. She steadied her aim, mentally superimposed the horrible image of Adonis over the target, and prepared to give it a chest full of holes. Then, in tones so low that Jim couldn't hear through the protective earmuffs: "I'll show you controlled."

❦ ❦ ❦

Through the open door of the bathroom, Harris could see late-afternoon sun angling into the bedroom. He lay in the claw-foot bathtub, legs drawn up—the thing was too short for him; he absently scrubbed at himself as the water cooled.

In spite of his worry and his intermittent nausea, he'd fallen asleep almost as soon as they got back to the Monarch Building.

Endless chiming noises had wakened him long after sunlight spilling over his eyes had failed to do so. Once he understood that the device that looked like a lizard's arm with a balled fist at either end was the handset of a telephone, or "talk-box double," he could answer it. On the other end was Doc, asking him to get ready for a trip in an hour or so.

Sitting in the tub, he reached out a finger and drew it over the cool tile of the bathroom floor, felt the texture, the roughness of the grout between tiles. The air just a little stuffy. Water nearly scalding hot when he'd drawn his bath, merely lukewarm now. It was all there with a level of detail he'd never experienced in a dream.

And it was so big. He'd found somewhere that no one else knew about. The map he'd seen suggested that this . . . place . . . was as big as the entire world he knew.

What the hell was he supposed to do about this? Go home and tell somebody? If he couldn't bring people back—preferably guys with minicams and sound equipment—he couldn't prove anything to other people.

And what if he *could* prove it? They'd want to come here, of course. There'd be a hell of a lot of press. Naturally, most people back home wouldn't believe it no matter how much press there was. Except big business; they'd be setting up McDonald's restaurants on every block as fast as they could bring in the yellow-arch signs. . . . That bothered him. It just didn't seem that Neckerdam would be improved by an invasion of junk food, tabloids, and grunge rock.

So hard to think about it. Every time he tried to put

the scattered pieces of his thoughts together, other things floated up to the forefront of his memory. Gaby telling him good-bye, Gaby running for her life. Gabrielle's gaze flicking away past him as though he were unrecognizable pixels on the TV screen. Sonny Walters' face, the Smile, floating forward on the audience's roar of contempt. Nothing seemed to banish these images.

With a defeated sigh, he rose, toweled himself dry and set about dressing in his new clothes.

He tried to let the view from his window distract him. The ninety-third floor of the Monarch Building afforded him an amazing panorama of tall, bizarre buildings and tiny cars moving along the tree-lined avenues.

He loosely knotted his tie and reminded himself that it was not the ninety-third floor. It was "up ninety-two." If he were to take the elevator down to the twenty-fifth floor, that would be "up twenty-four," even if he started out above that floor. The ground floor was "down," the basement was "down one." It didn't make much sense, he didn't like it, and he knew he'd never remember it; but trying to figure out all the differences was a helpful distraction.

Differences. Like the skyscrapers all around the Monarch Building. Half of them were cylindrical towers, capped with pointed cones for roofs or with battlements like the tops of medieval castles. The other half tended to be more like the skyscrapers he was used to, comforting in their squareness, though they all had the kind of art-deco-era architecture he associated with the Empire State and the Chrysler Building.

Some of these were odd, all bright and garish. The one opposite the Monarch Building was a checkerboard of alternating squares of white and green marble; back home, no one could have found investors to build something so ghastly. He hoped not, anyway.

The Monarch Building itself took up a city block, without the setbacks that characterized the Empire State Building and other skyscrapers from its era. It was an unsettling black and had broad ledges every twenty stories; he couldn't see the next one down, but had given them a good look on their return last night. On each ledge was a line of white marble statues of monsters like griffins and rampant dragons, men and women in medieval dress, odd symbols he could not recognize.

A single sharp rap on his door interrupted his thoughts. "Come in."

Doc entered. He wore the same clothes as last night, and though no sign of lack of sleep marred his face, Harris thought he could see a certain weariness in the man's posture. "Are you ready to go?" Doc asked.

"I guess. Where are we going?"

"A construction site. I'm looking for someone who can help us. I want him to see you, to convince him that the gap between the two worlds has indeed been bridged."

In the elevator down, Doc handed him a paper bag and a strange ceramic cup—it was capped by a hinged top like a beer stein. In the bag was a pastry something like an eclair, but the filling was meat and the breading reminded him of a bagel. The stein was filled with a thick, hot liquid as bitter as bad coffee, but tasting like unsweetened chocolate. Harris grimaced over the flavor but guessed that it was strong with the caffeine he needed.

In the basement garage, Fergus slid out from underneath Doc's top-down two-seat roadster and cheerfully told him, "It's ready, sir; all patched. Try not to drive over the potted plants next time." Harris wondered if the mechanic ever slept.

This car, lower than Jean-Pierre's but just as long, had a different sound to its engine, a throaty growl that told Harris that it was a different class of vehicle. As he and Doc roared out of the basement garage, it sounded like a leashed lion. Harris washed that thought away with the last of the bitter chocolate. "Did you get any sleep?"

"No."

"Well, thanks for driving, then. Did you get anything figured out?"

"Yes." Doc turned right onto the main street the Monarch Building faced and blasted his way into the southbound traffic. Harris estimated that this would be somewhere near Fifth Avenue if he were home. But the real Fifth Avenue would be southbound only instead of having two directions of traffic separated by a tree-filled median. It wouldn't be thick with the antique autos he was growing used to. There would be lanes painted on asphalt instead of a brick surface with metal tracks set into it for the frequent rail-bound red buses they passed. Taxis wouldn't be Christmas green. One vehicle in twenty wouldn't be a horse-drawn cart, for Christ's sake.

"Well, what?"

"First, unfortunately, none of the men we took has talked. I doubt they will; they are a very confident lot. They're in the prison of the Neckerdam Guard now.

"Second, though, I do have results from your valence tests of this morning."

Harris grimaced. The last thing Doc and Alastair had done before he'd been allowed to go up to his room was take him into a small side laboratory and load him into a preposterous upright glass cylinder capped with electrical apparatus. Harris hadn't been alarmed until the two men drew on thick goggles with lenses that were almost black.

Then they'd fired up the equipment, the noise of transformers and discharging electricity striking fear into Harris' heart. That was only the start; things got worse when a continuous chain of green lightning poured into the cylinder and washed over him, rattling Harris' teeth and standing every hair of his body on end.

But that had been over soon, and they'd sent the shocked (and, he suspected, smoking) Harris up to his room immediately after.

Doc continued, "The Firbolg Valence was zero. Meaning that you're not Gifted. You can't influence your surroundings except through normal means."

"You mean, not like Alastair does with his medicine."

Doc nodded. "But you have a Tallysin Aura like none I've ever seen. That's what Alastair sees around you. With normal people—" he ignored Harris' bark of laughter "—it shows up among the Gifted. In your case, when I subjected your aura to analysis, it indicated that you were . . . from somewhere else." They roared by another red rail-bus, and Harris barely glimpsed the man dancing merrily atop the vehicle.

Harris glared. "I told you *that* last night. So tell me, where is this 'somewhere else' of yours?"

There was a stoplight on the median ahead. It was different from the ones Harris was used to. It didn't change colors; a black-and-white sign swung out of the pole's summit, reading "Halt." Doc's car and the other traffic slowed to a stop at the corner.

Doc took his time answering, not speaking until long after the "Halt" sign snapped back into the pole and was replaced by "Go."

They left one cluster of skyscrapers and too-tall round towers behind and headed into a second one, near what should have been the financial district. Harris looked around to see if he could spot any familiar landmark, but there was nothing until a side street gave him a glimpse of the distant Brook—the *Island* Bridge.

"Some of the old stories say that there used to be two worlds," Doc said; his voice sounded as though he were reciting. "The fair world and the grim world. On one lived the fair folk, on the other the grim folk. And it was easy to go from one to the other.

"The fair folk were our ancestors, in our thousand clans: light, dark, and dusky. Smaller than people today, of course, and knowing many things that modern man has forgotten. Ignorant of many things modern man has learned.

"The grim folk were barbarians. They were bigger than our ancestors, stronger, more constant in size and form, but savage. Bloodthirsty men who preferred killing to lovemaking or anything else.

"And the grim men were entirely immune to iron and iron's daughter metals."

Harris frowned as what Doc was saying sank home. "Hey, wait a minute."

"Some of the men and women of the grim folk were better than others. More beautiful, more tolerable. They came to live on the fair world. And they were more prolific than the fair folk, more fertile. Those of our ancestors who wanted to have larger, healthier families found it no hardship to bring some of the grim folk into their bloodlines. And while this was going on, while these crosses were taking place, it became harder and harder to move between the grim place and the fair place."

"You think I'm from this grim world."

Doc nodded. "I've been rooting around in antique records and collections of legends, calling to experts on the talk-box, since you went to sleep. A lot of them put credence I never would have imagined into this twin-world idea."

"So I'm a savage." Harris felt himself get mad.

Doc cracked one of his rare smiles. "And most of us are the descendants of you savages, too. Caster Roundcap, an arcanologist I talked to this morning, who takes this sort of thing seriously, suspects that most modern men owe a quarter or more of their ancestry to the grim men. It explains a lot. A greater resistance than our ancestors had to iron poisoning. Increasing uniformity in the size and physical nature of people over the last three thousand years, something that still confuses arcanologists."

Harris sat back, his thoughts running around in circles. They thought he was a caveman. Some sort of Neanderthal.

But, wait. If his people were the ancestral boogey-men of the fair world folk, what were *their* ancestors to *his* people? He shot Doc another glance, looking again at the sharp-pointed ear revealed by the wind whipping at Doc's hair.

Then another thought occurred to him. "Wait a minute. There's no way."

"Why not?"

"Something I learned in college. I was a theater major. That accounts for my glittering job prospects. When people move apart and live in isolated communities, their language changes. That's where dialects come from. After long enough, the languages are almost completely different. It takes a scholar to figure out that they're related."

"True."

"But you're speaking English. Weird English, maybe. But I understand it."

"We are speaking Low Cretanis."

"I don't speak Low Cretinish at home."

Doc shrugged. "Perhaps your speech adapted itself when you came here, a mystical transformation. It's something I admit I hadn't considered. It's a good question. But you're speaking the vulgar speech of the Islands, regardless of what you spoke on the grim world."

"The hell you say." Harris thought furiously, then recited: " 'The play's the thing/Wherein I'll catch the conscience of the King.' There, did that rhyme?"

Doc looked startled. "Yes." His lips began moving silently as though he were reciting to himself.

"What are the odds of a random rhyme surviving some sort of hocus-pocus translation like you were suggesting?"

Doc didn't answer. For the first time since Harris had met him, he looked stunned. "That was William Shakespeare."

"Yes!"

"*Hamlet, Prince of Denmark*. Act Two, Scene Two."

"Yes, goddammit, yes! How do you know that?"

"There's no need to curse . . . Shakespeare was an insane fabulator several centuries ago. He wrote plays about places that never existed. They've survived as classical examples of fantastic literature. There has never been any proof that he himself really existed; it's long been suspected that Shakespeare was a quill name for Lord Conn MaqqMann, the poet who 'discovered' his work."

"No, he was *real*. Where I come from. And Denmark was real, and Richard the Third was real, and England was real, and William Shakespeare wrote about them." Harris blinked. "Okay. So there are some people who think somebody else wrote the plays for him. But they don't deny he existed. And we're speaking the modern version of his language, English, whether you like it or not."

Doc pulled over and parked beside a high, rickety wooden fence and looked closely at Harris. "Of all the things I have seen since you arrived, I think that disturbs me most. For everything else there is a reason. Not for this . . . duplication."

"Sorry." Harris waited a long moment. "Shouldn't we get going again?"

"No. We are there."

Harris looked up. Over the fencetop, he saw the metal girder framework of a skyscraper under construction.

Phipps entered the Manhattan office of his employer and cursed to himself as he felt his armpits go suddenly damp. The air-conditioning never seemed to help. He didn't know why his employer affected him this way. The old man might be murder on those who stood in his way, but he was always solicitous of his own people. Fixing their ties, inquiring after their families, giving them little gifts and big bonuses. And yet there was something about him, as though he were a hooded cobra hiding inside a teddy bear.

The old man sat in his leather-bound throne of an office chair behind his gleaming desk and smiled. "Bill. How's the arm?"

Phipps, rueful, gestured with his right arm. He didn't move it much; in its cast, hampered by the sling, it wasn't very mobile and still gave him shooting pains. "Could be worse. I can't wait to catch up to the guy who kicked me. He got his lucky shot in. Next time I kill the son of a bitch."

"No need to curse, Bill. But, yes, you'll get that chance. Do you have some news?"

"We found her." Phipps set the manila folder in front of the old man. His employer flipped it open and peered at the files and photographs it contained.

"The woman is Elaine Carpenter, born Elaine Johnson, one of her friends from high school. The man is James Carpenter, her husband. She works with a suicide hotline part-time. He's a tax lawyer. They live in Connecticut, and this Donohue girl is staying with them."

"Good, good. How did you find out?"

"I had Costigan make up some of those instant business cards out of a machine. General Carpentry. Gave one to every apartment manager on the block and quoted nice high rates. But for the manager of the girl's building, he had a special offer. A low, low introductory rate. And—surprise!—it turns out the manager had a door he wanted repaired. We gave it to him dirt cheap . . . and while Costigan was doing the repairs, he asked the manager how the door got broken." Phipps smiled in rich appreciation. "The manager told him the story. Also, how he had to collect the girl's mail and send it to her, since her keys were lost. Costigan got him alone and asked him a few questions."

"And?"

"And then he finished fixing the door."

"No, I mean—the manager?"

"Oh. He's gone on a river cruise. He may pop up in a few months."

The old man crinkled a smile at Phipps' word-play. "Good. We'll visit Miss Donohue again tonight, after the house is asleep. Do you have a man in place?"

"Naturally. I'll have the device out to him within the hour."

"Excellent." The old man waved him away. But as Phipps reached the door, he called, "Bill?"

"Yes?"

"If you had the choice, would you lead an army, rule a nation, or retire to a life of decadent self-gratification?"

Phipps smiled. He never knew whether the old man were testing or taunting, so he always answered honestly. "I'd take the army."

"I knew it. Go on, then. Get someone who is good at intrusion. And make yourself ready at moonrise."

CHAPTER EIGHT

The site foreman, a squat man who waddled comically as he walked, but looked as though he could bench-press an I-beam, guided Doc and Harris to the open-faced elevator. He handed a pair of long-cuffed leather gloves to each of them. "Joseph's up eighty," he said. "My best man. He's not in trouble?"

"No trouble," Doc said, and put the elevator into motion. He donned the gloves, and Harris followed suit.

As the elevator rose, Harris watched the metal girders flash by. "These look like the ones at home. Steel I-beams and H-beams."

"Yes."

"They're steel? I thought you people had a problem with that."

Doc nodded. "That's why he gave us gloves. You don't need them; I do. Workers wear very heavy protective gear so they never touch the metal. Hundreds die every year from heat; and in spite of the fact that they try to hire only those with some immunity, many others die of poisoning. But if we're to have modern towers, we have to have steel frames." There was a melancholy light in his eye that Harris found unsettling.

Harris drew off his gloves again. "I guess when you

82

put up all the wood and Sheetrock around the girders, it's safe to live in."

"Not entirely. I invented a process to bond neutral agents against the steel when it's all erected, and that is how the Monarch Building was crafted; but not every builder uses it, as it's costly. And when buildings that don't use it get old, cracks open, rain leaks in, rust seeps through, and rust poisonings take place. A particular problem in the tenements, where rust poisoning makes hundreds or thousands of babies mind-damaged every year."

"Oh." There was not much Harris could say to that. It all sounded very familiar, and he was struck by how much things were the same between this fair world and his grim world, despite their many differences. "You helped build the Monarch Building?"

"It's what I do. I design things. Buildings, aircraft, devices. But there tend to be interruptions. Such as when people try to kill me. The Monarch Building is one of mine."

Harris heard metallic clanking and banging long before Doc brought the car to a halt at one of the unfinished upper levels. In front of the car was a wooden platform; beyond that, open air a long way down. Harris stepped out on the platform but stood well back from the edge; he managed to quell his stomach's mild rebellion as he looked around.

He stood on the only flooring to be found on the whole level. But all over "up eighty" and the floor below, men worked, creating the cacophony Harris had heard.

One story down, odd metal contraptions were set up on small wooden platforms. Each device looked like a small metal cauldron on a stand; affixed to the cauldron was a crank-operated attachment. Men worked the cranks to blow air into the cauldrons, super-heating the contents to incandescence.

Harris watched one of the men take a pair of tongs, fish around in the glowing mass within the cauldron, and then expertly flick something up into the air. A man on

Harris' level caught the cherry-red flying thing in a brass bucket and immediately used tongs of his own to fish it out; Harris now saw that the thing was a big rivet. The bucket-man shoved the rivet into holes bored through a girder and the bracketlike framework it rested in. Two waiting men, one on either side of the girder, stepped into place; they carried coppery cylinders attached to firehoselike tubes stretching out of sight below. Each positioned his device over one protruding end of the rivet; there was an angry *brrraaapp*, like a short burst from a high-pitched jackhammer, and the men stepped back, satisfied.

All over the naked steelwork of the skyscraper, the same scene was being played over and over again. Other crews of men guided crane operators moving more girders into position, lowered them into place, fixed them there with temporary bolts.

These were men of all sizes, ranging from some three-quarters Harris' height to others nearly as tall as he. Most had nut-brown or red-clay-colored skin; they were earth-toned from head to foot because of the brown leather pants, jackets, and gloves they wore. Only their cloth caps, in red, green, yellow, and other colors, and the orange-red hair some of them had, gave them any color. They walked fearlessly on precariously narrow girders as though they couldn't see the thousand feet of open space between them and the ground.

And one of the men, positioned at a far corner of the building under construction, towered over the rest.

He was a freak compared to the others. If Harris gauged his size correctly, he was enormous, the height of an NBA basketball player, the build of a boxer. He was nut-brown like most of the rest, but his hair was a long blond cascade. Unlike the others, he wore only boots and a pair of lightweight tan pants. He had two partners, one catching the rivets and the other helping him drive them into place; normal sized for men of Neckerdam, they looked like midgets next to him.

Doc spotted the gigantic man and headed toward him—casually walking out onto the metal that stretched web-like over that long, long drop to the ground.

Harris froze where he was. Doc reached the first upright girder and began to edge around it, then realized that Harris was no longer behind him. He looked back and after a moment said, "Stay here. I'll return in a minute." He stepped around the upright barrier and continued onward.

Something wilted inside Harris. He knew that, in Doc's eyes, he had to have just ceased being an adult human and had become a child. Dammit.

He sat down and yanked off his shoes and socks. If he were going to do this, he wouldn't do it on slick leather soles. Then he rose, poised for a long, long moment at the edge of the wooden platform . . . and stepped out onto the cool metal girder.

One step. Still alive. Two steps, still alive. He reminded himself that as a kid he was always good at walking on the top of the curb, graceful and balanced.

Then he looked down, watched the girders of the steel skeleton growing together far, far below, and he was suddenly reminded that a fall off an Iowa City curb led to a four-inch drop. This sudden impulse of his would kill him if he slipped. A wind brushed at him and his stomach lurched.

He reached the first upright girder and clung to it. Still, there was no going back. He edged around the obstruction to the horizontal girder on the other side and kept going, making slow and steady progress, grabbing hard onto each upright beam as he came to it.

He heard a dry chuckle from one side. There stood the partners of the giant construction worker, one girder-length off to his left. They leaned casually against an upright, helpfully staying out of the way of this high-steel virgin, and lit smoking-pipes as they laughed at his progress. Then one of them glanced down at Harris' bare feet and his chuckle choked off. Harris shot them both a scowl and kept going.

An eternity later, he crept around the final upright. Ahead stood Doc, his back to Harris. Doc faced the big, bare-chested worker, and Harris realized that his estimation of size was correct; the worker towered over Doc, more than a head taller than the white-haired man.

Doc must have heard Harris' approach; he turned. "Joseph, this is Harris Greene, the grimworlder I told you of. Harris, this is Joseph."

Harris said, "Hi," looked up into Joseph's face . . . and froze.

Joseph's features were just somehow wrong. He had high cheekbones, wide-set eyes, a wide mouth—a strong combination. But there was something incomplete about his features, as though he were a doll who had not been detailed after emerging from the mold, or a cartoon character suddenly brought to life in the real world. Seen by himself, he might have been considered handsome. But alongside Doc, the perfection of his features seemed alien.

Joseph, expressionless, gave Harris a slow nod, then returned his attention to Doc. "I don't want to remember that. I don't want to remember you. I have a life now, and good pay for easy work. Don't drag me back into your circle." His voice was a deep, throaty rumble; Harris thought he could feel it vibrating in the steel under his feet.

"Joseph, this is important. Angus Powrie and his new master are up to something. Using devisements and devices worthy of Duncan Blackletter himself. Sending agents to the grim world and bringing people like Harris back.

"You owe it to me. I freed you. Now I need you."

Joseph stared. His expression did not change, nor did his eyes, but something did, and Harris imagined the huge, unfinished man swinging out an arm and casually batting Doc off the girder. Doc must have felt it too; he took a step back and balanced himself for trouble.

But Joseph crossed his arms over his chest and sighed. "Death follows you, Doc, and strikes down those who help you and love you while leaving you unharmed. But you're right. I owe you a debt. I will pay it. I hope you don't kill me in collecting it."

Doc was silent a long moment and Harris wished he could see his face. Then Doc said, "Did Duncan ever talk about the grim world?"

"Yes."

"Did he know devisements to take people there?"

"He went there. Not long before you caught up to him. He took gear and spent a day in that place. He left the gear there. When he returned, he said the grim world was ghastly. I think he loved it."

"What sort of gear?"

Joseph shrugged. "Crates. Boxes. He took gold to spend."

Doc fell silent. Harris broke in, "So did he have one of those conjurer's circles? Do you know where it went?"

"He did. In his conjuration laboratory. It went to the grim world, as I said."

"I meant, where *in* the grim—"

Doc said, "Wait. I don't remember a conjuration laboratory. Was this at Wickhollow?"

"Yes. It was well-hidden. You never asked about it. You just wanted help dealing with your dead friends."

Doc didn't answer for a moment. Then, his voice more quiet: "We'll go there tonight. You need to show me this laboratory."

"Meet me here at four bells. Leave me alone until then."

"Thank you." Doc turned to leave, and Harris began to grope his way back around the girder he clung to.

But Joseph spoke again. "Goodsir Greene."

Harris looked back. "Yes?"

"If you are not bound to this man, leave him. Else you will die with him."

Harris looked away from Joseph's glum features and didn't reply. He just crept back across the girders.

☙ ☙ ☙

"What did he mean?"

"About what?" Doc drove back to the Monarch Building more slowly than he'd left it; there was a shadow of gloom over his features.

"About your friends."

Doc was slow in answering. "Joseph was made by a deviser named Duncan Blackletter."

"Made?"

"He is not a man. He is a thing of clay and powerful devisements. One with a beating heart and, I think, a soul fit for rebirth. But he was Blackletter's slave, and did many bad things for him. He had no will of his own where Blackletter was concerned."

Harris thought about Joseph's unfinished face. It didn't look like clay. But he didn't look exactly human, either. "Was this Blackletter guy . . . the one who gave you all that trouble a while back?"

Doc shot him a sharp glance, then nodded. His voice was weary. "Duncan was a very bad man. Full of charm and good cheer even as he was murdering people. He set nations against one another to advance his businesses or to obtain knowledge.

"The last thing he did was to make plans to enslave the king and queen of Novimagos. He managed to do great things for Novimagos, anonymously. He built up a debt they could not repay and used dark devisements to tap it so he could bind their will to his. That's what he was about when my associates and I caught up to him in his home in Wickhollow, twenty years ago."

"Twenty?" Harris had to reevaluate Doc's age. "You don't look it, but that makes you forty at least."

Doc managed a faint smile. "At least." Then the smile faded. "Duncan and I fought. The old way. Not with guns or swords but with strength of will and old, old ritual. I was able to redirect his will against him, and he was destroyed, consumed by fire. I nearly was.

"But I'd had to concentrate all my attention on him. While my associates fought his allies, Angus Powrie and

Joseph among them. And died, one by one. Micah Cremm. Siobhan Damvert, Jean-Pierre's mother. Whiskers Okerry. All dead." Doc's voice was barely audible over the engine noise.

"I'm sorry."

"They were neither the first nor the last. Joseph is correct, Harris. Death wanders around in my shadow. My associates know it and stay with me anyway. But as soon as we can find your path back to the grim world, you will go, and be safe."

"Yeah." Safe to do what? Harris shook his head and tried to think of something else.

Just before dusk, as they rode in the vast red limousine Harris had seen last night, Alastair explained things to Harris.

"One bell" was midmorning. Two bells was exactly noon, straight up. Three was midafternoon; four near dusk; five was the shank of the evening; six was midnight; seven was the quiet time of the night—as quiet as a wide-awake city like Neckerdam ever got—and eight bells was around dawn. Each of the bells, so named for the ringing of the clock bells that marked their passing, was divided into twenty chimes; some clocks rang off the chimes as well. A chime was made up of five hundred beats, also called ticks.

Harris did some mental math and calculated each bell at about three hours, each chime at nine minutes, and each beat—what? a little over a second. As confusing a nonmetric system as he was used to back home.

So as the sun set far to the west of Neckerdam's stone and steel canyons, Jean-Pierre, driving, pulled up beside the Bergmanli Elevations building site and honked.

Joseph, clad in his work clothes and an enormous yellow shirt, emerged through the fence gate. He walked awkwardly, as though he were new to locomotion. He climbed into the car, settling alone into the rear-facing seat opposite Doc, Alastair, and Harris.

"You must be Joseph," the doctor said. "Alastair Korn-bock. Grace on you."

The man with the unfinished face gave him a little nod.

"Care for something to eat? We'll have better pick-ings before we leave Neckerdam."

Joseph shook his head.

Alastair reached into the little red satchel he'd brought and dragged out a green glass flask; he waved it hope-fully. "Uisge?"

Joseph shook his head.

Alastair sighed, uncapped the flask, and took a sip. "This is going to be a long drive."

He was right. A strained silence settled over the car. Jean-Pierre seemed strangely stiff during the drive; Noriko kept her attention on him, and Harris felt, in spite of the emotional detachment she projected, that she was concerned for him.

Doc spent his time disassembling the volt-meter the ersatz musician had carried. "Interesting design," he said quietly. "Old techniques, decades old, but very creative. I think I can improve on it, though." He seemed disturbed by the design of the device and spoke very little after that.

They took the Island Bridge to Long Island; it amused Harris to learn that it *was* called Long Island. Some things obviously translated quite well from the grim world to the fair one. The community on the far side of the bridge was Pataqqsit, and in the twilight it seemed to be half city, half green park.

On the far side of Pataqqsit, where traffic thinned so that the red limousine was often alone on the tree-lined road, Harris saw the first windmill. It was tall and more slender than the archaic sort of grain-grinding mills he'd seen in photographs.

Then they topped a hill and he could see what looked like an ocean of the things laid out below him; the road cut through an enormous field full of windmills. "Jesus," he said. "What's all this?"

"Wind farm," Alastair said. "Otherwise Neckerdam would have no way to power her lights, her underground trains and high-trains, or anything."

"What about coal? Oil?"

Alastair laughed. "While we're at it, why not lean out the window to empty our bowels instead of using the water closet?"

Doc didn't look up, but his tone was admonishing. "Alastair."

Harris frowned. "Then what do cars run on?"

"Alcohol, most of them." Alastair fondly patted his red medical bag, where he'd replaced the glass flask. "Oh, not the good stuff, of course. That's for fueling people."

Noriko turned back to face them. "I once owned a two-wheeler that ran on gas I bought from chicken farms and sewer plants."

"Chicken—methane. Of course. This place is an environmentalist's dream." Harris turned away to watch the windmills pass by and wondered why their answers annoyed him.

Probably because their responses were so unquestioning. But that didn't make much sense. He'd seen no sign that the normal people of Neckerdam were fanatically devoted to the clean, organic, *tedious* causes some of his own friends back home were. So why didn't they use all the same things the grimworlders did?

A few miles further on, they reached a large stone sign reading "Wickhollow." At Doc's direction, Jean-Pierre drove through the quiet town with its curiously irregular brick homes and turned down a blacktop country road, then took a narrower dirt road that led far away from the lights of the town. Finally, where trees and thick underbrush gave way to a good-sized clearing, he pulled to one side and stopped the car.

In the light cast by the nearly full moon, Harris could see a large black rectangle in the center of the clearing. On the blackness was a lot of standing rubble, some of which looked like remnants of a chimney. He followed the others as they piled out of the car.

It must have once been a huge house, Harris realized. The black rectangle was an enormous array of foundation stones, now cracked, with weeds growing through them. The blackening looked like old fire damage. After the house had burned, someone had pulled down much of the remainder and scattered the pieces all over the lot.

Doc walked out onto the foundation, looking here and there, pausing for a long moment beside an unmarked section of stone, staring down at it with eyes out of memory. Then he shook himself and looked back at Joseph. "The conjuration laboratory?"

Joseph moved out on the foundation and moved around until he found what he wanted: an irregularly cracked section of stone, an oval roughly five feet long and four high, piled high with a mound of fallen rubble.

"Just below where Duncan died," Doc said, his tone low.

Joseph had to clear the rubble away before he could get at the foundation stone beneath, and this he did with terrifying ease, scooping up thigh-high piles of stones that must have weighed hundreds of pounds and hurling them off the foundation. Then he stepped aside and waited.

"How do you open it?" Doc asked.

"I do not," Joseph said. "It's a deviser's laboratory."

"Ah." Doc closed his eyes.

Harris saw his lips move as he murmured silent words. For long moments nothing happened; then there was a faint vibration in the ground.

A square portion of the foundation stone cantilevered upward, revealing a rectangular black space below. A dry, musty smell wafted out. Doc opened his eyes and nodded in apparent satisfaction.

Alastair brought an armful of long, clumsy-looking flashlights out from the car's trunk—boot? Harris remembered them calling it a boot, like the British—and passed them around. They all lit the ungainly devices and shined their beams down on the dull gray steps heading into the earth. Doc led the way down.

The conjuration laboratory of Duncan Blackletter turned out to be a large, simple chamber. Two facing walls were covered in bookshelves, many of them now collapsed with rot and age and the weight of the volumes they held. In one corner were a plush chair, rotting and bug-eaten, and a collapsed mass that must have once been an uncomfortable cot.

Most of the floor was decorated with what Harris now recognized as conjurer's circles: unbroken rings of paint or carefully laid-out stones, decorated along the rims with painted symbols that looked a little like *Ms* and *Ws* and *Hs*—two or three vertical lines connected at the top, middle or bottom by short horizontal lines. The writing style didn't look at all familiar.

Jean-Pierre cast his flashlight beam again at the standing shelves of books. He looked tense and grim. "With my luck, we'll be digging our way through that until I'm grayed with age."

Alastair peered into the younger man's dark hair. "Too late. Going gray already."

"I am not." Jean-Pierre, scowling, pulled down a lock of hair and put the flashlight beam on it.

Alastair moved to the bookcase. "Stop worrying. It's good to get older."

"You're lying to me."

"The blood cools. Women become . . . less important, somehow."

"I'll die first."

Harris saw Doc smile, just a little, before the man moved to join Alastair.

It wasn't as bad as they had feared. Duncan Blackletter had kept a very organized library, and Joseph remembered which volumes had served it as an index. They were rotted now, whole sections falling to pieces no matter how carefully they were opened, but the pages pertaining to special sendings of conjuration circles were intact. Within an hour they'd found the bookshelf where the appropriate reference works lay and busied themselves looking through the aged and damaged volumes.

Harris found that he wasn't much help. Most of the works were written in that alphabet he couldn't read. Jean-Pierre described it as the old alphabet of Cretanis: "Harder to learn than the modern Isperian alphabet, and mostly forgotten these days. They don't even teach it in school."

Noriko, Joseph, and Harris, unschooled in the antique letters, went back up into the fresh air and left the other three to do the academic research. Harris brushed some of the dust off a level slab of rock, then sat. Noriko announced that she would stand watch. She disappeared into the surrounding woods.

Joseph walked awkwardly among the ruins, never slowing, never stopping for a good look, never evidencing any emotion . . . but the giant's hands would occasionally tighten into fists.

After a while, curiosity got the better of Harris. "Hey. Joseph."

Joseph, poking around in the wreckage of the chimney, looked over.

"If it bothers you so much, why don't you take a walk? Get away from it for a while. I'll honk if we need to leave."

Joseph shook his head. "Too late for that. I am back. Back where I was born. Doc has summoned up the memories. A walk will not bury them again."

"Did you really—" The question was half-out before Harris realized what he was about to ask. He cut it off and frantically searched for another way to finish the question.

"Kill them?"

Harris winced. "Well . . . yeah."

"Yes, I did." Joseph moved up in front of Harris and leaned against the upright section of chimney. "I injured Doc and killed Whiskers Okerry. It was easy. I held him over my head and twisted him until his back broke. He lived for a while. Long enough to see Angus Powrie break Siobhan Damvert's neck."

The giant's tone was so calm that it took Harris a moment to grasp what he was hearing. Gooseflesh rose on his arms. "Jesus Christ, *why?*"

"I had to. Duncan told me to."

"And you did everything he told you to do?"

"Everything." Joseph reached up to rub his forehead. "The words are gone now. The ones once written here; Doc took them away. While they were on me, I did everything Duncan bade." His face hadn't changed, but there was something in his eyes, dark shadows of pain, that suggested Joseph hadn't mentioned the worst of the things Duncan Blackletter had made him do.

It was another moment before Harris realized the rest—the fact that Angus Powrie had murdered Jean-Pierre's mother. No wonder he had become so hyperactive when he learned that Powrie was back.

Harris didn't ask anything more; he let Joseph return to his lonely thoughts.

The limousine, black as a moonless night, glided to a stop behind the anonymous brown Dodge van. A round face appeared in the van's rear window, and its owner gave the limo a thumbs-up sign before disappearing.

Phipps shut the engine off and glanced back at his passenger. "He says she's still in the house." He picked up the object lying on the seat beside him—a device shaped like a volt-meter—and keyed it on. After a few moments he added, "He's right. Your signal and Adonis' nearly drown it out, but it's there."

The old man looked around until Phipps pointed to a specific house—two stories, brick, nicely appointed. "Ah. Lights still on, I see. Night owls. We'll wait until they're asleep."

"Yes, sir." Phipps pulled the stun-gun from his pocket and checked it to make sure it was still charged. Then, his revolver. Left-handed because of the damned injury to his other arm, he clumsily pressed the catch and swung the cylinder out to make sure it was still loaded with the .357 hollowpoints.

CHAPTER NINE

Doc, Alastair, and Jean-Pierre spilled up out of the underground lab as though they'd been driven out by a smoke bomb. Doc gave the foundation stone a push; it was an effort, but the stone fell into place with a boom. Then they headed for the car; Harris scrambled to catch up to them. "What's up?"

"We have it," Doc said. He clutched a sagging leather-bound volume to him as though it were precious treasure. He reached in through the driver's window and honked, then climbed into the back; the others resumed their seats, Noriko returning fast enough to beat Joseph into the car. In moments, Jean-Pierre had them rolling back along the road that had brought them.

"So what does that mean?" Harris persisted.

"A complete ritual set," Doc said. "The devisement to take you back to the grim world, Harris. We'll be departing from the conjurer's circle where you arrived."

"*We*? Who's going with me?"

"I am. You need to find Gaby, and I need to find Gabrielle, and we must find out if they are the same woman. Gaby is in danger, and so Gabrielle probably is, too. I want to waste as little time as possible. We need to get clothes and gear back at the Monarch Building, anything you think will not stand out too much in the grim world, and then return to Heinzlin Corners."

"So how does it work?"

Doc patted the leather volume. "The usual way. You assemble sacrificial goods, set up your ritual field, make your invocations and pleas, focus your mind and intent, and it happens. In theory. Each devisement is unique, of course, with variations for the types of the sacrificial items, the exact nature of the invocation and the godly aspect to whom it is addressed, the precise construction of the conjurer's circle—"

"I'm sorry I asked. This is starting to make my head hurt."

Doc smiled. "There is also an expenditure of personal energy, a telling one. Alastair will be performing the ceremony tonight—"

Alastair perked up. "Thank you for telling me."

"— so I will not be excessively wearied by the transfer. That way I should retain the wherewithal to send us back when we wish.

"But listen to me, Harris." Doc's expression, momentarily illuminated by moonlight, had become somber. "If we are separated or I do not survive, I need you to bring Gaby to the conjurer's circle precisely a day after our arrival. Exactly eight bells after the devisement is cast, the far conjurer's circle becomes alive again and sends everything within it back to the fair world. It is a process that does not require the deviser be there. Do you understand?"

"Yeah. It's a deadman switch. I can send her back without you." Harris thought it over. "That's what happened in Central Park. I was standing on the conjurer's circle when the time came up."

"Yes."

"Well, don't make me use the deadman switch. Alastair and Noriko will come across and make me explain why. I don't want to have to do that."

"That's true. I wouldn't want to."

❦   ❦   ❦

Doc's room in the Monarch Building was barely larger or more personal than the one Harris had been given. Harris spent a couple of minutes picking through the man's wardrobe and looking for appropriate clothing. He gave up quickly: "There's no way we're going to make you blend in, sorry. So take this ruffled white shirt job and the brown pants and vest. We'll pass you off as a sixties burnout case or a disco revivalist."

Doc looked confused by the terminology, but retreated to his water closet to change.

Harris nosed around a bit while he waited. The books on Doc's low bookshelf looked like technical manuals, but their titles suggested they were textbooks written by New Age gurus: *Kelloqq's Musings on Excarnation Theory*, *Groundline Interaction With the Tallysin Aura in Controlled Environments*, *Traditional Dances and Heightened-State Mental Acuity*. Harris grimaced.

"Goodsir." It was a woman's voice, low and urgent, with a bit of mechanical hiss over it.

Startled, Harris spun around. There was no one behind him—but against the wall, Doc's talk-box had come alive.

And there, staring at him from the screen, was Gaby.

Again she was against the stony background and wearing the slinky dress he was really beginning to appreciate. He had a sudden urge to see the whole costume. He had another urge to help her take it off.

"Hi." He moved closer to the set, afraid with each step that she'd disappear. "Are you talking to me now?"

"Do you really know me?" Her expression was somber, tense.

"I thought so, yeah." Bitterness gnawed at him. "I guess maybe I didn't."

"Tell me *what* you know—"

Harris heard Doc open the bathroom door. Gabrielle heard it too, looked startled . . . and her picture faded to a little white dot. Harris cursed.

Doc emerged. He wore the clothes picked out for him; his hair, drawn back in a braid, concealed his ears. He looked no stranger than some musicians Harris knew. He gave Harris a curious look. "Who were you talking to?"

As Alastair drove them back to the rented house where the conjurer's circle lay, Harris told Doc about the conversation. Doc looked briefly annoyed that he'd missed Gaby—rather, that she seemed to have deliberately avoided him.

At the little estate on Heinzlin Corners, Alastair walked around the conjurer's circle and, consulting one page of Duncan's book, adjusted the placement of some of the rocks; he told Harris that he was performing corrections. "Someone who knew what he was doing has meddled with this," he said. "Made a trap of it. If I'd left it as it was, gods only know what you'd have been when you got there."

Meanwhile, Doc checked over his gear. A small, brassy-looking revolver worn in a shoulder holster under the shirt; a leather pouch full of little devices on his belt; the assassins' "volt-meter" in his hand. "The charge on you should wear off as soon as we reach the grim world," he told Harris. "But with study I may be able to key it to find Gabrielle. It seems evident that the kidnappers used something of the sort to find her originally. And this device was a little antiquated. I've made some improvements to it."

Harris wore Gaby's fanny pack with her possessions in it. Alastair solemnly offered him a pistol like Doc's, but after a moment's thought Harris shook his head. "I'd just shoot myself in the foot," he said.

A chime later Alastair got things under way. First, he asked, "You're sure you don't want me along? Or the others? Or some troops?"

Doc shook his head. "If we haven't returned in eight

bells, we have both failed. You are the only one left who understands Duncan's work well enough to try again. You have to stay. And the more of us who go, the more we will be conspicuous. So, no." And that was that.

Doc and Harris waited in the center of the conjurer's circle. Alastair, his face lit from below by the oil lamp that rested beside the book, hovered over the proper page. He began reciting words in a language Harris did not understand—thick, gooey words that put Harris in mind of a preacher trying to cough up a peanut butter sandwich stuck to the roof of his mouth.

The recitation went on and on, long enough for Harris to become bored and restless . . . until he began noticing things.

Such as the way the pines nearest the conjurer's circle were beginning to shed their needles—they'd already looked a little bare, and now even more needles began raining down on the ground.

Such as the way the wind was stirring, tugging at Harris' clothes and hair, feeling almost like tiny, delicate hands playing with him.

Such as the way the moon and stars suddenly felt like eyes staring down on him.

Harris brushed away the gooseflesh rising on his arms. Then, all over Neckerdam, clocks mounted high in impossible skyscrapers began solemnly bonging off six bells, not quite in chorus.

When the nearest tower chimed for the third time, it happened: the world changed shape. He saw the trees growing tall, the kneeling Alastair stretching all out of proportion.

The first sensation of dizziness touched him. Harris didn't wait for it to worsen; he dropped to one knee and put his hands on the ground for balance. Alastair, still chanting, his words deepened and coarsened by what was happening, was suddenly twelve feet high and still growing. Doc awkwardly dropped to sit beside Harris, dizziness and annoyance clear on his face.

Then the pop.

The trees were suddenly gone, and Alastair with them. The stars above were gone, obscured by clouds and haze, but somehow the sky was friendlier—there were no malevolent eyes staring down at them.

Central Park.

It was as if Harris had been wearing a heavy weight of tension around his neck on a cord ... and the cord were suddenly cut. He felt light, and light-headed. He was home.

The old man felt the faintest chill, like a cold trickle of water down his neck and back. He rubbed his neck to be rid of the sensation.

He didn't like that. His instincts were very good. It didn't pay to ignore them. "Bill, check to make sure she's still there."

Phipps obligingly picked up the tracing device and switched it on. After a minute, the little screen glowed green.

"She hasn't budged. Wish she'd go to sleep. I . . . " His voice trailed off.

The old man waited an impatient moment. "Yes, what?"

"Nothing, I think. Caught a faint blip way off at the edge of the screen. Just a spike, faded in and out. Sort of like the way the neopagan festival we scanned kept futzing with our readings. It's gone now."

The old man sat back, scowling. He had to fight back a sudden urge to take the tracing device and go roaring off in the direction of that phantom blip. But as close as he was to finishing this long, long stage of the plan, it wouldn't do to go running off like a reckless youth.

The chill faded, but his unease did not.

During the cab ride, Doc was fascinated by the sights and sounds of Manhattan. His head whipped around as he stared at the clothes people wore, at the cars, at the skyscrapers—buildings no taller than Neckerdam's tallest, but very different in style and construction. He said nothing, though at several times he seemed to want to.

At Gaby's apartment building, Harris pressed the buzzer for her apartment, but no one answered. However, her keys gave him access to the lobby, and three flights of stairs later he and Doc stood outside her door.

Or, rather, her brand-new door. That's right, Mr. Crenshaw had said that somebody had smashed her door to pieces. The new one didn't open to their knock. Worse, her door key didn't open it.

"She sure got it fixed fast," Harris said, grumbling. "Any reason we need to go in? I can make the calls from my apartment."

"We need to go in. I want to see if her kidnappers left any sign behind."

"Can you pick the lock or something?"

"Something." Doc wrapped his hand in his handkerchief. He looked back and forth along the hall, then gripped the knob and tried to turn it.

Nothing happened for a long moment—except Doc's arm trembled almost invisibly, and a vein stood out on his wrist. Then, with a sharp cracking sound, the lock turned in his hand. Broken. He pushed it open, glanced nonchalantly at Harris, and entered.

Harris found the light switch by feel but didn't turn it on until the door was closed behind them.

Gaby's tidy one-bedroom apartment. Her furnishings were old but clean; her walls were decorated with framed prints and posters, some of which he'd given her. Harris walked Doc around, explaining things to him: *TV Guide* and bug-bombs and junk food leftovers and why the TV received but didn't call out and dishwashers and blue toilet drop-in tablets and clocks with LCD displays; the list went on and on. Partway into it, Harris realized that this was just the sort of stuff *he'd* been asking during the month-long day he'd spent in the fair world.

Finally Doc settled in to look over the traces of intrusion—signs of violence in the living room, footprints that were too large to belong to anyone but Adonis. "Make your talk-box calls," he said.

"Sure. It may take a while. It's one A.M.—uh, nearly seven bells—and I'll be waking people up. Conversations won't be too friendly."

Doc tried not to show his irritation. He couldn't make his thoughts run in the same direction, couldn't focus them. Each one wanted to go its own way, to marvel, to deduce, to condemn.

The grim world. He supposed he'd always believed in it. So many of the legends of his youth had their bases in scientific truths. But this world was nothing like he imagined it to be.

Animals didn't befilth the places where they lived, but the men of the grim world did. His nose was sharper than most men's, but surely they couldn't all be immune to the bad mechanical smell the automobiles spat out.

He wished he could read the writing that decorated the ground-floor exteriors of so many of the buildings, but the cursive script was difficult to decipher and so many of the words meant nothing. Did these scrawls act as wards against bad devisements, appeals to the gods, simple territorial markings?

And the buildings themselves—the men of the grim world must not have come from a tradition of defensive buildings. So many of their structures had windows on the ground floor; some of the high-rises seemed to be made *entirely* of windows. He resolved to look into their techniques of construction; not many of the architectural styles he'd seen here had appealed to him, but that one had.

The grimworlders' technological achievement was amazing. Talk-boxes that people could effortlessly carry, in singles, doubles, and triples. He hadn't yet seen any portable quadruples—no full-picture send and receive in a hand-carry device. But shows from all over the world came in on the triples.

Harris had said they had aircraft that surpassed the speed of sound, and he desperately wanted to see one in flight.

Human skin colors he'd never seen before. Browns so deep as to be almost black. Yellow tones. But as on the fair world, the darks and duskies of the grim world didn't seem to have all the advantages of the lights.

The language. Harris had been right. Doc recited poetry to himself to test its rhyme and scansion. His words were the same they had ever been; no mystic translation had taken place. So Low Cretanis and English were dialects of the same tongue. He'd also heard dusky men of the grim world shouting in something like Castilian.

It made no sense. He could think of no way for languages to stay so similar if they hadn't been in constant contact in the centuries since the worlds drifted apart. Yet somehow they had.

Other similarities. The cars were as related as the languages; he was certain that he could drive one of the automobiles of the grim world, even if they did have only one gear. Dwellings here were broken down by familiar human needs: parlors, bedchambers, kitchens, privies.

So much iron. He'd burned his hands half a dozen times since he'd arrived, as if every other thing he touched had just been resting on a hot stove. No use letting Harris know; there was nothing he could do about it. Doc hadn't thought to carry gloves—a careless error; he was annoyed that he hadn't given it more thought. Now he just let Harris precede him everywhere. He'd pick up gloves as soon as he could.

So much to learn . . . but for now, the only thing he could afford the time to learn was the nature of Gabriela Donohue's attackers.

Harris had to use the phone in the bedroom; the one in the living room had been torn free from its old-fashioned wall connector. The bedroom was stuffy, so he opened the window over the fire escape and looked out on the sparse 11th Street traffic while he called.

"Hi, it's Harris. I'm looking for Gaby. It's kind of an emergency. Are you sure you don't? No, sorry, I wasn't implying anything. I know it's late, I'm sorry, bye."

But the third call was to Elaine's, and a second later Gaby was on the line. "Harris, are you all right?"

"I'm fine." *I almost got my leg cut off but a magical doctor put me back together.* "How about you?"

"I'm okay. I've been so worried. Did the police find you? Where are you?"

"Your place. No, I haven't talked to the police. They're kind of low on my priority list."

"Did you talk to Leo next door? I asked him to kind of keep an eye on my place. If he hears something suspicious he may call the cops."

"We'll keep quiet."

Doc appeared in the doorway, the volt-meter in his hands. Harris said, "Doc, I have her."

"So do I, I think. I rekeyed this to show myself . . . and I read another signal, probably hers. She'd be nearly due east of here, ten or fifteen destads, I think."

"Who's Doc?"

"A friend, Gaby. Wait a minute—you mean you don't know him? Doc, with the Sidhe Foundation?"

"Huh?"

Harris looked up at Doc. "She says she doesn't know you from Adam. What's a destad?"

"Two thousand paces—ten stads. If her signal strength is similar to yours, she is—"

"Ten or fifteen away. Right." Harris did a rough conversion: one pace would equal about one yard. That made her twenty to thirty thousand yards. Sixty to ninety thousand feet. Divide by five thousand . . . "Yep. That puts her out somewhere near New Rochelle, all right. Gaby, Doc here has a gizmo that you have to see. It shows that you're at Elaine's."

"You've got to be joking."

"No . . . Oh, shit. If Doc has this thing working right, then the old guy . . . Gaby, the old guy has to have one of these, too. He probably knows where you are *right now.*"

He heard her hiss of breath, then: "Stay there. I'll get there as fast as I can." And she hung up.

"Dammit." Harris slapped the handset down in its cradle. "She's coming here, Doc. It'll be a little while."

Doc nodded. "That will give me more time to collect scrapings and measure aura traces. There was something very ugly in these quarters a few hours ago . . . and if I read the signs right, Adonis was not the ugliest."

CHAPTER TEN

Doc closed his right eye and returned to scanning the living room. It wasn't easy; though his Gift was very strong and well trained, ever since he'd come to the grim world it had been very hard to call upon.

It was too bad Alastair wasn't here; the doctor's good eye was so much better than Doc's. Alastair might have been able to make more of the faint haze of aura that still hung in the apartment. All Doc could see was traces of two aura presences. One was obviously "Adonis"— dim, channelled anger and animal spirit.

The other, almost washed away by Adonis' trace, was dark and very complex. Someone with the Gift. Maybe even a deviser. Doc had seen the auras of many of the Gifted and a few devisers . . . and this aura trace was starting to look familiar.

Almost as familiar as his own. Doc found himself swallowing as his stomach rebelled. It was different from the aura he remembered, but not more different than could be accounted for by twenty years of profaning the spirit.

Duncan's aura. Just older. Bleaker. Purer. He'd started to suspect when he studied the tracing device, but it had been easier not to believe.

These thoughts held Doc's attention so completely that he never heard the faint creak of footsteps out in the hall. He didn't recognize danger until it was on him: the door slamming inward, two men in street clothes and coats pointing guns at him, shouting words in angry tones.

Solemnly, he raised his hands, with a little prayer to the gods that this gesture was universal.

"Lights going out, sir."

The old man started out of his doze and looked over at the Carpenter house. The porch light was now off, and as he watched, the last of the bedroom lights went out. "Ah. Very good. We'll wait a few minutes and then go in."

"Sir . . . Things would be easier and safer if we just eliminate her."

"I want to study her."

"Yes, but—forgive me—wanting to study her has caused us a lot of problems so far."

"You're entirely correct." The old man sank comfortably back against the soft seat. "William, does gravity ever bother you?"

"I never gave it much thought. It's not as though I have a choice."

"Ah, precisely my point. William, all existence tries to dictate what you can do and not do. I find it tremendously galling that life insists that we use mechanical devices to escape gravity's bond. That we find ourselves inconvenienced by luck or practical considerations. That we die. Freedom consists of telling the universe what to do. Not the reverse."

"I don't get you."

"Well, in the short term, it means I have chosen to study Miss Donahue before we eliminate her. I have *decided*. And regardless of the relative importance of that study, I refuse to let man or god stop me. My wish is more important than theirs. Else I'm just another bee in the hive. Do you understand?"

I understand you've got some busted gears. "Yes, sir."

❧   ❧   ❧

Harris finished stuffing Gaby's pocketbook and address book back into her pack. He rose to shut the window again—and felt it shake under his hand as the apartment door slammed open. Someone in the living room, an unknown male, shouted "Police, don't move!"

Cops. That was okay. He had a right to be here. He might be arrested, but Gaby would show up and fix things.

If she made it home.

If she weren't grabbed again on the way.

And if she were, and he were in jail, he wouldn't be able to help her. Dammit! He could run out on Doc, or stay here and perhaps not be available when Gaby needed him. Swearing to himself, he stepped out through the window onto the fire escape, then began descending as quickly and quietly as he could.

He got to the bottom of the fire escape on the second floor. Below was the sidewalk along 11th Street. He climbed over the wrought-iron railing and lowered himself partway down, then dropped to the concrete, jarring his feet.

So what had happened? Probably Leo Crenshaw next door, being a dutiful neighbor. Such a nice guy. Harris felt a sudden urge to throw the man out his window.

He heard a scream from the window he'd just left.

A man's scream. He thought it was Doc's.

Phipps left the limousine and joined the men from the van. They sent Adonis around to the back of the house— instructing it very carefully, as they always had to do, where the various hands of the pocket watch had to be before it walked through the back door. Then Phipps and two of his men moved up to the front door.

The old man watched and waited. He smiled; they were so close to his dream. It was like the end of a huge, exquisite meal, and the masterwork of a dessert had just been laid before him.

He watched one of Phipps' men—was it Dominguez, the one with all the tattoos? no, Kleine, the one with

the charming children in all the wallet photos—kick in
the front door. The three men rushed in. One of them
closed the door immediately.

Minutes passed. Lights went on and off at various places
in the Carpenter house. There were no gunshots, and
the old man nodded approvingly. Knives were much better.
Less apt to wake the neighbors.

But Phipps and all the others came trotting back out
of the house . . . *without* the Donohue woman. Phipps'
face was rigid as he climbed back into the driver's seat.
"They're gone," he said.

The old man raised his brows. "Interesting."

Phipps picked up the tracer and turned it on. "The
cars are still in the garage, and the place was locked up
tight. Maybe they spotted us— Dammit!"

"Is she not registering?"

"No, she is. Her signal's getting fainter. She has a big
head start. But that phantom blip is back." Phipps scowled
at the device, then handed it over to the old man.

The screen showed a big, fuzzy blur in the center. That
represented the overlapping emanations from the old man
and Adonis. The old man tilted and rotated the device
until he picked up the fainter glow that had to be the
Donohue woman.

But there, in the same direction, at the edge of the
screen, was a new glow. Faint, fading in and out. But if
he read its characteristics right, it was a strong signal,
far away, at the limits of the device's ability to detect.

He bit back on a curse. "Let's go. The Donohue woman
first. Then we find out who our new friend is."

Phipps put the limo into motion. The van carrying the
other men and Adonis lumbered into line behind.

One man kept Doc under the gun while the other
quickly checked out the other rooms in the apartment,
then stood Doc up against the wall and patted him all
over. A search for hidden weapons, Doc guessed, and
they found his pistol immediately. The man doing the

patting pulled it free, saying "Lookee here. Don't tell me you have a license for this."

"I—"

"Shut up. I'm required to advise you of your rights. You have the right to remain silent . . . "

The man gave Doc a halting, badly memorized litany of his rights—good to know, he thought, and committed them to memory as they were spoken—while finishing the search. Then the man twisted his arm up behind him, obviously to conduct him to whatever served them as a gaol. Or so Doc thought.

Then pain, horrible burning pain clamped onto his wrist. It shot like fire up his arm and through his body. He heard the bellow of agony tear free of him, felt his knees begin to buckle, saw redness cloak his vision.

Torture. Harris didn't say these police were torturers. *Murderers.* He twisted, brought his other elbow into his torturer's gut, and was rewarded with a grunt of pain from the man. But the pressure on his arm didn't let up, and shock was already robbing him of his strength. With his free hand he shoved against the wall, pushing them both backward—

Then the second man hammered his head, once, twice, with something small and metal-hard. All strength left him and he crashed to the old, gray-green carpet.

As Doc's senses dimmed, he felt them twist his other arm around and shackle it, too, with the poisonous metal. Pain tore through his other arm.

"Christ, Jay, what's going on with his wrists?"

"Hell if I know. Maybe they were already like that."

Doc tried to speak, but the pain was too intense. Only a faint hiss emerged.

"Get the cuffs off him."

"Hell you say. He'll be all over us again."

"Then get on the phone and call this in. We're going to need . . . "

That was the last he heard.

Harris' stomach did flip-flops: what were they doing to Doc up there? Why? Had he been stupid enough to attack the cops?

Hell, "cops" didn't mean anything to Doc, and there was no telling what he might have done. At least there hadn't been any gunshots. Harris got to the corner and looked up the street. There was no police unit parked within sight; they must have arrived in an unmarked car. And in a couple of minutes, they'd be leading him down in cuffs . . .

Cuffs. Did New York cops use steel handcuffs, or nickel-plated? Oh, hell.

Harris ran to the entrance, praying he'd remembered to take Gaby's keys—and there they were, still in the fanny pack. Once again they got him through the main door.

He ran up to the third story two steps at a time, then slowed for the last flight.

No one in the hall outside her apartment. Mr. Crenshaw would be in his room, waiting for someone to tell him everything was all right.

Harris moved up to the door. It was ajar a couple of inches. He faintly heard someone talking. Peeking in, he could see Doc's feet. Doc had to be lying on his stomach. The man's legs shook.

Harris hesitated. If the cops had cuffs on him, Doc could die before they figured it out. But if that wasn't what was going on, Harris could be throwing away years of his life.

Or getting killed.

False bravado steeled him against that last thought. *Hell, I almost got killed just showing that I could walk on I-beams.* He threw the door open and charged.

One man, black and in good shape, was just emerging from the kitchen. The other, white and big, was kneeling over Doc's body in the middle of the living room. There was something going on with Doc's hands . . .

The men were caught off guard. Harris stopped over Doc's body and rotated into a side kick that caught the black man right in the balls, folding him up like a hinge; he fell to his knees.

Harris, still recovering, drove a knuckle-punch into the second man's neck; then he had his balance again and brought his foot up in a forward kick against the man's face. The white man, already grabbing at his injured throat, went over backwards, hitting the floor with a boom that shook the walls.

A glance for the black man; that man was up on shaky legs and was clawing awkwardly at his coat pocket. Harris stepped in close and spun. His backhand cracked into the man's temple, dazing him, and a follow-through punch combination to the gut and ribs put him down.

Less than ten seconds from start to finish. Harris stood over the bodies of the men he'd beaten and trembled as though he'd run a marathon.

He'd just beaten up two cops. His life was over.

Doc. The white-haired man lay still as death . . . and his *hands*. The flesh around the wrists was blackened as though it had been exposed to an acetylene torch. Blisters radiated away from the handcuffs, covering his hands, continuing up under his sleeves. His breathing was fast and shallow, like a dog's pant—but at least he was breathing.

Harris hurriedly took the cops' guns, then shut the door to the apartment. A minute's worth of searching yielded the handcuff keys in one of their pants' pockets.

Harris unlocked the cuffs on Doc, then delicately pried them free of his flesh. Blisters broke as he did so, and clear fluid ran across the man's burned wrists; Harris had to swallow down revulsion as he got Doc free of the restraints.

Now what? Tossing the cuffs across the room didn't magically cure Doc. His wrists still looked terrible. He was still out cold. And the cops wouldn't stay unconscious forever. They'd wake up mad . . . and more were probably coming. Dammit!

Wait a second. He'd been through their pocket goods

while looking for the keys, and . . . Harris scrambled over
to where one officer's wallet lay; he flipped through it.

Driver's license, Jay E. Costigan. Credit cards. Money.
No badge. No police ID.

He dug out the black man's wallet. Same story. And
this man had in his pocket a volt-meter device like the
one Doc had taken from the attackers at the Monarch
Building.

They weren't police. They were more of the men who'd
grabbed Gaby. But that meant the cops wouldn't be coming for him: good.

He left Gaby's apartment, ran to the next door up the
hall, and pounded on it. Mr. Crenshaw was a bit of a
nosy pain, but he was always willing to help—

Crenshaw shouted from beyond the door, his voice
wavering, "Go away! I have a gun! I've called the police!"

For a moment, Doc imagined he was back in the burning house in Wickhollow, watching fire claim the body
of Siobhan Damvert, feeling fire climb his sleeves and
back.

Then, even through the cloud of pain, he knew. Poi-
son. He was badly poisoned and probably in shock. And
he was upside down—being carried by someone with a
jarring gait. He opened his eyes.

The backs of gray-clad legs, slowly and shakily descending a dark stairway. Every step shot pain through Doc's
arms, which hung limp. "Harris?"

"Doc? Thank God. Can you walk?"

No. He wouldn't manage ten steps. "I . . . yes."

Harris waited until they reached the next landing, then
lowered Doc as carefully as he could. Doc couldn't bear
to soften the descent with his arms; he took it on his shoulder and neck and let himself roll down until he was on
his back.

Harris, sweating profusely and stinking of effort, stared
helplessly down at him. He reached for Doc's hands,
obviously thought better of it, and knelt beside him. He

grabbed him around the torso and helped him sit up. Even that effort was almost too much; Doc almost passed out just getting upright. But a minute later Harris got Doc up on his feet, pulling Doc's arm over his shoulder. Doc didn't let him know how much that hurt.

They took the stairs as fast as Doc's weakened, rubbery legs would allow. "We're on the second floor," Harris said. "Almost down. Gaby's next-door neighbor heard enough to scare him and he rolled the cops. The real ones, I mean. I can hear a siren. Man, I've got to get you some medical help."

Doc couldn't lift his head but could shake it. "No," he whispered. "They would kill me. By accident if nothing else. Get me clear of here."

A dozen more bone-jarring steps and they were at the front door, then beyond. There was no traffic on the street, but the sirens were getting louder. Harris got Doc down the concrete steps and to the sidewalk, then turned away from the sound of sirens. "Easy does it. Look casual. Look *drunk*. If we can make it a couple of blocks, we can get to the subway and be away from here."

Something stirred at the back of Doc's memory. It was so hard to think . . . "Gaby Donohue was returning home."

"Shit."

"No need to curse."

"Right, right. I've got no reason at all."

CHAPTER ELEVEN

Gaby put down the phone, took a deep breath, and told Elaine and Jim, "We need to get out of here." Then she explained.

It was a nerve-wracking ten minutes. They dressed, crept out the back door into the darkened yard and climbed clumsily over the back fence. A few minutes later and a block away, they were hammering on the back door to the house of one of Elaine's suicide-hotline friends.

A good friend. She heard what Elaine had to say and volunteered Gaby her car with no hesitation. Then she set about opening up the bed in the couch for Elaine and Jim.

So her departure had come off without a problem. Her arrival at home was another matter.

When she pulled onto her own street, she saw the official vehicle, a squad car, parked right in front of her building. Something had obviously gone wrong here.

No parking available—as usual. She parked in a tow-away zone around the corner and ran up the stairs to her floor. She took a deep breath as she saw a uniformed officer emerging from her door. "Hi," she said. "I live here."

The officer smiled. It wasn't an amused smile. "Go right in."

※ ※ ※

Three minutes later the black limousine cruised past the same block. The old man in the backseat looked over the police unit and made a disgusted noise. "Tell the van to stay and watch. We'll follow the other signal."

Harris couldn't have had more trouble juggling cats. He had to walk and support Doc—not easy, as the man was half-unconscious and *heavy*. He had to make sure all the stuff he'd taken from the apartment didn't spill out of his pockets, and that included three revolvers and the damned volt-meter gadget. Thank God these ugly slacks with the dorky high waistband had deep, deep pockets. And he had to figure out what to do next. Doc wasn't conscious enough to do much thinking.

Run. That was first. Just outside the building's main door, they'd turned left, toward Bank Street, and rounded the corner before the sirens arrived. Harris heard the police car pull up in front of the building and cut its siren. The two of them weren't spotted, a little bit of good luck mixed in with all the bad. Now they were headed toward the nearest subway station he could remember, at 7th Avenue and 14th, and he felt fresh out of ideas.

Why was that? Used to be he was full of ideas. Just in the last day, though, Doc and the others had been doing all the thinking for him. Hell, he'd been letting Zeb do all his thinking before that. He was out of the habit.

It was time to think again, and to think analytically. Like dissecting an opponent's technique before moving against him.

Problem. Doc was hurt and had refused medical aid. That meant Harris had to do everything for both of them. No solution for it. Except maybe to get help Doc would accept. Harris could trust Zeb and make Doc accept it; maybe he'd stop by and visit his manager. Ex-manager.

He noticed under a streetlight that Doc's hands seemed to be a little better; the blisters hadn't faded, but they had closed and the flesh around the wrists was showing

a little pink among the gruesome cracking expanses of
black. That was a hopeful sign, but he didn't put much
stock in it.

Problem. Somebody was after Gaby, and he'd have to
track her down again. She probably wouldn't go back to
Elaine's.

Wait a minute. He let go of Doc's arm with his right
hand and began fishing in his pocket. The gizmo. Still
there; he dragged it out, looked at it, and pushed the
only switch to turn the thing on. It made a low buzzing
sound and the little screen, set where a volt-meter's dial
would be, began to glow.

It was like a radar screen, but gold-toned and without the rotating line he was used to from TV. In the center
was a big, fuzzy glow; it had to be Doc. Further away,
another dot, also bright . . . headed more or less in his
direction.

No, *two* dots. The second one was a lot closer and
fainter. It wasn't on-screen all the time.

Two dots, and only one of them could be Gabriela.
Okay. Maybe, if the dots didn't fade out completely, he
could find her again with this thing.

Problem. Cops would be looking for him and Doc. Harris could blend in with a crowd . . . once he got some
new clothes. Doc couldn't, not as easily.

Both the faint and the strong signal had gotten closer
and brighter as the two men walked, but as they descended
the steps into the station, the fainter signal abruptly faded
and disappeared. By the time they got to the bottom, the
other signal had dimmed to nothing. The big signal in
the center, Doc's signal, was as strong as ever.

Harris stared perplexed at the screen for a moment,
then looked back up the steps. "Doc. Can you stand by
yourself for a moment?"

Doc didn't look up or speak, but he nodded.

Harris carefully leaned him up against the wall. "I'll
be back in just a second." He walked up the steps.

The brighter signal increased in intensity as he ascended,

and by the time he reached street level again the fainter signal had returned.

Interesting. Did concrete block transmission? It looked like it. Harris trotted back down the stairs and watched two of the signals fade again. That meant he couldn't find Gaby while he was below ground.

It also meant the other guys might not be able to track *Doc* while he was below.

Harris shut the device off and pocketed it, then slid back under Doc's arm. "Doc, we need to ride the subway for a while. I'll tell you the rest when we're moving."

Phipps watched the new signal brighten on his tracer as they got closer and closer. Then, in a matter of seconds, it faded to nothingness.

The old man must have detected something in his posture. "What is it, William?"

Phipps wordlessly handed the tracer back.

He braced himself. Sometimes the old man took bad news by "keeping in practice"—calmly, coolly pulling out his favorite automatic and extinguishing someone at random. Phipps was the only one within easy reach.

But the old man simply sighed. "Home, William."

Harris and Doc traveled for quite a while, changing subway lines a couple of times.

After that, it only took one call to find her. Harris could have cheered when she came on the line: "This is Gaby."

"It's me."

"Let me call you back."

He gave her the number.

A minute later the phone rang under his hand. He picked it up. "Hi."

Her voice dropped nearly to a whisper. "I'm at another phone. I didn't know if they monitored incoming calls."

"Good thinking. Creative paranoia is probably very helpful right now."

"What the hell went on in my apartment?"

"Two fake cops jumped in and grabbed my friend Doc. They must have been waiting around for you to come home. We got out of there. Did the real cops get the guys I left there?"

"No."

"Damn. Did you tell the cops I was supposed to be there?"

"Give me some credit for intelligence, all right? I said that I got an anonymous call saying that the people who grabbed me before knew I was staying with Elaine. So I decided to go home instead."

"Thanks."

"No, thank *you*. The cops in New Rochelle say somebody broke into Elaine's house after we left. So you score big points there. Did you use that device you were talking about to find me?"

"No, I used my poor, misfiring brains. I figured that even if the police were through with you, you wouldn't want to leave them so fast . . . knowing there was somebody after you. So all I had to do was find out which precinct was nearest your place. Sixth."

"Yeah, I'm getting to be a fixture here. They have kind of a museum display in their squad room, and I'm on a first-name basis with every bit of memorabilia."

"I need to talk to you, Gaby. I can fix it so the guys after you can't follow you."

"How?"

"This tracer thing doesn't work if you're in the subway. When you leave the police, take a cab and see if you can get the driver to lay down some rubber. You have to shake off anybody following you, at least for a minute or two. And use that minute to get down to the subway. Meet us at the platform at Eighty-sixth Street and Lex."

She was long in answering. "It may be a while before I can get out of here."

"We'll wait. I'll be easy to spot. I'm wearing the gray suit my grandfather was buried in."

"Okay."

Harris hung up and returned to the bench where Doc sat.

A couple of hours had worked changes on Doc. He now wore sunglasses, a sweatsuit jacket, and the *Phantom of the Opera* T-shirt Harris had bought in a corner store during a brief solo return to street level.

Harris had also been at him with tricks barely remembered from his college theater career. Doc's hair was now gray—streaked with shoe polish applied with a toothbrush in the bathroom. His skin was dark with the orange-brown tan that came out of a bottle. He looked older, his features lined with makeup pencil. Harris could have put an additional twenty years on him—Elmer's glue, toilet paper, and makeup base could do an amazing job of simulating wrinkled, sagging skin—but he hadn't wanted to get too elaborate. This disguise might be adequate to keep the police from noticing Doc if they had a description of him from witnesses outside Gaby's place.

Doc's wrists were bound up in bandages, but his hands, where they showed, looked better anyway. Dead flesh was slowly peeling away, revealing pink skin beneath. Doc was a long way from being healthy, but the injury was healing much faster than any burn Harris had ever seen. But then, it wasn't exactly a burn.

And Doc was more alert. He looked as happy and energetic as the losing quarterback in the Super Bowl, but he was awake and could walk under his own power.

He looked up as Harris returned. "You found her."

"Yep. We'll meet her where I told you."

"We cannot wait for tonight, Harris. The deviser chasing Gaby will catch up to us. He is very capable. Or all the iron around us will kill me. I'll begin the ritual as soon as we return to the park."

Harris sat down beside him. "You don't have the book."

"I remember the ritual. I remember everything." He made it sound like a sentence handed down by an unfriendly judge. "Not always when I need to, unfortunately."

"Are you up to it? You made it sound like it wore people out. You're already wiped out."

"I can do it."

"That's not what I asked."

Doc looked at him wearily. "Harris, it does not matter. We can't protect her here. We have to get her back to the fair world."

The phone jarred Phipps out of his sleep; he answered it out of reflex. "Six one two. No, wait—"

"You're not at your extension now," the old man chided him. "But you will be. Fast. I have one of them again, William."

"Don't you ever sleep? Never mind. I'll be right there." Phipps hung up. The old man's office was only an elevator ride away from his bedroom, an arrangement that the old man found convenient. Groggy with lack of sleep, Phipps staggered to his feet.

It wasn't dawn yet, but the traffic of men and women through the subway system had started to pick up when Harris spotted her coming off the uptown number six. He waved and she ran to him.

She wrapped herself around him, held him close. For a moment, he floated around in the suburbs of heaven.

She pushed him back to look at him. "You're really okay."

"Yeah."

"That suit sucks."

"You romantic thing, you."

She looked uncomfortable. He knew her too well, knew she'd just remembered yesterday's dinner. He let her step away from him.

He turned and gestured. "Gaby, this is my friend Doc."

Doc made the effort to stand and gave her a little bow.

She gave him a searching glance. "Doc what?"

"MaqqRee," Doc said. "You may call me Desmond if you prefer."

"Desmond," she repeated. Harris saw her struggle not to wince. "Doc is fine," she said, then looked at Harris. "Okay. You think you can tell me what's going on?"

"We need to go over to the conjurer's circle in Central Park. I mean, the circle of white stones."

"But if what you said was true, as soon as we go up, their tracer thing will show where I am. If it really exists."

Harris pulled the tracer out of his jacket pocket and turned it on. Doc's glow at the center of the screen had completely absorbed Gaby's.

"That doesn't show anything."

"It will when we reach the surface," Doc said. "And it will let us know how much time we have."

The three of them reached the circle of stones and Doc immediately began setting right those that had fallen over or been moved.

"So where were you all day?" Gaby asked, maddeningly persistent.

"You won't believe me. Not until Doc shows you this trick," Harris added. "I've got a question for you. Gaby, have you ever heard of anybody who looked like you, had sort of the same name? I've seen a woman called Gabrielle. Your spitting image. Nobody knows much of anything about her."

Even in the moonlight he could see her swallow. "No."

"Did you just accidentally say no when you meant yes? You always said women don't really do that."

"You bastard." The heat in her voice surprised him. "Don't make a joke out of this."

"Then don't lie."

She tried to glare at him, but she looked guilty instead. She stared down at the grass. "Harris, don't laugh, okay? But I've always felt connected to somebody else. I mean, I've always had these dreams about meeting a sister I never met. When I was a kid I used to drive my parents crazy—'Are you sure I wasn't twins? Did you leave another baby at the hospital?' That sort of thing."

"What did they say?"

"They said that reading too much was rotting my brain."
She looked up again and tried to gauge his expression.

"Oh, yeah. Hell, they said that the last time I saw them."
Harris turned the tracer on again. The bright glow was
still distant—but now it was moving slowly. "Doc, I think
they're onto us."

Doc nodded. His circuit done, he knelt in the circle's
center and began unloading things from his pockets—
gold coins, a small gold cylinder with an opening at one
end, tiny statuettes carved of stone.

"Give me that thing." Gaby took the tracer from Harris' hand and trotted off a few dozen yards, looking intently
at the screen. She wandered back and forth out on the
grass for a minute, long enough for Doc to start chanting, before she returned.

She handed it back to him. "Okay. It picks *him* up. It
picks up this other signal. I'll take your word for it that
the glow in the middle is me. What's he doing?"

"I know it sounds like he's trying to cough up a hairball,
but it's all part of the ceremony." Harris eyed the tracer
screen with concern. The incoming signal, still northeast, was getting closer, faster than he liked. "Doc, can
you snap it up?"

Doc shook his head, not interrupting the flow of foreign syllables.

Gaby eyed the distance to the nearest stand of trees. "Look,
if that really is them, we ought to get back into the subway."

"We'll be fine." Harris spoke with confidence he didn't
feel. "When Doc finishes, they won't be able to get at
us. You need to trust me about this."

She gave him a hard look. "You're making it hard. Not
telling me what this is all about."

"You *really* won't believe it until you see it."

"Try me."

Doc interrupted his recital. "Harris." His voice was
rough and weak, and Harris could see sweat pouring down
his face. "Almost done. Are you staying?"

"Hell, no." Leave Gaby to go back to the fair world alone?

Harris took a last look at the device. The incoming patch of light was very close now; its edges nearly touched the edges of Doc's glow.

Doc began his chant again.

Gaby looked suspiciously at the two men, then her eye tracked something behind Harris. He turned to look . . . and saw the park grass writhing, curling and dying in a wave front spreading out from the circle of stones.

"See?" he told her. "It's real."

"This is your trick?"

There was a sharp crack from the east, and a little spray of dust kicked up two inches from Doc's knee.

Doc flinched and bent to be lower to the ground, but he kept chanting. Harris swore and looked toward the source of the noise—where a half-dozen men, bobbing pale faces out in the darkness, were running at them from the direction of the Met.

Gaby grabbed Harris' jacket. "God, Harris, we've got to get out of here." She dragged him half off the circle.

He grabbed her around the waist, spun her down to the ground as gently as he could. "Not yet."

She looked at him, her eyes wide, as if he'd pulled off a Harris mask to reveal the face of Adonis beneath it. She hit his shoulder. "What the hell are you doing? *We have to go.*"

"Not yet. Trust me."

Another crack, another section of ground twitched as if hurt.

Dammit, dammit, dammit! Harris bore Gaby down, flattening her by sheer weight, covering her as much as he could. He pulled one of the fake policemen's pistols out of his pocket, saw her eyes get even wider.

He aimed it in the direction of the oncoming men.

No. If he missed, he might start raining bullets down on the museum. There could be people over there. It would be enough just to make them duck for cover. He lowered his arm a bit, aiming into the ground thirty or forty yards away, and pulled the trigger. He was startled by the way the gun kicked in his hand, by the painful loudness of the shot, but he brought the gun back in line and kept firing.

The three closest faces disappeared. He marveled that he might have hit them anyway. Then the three men returned fire from prone positions. Dust kicked up around Doc, and something high-pitched whistled inches over Harris' head.

His gun clicked on empty and he dropped it. He began groping around in his pocket for another revolver.

Gaby hit him again, ineffectually. "Get off me." There was fear in her voice. He felt a moment of pain as he realized it was him she feared.

He got out the second captured revolver and aimed it.

"Harris, you're crazy."

Harris began firing again—one shot, two. There were only two faces out in the darkness now, and one of them was shouting to the others. The return fire abruptly stopped. The two faces kept coming, one of them much higher off the ground than the other.

Gaby's hand clamped down on Harris' balls with a grip of steel. He jerked in pain and fired an accidental shot into the air. "Jesus, let go!"

"Let me up, or *I Will Tear It Off!*"

Harris writhed. It hurt worse that way, but he couldn't help himself. And that face was getting closer—

That face. Adonis, not more than ten yards from the edge of the circle. Harris took aim and fired. He missed; he couldn't hold his aim steady. Not with a furious nutcracker clamped on him.

Five yards. Adonis was so close that Harris wouldn't be able to get to his feet in time. Harris fired again.

The shot hit Adonis in the nose. A gross spray of blood and meat, black in the moonlight, blew out the back of Adonis' head.

Adonis jerked to a stop and looked surprised.

Then it kept coming.

And it began to grow, stretching unnaturally just before it reached the boundaries of the circle. Moving too fast to slow down, Adonis, ten feet tall and growing, reached the edge—and stopped there like a mime running into an imaginary pane of glass.

Doc fell over on his side and turned to look at Adonis. He was in time to see the old man, a stretched, twelve-foot-tall version of the old man, stride up to the edge.

The old man's face, twisted in anger, peered down at the three of them—and Gaby, finally seeing what was going on, gasped at the sight of their elongated attackers. She let go of Harris.

Doc looked at the old man. He said a single word: "Duncan." His tone was pained, not surprised.

Then the world popped.

The bubble of light in the conjurer's circle dwindled to nothing. Adonis and the old man just stood there as Phipps tentatively approached.

It was bad. The old man's shoulders were shaking. "Sir?"

The old man spun on him. It was his I'm-just-about-to-lose-it look, all trembling anger ready to erupt. "It was him," Duncan hissed. "He's found me. Like he always does."

"Sir, we need to get back to the cars. The police will be coming."

The old man looked at him as though he'd spoken in a foreign language, then finally nodded.

The other men had hung back, brushing off their clothes. As he reached them, the old man quietly asked Phipps, "Who started shooting?"

"That was Kleine, sir."

"Kleine!" The old man smiled at the startled gunman. "How is your lovely daughter?"

"Uh, just fine—"

The old man drew his automatic and shot the man between the eyes. Bloody matter blasted out the back of Kleine's head.

Unlike Adonis, the gunman didn't keep going. He just fell over backwards.

The rest of them hurried back to the cars.

CHAPTER TWELVE

Harris rolled off Gaby and gulped in the air of Neckerdam. The stars above the city glittered down at him.

Nobody was *shooting* at him. But his arms were still shaking.

Gaby rose, looking around. "What the *hell* is happening here?"

"Doc!" That was Alastair, pelting up the roadway leading to the manor house. He skidded to a halt beside the collapsed body of his friend and knelt to check his pulse.

"They shot at us," Harris gasped out. "I don't know if he was hit." He reached over to pick up the guns he'd dropped—and froze. They lay where they'd fallen, but they were now deformed, twisted as if exposed to some enormous heat. Like Gaby's pepper spray.

"What the *hell* is happening here?"

Alastair gingerly probed around Doc's back, then peeled him out of the sweatsuit jacket. "I don't think he's been hit. A bad poisoning, though. I wager he ignored it."

"Much as he could." Harris wearily tried to sit up, then decided against it. His groin still hurt. Better just to stay here for a minute.

"And then commencing a devisement like this. Exhaustion and shock. The idiot."

Gaby stood over Harris and glared at him. But her voice

was deceptively sweet. "Are you going to tell me? This is the last time I ask nicely."

Weary, he grinned up at her. "Welcome to Neckerdam. Gaby, meet Alastair Kornbock. Alastair, Gaby Donohue."

"Grace, child. Harris, help me carry him to the car, will you?"

Doc didn't wake up, but didn't get worse. They got him up to his room in the Monarch Building and Alastair sent the two of them away.

They found Jean-Pierre and Noriko back in the lab. Jean-Pierre spotted Gaby, put on a predator's smile, and walked up to her as if dragged by magnetism. "Harris, introduce us."

"I'm surprised to see you two awake." Dawn was finally lightening in the east, but Jean-Pierre and Noriko looked alert.

"We were preparing to spell Alastair out at the estate. Harris, your manners."

"Oh, yeah." Jean-Pierre's sudden, deliberate charm put Harris off. "Gabriela Donohue, this is Jean-Pierre Lamignac and Noriko Nomura."

Noriko bowed.

"Grace," said Jean-Paul. "So, you are the famous Gabrielle. Doc's description does not do you justice." He bent to kiss her hand.

She watched this with a bemused expression. "You remind me of my uncle Ernesto."

"Truly?"

"Yes. He's in jail where he belongs."

He straightened, his expression confused, and she turned away from him. "Harris, your friend Doc is in bed, all your fires are put out . . . it's time for you to give me some answers."

Gaby caught on faster than Harris had. "Wait a minute. When you say 'Sidhe Foundation,' you don't mean the pronoun. You mean like in 'banshee.'"

Jean-Pierre winced. "No. Daoine Sidhe. But like the Bean Sidhe, they're almost gone."

Gaby's face was an interesting study; Harris could almost see the thoughts clicking through her head like coins through a mechanical change-counter.

She looked at him. "Pop's half-Irish," she said. "And a fireman. A great storyteller both ways. He had lots of fairy tales for all the kids."

"So this means something to you."

"Oh, yes. Either you slipped me a tab of LSD, or we're in the land of the little people." She glanced at Jean-Pierre and Noriko. "Only they're not so little."

Harris finished up his account: "So just as we were popping out he saw the old man and called him 'Duncan.' I can only guess that means the old guy is Duncan Blackletter."

Jean-Pierre paled and lost all the charm he'd been beaming at Gaby. "Doc killed Duncan Blackletter."

"Don't count on it."

"Gods. Then *I'll* kill him."

Gaby broke in, "I have a question. The way you've been talking about 'protecting' me—am I your prisoner?"

Noriko and Jean-Pierre looked at one another.

"Of a fashion," she said.

"Of course not," he said.

"Which is it?"

"You are not," Jean-Pierre stated firmly, before Noriko could speak. "You are our guest. We will defend you with sword and firearm as long as you choose to accept our aid."

"Thanks." Gaby rose. "For right now, though, I'm going to take a walk."

Jean-Pierre rose also. "I will be pleased to accompany you."

"I mean, I'm going *alone*."

He frowned. "That is not advisable."

"I know. I'm doing it anyway."

"Why?"

"To prove I can. If the only way I can go somewhere is with one of you hanging off my arm, then I'm your prisoner. Right?"

Jean-Pierre tried being patient. "Doc would want—"

"Come on, Jean-Pierre. Do I walk, or am I your prisoner? You just said I wasn't. What's your word worth?"

Harris winced. He already had the impression of Jean-Pierre that Gaby's words would cut deep.

Jean-Pierre's face froze into a blank, cold lack of expression. "If you are foolish enough to go . . . I will not stop you."

"Or send anyone else to follow me."

"Or that, either." Jean-Pierre looked very much as if he'd benefit from half an hour of outraged swearing. "Please do not. *They* are out there. If you go, you expose yourself to danger. They have tried to kill Harris already."

She glanced at Harris. He gave her a private little nod of confirmation.

"Okay, it's dangerous." She did not look happy at the prospect. "But I'm doing it anyway. So sit." She took a tentative step toward the door.

Harris cleared his throat. "Gaby, you want some company?"

"You're damned right I do."

He rose. "Mind if I go upstairs to change?"

"I have grass on my ass, too, and you put it there. No, let's just go." She had on her tougher-than-nails expression, but Harris could hear the distress in her voice: she wanted out, *now*.

"Right. Never mind." Harris checked his pockets. Doc's gun, the volt-meter, and the big silver coin he'd been given about a day ago. He hoped these would be all he'd need.

It would otherwise have been an enjoyable walk. The morning sun was sending tentative streamers of light down into the street as they headed uptown from the Monarch Building, and even at this hour the street was alive with traffic. Fruit stands were already set up, if they'd ever been taken down, and a boy wearing shorts and a beret with his long-sleeved shirt hawked newspapers with a sales cry of "Oyez, oyez!"

Come to think of it, the street had been alive at every hour he'd passed along it. Neckerdam didn't sleep. He liked that. But he'd enjoy it a lot more if he didn't look behind every bush and in every storefront expecting one of the Changeling's men to come leaping out at him.

"You jumped on Jean-Pierre pretty hard. Were you just testing the limits, pushing the rules as usual?"

She smiled. "I don't have anything against him . . . but from the way he talked, I felt like I was some sort of package to be stuck in a storeroom. I hear talk like that, all I want to do is slap it down." She shrugged and changed the subject. "I'm sorry if I hurt you."

He forced a falsetto: "No problem, didn't hurt a bit."

She laughed. He thought, maybe if he built up a large enough supply of her laughs, then she'd reconsider things.

Gaby continued looking around her, wonder on her face. "God, this place is *great*."

"You sure are taking it better than I did when I first arrived."

"Maybe. It's all very familiar. Like the kinds of places I dreamed about when I was a kid. It's hard not to believe in a place you already sort of know." She shrugged. "You know, when I was little, I didn't want teddy bears or Barbie dolls. I always wanted my pop to find me a stuffed toy no one else had. An eight-legged horse."

"Why the hell would you want an eight-legged horse?"

"It was supposed to be Sleipnir. The horse of Odin. From Norse mythology. Anyway, I bet I could find an eight-legged horse here. It's the kind of place where it would fit right in. Hey, listen to that."

They paused on the sidewalk near the door into a restaurant; the neon sign above the door read "Tifania's." Each patron who entered or left—and there were quite a few—let a wash of music escape. Harris heard a pretty jumble of many stringed instruments.

With the music came the smell of fresh bread. Harris' stomach suddenly woke up. He gestured toward the door. "After you."

The corner bar and the restaurant tables took up about half of the establishment's large main room, while the dance floor and a raised band platform took up the other half. Even at this hour the band was playing merrily away and the dance floor was crowded.

Young men and women of the fair world, even more brightly clothed than the average people on the street, were doing circle dances or paired off in something like a double-time ballroom dance. Some of the music called for steps that looked like sword-dancing without any swords on the floor.

The band played more of the Irish-style music. The instruments were mostly woodwinds and strings; the standout performer, a dumpy man with nut-brown skin and a goatee, battered away at a hammered dulcimer with skill that Harris found amazing.

A waitress with sand-colored skin and an abbreviated dress of headache-inducing red seated them in the restaurant section. There were no menus; Harris asked for the house special, while Gaby ordered a drink by pointing and asking for "what he's having." On the tables were cloth napkins, two-pronged forks and sharp knives, nothing too strange to their eyes.

"So, you got me to Neckerdam," Gaby said. "If it's real. No, I'm not really doubting it. I'd rather enjoy it. But I was going to ask—what now?"

"I wish I knew. It really upset Jean-Pierre to hear that Duncan Blackletter is on Earth—on the grim world. So they probably don't know what the hell they're going to do yet."

She made a face. "I was hoping you had some sort of plan in mind. Sic the police on the bad guys, put them in jail, and everybody go home."

Harris' gaze was drawn to a man at a nearby table. He was of greater than average height for the Neckerdam people, nearly six feet, and well-built; with his thick red hair, green suit, and pipe, he looked like a human-sized leprechaun who'd spent a few months on a Nautilus machine. He kept looking at Gaby as though he recognized her.

Harris tensed. Maybe Duncan's people had caught up to them already. Maybe he should have told Jean-Pierre to stuff himself and that Gaby *was* a sort of prisoner for now; at least she'd be safe.

The red-haired man stood and came their way. As inconspicuously as possible, Harris slid his hand into his pocket and got a grip on Doc's pistol. He was suddenly a little light-headed. Prefight adrenaline.

The redhead came up to the table and beamed down at the two of them. "Grace," he said, and turned to Gaby. "Pardon my manners. Are you two lovers?"

Gaby looked at him, wide-eyed. "*Excuse* me?"

"Well, you don't act like lovers. So I wanted to ask if you would join me on the floor." He gestured toward the dancers with his pipe.

"Oh." She glanced at Harris a little guiltily. "Well, thanks, but no thanks."

The redhead spread his hands in a comfortably familiar "can't hurt to ask" gesture. "Well, then. How about to bed? My flat is close, and I treat the ladies well."

Gaby gaped at him a long moment and didn't answer. Finally she managed, "Thank you, but not this morning."

"Ah, well. Fair morning to you, then." His step jaunty, the redhead returned to his own table.

Harris tried to unlock his shoulders. His hand didn't want to let go of the gun. He managed it anyway. "Son of a bitch has a lot of nerve."

"Maybe. He was very polite, though. I've heard lots worse." She glanced at him, then smiled. "Harris, you're blushing."

"No, I'm not." He found himself annoyed.

"Yes, you are. But never mind."

Harris was saved from offering a rejoinder by the waitress' return. His "house special" turned out to be a ball-shaped loaf of fresh, mealy bread, a little bowl of jam, and a crock of potato-and-sausage hash. He tore into it, prepared to devour just about anything to satisfy his hunger, but it turned out to be good—spicy and filling.

Gaby started to sip her drink, then looked at it warily. "Maybe I'd better not."

"Why?"

"Well, some of my father's stories . . . you eat their food, you don't come back."

"I ate their food. And I came back." Harris shrugged his unconcern and attacked his hash again.

"True." Gaby sipped her drink. "Hey, ginger beer!"

"Blech."

"No, it's good. Care to try a sip?"

"Thanks anyway. The last time I took a drink, I ended up in Neckerdam."

That earned him another smile. "Okay." She watched the crowd, alert, soaking up the local color with her journalist's eye. "Interesting," she said after a while.

"What is?"

"Differences. Women with purses, that's the same. But they leave them unguarded on the tables to go over and dance, and they're still there when they get back. I saw a guy standing at the edge of the dance floor who seemed to be looking one over, but the other people eating are keeping an eye on *him*."

"Canary yellow suit and red tie?"

"That's him. Then there's the guy who came in with the rifle."

Harris looked around, startled. "I didn't see him. Where?"

"Oh, he doesn't have it now. He left it with the hat-check girl by the front door."

"Jesus."

"Nobody thought anything about it! And then there's the hookers."

"Where?"

"Exactly. Where? This isn't exactly a family restaurant. They're groping each other to distraction out on the dance floor. When the music suits it, that is. And there's kind of a meat market attitude to some of them here. But no one I can identify as a hooker. I didn't see any on the street in the blocks we walked from Doc's building . . . and this is not the jazziest block we came through."

"You're right. Well, it's going to take a while to figure this place out. We have to *live* to figure it out, though."

"We'll go back as soon as you're finished eating. Promise."

Harris' coin was easily enough to cover the charge; the waitress came back with a handful of coins—big copper ones, small copper ones, small silver ones. He slid one of the silver coins under his plate as a tip and hoped he'd guessed right.

The waitress, hovering, asked Harris, "By your leave— are you two lovers?"

Used to be, yeah. He glanced at Gaby. She wore her uncomfortable look again. "No."

She smiled. "My duty ends in a chime. Care to come to my flat for lovemaking?"

He forced a smile and hoped that he wasn't blushing again. "Well, thank you. I'm flattered. But my own, uh, duty calls. Maybe some other time."

"Well, then. I'm Miarna." And she was gone.

Harris clutched his heart for comic effect.

Gaby smiled uneasily as she stood. "People aren't exactly repressed here."

"Nope. One more difference." He rose. "If we don't want those differences to trip us up, I suggest we go and learn what they are."

Duncan Blackletter and Adonis knelt in the center of Duncan's ritual circle. This was no improvised thing made of rocks or paint; the inner and outer circles, like the words that lay between them, were of gold laid with an artisan's skill into the veined green marble floor. Candles rested in notches cut for their presence; the gold incense burner, from which the bitterly strong smell of myrrh exuded, rested on its own upraised marble stand.

He breathed in the incense, focused his mind on the task at hand, and called upon the Crone.

On the grim world, she was so quiet, so deeply asleep, so close to death that it wrenched his heart whenever he invoked her. She was his favorite: the snipper of lifelines, the weaver of epilogues, the spirit of endgames, the weathered grandmother smiling fondly at her descendants while knowing that one day she must take their lives, too.

Perhaps, when all was done, he could speak some word or play some music so loud and glorious that it would awaken her here, too.

His sideline thoughts were drawing him out of his focused state. He put them from his mind and concentrated on finding the spirit of his goddess.

We sit within your sight, he thought. *Tiny specks within the great circle of your eye. With all my heart and spirit, I beg of you, open your eye, cast your gaze about, and tell me: Are we the only ones? The last two straying motes left to be swept away?*

Again and again, he repeated his prayer, as though with each repetition he could hurl it farther and farther into the depths of the goddess' sleeping mind. With each completion he felt himself grow farther from his body, from the aches of age and joys of life, and he knew the familiar fear: would this be the time that the goddess just took him, cut him free from his life as easily as cutting a thread with shears?

Are we the only ones?

"Yes." The word sighed out of Adonis' gaping mouth, distant and fuzzy and indistinct, as though numberless worms deep in his chest had taken that moment to look upward and issue one word. The interruption jarred

Duncan out of his concentration, snapped him back to resentful wakefulness.

"Damn you, Adonis, I have to begin again." He automatically raised his hand to punish the creature and Adonis shrank away from him.

But Duncan froze, perplexed. Adonis never spoke. It couldn't; it lacked the equipment.

This was the voice of the sleeping goddess.

Duncan swallowed hard, afraid to speak again. But he had to be sure. "Are we the only ones?" he asked again, aloud.

Again, the word wafted out of Adonis' mouth: "Yeeessss." The creature's lips did not form to shape the word, and its eyes grew round with confusion. Even Adonis did not know how it was speaking.

The candles guttered for a moment, then grew brighter again, and Duncan felt the last of his rapport with the goddess slip away like the last memories of a dream. She was gone.

Duncan took a long moment to slow his racing heart, then forced a smile for his imbecilic companion. "Adonis, we've done it. Are you ready to home?"

Adonis' face twisted into something like a child's smile; its eyes grew bright and happy.

"Good. Let's pack. We have a lot to do."

CHAPTER THIRTEEN

Joseph looked up into the eyes of the man he held over his head. Whiskers Okerry, his face twisted with pain and effort. Above him, ceiling beams burned and gray-and-white flame licked off in search of more victims. All Joseph had to do was hold Okerry a little higher and the man, too, would begin burning.

He didn't. It didn't matter that he didn't want to. He hadn't been told to.

He exerted himself and heard the meaty crack of the man's back. Okerry's eyes widened. From pain, from realization that nothing he could ever do would fix what had just been broken, Joseph didn't know.

Almost tenderly, Joseph set him in the room's one corner that fire had not yet touched.

Speak, he told himself. *Tell him you would rather be dead than do this. Speak.* The words welled up in him. But he could not utter them, could not give them to the dying man as one last comfort.

Duncan wouldn't let him.

The words got bigger within him.

Speak.

Scream.

Joseph thrashed and heard himself shout. In the first moments of wakefulness, he felt his legs somehow hampered by cloth, felt his foot hit the footboard of his bed. Wood cracked and fell to the floor with a bang; the end of his bed collapsed.

He sighed. He'd kicked the footboard off again. He opened his eyes. A little light lurked behind his bedroom curtains.

He should be sweating, the way real men did.

"Joseph." A woman's voice from the other room.

Not alarmed—what could hurt him?—he rose and, naked, walked into the front room. Before he even faced it, he could see the glow shining from the screen of his talk-box.

It had been off when he went to bed last night. He moved to stand in front of it.

A woman stared back at him from the screen. She was beautiful, solemn. He could not determine the color of the dress she wore; even if his were not a gray-shade talk-box, his eyes did not offer him the range of colors that human eyes did.

She did not react to his nakedness. "Joseph," she said, "Duncan Blackletter is looking for you."

"He's dead," he said.

"No. He's just been living on the grim world."

He knew it was the truth. The gods did not love him enough for Duncan Blackletter to be dead. "Who are you?"

She hesitated. "My name is Gabrielle."

"Leave me alone." He turned off the set, and she faded to a tiny white dot.

Harris, still blinking sleep from his eyes, walked into the laboratory with the new box in his hand.

Doc, Alastair, and Gaby sat on bar stools at one of the tables. Gaby was wearing a belted knee-length dress in dark green, obviously one of the fair world styles, and black pumps. Doc looked like his former self, with weariness in his eyes and darkness under them the only visible signs of what he'd gone through. Seeing Harris,

Doc smiled and smacked his hand on the tabletop. "It works."

Harris looked at him, confused, and waved the box, a black metal thing about the size of a VCR tape. "I found this on my bed when I woke up. The note said to turn on the switch and come to the lab."

"My note," Doc admitted. "And my box. Yours, now."

Harris moved over to join them. The table, he saw, was piled with food—more of the meat-filled pastries, a big platter of cold cuts and bread.

Alastair waved a hand over the mass: "Care for anything?"

"My stomach isn't awake yet. God, I must have slept almost a whole day. I'll take some of that chocolate drink if you've got it." Harris took an unoccupied stool. "So what's the box?"

Doc gestured at the volt-meter on the table before him. "I rekeyed this to show you, as it did the first night. But it doesn't. Not while you carry that box. It's something I've made to conceal your presence."

"Great." Harris slipped the box in his jacket pocket. "You whipped this up just today?"

"During the night."

"Should you even be out of bed?" Harris peered at Doc's hands, but they were back to normal. Doc obligingly turned them over so he could see both sides.

Alastair paused with a silver container filled with milk poised over Harris' chocolate. "He should not. He's still dragging his feet out of his grave."

"That's what I thought. I'll take it black, thanks."

Alastair blinked. "But you asked for milk."

"I did?"

Gaby looked amused. "I've already been through this once today. The nasty chocolate stuff is called 'xioc.' So when you put milk in it, it's 'xioc au lait.' Get it?"

"I'll take your word for it." Harris took up the mug and sipped, winced once more at the drink's harshness. "I've changed my mind. I'll take the milk." He turned back to Doc. "Does this mean that Duncan Blackletter's people can't find me now?"

"I think so . . . at least, not by using a device like this. Now I need to make another one for Gabriela. Unlike you, she registers on both settings. Her Tallysin Aura has elements like yours, an outsider's, and elements like one of the Gifted."

"Meaning they get to track me down on both worlds," Gaby mock-grumbled. "Between that and the fact that they tell me they don't have any blue jeans on the fair world, I'm getting pretty annoyed."

Harris smiled. "You loved this place yesterday. You fall out of love fast."

The words were out of him before he realized what he was saying. He saw her expression of hurt surprise. He suppressed a wince and waited for the moment to pass. "So, what's on the schedule for today?"

"Tests," Doc said. "We know Gaby is Gifted. We know she must be tied up with Gabrielle somehow. But she says she's never manifested any sign of the Gift. We have to find out what that means."

"You going to put her in the big glass tube and fire lightning into her brain?"

Gaby's eyes got big.

Doc nodded, oblivious. "Yes, the Firbolg Valence is first on the itinerary. And you? What would you like to do?"

"I don't know. Do you know where I can find a weight room?"

"A what?"

"A gymnasium, maybe?"

"Ah. Down three, next to the gun practice range. Private, for the use of Foundation associates; use the Foundation elevator."

"Doc, is there anything this building *doesn't* have?"

"I don't think so. Suggest something. I'll have it put in."

The gymnasium had a wooden parquet floor that hadn't seen a lot of use. Only one of the banks of lights against the high ceiling was on; this gave the place an air of emptiness and gloom, like the sports arena of a losing team after the crowds had gone.

Most of the way through his warm-up stretches, Harris lowered himself into a front split, right leg forward, left leg back as straight as he could manage—which wasn't as straight as he'd like. He used to be a little more limber. He held the pose, then bent to touch his forehead to his knee in spite of the protest from offended muscle groups. He reversed his pose, bringing the left leg forward.

The chamber's dim atmosphere was fine with Harris. He'd always liked prowling around where he wasn't supposed to be, and being here felt like that. It was a habit that had gotten him in trouble with school officials and police a couple of times when he was younger.

And the gloom reflected his mood. Much as he wanted to be with Gaby, help keep her spirits up during the tests, he knew he'd probably say something stupid, hurtful. Knew that her eyes no longer lit up when he appeared. Most of the time, when she saw him she looked guilty, unhappy.

Finished with the front splits, he turned sideways, his legs straight out to either side, and bent forward, trying to touch his forehead to the floor. He never could quite manage to split his legs out to a 180° angle, but he could get close. His muscles protested as he pressed his forehead to the cool floor; he held the pose.

He relaxed and rose. Enough stretching. He lowered himself into horse stance to begin the first of his forms exercises . . . and spotted someone in his peripheral vision. He turned his head slightly to get a better look. It was Noriko, lingering in the shadows near the door.

Come to study him, as she studied everything, with her solemn expression and unblinking gaze? He smiled to himself. Well, as long as he had an audience, he might as well put on a show.

He decided against one of his traditional forms sets and instead conjured up the mental image of Sonny Walters, positioning him in the far corner of an imaginary boxing ring. It was time to replay that fight, see where it had gone wrong. Do it right this time.

Hands high, body in motion, Harris advanced on the Smile.

He still had to advance. Sonny had the reach on him; there was no other way to fight it. No mistake there.

In the real fight, after the first couple of rounds, Sonny had begun nailing him just as Harris moved in close enough to strike and just before Harris drew back out of Sonny's range. Transitions, just as Zeb had said. But why not before—why not in the first two rounds?

Sonny must just have been studying Harris. Soaking up a little punishment while he catalogued Harris' inventory of moves and approaches. Okay, then. Harris moved into range of the phantom Sonny's attacks, and his sparring partner didn't attack. A few inches closer, still bouncing and weaving, and Sonny was in range of Harris' kicks, but still didn't strike. That was the way Harris remembered it.

Harris moved into arm range and threw a left-hand feint. The phantom Sonny blocked, came back with a right hook. This time Harris knew not to try to stop it with his knifehand block; strong enough for most opponents, that move wasn't strong enough for Sonny Walters. Instead, he threw a middle block, bringing his left forearm in on Sonny's extended arm, battering it out of line.

A good pose from which to launch his spinning backfist. He started a clockwise spin but only turned a few degrees, then disengaged his left hand and snapped it into Sonny's exposed face, right into his nose. The phantom looked surprised, moved back an involuntary step, and took Harris' follow-through right front kick right in the guts.

Zeb had *said* to work on his stomach; why hadn't Harris listened? Zeb must think he was a complete idiot. Harris had marched in, mistaken Sonny's cool, collected analysis for passiveness, and settled into the tactics that would lead him to painful defeat.

Not this time. He kept his own critical faculties working. Sonny *had* kept his guard lower than usual, probably protecting pained ribs. Harris exploited that now; every one of his combinations included at least one blow aimed at the bigger man's torso, and it was often one of his more deceptive blows. He didn't have to hit hard, not yet; he just had to leave Sonny with the impression that he could get through to his gut anytime he wanted.

All the while, his silent audience, Noriko, watched. Harris caught sight of her whenever the phantom fight faced him in the right direction. She had to be taking stock of his style, looking for weaknesses . . .

No, that wasn't right. There was something about the way she stood. She had her back to the wall but wasn't leaning against it. Her arms were crossed, but it wasn't a relaxed pose, and seemed just a little awkward and uncertain. It reminded him of something, someone else.

Then she turned away and moved toward the door, and Harris had it. High school algebra, and Mary Francis Richards tensely standing by as class let out, trying to figure out how to ask a question of the teacher without sounding stupid; she never could stand for people to think ill of her. Her pose had been the same. That didn't seem right, not like Noriko, but . . .

Harris gave a flick of his fingers. The phantom Sonny, an annoyed look on his face, disappeared. "Noriko."

At the door, she turned. "Yes?"

"Were you going to ask me something?"

She didn't answer.

"Go ahead."

She took a long breath. "Would you . . . would you teach me how to kick as you do?"

"Sure."

Noriko blinked and came forward a step. "When?"

"Well, if we get started right now, we can be through in three or four years."

She managed a little smile. "I would not be intruding?"

"Nope. Tell you what, though. If you teach me a little about the way you use that sword, we can call it an even trade."

"I would like that." She moved forward to join him.

"That was hard for you, wasn't it?"

"What?"

"Asking."

She took a moment to answer. "Maybe."

"Well, try to take it easier on yourself next time. I don't bite." He shrugged. "Is that what you wear to work out?" Her outfit was gold-yellow and cut much like her evening pants suits, but was not new and looked more like common linen than silk.

"Yes. Is it suitable?"

"Just fine. So. We'll start with a little history. What I do is called tae kwon do, which means the art of kicking and punching. Truth in advertising. It was developed in Korea, a country in the same place as your Silla . . . "

Duncan spoke the last words. As ever, they were like a switch, turning on the tap to the reservoirs of his endurance. He felt strength flow from him, a sensation that was simultaneously comforting and worrisome.

Then there was nothing but the sound of the wind in the trees around his outdoor stone circle. But he could feel the energy hovering out there, just at the limits of his circle; it built in focus and intensity, wove itself into a pattern too complex for any but the most sophisticated devisers to comprehend.

Behind him, one of the men coughed. Costigan, probably. The cool winds flowing over this upstate campsite were aggravating the young man's injured throat. Duncan shook his head. He'd have to get the boy to a doctor. And Phipps, too, to repair his broken arm. Duncan had chosen the two of them and Dominguez for their knowledge and loyalty, not for their current physical condition, because the latter could be dealt with once they were on the fair world.

There it was—the shriveling of grasses as the devisement demanded more power than Duncan had given it. Like a shockwave, the ripple of death spread away from the circle, consuming the lives of plants and insects before it.

Then the trees began to stretch . . . He heard his men gasp.

A moment later, it was over. One big, ear-hurting pop, and they were somewhere else, at one end of a vast wooden hangar.

And fair world men waited there. One was Angus Powrie, rushing across the border of the conjurer's circle painted on the floor. The redcap helped Duncan to his feet. "Sir. Glad to have you back at last."

Tired by his devisement, Duncan leaned heavily on the redcap's arm. "I'm so glad to be home, Angus. I'd like you to meet my chief lieutenants: Costigan, Dominguez, Phipps."

The three grimworlders still stared around, trying to take in the changes they'd just experienced. They snapped to attention for the introductions.

"Graces on you," said Angus. "Big ones. I like that. My own chiefs, Alpson, Moon, Captain Walbert, who'll be your personal pilot, are in Neckerdam. And what—" he stared openly at Adonis "—in the name of all the gods is *that*?" The redcap began laughing.

"The best I could do." Alastair gave an embarrassed shrug. "Devisement is not an easy process on the grim world, and I had to work with the materials I had available. This is Adonis, which is, as they say, better than nothing. No replacement for Joseph, though.

"Now. My list is done. We can begin cutting."

Angus left off his chuckling and nodded.

"And your list?"

"Done . . . but for the additions you so graciously sent us." The redcap's voice was anything but gracious.

"Ah. Well, we will eliminate them as well. Once that's done, we can begin rebuilding. Building a new world." Duncan looked over the small fleet of aircraft arrayed in the hangar, especially the largest of the ships, the one with the name *Storm Cloud* painted on its side. "You've done quite well, Angus."

"I want you to have all the conveniences you need."

"Angus? Is the ceremony done?" That call came from the far side of the hangar, and the speaker soon trotted into view: a blond man, elegant, almost inhumanly beautiful. "It is," he continued. "I wish you'd told me." The blond man slowed to a walk, approaching almost tentatively.

Angus waved him over and brought him face-to-face with Blackletter. "Duncan, let me present the boy, Darig. He has learned the business well. He will make you proud. Darig, this is the great man himself."

Duncan took the young man by the shoulders and stared intently into his face. "I have not seen you since you were an infant."

"I know, sir."

"You are as handsome as your mother hoped you would be."

"More so, I trust."

Duncan smiled. "You know you will have to go to the grim world for a while."

Darig shook his head. "I'd rather stay."

"Well, if you do, you'll have to die." Duncan's tone was friendly, reasonable.

"I know." Darig smiled shyly. "I'd like to die as my world does. Help bring it about, even. Have you any need for a sacrifice to the gods? I've always fancied dying on an altar. Perhaps seeing my own beating heart before death takes me."

Duncan beamed down at Angus. "You were right. He does make me proud."

Harris settled into a schedule. Up just after dawn. Down to the gymnasium for a workout alone. Noriko would join him for instruction. Then she'd teach him for a while—techniques with knives, her sword, some of the grappling and tripping maneuvers she'd grown up learning in the land of Wo, not too different from the little bit of hapkido he'd learned once upon a time. When he told her that he barely knew one end of a gun from the other, she began taking him to the range on the same floor for practice with firearms.

Back to his room for a bath and clothes. Then he'd descend to the lab floor to graze from the food perpetually laid out on one of the tables. He might bump into anyone there, but it was usually Alastair, eating, smoking, reading Neckerdam's newspaper, happy to talk. Doc was sometimes on hand, doing tests on Gaby, assembling a piece of equipment, or testing the reactions of chemicals introduced to one another; at such times, he would usually not notice any greeting short of a gunshot.

Then it was back up to his room to watch the talk-box for the rest of the day.

The programming was mostly local broadcasts from Neckerdam nightclubs—live music. Good stuff. Some sounded like big band music, torch songs, swing—but with more strings than brass. Some was the vigorous, fast-paced stuff that sounded like Irish dance music.

After a couple of hours, he'd had a month's worth of Neckerdam music. But he left it on and kept watching.

Because if he went down to the lab, he'd get in the way of Gaby's tests. If he went to the library, he'd probably bump into Gaby there, too—it seemed to be her retreat for the occasions she could escape Doc and Alastair. If he went for a walk outside, the Changeling's men might be waiting, might kill him on sight. Maybe he should take a brisk walk out on the eightieth-floor ledge and say hello to the gargoyles and griffins.

He'd get hungry in the evening, go down to the lab floor for another grazing run, then return to his room to lie awake on the bed until he could drift off to sleep.

By the second day of his new routine, he was sick of it.

※   ※   ※

At breakfast of the third day, Alastair took a call from the lobby. He hung up and said to himself, "This should be interesting."

Harris, Jean-Pierre, and Gaby heard him; Doc, across the room, did not. Harris asked, "What should?"

"That was the elevator captain. Joseph is on his way up."

"You're right. It should." Harris rose and looked around. "What do you need?" asked Alastair.

"A hammer and chisel. I'm going to try to get Doc's attention."

They were waiting for him when Joseph, somber as ever, stepped off the Foundation elevator. The giant was dressed in lighter, brighter garments than before, not work dress, and carried an enormous green cloth bag over his shoulder. Harris saw Gaby shudder; doubtless she was remembering her last experience with large cloth bags.

Doc stepped forward. "Grace on you, Joseph. I'm surprised. I thought that this was the last place you'd ever wish to visit."

"It was," Joseph said. "But I am ruined for work. Ruined for living. The dreams wouldn't let me go. You stirred them up. I cannot work or sleep. So I am here."

Doc considered a brief moment. "Joseph . . . Duncan is still alive."

"On the grim world. I know." He gestured at Gaby. "She told me."

They all gave her a look. She shook her head and asked, "Was it on the talk-box?"

"Yes."

"Then it was Gabrielle. The twin I've never met."

"It does not matter," Joseph said. "Duncan must die, or I must. So here is the place I must be."

"And you are welcome," Doc said. "Jean-Pierre, would you set him up in a room?"

Jean-Pierre and Joseph left for the residential floor; Gaby, visibly upset, took the stairs up to her room. Doc returned to his experiments, Alastair and Harris to their breakfast.

"Joseph acts like he expects the hammer to fall at any time," Harris said. "Poor guy."

"One of several." Alastair gave him a sympathetic look. "Harris, why don't you go home?"

"Back to the grim world?"

"You can go back anytime. It's not a trivial effort, but we can do it. Doc has recovered, and I can also do the ceremony. All we have to do is find a spot that's usually clear on both worlds. You were talking about a spot on something called Liberty Island."

"No, thanks."

"Why not?"

"Do you want to get rid of me?"

"No. I just want to know why you're so determined to stay in a place that makes you so unhappy."

Harris grimaced. "I don't want Gaby to feel alone. You know, surrounded by strangers."

"*Strangers.* Harris, she's fitting in better than you. We haven't had one jot of success trying to figure out how she can use that well of Gift power she has, but she learns, she asks questions, she suggests, she makes Doc think—I'm a betting man, and my money says Doc will ask her to stay as an associate when all is said and done."

Harris scowled. "She won't."

"Perhaps not." Alastair drew on his pipe and blew a perfect smoke ring toward the ceiling. "You know she's fretting. Says it's almost time for the homelords to collect her rent. Says her parents have to be going mad with worry."

"Yeah, mine too, probably."

"But you won't go back, not even for a day, to straighten out affairs. Why not? Are you afraid you wouldn't be able to return?"

"That's not it." He chewed over his reply. "Alastair, if I go back . . . maybe people would be relieved if I didn't return to the fair world at all."

The doctor gave him a puzzled look. "Even if it's true, and I don't think it is, what does that matter?"

"It matters. If I go, I might lose my nerve and not come back. If I don't go, that can't happen."

"Have you lost your nerve since you've been here?"

"I guess not. But I don't want to give myself the chance."

Alastair's expression remained confused. He stared up at the ceiling as if enlightenment might be waiting there.

CHAPTER FOURTEEN

Day four.

As he rose past up ninety, the laboratory floor, on his way to the residential floor, Harris heard his name called. He pulled the elevator's lever back to neutral and beyond, bringing the car down level with up ninety.

Jean-Pierre waited there and yanked the exterior cage open. Harris did the same for the interior cage.

Jean-Pierre held a folded paper packet out to him. "Almost missed you. Gods, you stink." He looked over Harris' boxing shorts and the towel around his shoulders. "You're spending far too much time in the gymnasium."

"I just get in the way up here." Harris accepted the packet; it was heavier than he expected. "What's this?"

"You know, there's a shooting range on the same floor."

"I know. Noriko offered to teach me to shoot."

Jean-Pierre beamed. "Did she? I made the same offer to Gaby." His face fell. "Not the only offer I made. I haven't quite persuaded her to bed with me. Do you know the trick?"

Harris glared. "You could kill yourself. Play on her sympathy."

"Ah."

Harris tried to let go of the sudden flush of anger. "So what is this?"

"Your pay, of course."

"Pay?" Harris popped the wax seal on the packet. Out from the folded paper slid a dozen libs, the big silver coins Harris had seen before, plus a few of the smaller silver decs and copper pennies.

"Every half-moon on the chime. Doc pays all his associates and consultants while they're working with him. It doesn't do to accrue indebtedness; there are devisers out there who could take advantage of it. So he pays off as fast as he accrues." He pulled the elevator exterior grate shut again.

Harris hefted the coins. "Well, that settles it. I'm going out."

"Out of the building? Not a good idea."

"You're damned right, it's not. But neither is staying here until I blow up from boredom." Harris pulled the interior grate closed. "I think I need to find a tailor. And do you know where Banwite's Talk-Boxes and, uh, Electrical Eccentricities is?"

Jean-Pierre looked surprised. "Brian Banwite? Doc sometimes uses him for specialty work. Good man. He's on Damablanca in Drakshire. Walk six blocks east, take the uptown underground to the Damablanca station. And look for Brannach the Seamer on the same street. My tailor."

"I'll do that, thanks." Harris sent the elevator into motion again.

Forty-five minutes later, he was clean and presentable, but instead of heading straight for the lobby he descended only one floor. Up ninety-one was where Doc kept his offices . . . and his library. Odds were good that he'd find her there.

Gaby was in her usual place, in the stuffed chair at the end of the smaller of the two long tables, where the light was best, and as usual she had a stack of books beside her. She didn't notice him as he entered; he silently closed the door behind him and studied her.

She was in the jeans she'd worn from the grim world and a flowing yellow blouse they'd given her here. She bent over her books, intent on them, her hair half-concealing her face.

So many times he'd seen her in just that pose. He found that his mouth was dry. It was suddenly impossible to look away from her. Impossible to accept that he couldn't just walk up to her, take her head in his hands, twining his fingers into the glossy heaviness of her hair, tilting up her chin to kiss him . . .

She brushed her hair back from her face and caught sight of him. She looked up, startled. "Hi."

"Hi."

"I haven't seen much of you lately. What have you been up to?"

"Actually, I was just obsessing about your hair."

She winced. "Harris."

"Yeah, I know. I shouldn't. I didn't mean to upset you."

"It's all right." He could tell from her expression that it wasn't. "Jean-Pierre was just looking for you."

"He found me. He forced a small fortune into my unwilling hands."

"So you're all dressed up to go out and spend it?"

He settled into the seat next to her. "Yeah, basically. I'm going to pay off a debt, then find a tailor and commission some blue jeans."

Her eyes got round. "I never thought of that. What a great idea! If I give you some of my money and my measurements—"

"Sure."

She tore a page from the back of the notebook she was writing in and began scribbling. Harris saw that she did already know the measurement system the people of Neckerdam used—a standard value called a "pace" broken down into fifty "fingers."

He glanced over the books she was browsing through. *Events of the Reign of Bregon and Gwaeddan in Novimagos, Volume One. The Full History of the World Crisis.* "Catching up on history?"

She slid the piece of paper and several of her own coins to him. "Yes, and you should be, too. Noriko told me a little about the recent history of the fair world, and it was too strange—I had to check up on some things."

"Oh, God, the journalist is running amok again." He folded the paper and tucked it and the coins away. "Things such as what?"

"Such as . . . about twenty years ago, in the Old World, which is what they usually call Europe, they had this deal called the Conclave of Masallia. A lot of the kings of the Old World swore undying affection for each other. A mutual protection pact. Then one of them flipped out and invaded his neighbor. Everybody was obliged by the treaty to side with both of them, so they sort of split down the middle and everybody attacked everybody. And since they all owned colonies in the New World and in their versions of Africa and Asia, pretty soon half the planet was at war. Sound familiar?"

"Like World War Two?"

"Well, closer to World War One, actually." She tapped another volume, *Mechanics of Systemic Economic Collapse*, the first one Harris had seen with a title that wouldn't have looked strange in one of his own college courses. "And here. About five years ago, the economic alliance of the League of Ardree, most of the nations of what should be North America, had a crash. For the last long while, they'd gone increasingly industrial, whole nations turning to production and importing almost all their food. Then there was a trade glut, a repayment problem at the international level, foreclosings, treasuries folding, an economic collapse affecting pretty much the whole world. The fair world is still recovering from it. You see it?"

"History was never my strong point. But you're trying to draw a parallel with the Great Depression."

"I sure am."

"I think you're reaching. A war followed by an economy going bust and you're talking about history repeating itself. That's pretty thin."

"Okay, try this. In the grim world, about the time we were having the Depression, Japan was at war with China."

"So?"

"So Noriko told me yesterday that her people, the Wo, are involved in a pointless war with the nations of Shanga. I looked them up on the map. Any guesses as to what Wo and Shanga correspond to?"

"I already know." Harris frowned.

"So it sounds like another mystery for Doc to go funny about. Like why English and Low Cretanis are the same language. Between that, and the routine with the guns and pepper gas and my wristwatch being all twisted when they got here when nothing else was, he's chewing on the furniture in frustration. How about you?"

"You know I don't chew furniture."

She gave him an exasperated look.

"Okay, okay, it's weird." He rose. "Did you find a Civil War?"

"War of the Schism, eighty years ago. The League of Ardree split into two pieces, basically north against south."

"American Revolution."

"The Great Revolt, about a hundred and fifty years back. When the League of Ardree was formed. The people of Cretanis call it the Ingratitude."

"Jesus."

"The Carpenter Cult."

"I *meant*, 'Jesus H. Christ, you're freaking me out.' Okay?"

"Sorry. I got carried away."

Harris stood. He did some mental calculations. "I don't know whether you ought to tell Doc about this."

"Why not?"

"Because if you're right, events here are sort of following the history of the grim world, and we have a general idea of things that are going to be happening over the next forty or fifty years."

"So?"

"So we can predict the fair world's version of World War Two. Should we?"

She frowned, considering.

"I'll think about it, too. But first I'm going to order us some jeans."

Once he was gone, Gaby finished up with the broader histories and returned to another subject: Duncan Blackletter.

Reports of him appeared occasionally in the newspapers, and Doc's library had scores of bound volumes of crumbling periodicals. Of course, there tended to be a problem figuring out when things happened.

By Novimagos reckoning, the current year was 28 R.B.G.—twenty-eighth year of the reign of Bregon and Gwaeddan, the current king and queen. Before these rulers were Gwaeddan's parents Dallan and Tangwen, who ruled forty-eight years: 1 R.D.T. to 48 R.D.T. Each royal reign reset the year to one, and each sovereign nation had a different chronology. Acadia, to the north, was in its eighteenth year under Jean-Pierre's widower father, King Henri IV—abbreviated 18 H.IV.R. It was maddening.

Still, there were a few benchmarks. Years were often translated to a chronology dated from the union of the nation of Cretanis, 1435 years ago. Most historical volumes translated one date from each reign to this dating system, usually referred to as "Scholars' Years." But not even Cretanis used that dating system routinely; they were currently in year 248 of the reign of their current queen, Maeve X. Gaby marvelled at her longevity.

Duncan Blackletter first showed up in Scholars' Year 1368, nearly seventy years ago. A young man then, leader of a gang, he was tried for the train hijacking of a gold shipment from Neckerdam to Nyrax. The gold was not recovered, and Duncan and some of his men escaped the next year. The dim photographs of him showed a lean, handsome, arrogant face; Gaby could recognize him beneath the years of the face Duncan wore today.

Over the years, Duncan's plans became more ambitious and deadly. He constructed a metal-hulled ship with a ram and used it to pirate shipping routes; it was finally sunk by the navy of Nordland, but he escaped. He exterminated an entire community in Castilia because its rulers would not share their scholarship with him. He used his growing fortune to finance the development of new and bigger explosives, then used them to blackmail entire cities. In Scholars' Year 1398, he nearly bought the kingship of the southern nation of New Acadia through political corruption in its capital, Lackderry. Two years later, he emerged as one of the forces behind the development of glitter-bright, the narcotic liquor that first appeared in the faraway land of Shanga.

It was then that Doc first appeared. Gaby found reports of a brilliant engineer from Cretanis named Desmond MaqqRee building a bridge across the River Madb in the Cretanis capital, Beldon. Doc had uncovered and thwarted a plot by Blackletter to assassinate the Queen. Gaby noted with interest some mild criticism in the newspapers that he had not been knighted for his efforts. This was thirty-five years ago, so she had to revise Doc's estimated age up again, to sixty or higher.

Not long after, there was an obituary notice for a Deirdriu MaqqRee. A suicide, she'd jumped from one of the high towers of Doc's bridge. She was survived only by her husband . . . Desmond. Doc.

There was no explanation, no other account of the death, no hint as to what Deirdriu might have been like or why she killed herself. Gaby fumed over the incomplete picture she was assembling. She kept at it.

Duncan had invested in munitions and reaped big profits during the Colonial War between Castilia and the nations of the New World. A few years later, Scholars' Year 1412, he was at it again. There were hints that he manipulated the kings of the Old World into the war called the World Crisis. The same year, the papers reported Doc refusing a commission in the army of Cretanis and being exiled from that nation; he accepted citizenship in Novimagos.

He was by this time appearing in the news as leader of the Sidhe Foundation, accompanied by an Acadian princess and other like-minded people; they settled disputes, turned the tides of some battles, and followed the trail of Duncan Blackletter across the landscape of the Old World.

Then it was Scholars' Year 1415. Obituaries for Duncan Blackletter, Whiskers Okerry, Micah Cremm, and Siobhan Damvert—the last survived by her grieving prince of a husband, only two years away from becoming king himself, and her grim twelve-year-old son Jean-Pierre.

The end of Duncan Blackletter . . . until his botched plan to kidnap Gaby resulted in Harris finding the fair world.

Gaby sat back from her studies. With so much history between Doc and Duncan, Duncan and Jean-Pierre, there was no way they were all going to emerge from it alive. She feared for Harris and her new friends.

Harris kept his fedora low on his face and left the Monarch Building by one of its side exits. He tried to use reflections in storefront windows to spot anyone who might be following, but couldn't spot anyone. If no one were following now, and if the device in his pocket were working right, then he'd be all right . . . but he felt more secure for having the hard, heavy lump pressed against his kidney, the revolver Noriko had given him.

Jean-Pierre's directions were on target. Damablanca turned out to be a narrow, winding street with two-way traffic moving between tall residential buildings of brown brick; only at street level, where storefronts were crowded with neon and painted signs, was there any color along the street.

And then, a few blocks later, there was Banwite's Talk-Boxes and Electrical Eccentricities, offering enough color and motion for any two normal blocks of storefronts. The shop's name was picked out in gleaming green neon Celtic knotwork letters and surrounded by a gigantic yellow neon oval; just outside the border of that oval ran a bronze model train, upside down when it turned to chug along the underside of the sign, always sending gray fog from its smokestack floating up into the sky. Like most of the ground-floor shops in Neckerdam, Banwite's had no windows at street level, but in the windows up one, Harris glimpsed dozens of talk-boxes and moving mechanical toys.

He shoved his way in through the front door, heard the clang of the cowbell hanging overhead, and walked in on a gadget-freak's vision of paradise. The shop interior was like a repeat of the exterior, only more crowded. In one corner was a gadget that looked like a diving suit's arms and legs sticking out of a water heater. A model aircraft with articulated pterodactyl-like wings hung from the ceiling. A grandfather clock with moving figurines instead of a pendulum behind the glass belled six, hours off from the correct time.

Brian Banwite stood behind the massive black-and-gold cash register at the main counter. "Help you, son?"

"You can take my money." Harris set a lib in front of him.

"Always glad to oblige. But you have to take something for it."

"I did that already." Harris lifted his hat. "Remember, about a week back, I stole a ride in the back of your truck—lorry?"

"That was you!" Banwite scooped up the coin and pocketed it. "Done, then. I knew you were good for it. You seem to have done well for yourself." He shot Harris a suspicious look. "You haven't fallen in with bad eamons, have you? No gangs, no glitter-bright?"

"A sort of gang, yes. The Sidhe Foundation."

Banwite sighed, relieved.

"You have a neat shop. Do you make all this, or just sell it?"

"Half and half. If it's electrical or mechanical, I can make it for you. Ask Doc."

"I'll do that." For politeness' sake, Harris took a walk around the shop, marveling at dioramas of moving figures, flashlights that were so small by fair world standards they looked almost normal to him, folding knives with extra tools like half-hearted Swiss Army knives. Then he tipped his hat to Banwite on the way out and went looking for the tailor's.

It was two blocks further on, much less conspicuous than Banwite's. The owner, Brannach, was a comfortably overweight pale man with bright eyes and big, blindingly bright teeth. He'd never heard of denim, but showed Harris his selection of materials.

One of them, demasalle— "That's more properly serge de Masallia, of course"—was the right stuff, but was available only in red and green.

"Can you dye it blue, like that?" Harris pointed to the one blue garment in the shop.

"With ease." The tailor looked uncomfortable with Harris' color choice, but said nothing about it.

So, half an hour later, poorer by about a third of his coins, Harris left. Three sets of jeans for Gaby, three for himself, ready within a few days; he'd have to pay the other half then.

It was just two errands, but he'd pulled them off without any of Doc's associates leading him around by the hand, without screwing up three ways from Sunday. He smiled at the skyscrapers of Neckerdam and turned back toward the Monarch Building.

Gaby accepted Alastair's proffered hand and stepped up out of the car. She looked dubiously at the mound of a building. "And these guys are supposed to be able to figure me out."

Doc joined them on the sidewalk. "If anyone can."

The building was a mountain of brick. This was no accident of design, no passing similarity. The structure was ten stories tall and took up an entire block. It rose in gradual, irregular curves, slopes, and cliff faces. Bushes grew from outcroppings—and from planters set outside the many lit windows. The shutters across the closed windows blended in with the surrounding brick in color and texture.

At street level, the doorway into the building was flanked by bearded men sitting against the brick front. One was gray haired, the other brown haired and much younger. Both wore stained garments in dull brown and green. Their eyes were focused on some distant point invisible to Gaby; they did not react to her or to the pedestrian traffic on the sidewalk.

The three of them entered the building's dark, low-ceilinged lobby. "What's their problem?" Gaby asked.

"Glitter-bright," Doc said. "Highly addictive, very destructive. It's illegal in most kingdoms, but sold everywhere. That's where crime makes a lot of its coin."

Several old men and women sat on the lobby's sofas, many of them reading newspapers, some playing chess. A set of wooden doors in the far wall vibrated with the music playing beyond. It was much like the music Gaby had heard several times in the fair world, but she had the impression that it was wilder, more powerful.

Doc's hand closed around her arm, bringing her up short. She looked around in surprise. She was halfway across the lobby, halfway to that set of doors, and couldn't remember getting that far.

"We don't want to go in there," Doc said.

Wrong, he was wrong. She could feel something pulling at her from beyond the doors, something very demanding and exciting. "Yes, I do. Why shouldn't I? What's in there?"

"A dance. A dance from the Old Country. Very potent." He drew her toward another doorway; she could see stairs through it.

She hung back, trying to pull free. "What's wrong with just taking a look?"

He smiled thinly. "Nobody just looks, Gaby. You join in. And if we were to join in . . . well, I would have a very good time. Alastair would probably die. And you would become pregnant."

"Oh, not likely. Even if I were interested, which I'm not, I'm on the pill. It's the wrong time of the month anyway."

He shook his head. "None of that matters."

"I'll just take a peek." She tried to pull away, but his grip was like metal. Protesting, she found herself pulled into the narrow stairwell and up dimly lit wooden stairs.

After a couple of flights, she realized that her breathing was slowing. It startled her; she must have been practically panting before. And the appeal of the dance going on beyond those closed doors was suddenly lost on her.

She gulped. "Doc, I'm sorry. I don't know what got into me—"

"I do. Don't concern yourself. It's the usual reaction. One good reason why people with a lot of grimworld blood shouldn't come into neighborhoods where the old customs are kept."

"On the other hand," Alastair said, "when I'm old and I've decided to die, this is the place and that's the way I'll do it."

After eight flights, Gaby swore to herself that she was going to start running again. And that she'd never again wear the damned heeled pumps Noriko had found for her. Her toes felt as though mechanics had been at them with pliers and her back was already giving her trouble.

In the narrow hallway up nine, Doc knocked on an unmarked door. It opened to reveal a woman who couldn't have been more than three and a half feet tall. She was middle-aged and heavily built, with a round, florid, happy face. She wore a bright red shawl and a dark green dress. Gaby decided that she looked like a large rose sprouting from an unusually hefty stem.

She beamed up at them. "Doc."

"Hedda." Doc stooped to kiss her. "I bring you Gabriela Donohue and Doctor Alastair Kornbock."

"Gods' graces on you." She stepped back to allow them entry. "You are the young lady with the troublesome Gift?"

"I'm afraid so." Gaby decided the woman sounded German.

"We will unwrap it for you."

The flat beyond was dim, its inadequate electric lamps illuminating age-darkened walls, but clean. Chairs, tables and sofas were drawn away from the center of the room, and a rug was rolled up against one wall. A dented platter painted with apples sat in the floor's center, loaded down with little pots and jars.

It was all very homey and charming, but there was something about the place. The shadows were thick against the walls and seemed darker than they should have been; Gaby fancied that she saw deeper blackness rising and ebbing within them. She smoothed down the hair on her arms where it tried to stand.

Hedda shut the door behind them. "We will do this very slow, with tradition and care. But first, there is something important I must know."

"What is it?"

"Would you like xioc? Tea? There is fresh pastry."

Kneeling, Gaby read the words aloud, the ones Hedda had spelled out phonetically on the piece of paper before her. She kept her thoughts focused on the words, on the smell of jasmine incense, on her contented state of mind.

Around her was the conjurer's circle she and Hedda had made together. The diminutive woman had told her to hold each piece of chalk, each little pot of paint. Only when Gaby had warmed it in her hands would Hedda take the item and begin working on the circle. The outer circle was of yellow chalk and an unbroken stream of yellow sand; the inner, the same but in red. The symbols between, carefully chalked in by Hedda and then painted by Gaby, each in a different color. It had taken nearly an entire bell to complete.

She reached the end of the last page. "Think of him as a smiling man," Hedda had said. "The eyes of a wise man, the smile of a lover. Light shines from his face. Call to the light. Beg it. Ask for the wisdom behind it."

She did, effortlessly holding the image in her thoughts, relaxed, clear-minded, waiting.

Nothing.

She heard Doc sigh. She opened her eyes. He and Alastair stared at her from their chairs outside the conjuration circle; Doc shook his head.

She looked at Hedda, unhappy. "I did it wrong."

"No, sweet. You did it right. Every step true." The woman looked apologetic. "What confused Doc confuses me. I could feel your strength when we put the circle together. You have Gift. I wish I had your strength. But it does not come out."

"You're having the exact same results someone like Harris or Noriko would," Doc said. "But unlike them, you're full of the Gift. Your well of power just seems somehow capped."

"Sorry."

"Don't be." He rested his chin on his hand and stared morosely at her. "We've learned some things, today and in my tests. We know what you can't do."

"Such as?" Her tone was sharp.

"Don't be annoyed."

"I just don't like being told what I can't do."

"So I gather. Gaby, your Gift doesn't follow the traditional patterns. You have no Good Eye; you can't see the residue of devisements. You don't see the future. You don't see events imbedded in the objects that have experienced them. There's no sign of a cord between you and some twin, real or mystic. You can't melt your flesh and reshape it."

"People *do* that?"

"Not many. It's a dying art."

Hedda smiled. "Which is sad. It can be such fun."

"Today, we learned that you can't project your voice to the ears of the gods. You make no links between objects or places, even with conjuration circles. You do not weave patterns of your Gift into things you make with your hands. You do not send your sight away from your body. You do not affect fire, water, air, or earth."

"Does that leave anything?"

Doc didn't answer. Alastair said, "Well, yes, countless things. But they are so rare, and often—I will be frank—so irrelevant that there are no tests devised for them." He gave her an apologetic smile. "For example, a few years ago, I tested a woman who showed sign of Gift but didn't follow the usual patterns. I found that her Gift was directed inside her. All her sons grew up to look just like her father. Identical, to the last mole and birthmark. Except for the one who looked like Kiddain Ohawr, the star of stage and screen. You can't imagine the trouble that caused with her family."

She laughed, then sobered. "You're saying that this Gift could be something totally useless."

Doc nodded. "Yes. That would be a waste. You have so much of it. But you should prepare yourself for that possibility. Hedda, I'm sorry. I've taken up your whole afternoon."

"But not wasted. You are always good company. And the young lady likes my pastries."

On one Neckerdam broadcast channel, the talk-box showed square dancing. Not too different from similar stuff he'd seen on the grim world. On the other channel, it was the game they called crackbat—part baseball, part jai alai. Harris settled on it and concentrated on trying to figure out the rules.

The little talk-box, the one that acted as his telephone, rang. He picked up the handset without taking his attention off the screen. The runner in his padded suit, still holding the flat bat with the net at the end, charged the base and whacked the ball out of the net of its defender. He crashed into the defender and both landed on the base. "Hello."

"Goodsir Greene?"

"Yes."

"This is Brannach the Seamer. Three days ago, you brought in an order for demasalle trousers."

"Oh, right. Hi. Grace on you."

"And on you. They're almost finished, but I needed to know if the lady's trousers were also supposed to have buttons for suspenders."

"Suspenders? No, no, no. Belt loops. They're supposed to be worn with belts." Another batter was up. The pitcher threw the ball and hit him with it. The crowd groaned; the batter walked dejectedly away from the base. The next batter up took his place. "Did you put buttons for suspenders on my trousers, too?"

"Of course, sir."

"My fault for not explaining things better. All six pairs need to have loops for belts, but no attachments for suspenders. Is that going to cause any trouble?"

This batter ducked the first pitch. He managed to sway back and catch the second pitch in the net. He spun around, hurling the ball far out beyond the base defenders, and dashed for the first base, his bat still in hand.

"No *trouble*, sir. I'm afraid I'll have to charge an extra four dec for the additional work. And they probably will not be ready for a couple of bells more. We are open until five bells, though, and they will certainly be ready by then."

"That's great. I'll be by then for them." He hung up, wondering why the runner on third base looked as though he were preparing to hurl his bat at the pitcher.

Harris hadn't felt imprisoned since he'd begun his walks outside the Monarch Building. He did follow Jean-Pierre's advice, not leaving at the same time or by the same door every day, varying his route, staying alert. Nothing ever happened.

It was time to further expand his options.

He stuck his head in the laboratory door. Joseph and Jean-Pierre were there. Joseph was lifting a barbell that looked impossibly heavy. Jean-Pierre, stretched out on a couch, took notes on a pad of paper. Harris waved to get their attention. "Hey, you guys, I'm going out to get my pants. Either of you want anything?"

"Hot xioc," Jean-Pierre said. "Joseph?"

The giant shook his head. He set down the barbell and began adding weights to it.

"Be back soon."

But instead of descending to the lobby, Harris went down two, to the garage. The mechanic, Fergus Boot-black, listened to his request.

"Take the Hutchen," Fergus said. "You *can* drive, can't you? Good. Are you carrying fire?"

"Fire? Like a cigarette lighter?"

"No, no, no." Fergus pointed his finger, miming a gun.

"Oh, *fire*. Yeah."

"Good. Oh, and Doc wants you and the lady Donohue to use the faraway ramp whenever you leave the building."

"Use the what?"

Fergus pointed to a shadowy far corner of the garage. There, a dimly lit concrete corner led away from the garage at a right angle to Harris' line of sight. "That leads to a ramp that comes out one block over. Anyone waiting for you outside the Monarch Building will miss you. Come back in the same way."

"Sure thing." He looked around. "What's a Hutchen?"

The Hutchen turned out to be an anonymously boxy dark green two-seater; it had a high clearance and looked a little like pictures of the Model T. Fergus had Harris wait a couple of minutes while he logged the car out on the records in his office, then showed him which button started the ignition. It took Harris a minute to reac-quaint himself with the concept of the choke, but fortunately he'd learned to drive on his grandfather's archaic pickup truck and not on a more modern vehicle. He groped around for the seatbelts for a long minute before realizing, dismayed, that there were none for him to find.

He managed to get the Hutchen into gear without embarrassing himself—the gearshift was an H-pattern, floor-mounted stick familiar to him—and carefully guided it into the opening Fergus had pointed out.

A long tunnel, four sides of concrete and bare lightbulbs overhead, it traveled at least a block. Halfway along, Harris was sure that he heard the rush of a subway train beneath him.

The ramp at the far end took him up to where the tunnel terminated in a large warehouse-type door. There had to be unseen operators at work; in the rearview mirror, he saw a similar door slide into place behind him before the exterior door slid open. Beyond, quick and noisy traffic zipped by in both directions. Streetlights gleamed atop Greek-style columns, moths fluttering their lives away around them.

At last, he was vehicular again. It felt pretty good. He eased the Hutchen forward; during a break in traffic, he turned left onto King's Road, staying alert to the simple fact that traffic here ran on the wrong sides of the road. It felt like he was sixteen again, with a freshly minted driver's license, trying to keep all the rules in mind at the same time.

Harris stuck his hand out the window and signaled, bicycle-style, the way the other motorists did it, for his right turn from King's Road onto Damablanca. He passed the glowing green-and-gold sign over Banwite's and threw a salute his one-time benefactor couldn't see.

There was no parking space open in front of Brannach's. Harris sighed and drove on past. Parking was better in Neckerdam than in New York, but he might have to go around the block once or twice before he found a spot for the Hutchen.

Still scanning for a place to park, he continued a block, then turned left onto the two-lane northbound-only avenue labelled Attorcoppe.

A horn blared behind him and he heard a sickening crunch, felt the Hutchen shudder as its right rear quarter slammed into something.

He cringed. He knew, without having to turn and look, what had happened. Coming off Damablanca, distracted, he'd gravitated like an idiot into the right lane. At least on this one-way street it hadn't been a lane full of southbound traffic. He slowed and looked over his shoulder at the car he'd hit, preparing to mouth an apology to its driver, something to tide him over the few seconds it would take to pull the two cars to the side.

In the glare from the streetlights, he saw that the driver of the car was staring at him, cursing. No surprise. Two of the three men in the car with him were also glaring.

The last man, the rear-seat passenger on the left side of the car, was half out of the window, reaching down for something bouncing and teetering on the car's running board. Harris glanced at it.

It was a Klapper autogun, the same sort of brassy submachine gun Alastair had used when the assassins struck at Doc's lab.

The same sort of gun the other two men in the car were now bringing up to aim at Harris.

CHAPTER FIFTEEN

"Damn it!" Harris hunched down, mashed the accelerator, jerked the car to the left.

There was a roar from the other car, like the world's loudest lawn mower starting, and Harris felt hail batter the side of the Hutchen. He flinched and ducked as low as he could. The shuddering went on and on.

He felt hot stings in his back and neck. It couldn't be gunfire—that would hurt worse, stop him, wouldn't it?

He wheeled left at the first cross-street, automatically slid into one of the lanes to the right of the median, and realized that all the traffic he could see was headed his way. Headlights ahead swerved and horns honked. There was a moment's break in the gunfire from the other car. Then it started again, from directly behind; the back of the Hutchen shook under dozens of impacts.

Harris swore. The car pursuing him was a long, low-slung, fast-looking job like one of Doc's. He wouldn't be able to outrun it.

One of the oncoming autos roared past him in the other lane. A few hundred feet ahead, both lanes were occupied by oncoming headlights.

Harris yanked the wheel left, aiming for a gap between two trees in the median. He felt a tremendous bang as his front wheels hit the curb; the Hutchen bounced up, slowed as it plowed through a bush planted between the trees, and rocked as it came down the curb on the far side.

An oncoming car in his lane screeched as it braked; it swerved but managed to skid to a stop just feet away. Harris turned right, finally traveling with the traffic.

There was the sound of an impact behind him, followed by a metallic crunch. Harris looked in the rearview mirror—to no avail; it was shattered, pieces of glass still falling from the frame. He glanced over his shoulder.

The pursuing car straddled the median. It was motionless, pinned between the two trees Harris had cleared.

"And then you returned to the Monarch Building?" Doc persisted.

"No, I went back and got our blue jeans."

"That would seem to be a foolish choice."

"Damned right it was. But I was mad." He shrugged. "After that I did come right back. You should have seen Fergus' face when I drove in and he saw what had happened to the Hutchen."

"And what about you, Harris?" Doc peered over Harris' shoulder. "How is he, Alastair?"

Harris winced as he felt the doctor's tweezers tug at his bare back again.

"Not bad," Alastair said. "A few pieces of shrapnel that probably used to be car door. Nothing serious."

Harris glanced again at the faces around him. Doc looked thoughtful. Jean-Pierre was frowning. Gaby was worried. Noriko's expression was, as usual, serene, but Harris thought he saw tension in her pose. And Joseph, standing near the door, arms folded, looked just plain mad.

Harris' attention was drawn to a jar on the nearest laboratory table. The jar held a brain and eye-stalks floating in what looked like red jelly, and he had the sudden disconcerting feeling that the eyes were looking at him. As soon as he glanced at them, the eyes looked away. He shuddered.

"Anyway," Harris continued, "my guess is that they were just getting ready to shoot me when I accidentally side-swiped them. I figure that the impact made the first guy drop his gun. I think maybe I was saved by my bad driving."

Jean-Pierre asked, "Did you ever return fire?"

"Nope."

"Did you drive past the car once it was stopped to see what condition the gunmen were in?"

"No."

"Did you contact the Novimagos Guard?"

Harris shook his head, impatient. "That's what I'm doing now, right? What are you getting at?"

Doc interrupted: "Who knew you were going out?"

Harris thought it over. "Jean-Pierre and Joseph. And Fergus."

"And who knew you were going to Brannach's?"

"No one. No, wait. I told Jean-Pierre and Joseph."

Jean-Pierre stiffened. "What are you suggesting?"

Harris looked at him evenly. "I'm not suggesting anything, JayPee. I'm answering questions. I know you didn't have anything to do with this. If you wanted something bad to happen to me, you could have arranged for it lots of times. Stabbed me in a back stairwell or something."

Jean-Pierre slowly relaxed back into his chair. "Well, then." He turned to glare at Doc. "Stop trying to pick fights, Doc."

Alastair slathered balm on the last of Harris' cuts and affixed another bandage.

Doc ignored Jean-Pierre. He said, "The Novimagos Guard found the car. It was wedged too firmly between the trees to drive clear; you chose very well. But the gunmen were gone."

"Great." Harris glanced back over his shoulder, saw that his cuts were all bound, and shrugged back into his shirt. "Thanks, Alastair."

Doc said, "I need to make some talk-box calls. And then . . . I'd appreciate it if you would arrange to go driving again."

"Oh, yeah? And how about gunmen?"

"There will probably be even more this time, and better armed."

"Great," Harris said. "Sign me up."

Gaby glared at him. "I think that too many days of being cooped up here have made you crazy."

"Maybe it'll be an improvement from when I was sane," he shot back.

"You want what?" Fergus asked.

"I want the Hutchen again," Harris said. "I'm stubborn."

"You mean you're mad. I haven't even begun the repairs."

Harris shrugged. "If it's drivable, it's what I want."

Fergus sighed. "Give me a few beats; I have to look over my notes." He turned away from the madman, sorrowfully shook his head, and walked into the little office, closing its door behind him.

Once inside, he kept a nervous eye on the door and picked up the handset of his talk-box double. "Morcymeath five nine one naught," he told the operator.

After a minute, he heard the click of connection, but no voice spoke. Fergus said, "It's me."

The other voice was low and smooth. "What?"

"He's coming out again."

"With anyone?"

"No, alone." Fergus paused a moment. "He'll be in the same car as before. It should be even easier to spot. It's shot up all to Avlann." He waited a moment longer, but the other voice didn't speak again. Fergus replaced the handset in his cradle.

He picked up the Hutchen's key and his notebook and consulted the latter as he walked back out.

"It should carry you," he said, not looking up. "The

Hutchen. But don't beat it too much about before I can repair it."

"I won't," Jean-Pierre said.

Fergus looked up, confused. Jean-Pierre stood beside Harris, both of them leaning against the wall, looking identically nonchalant.

"Oh. Both of you? Or do you want a different car, Highness?"

"In fact, we'll need the slabside lorry instead."

Fergus looked in some confusion at Harris. "I'm glad you changed your mind. I'll just get the key to the lorry."

Harris shook his head. "Not yet. Stay here. Doc will be here in a second to talk to you. He's just up in the building's switchboard office."

Fergus's stomach went cold.

He threw his notebook into Jean-Pierre's face and sprinted for the stairwell.

He was two steps from it when an impact like a sledgehammer blow hit the small of his back. He smashed into the wall beside the door, staggered backwards, and felt his head crack on the concrete floor of the garage.

Harris stood over the unconscious mechanic and searched him for weapons. Fergus carried nothing but the tools in his belt.

Jean-Pierre joined him. "I have never seen a jumping kick like that."

"Flying side kick. Best used against immobile targets and blind men. But when it connects, it tends to smart." Harris unbuckled the tool belt and pulled it free of Fergus. "Say, what's all this 'Highness' stuff, anyway?"

Jean-Pierre shrugged. "By an accident of birth, I am prince and heir to the kingdom of Acadia."

"Hey. Nice work if you can get it."

The other man smiled thinly. "If I thought it was such nice work I would not be here."

🌿   🌿   🌿

Fergus felt pain in his back and heard a murmur of voices. He forced his eyes open.

Doc's face hovered above him. Fergus closed his eyes again.

He felt Doc seize him by the lapels; then he was swung through the air. His back slammed into the wall and the pain grew. He dangled in Doc's grip, his feet well off the floor, and opened his eyes again.

Doc's face was set in angry lines. Behind him waited his associates, the two grimworlders, and the huge man named Joseph. Their expressions were unforgiving.

Doc said, "Do you want to go to gaol, or do you want to walk away?"

Fergus felt a little surge of hope rise through all the fear. "Walk, please."

Doc dropped him. Fergus' heels hit the floor but his legs would not hold him up; he slid down and sat, legs drawn up, at Doc's feet.

Doc glared at him. "You have to do two things. First, tell me everything you know about the place you called to—Morcymeath five nine one naught."

"It's the number he gave me." Fergus heard his voice quavering, but he couldn't stop it. "It belongs to a man named Eamon Moon."

"Tell me about him."

"My height. Lean, like Jean-Pierre. The ladies all seem to like him and he spends a lot of money on them. He has a flat in Morcymeath."

"That's all you have?" Doc shook his head. "It's not enough. Take him to gaol."

"No, *please.*" Fergus frantically searched his memory for things to say, presents to give Doc so that the man might think better of him. "I met him at the Tamlyn Club once. He has a regular table there. I saw him meet another man there once."

"Describe this other man."

"A strong-looking redcap, a graybeard from the old world. He has a lowland accent."

"Angus Powrie." Doc thought about it for a moment. "Very well. That's enough for us to start.

"Second." The anger he turned on Fergus made his previous attitude seem like one of affection. "Why?"

Fergus felt his breath catch. The anger he'd held down for years threatened to surface. It wouldn't do to vent it on Doc if he still had a chance to get away. But he couldn't keep the resentment out of his voice. "It's not my fault. You're to blame."

"Explain yourself."

"*Ten years* I've worked for the Foundation. Every year I apply to be a full associate. Every year you turn me down, keep me chained in this hole." He gestured at Jean-Pierre and the rest. "I could have been one of them, but you just wanted me to keep their cars running. *I'm as good as they are*. She—" he pointed at Gaby "—is here less than a week, and already you're talking about taking her on, too. What about me?" His voice cracked on the last word.

"No doubt you've told this to others. At a pub, say, after hours."

Fergus didn't answer.

"And, no doubt, one day you found a friend in Goodsir Moon. He bought you drinks and told you, yes, you are as good as they are, but they hate you and laugh at you."

Fergus felt a flicker of confusion. That was exactly what had happened. "Maybe."

"They don't deserve you, Fergus." Doc's tone was harsh. "You know, you could do your family a lot of good with just a few more coins every moon."

The mechanic didn't answer. His anger was gone, replaced by a cold sickness. If he concentrated hard, maybe he could keep from throwing up on Doc's boots.

Doc stared down at him a long moment. "Alastair, take him to Galt Athelstane at the guard station. Tell them to hold him until his words prove true. Or forever, if they do not."

❀   ❀   ❀

The next evening, Harris and Doc walked into the Tamlyn Club with the confidence of the wealthy dilettantes they saw all around them. "Goodsir Cremm's table," Doc said, and the maître d' led them across the crowded floor.

The club was huge, a vast expanse of tables dressed in gold tablecloths and decorated with fresh flowers, white china, and gleaming silverware.

Green-jacketed waiters served brightly hued patrons. On stage, Addison Trow and his New Castilians, in matching white jackets and blood-red pants, played for the dining audience. Their sound was like big band played entirely on strings and woodwinds. Harris decided that he liked it.

The maître d' brought them to the table where Alastair sat. The doctor glanced up at them, looked away, and did a classic double-take, breaking into a wide grin. He waited for the maître d' to leave. "I didn't recognize you two."

"That's the idea, isn't it?" asked Harris. He and Doc sat.

Doc's skin was the color of a deep California tan, just slightly lighter than the suit he wore, and his short-cropped blond hair matched his tie. Harris was as dark as old wood and he knew the Van Dyke beard and mustache he wore dramatically altered the lines of his face.

"Where did you get all that?"

"Doc showed me to Siobhan Damvert's old makeup kit. The makeups were mostly too old and dried up, so I sent out for more, but the hairpieces were mostly in working order." Harris gingerly touched his beard; the spirit gum was holding fine.

"Harris has a fine hand for this sort of work," Doc said.

"He does," Alastair said. "Very well. If you'll try not to be too indiscreet about it and take a look at the tables nearest the stage . . . The small round one with only one man at it. That's Eamon Moon."

Harris turned as if to watch the band and spotted the

man Alastair described. Moon was a lean, handsome man with a pencil-thin mustache and a sophisticated look. He sipped from a wineglass while smiling at the musicians.

Alastair continued. "He's been here most of the afternoon. Sitting alone, but occasionally people come up to talk to him. It looks like social contacts for the most part, and I've recognized a couple of royal ministers and one captain of the guard among those he's spoken to. Others have the look of strong-arm men about them. They don't stay long after he speaks to them."

"Noriko and Jean-Pierre went through his flat," Doc said. "It seems barely lived in. The talk-box was attached to an interesting device. A wireless transmitter made for cabled doubles to plug into. I think it must send his calls on to another site."

"Not here. I've seen him take no calls."

"Go home and get some rest."

Alastair nodded. He drained the last of his uisge glass, made a face that suggested both pain and contentment, and left.

A waiter asked Harris and Doc whether they were here for dinner or drinks. Doc ordered wine.

Harris discreetly watched Eamon Moon. The man did little but listen to the musicians, sip his drink, and exchange words with other patrons as they passed his table. "Boring guy."

"Where's his fire?"

"His gun? I don't know. Do you?"

"Yes."

"Well, where?"

"My point is that you should be able to tell me."

"Oh." Harris looked a little more closely. "This is where all these damned baggy fair world clothes are going to trip me up."

"There's no need to curse, Harris."

After two more of the band's songs, he said, "He's a compulsive kind of guy. Does everything the same way.

Lifts his wineglass the same way everytime. Checks his pocket watch every so often."

"Yes."

"Left armpit."

"Yes. How do you know?"

"He checks it every time he pulls out his pocket watch, doesn't he?"

"Very good. Where is his bodyguard sitting?"

"Bodyguard?"

The band's instrumental number ended. The crowd applauded. A large, dusky-skinned musician stood and took center stage; at the back of the band, a bagpiper stood.

The piper began to play an eerie, unhappy wail. In an earthquake rumble of a voice, the other man sang,

He tells me again, "I can do you no more,
No work to be had," and he shows me the door.
Long day of walking, I'm sore o' the foot,
Naught to show for it but a hole i' my boot.

The door to my flat does not yield to my knock.
The boy says my lady has changed out the lock.
And through the barred door all the world hears her
     say,
"From my room and my bed I must turn you away."

The rhythm was wrong, the instrument was wrong, the setting was wrong, but Harris felt a sudden shock as he recognized what he was hearing. He put his head down on the table. "He's singing the blues."

"What do you mean?"

"That's what we call it on the grim world. The blues." Harris lifted his head to stare imploringly at Doc. "But, oh my God, on the *bagpipe*?"

"That's the way it's done. What else could sound so soulful?"

"Do you suppose anyone would get mad if I beat both of them to death?"

"I think it would spoil our watch."

"Oh, yeah." Harris suffered through eight more stanzas of the mournful musician's troubles. He felt much better when the singer and piper sat to the audience's inexplicable applause. Two other musicians rose and began a duel of hammered dulcimers.

Harris' relief didn't last long. Angus Powrie appeared at Eamon Moon's side and leaned over to speak in the man's ear. Harris stiffened.

"Better than I had hoped," Doc said.

Powrie didn't stay. He clapped Moon on the back with rough familiarity and walked toward the exit.

Doc dropped a coin on the table and rose. "A change in plans," he said. "I'll follow Powrie. You call the Foundation and have someone come out to join you. Jean-Pierre, preferably. Keep watching Eamon Moon."

"Right."

Doc walked after Angus Powrie with studied casualness.

Harris signaled the waiter. When the man came over, he said, "I need a talk-box for an outside call—oh, hell."

Eamon Moon was on his feet, placing coins on his table. So was the thick-waisted, gloomy man Doc had identified as his bodyguard.

"Never mind," Harris said, and waved the waiter away. He kept his face turned toward the band but watched Moon and his man leave the club. Once the bodyguard was out the door, Harris followed. He struggled to keep his breathing regular.

It got worse. As soon as he got out to the sidewalk, Harris saw Moon and his bodyguard pull away from the curb in a gleaming red convertible.

Harris cursed. Doc had the car. He looked up the street. There was no taxicab in sight, just a steady stream of oncoming traffic, and Moon's convertible would be out of sight in a matter of moments.

He sprinted after Moon's car. It trailed away, shrinking into a distinctive pair of taillights in the distance. Harris had to have a car, and fast.

He crossed into the roadway, glancing back. Two cars back was a low-slung roadster, a gleaming black. Harris put on a burst of speed, crossed the lane empty of oncoming traffic, and made a leap for the roadster.

He landed clean on the running board and grabbed the top of the door.

The car was filled with kids—they looked like they were barely in college years, two boys and three girls, ranging from very fair to nut-brown, all dressed up in eye-poking colors. They all wore identical straw hats with red hatbands and looked at him wide-eyed.

"I'm with the Sidhe Foundation," Harris said. The cliché was out of his mouth before he could check it: "Follow that car."

Their sudden, united cheer startled him; he almost fell off into the street.

Doc, in his roadster, kept two cars back from Angus Powrie's taxi. That massive green vehicle, shaped something like a giant scarab beetle, headed south on King's Road, keeping a steady pace. Then it turned left onto Island Way, the highway that crossed the Island Bridge, and put on a burst of speed.

Doc shook his head. Powrie, canny after decades in the criminal life, had to have spotted him. The redcap wouldn't be leading him anywhere. Doc pulled the too-warm blond wig off, dropping it on the seat beside him, then accelerated and whipped around the car ahead of him.

The cab's wheels screamed as it turned right, too sharply, and disappeared behind a long residential building. Doc sent his more maneuverable roadster into a tighter turn and got the cab in sight again. It was accelerating, a straight-line run past cross-street after cross-street.

Doc stood on the accelerator and gained on it. Within a block, he was on the taxi's bumper. He made sure his automatic pistol was still in the shoulder holster.

The driver gave up. He pulled to the curb and switched off the red light on the hood that said he was engaged. Doc pulled in beside him and jumped out, leveling his gun at the taxi's occupants.

Occupant. The streetlight showed only the taxi driver, a man with a lined face and a startled expression. The driver raised his hands.

"Where is he?"

"Most amazing thing I ever saw," said the driver. "Dropped me a full lib and said to keep going. Just off Island Way, he jumped clean out of the car! Hit so hard he bounced. Did you ever hear of such a thing?"

Doc sighed and holstered his gun. Well, at least Harris and Jean-Pierre still had Eamon Moon under observation.

"Are you really with the Sidhe Foundation?" asked the driver. She was tiny, blond, and naturally wide-eyed even after her composure returned.

"Yes, I—"

The boy beside her asked, "Are you after a gunman? A spy?"

"Well—"

"Do you know the prince? He's to swoon for."

"I think he's wearing makeup. Are you wearing makeup? Your face is running."

"How did you get so big?"

Harris stretched on tiptoe. Over the roof of the car in front he could still see the taillights of Moon's car. It was turning. He crouched again, holding tight. "Take a right at the next street."

The girl braked and turned expertly; the maneuver pressed Harris against the door. "How do you join?" she asked. "Is there a test?"

Suddenly there were no cars between the kids' and

Moon's. Harris returned to a crouch. "Hell if I know. I just sort of fell into it."

"Well, that's not very helpful. You can't plan to fall into things, can you?" She didn't wait for an answer. "Is that the one, the red Bellweather?"

"Yeah. Is that what it is, a Bellweather?"

"Last year's."

"How do you know?"

"By the taillights."

"That's good, very good. You know a lot about cars?"

"I love cars. I plan to be very rich so I can have one for every day of the moon."

"Good plan." The car made another right turn; he held on tight as the girl followed. "That taillight thing is a good trick. Learn lots of neat stuff like that. It'll probably improve your odds with Doc."

"Truly?" She beamed a smile like a headlight at him.

The boy beside her asked, "He lets you call him Doc?"

They were on a broad four-lane that ran along the shore of what would have been the Hudson River. Between warehouses and dark businesses, Harris had frequent glimpses of the river and of the piers arrayed along it.

Ahead, the Bellweather turned left beside a large warehouse building. Harris said, "Stay on the road. But go slow, please."

They cruised past. Harris saw the Bellweather stopped in front of a big warehouse. The car honked. Just before the building hid them, Harris saw the big door begin to slide open, light shining from beyond.

They passed in front of the office building in front of the warehouse, a part of it. The painted sign above the main entrance, dimly lit by a small spotlight, read "Aremorcy Waterways." "Okay, can you stop here?"

She pulled the car to the side and braked. He stepped off, staring at the building. A heavy, monolithic thing of dark brick. Three stories. Shuttered windows on the upper stories. "What street are we on?"

She laughed at him. "Western High Road. How many roads do you think run along the river?"

"Oh."

"Are you carrying fire?" asked the older of the two girls in the backseat.

The boy in the middle asked, "Doesn't the Foundation give you an auto?"

"Can I drive you somewhere else?" the driver asked. "The guard-station?"

He smiled at her. "Sure." He stepped back up on the running board. "How about the Monarch Building?"

"Oh, good."

Back in the laboratory, Doc managed a derisive snort. "Perhaps if I'd enlisted the aid of a car full of university students, I'd not have been outmaneuvered so easily. No, you did very well, Harris." He turned to face everybody. "Harris, Gaby, the rest of us will be visiting this place in Morcymeath. It's likely to be the center of their activities in Neckerdam. This will be a raid, possibly very dangerous. The two of you will stay here."

Harris started to nod.

Gaby said, "No way in hell."

Everyone looked at her. Doc said, "Why not?"

She took a deep breath before answering. "Doc, I'm not going to let you all go out and risk your lives for me. Not while I stay safe on the top of your ivory tower. What if you got hurt? What if you got *killed*? How could I live with that?"

Doc shrugged. "It's what we've chosen to do."

"Well, it's what I—" She looked startled. "It's what I'm choosing to do."

Harris saw Doc's face brighten and Joseph's face fall. The taciturn giant looked as though he'd just come to the funeral of a friend.

In spite of his smile, Doc said, "You're not trained in it, Gabriela."

"So tell me where to go and what to do so I don't put any of you in danger."

Harris fumed. If she went, he had to go. He fought down the urge to strangle Gaby.

Doc looked at Harris. "Do you agree with her?"

"Oh, absolutely." Harris spoke the biggest lie of his life with utter conviction. Gaby turned her smile on him. That made it a lot better.

"Then you're a pair of fools. Make yourselves ready."

In the bouncing back of the Sidhe Foundation's delivery truck, Harris sat on a bench and unfolded one of Fergus' maps of Neckerdam. He saw that if this were Manhattan, Morcymeath would have been the entire southern tip of the island, and there were more piers here than in the corresponding area on the grim world.

He glanced around at the others arrayed on the two benches. Everyone but Doc and Jean-Pierre, who were in the truck's cab. Alastair had his Klapper autogun partially disassembled; as he put it back together again, Gaby watched in grim fascination. She held a tarnished bolt-action rifle; it looked incongruously big and old in her hands. There were wooden cabinets bolted to the truck walls above their heads; Harris had already seen the weapons racked inside them, had been given more firepower than he'd ever carried before. This was a primeval SWAT van.

Joseph, beside him, looked gloomier than ever. Harris nudged him with his knee. "Hey. What's eating you?"

"You and Gabriela should not be here."

"Tell me about it. What about you?"

"I am hard to hurt."

"You stand in front, then."

"I will."

"I was joking."

They all slid a few inches toward the cab as the truck slowed and stopped. The lightbulb against the van roof went dark.

A moment later, Doc pulled open the back doors of

the truck. Atypically, he wore black clothes and his hair was tucked up under a black felt cap with earflaps; it looked hot. "Out, and quiet," he said.

They disembarked into the deep shadow cast by the monstrous skyscrapers of Morcymeath. Though a few of the buildings had windows lit, at this hour most of Neckerdam's businesses were closed for the night, and Doc had chosen a dark side street.

Two other trucks were parked behind Doc's. Harris saw people climbing out their rear doors. They seemed young but quietly professional, perhaps a dozen men and half a dozen women, all clad in uniforms made black by the night.

Doc waved one over. The burly, bearded man who approached was better dressed than the others; in addition to the uniform trousers, tunic, boots and holster belt, this man had elaborate gold trim on the tunic and a hip-length cloak. He saluted Doc—at least Harris assumed it was a salute; the man held his open palm on his breast for a moment as though he were listening to "The Star-Spangled Banner."

Doc returned the salute. "Good to work with you again, Lieutenant Athelstane," he said. He gestured at the hulk of a building down the block and across the intersecting street. "Position your men on the south, north, and west sides; my associates will be on the east. There's the chance that this is a legitimate business, so be cautious. But I think it's more likely this will be similar to any glitter-bright distillery raid."

"Meaning they'll fight like trapped rats."

Doc smiled sourly. "Rats with autoguns. You're to wait for my signal, but use your discretion. If you hear shouts or gunfire, don't bother to wait. Dismissed." They traded salutes, and Athelstane turned to rejoin his troops.

As the lieutenant led his people away into the darkness, the others clustered around Doc. Jean-Pierre was not in his usual elegant dress; he wore baggy workman's clothes and a cloth cap.

Doc said, "We have to assume the doors are watched. Noriko, you and I will creep up beside the front door and wait for Jean-Pierre. Alastair, I want you and your Klapper on the other side of the street on the north corner for fire support." He frowned at Harris. "You're not carrying a long arm."

"I've never fired a rifle. I took a couple of revolvers from the truck, on top of my usual." Harris patted his coat pockets, felt the reassuring weight of the weapons and ammunition they held.

"You'll need to be close, then. Like Alastair, but south corner. But you won't be entering; stay at that position and keep any gunmen from leaving the building."

"Sure."

Doc looked at Gaby. There was nothing but joyless resolve in her expression. "Jean-Pierre, how is she with that?"

"Straight and true."

"Gaby and Joseph, stay here with the truck. You're our final line of reinforcement on this flank. Don't act unless you have to. Any questions?"

There were none. Doc nodded at the rest of them, then he and Noriko melted away into the shadows.

Harris looked at Alastair. The doctor gestured for him to wait; then, after several seconds, pointed at the wall behind Harris. Harris moved there and walked in the deep shadow beside the wall, while Alastair matched him beside the building across the street.

Harris' heart pounded. Prefight jitters again. He concentrated on his breathing, tried to make it slow and even.

In a minute, because of Gaby's damned insistence that she come along, he might have to shoot somebody.

Kill somebody.

He reached the corner of the building, the closest approach to the cargo house, and stopped there within its shadow.

A few feet ahead, cars were parked along the sidewalk. Beyond them was the broad four-lane street, and beyond that was the combined warehouse and office he'd seen before. There were no cars parked in front of the office. Traffic was not heavy, but the cars that did pass were moving fast.

Across the side street to his right, Alastair had set up just short of the corner of his building. The doctor's attention was fixed on the front of the building they would soon be assaulting.

He took another look at the building, evaluating it in terms of what Doc planned for them to do. In the middle of the building face there was an inset a dozen feet deep; there, the steps of a stoop rose half a dozen feet to the heavy, round-topped wooden door that seemed to be the place's main entrance. There were shuttered windows above the entrance, and Harris could see another window on the right wall of the inset; if there was yet another window on the left wall of the inset, Alastair would be able to see it. Harris saw no street-level stairwells leading down to a basement entrance.

Doc appeared on the stoop as if by magic. He stood to the left of the door, back flat against the wall. Harris could see only his face—in profile, turned toward the door—and his left hand. Doc gestured, and Noriko appeared almost as suddenly, climbing up over the right concrete banister of the stoop. They flanked the door and froze into immobility.

From his pockets, Harris drew out the two pistols he'd been given in the truck. They were both bigger than the one he'd been carrying, the one he still wore just over his kidney. Instead of having swing-out cylinders, they were break-loaders, long-barrelled weapons, comfortingly heavy. He broke each one open to make sure it was loaded.

Jean-Pierre, carrying some sort of clipboard and a package wrapped in brown paper, breezed past him with a wink. He had copper-red hair and a bristly beard to match, courtesy of Harris and Siobhan Damvert's makeup case. "You'll do fine," he whispered.

Jean-Pierre dodged traffic to cross the street, then trotted up the stoop of the office building and knocked loudly.

There was no immediate response. Harris saw him stand there, slouching, the bill of his cap drawn low, as relaxed and indifferent as though he weren't flanked by two people carrying dangerous weapons.

Harris saw a little rectangle of light appear in the doorway at about face-level. A small panel, like Harris had seen in movies about speakeasies. A face appeared in the opening.

Cars roared by and Harris couldn't hear any of Jean-Pierre's words. He could see Jean-Pierre offering the package, gesturing with the clipboard, shaking his head.

The little panel closed. Jean-Pierre froze.

Doc swung around and put his fist through the panel. Harris heard a crack of wood. Doc jammed his arm in the hole, almost to the shoulder, then pulled. He yanked the man's head through the hole, splintering wood above and below. The man squealed, harsh and loud as an angry wildcat.

Harris moved forward to kneel behind the nearest car. He set one of the pistols down beside him, brought the other one up in a two-handed grip, and readied himself to kill.

CHAPTER SIXTEEN

Across the street, Doc shoved the guard, then yanked hard. The guard's head, now bloody, emerged a second time. This time he didn't scream. But the door didn't budge.

Jean-Pierre pulled out his pistol and fired it at the lock, two quick shots. Harris saw one of the passing cars swerve at the sudden noise. Doc yanked again and the head of the guard bobbed, but the door still didn't move. Harris thought he saw Doc curse.

The shutters above and to the right of the stoop swung open. Harris saw two men lean out into the light. One held an autogun.

"Shit, shit, *shit!*" Harris aimed at the window and squeezed off a fast shot. He saw the man in the window flinch. It was too dark to line up the gun's sights; he thumbed the hammer back and aimed as best he could for the second shot, the third, the fourth, the gun kicking in his hand.

The men in the window dropped back out of sight. Harris cocked the revolver again and sighted in on the window, waiting.

Across the side street, Alastair opened fire with the autogun; Harris flinched at its jackhammer roar. The doctor hosed down the left wall of the inset. There had to be a window there, too, and it must have opened.

There was gunfire from the far side of the office building. Harris saw Doc curse again. The building's door still stood resolutely closed. The thing had to be massively reinforced.

The man with the autogun appeared in the window. Harris fired. This time he saw the man jerk and drop back. The autogun fell; Jean-Pierre, his attention on the windows, caught the weapon before it hit concrete. He swung around and, like Alastair, directed gunfire against the window Harris couldn't see.

A quick exchange between Doc and Noriko. Harris saw her draw her blade, a silvery line glinting in moonlight. Doc released the guard; the man hung in the doorway. Doc stooped and cupped his hands.

Noriko stepped into the stirrup his fingers made. Doc straightened, swinging his arms up. Suddenly Noriko was flying, leaping up to the window Harris was covering. She got one hand on the pane and came down with her knee on the sill; Harris saw her face twist in pain. Then she slashed at something beyond the window and scrambled in, disappearing from sight.

A blur of pink to Harris' right. He glanced that way and saw Joseph charging toward the front of the office.

Joseph ran like a child, with tottering, off-balance steps, his arms waving awkwardly out in front of him. He didn't pause for traffic. A gleaming green Hutchen swerved to miss him; the driver honked and kept driving.

Joseph hurtled up the stairs. Doc and Jean-Pierre leaned out of his way.

The clay man hit the door like an awkward football lineman in full charge. The door didn't slow him; it just broke with a noise like a gunshot and was instantly gone. Harris didn't want to think about what had become of the guard behind it.

Jean-Pierre charged in after him, the autogun pointed high, and Doc followed.

Alastair emerged from cover and crossed the four-lane, dodging traffic. He paused at the corner of the inset, scanning the entrance and the window he'd fired on. Then he scrambled up the stairs and disappeared into the office building.

And then there was nothing but muffled gunshots. Shouting that Harris couldn't make out.

He concentrated on his breathing again.

How many shots had he fired? He broke open the gun in his hand, ejected the brass. One cartridge was still unfired. He replaced it in the cylinder, then reloaded the weapon from the ammunition in his pocket.

They started firing on Joseph the moment he crashed through the door: two autoguns, pistols he couldn't number. He dimly felt impacts before he plowed through the line of gunmen, cracking limbs and ribcages, scattering them.

It was sad. But perhaps if he broke them now no one would have to shoot them later.

Ahead, more men were rolling a metal door into place, blocking the opening into the warehouse beyond. Joseph picked up speed.

He hit the metal door as hard as he'd ever hit anything. He heard its scream of protest, felt it buckling under his mass as though it were a light roasting pan. It tore free from its housing and crumpled around him as he drove it before him; he went off balance and tripped, skidding across the concrete on his malformed metal sled, scattering more men.

Harris watched as, across the street, one of the sections of concrete sidewalk levered open. It was just like the hidden door at Duncan's Wickhollow house. He came alert, closed his pistol, aimed it across the hood of the car.

A man's head rose from the hole and looked around; he didn't spot Harris. He climbed out of the hole. In his hand was something that looked like a sawed-off shotgun. It was Eamon Moon, now dressed in what looked like a scarlet silk robe.

Harris let him get completely out from the hole. Moon took a couple of furtive steps toward the open office door. His intention was obvious: sneak up on the Sidhe Foundation people from behind. Harris shouted, "Don't move!"

Moon turned and yanked the trigger.

Harris felt blind fear as he saw a gout of fire emerge from the weapon barrel. The other side of the car he crouched behind screamed and crumpled in protest.

Harris fired. Moon jerked as if punched in the gut and stared stupidly at Harris.

Then he aimed the gun again.

Harris fired a second time. Moon took a staggering step back toward the hole and fell to the concrete. Harris stared at his unmoving body.

He'd just shot a man. He paused, expecting . . . expecting he didn't know what. Nothing happened except he found that his mouth was dry.

What now? If men came pouring out of that hole, Harris wouldn't be able to stop all of them. They'd be able to hit Doc and the others from behind.

He half turned. "Gaby, get up here!"

"I hear you." Her voice, coming from right behind him, made him start. He craned his neck to look back. She was standing where he'd been just a few moments ago, at the corner of the building; all he could see was some of her rifle's barrel, protruding beyond the corner, and a little of her silhouette behind the building edge.

"I have to go block that hole." He grabbed his second handgun and sprinted across the street, stuttering a step to avoid running in the path of a northbound limousine. Once past the brick roadway, he moved cautiously up toward the dark hole, both guns out in front of him.

Concrete steps leading down into darkness. If he got close enough, anyone down below would be able to see him.

The thought of somebody lurking at the bottom of the steps, a shotgun ready, drove all the air out of his lungs. He circled around the hole, coming up on it from behind

the tilted slab of concrete. That put him right beside
Eamon Moon. He took a soccer-style kick at Moon's gun,
clattering it up against the side of the building, then put
his shoulder to the slab and shoved. It obligingly keeled
over and fell back into place, making an enormous hol-
low boom and stinging his feet through the leather soles
of his shoes.

Situation under control . . . for now. He picked up
Moon's gun and trotted back across the street, keeping
the slab, the dead man, and the bottom of the stoop in
view. He knelt down behind the cover of the car. There
were more shots from inside the building.

Harris could see Moon's eyes staring up at the stars,
unblinking. He had the uneasy feeling that if he stared
long enough, Moon would look up with a hurt expression and point an accusing finger at him.

Well, let him. Harris couldn't afford to worry about it
now. He kept his aim on the building.

Noriko found a second-story window, allowing her to
look into the cargo house. Immediately below her were
enormous shelves piled with wooden crates and cardboard boxes. Below and to the left was the doorway into
the office building; Alastair and Jean-Pierre held it, firing short bursts into the cargo house, keeping the
Changeling's men under cover. She could see Doc and
Joseph, the former leaping clean through a set of shelves
to open fire on defenders on the other side, the latter
advancing on gunmen with a mangled metal sheet held
before him as cover.

Gunfire sounded from the far side of the building. That
had to be the men defending at the exterior door, in battle
with Lieutenant Athelstane's soldiers.

She squeezed through the window and, catlike, dropped
to the nearly empty top of the shelving below. The impact
made her bruised knee smart more. Thin board bent beneath
her feet but did not give way. The shelves themselves, massive and rock-solid, stood firm against the impact.

She raced forward along the shelf-top, toward the broad center aisle between the ranks of shelving, and gauged her leap. It was fifteen feet, a distance she should easily manage—on an unimpeded dirt track, on an unhurt leg. If she failed, she'd crash into the shelves on the far side.

She picked up speed in the spare few steps before the end . . . and then she was airborne, flailing the sword in her right hand and the sheath in the left for balance. She heard the whistle of a bullet inches from her head.

Noriko came down on the far shelf-top with two feet to spare, but stumbled as her hurt knee gave way. She fell forward, slamming down on the cheap wood of the shelf, knocking the wind from her. She heard her sheath clatter to the concrete floor before she realized she'd lost it. But she was up in a second, ignoring the pain in her chest and leg, and leaped for the top of the next set of shelves over, a much shorter jump than her first one.

Two more bounds and she was at the shelf next to the side door. Below, two men with autoguns stood at the door, firing out through slits cut in the wall. Beside them, two cars, a hardtop sedan and a canvas-topped red roadster, waited—escape vehicles for the Changeling's men. She saw no one through their windows; they hadn't yet decided to retreat.

She stepped off the top of the shelf and dropped more than a dozen feet, landing on her back on the canvas top of the roadster. It held up against the impact, threw her a pace back up into the air; she rolled, coming down in a crouch beside the car. Her knee held.

One of the autogunners saw her just in time to turn and take her sword-thrust in the chest. He fell back against the wall. The other didn't have time to turn; her bloody sword-point pricked at his throat just as he realized something was horribly wrong. He stiffened.

"Drop the gun," she suggested. "Open the door. Or join your friend in your next life."

Out front, the concrete slab levered open again.

Harris glanced back at Gaby, saw her rifle barrel still protruding from the corner. He brought his revolver up, aimed at the hole again, and sucked in a lungful of air for another shout.

Alastair's head popped up. The doctor turned for a quick look around, caught sight of Harris, and flinched back out of sight.

The halls of Aremorcy Waterways were frantic with activity. Blue-uniformed members of the Novimagos Guard hustled captured gangsters through the tile-walled halls. Other guardsmen, guns drawn, burst into darkened offices to ferret out gangsters who might be hiding. Doc's associates collected in the cargo house, prowling among the shelves and stacks of wares, using crowbars to pry open interesting-looking containers.

Harris walked through the confusion, glancing numbly at the arrests and the searches. Novimagos guardsmen passed him in the hallways, not seeing him. It was as though he were a ghost. Maybe he was close enough to death that all he needed to do was squint to see the spirit of the man he'd killed.

He passed through the door out of the offices and into the cargo house. Noriko spotted him at once and came to him, favoring her left leg. Something about his expression must have told a story; she asked, "Are you hurt?"

"I killed a man, Noriko."

She nodded, sympathy briefly evident in her eyes. "And it feels bad."

"No, that's just it. It doesn't feel at all. I keep waiting for it to hit." He shrugged. "Isn't it supposed to?"

"If you hadn't shot him, he would have shot all three of us. I don't think Alastair could see him from his corner. It was the right thing. We owe you our lives, Harris."

He frowned. "I don't get you."

"The man with the Klapper."

"No, the man on the sidewalk—oh." Harris sagged. "You mean I got the guy in the window, too. I shot *two* men to death tonight." He took a deep breath and waited. Maybe now something would happen to him, some blast of guilt like a lightning bolt from the hand of Zeus.

Nothing did.

Doc called, "Noriko? Tell me what you think of this."

She gave Harris an apologetic look and headed Doc's way. The investigation wasn't waiting for the lightning bolt of Zeus.

An unaccustomed weight in his coat pocket reminded him that he was still carrying the dead man's gun. He pulled it out to look at it.

It was strange. It was as long as a sawed-off shotgun, but with a single barrel and a large cylinder like a revolver's. It had a swing-out cylinder like his small revolver. He pressed the catch for it and popped the cylinder out. It held four shotgun shells. He closed the weapon.

There was a loop of white cord tied to the front of the gun, just under the barrel. The cord continued along the left side of the barrel and was tied off to a knob near the trigger. He could tug on the cord and draw the loop closed.

Alastair, visible between crates on the far side of a set of shelves, said, "It's a Wexstan."

"It's weird."

"Sportsman's weapon. For birdstalkers who liked to get close to their quarry. Also for snakes that get too close." He came around the set of shelves to give the thing a better look. "This is the way gangsters modify the things. See the loop of rope? Drop it over a victim's head and draw it tight over his neck, and you ensure cooperation. If the victim tries to yank free, he'll probably yank the trigger. That's the end of the victim. The gangster can draw the loop tighter to control his victim. It's very good for kidnapping."

"Charming." Harris handed the weapon off to the next guardsman.

❀   ❀   ❀

The second floor of the office building had been arranged into bedrooms and barracks rooms. Lieutenant Athelstane reported that the building had, until recently, housed more than the thirty or so men the raid had killed or captured. "We have a singer," he told Doc. "But he won't perform in sight of the others."

"Let's find him a private office," Doc said.

One of the offices downstairs was actually set up for business, with a desk and an adding machine nearly as big as an old-fashioned cash register. Alastair brought in extra chairs for Doc's associates.

Athelstane dragged in one of the captured gangsters. This man had a square face and slack expression under intelligent-looking eyes. His ears rose to a dramatic point; his hair was blond and he was clean-shaven. He was dressed only in trousers, and his hands were shackled in front of him with handcuffs the color of tarnished copper. Athelstane shoved him into the chair behind the desk; Jean-Pierre turned the desk lamp so it shined into his face. The man's eyes watered from the light. He grimaced but didn't complain.

"You know who I am," Doc said. "You know my reputation. These are the terms: You cooperate. I decide later what it's worth to me. Lie to me and it's not worth much. Give me the keys to the city and it can be worth a lot. That's as explicit as it gets. Yes or no."

The man said, "Yes."

"Your name."

"Swyn Alpson."

"Who do you work for?"

"Aremorcy Waterways."

"You've just insulted my intelligence."

The man shifted, restless. "My boss is Eamon Moon. I do most of the work he's responsible for. But Angus Powrie gives Moon orders, and he and Darig MacDuncan give each *other* orders. I don't know which one is the boss, but Angus calls Darig 'sir' and Darig calls Angus things like 'toad' and 'bug'."

Harris leaned forward to interrupt: "'Bug'? This Darig guy is the Changeling, then."

Alpson nodded. "He calls himself that, yes."

Doc said, "MacDuncan. 'Duncan's son.' Is he?"

"I don't know whose son he is."

"Is Darig a deviser?"

"No. Don't think so."

"But you have a deviser in your gang."

"No. Darig just gets packages with things in them. Books. Instructions. From a deviser. I don't know who."

"Does Darig show any sign of any Gift?"

"No."

"Why do you call him the Changeling, then?"

Alpson shrugged. "He likes it. He tells us to."

Doc sat back, frowning. "Where are they? Angus and the Changeling?"

"Went to the airfield early this evening. Angus went off to fetch Eamon back first. Eamon's supposed to be here when Angus and Darig aren't. Angus came back full of spite about you—" he nodded to Doc "—don't know why, and then he and Darig left. With the old sodder."

"Who is that?"

"Name is Blackletter."

Harris saw Doc and Jean-Pierre stiffen. His own back was suddenly tense.

Doc drew a long, slow breath. "Tell me about Blackletter."

Alpson twisted his mouth, an expression of distaste. "Came a few days ago with three big, stupid-looking men, and a bigger, stupider-looking *thing*. Took charge; Angus and Darig both call him sir. They talked and talked, like getting reacquainted." He gave Doc an evaluative look. "I heard some of what they were talking about."

Doc waited.

Alpson shrugged. "Blackletter asked about the list, whatever that is. Darig said it was all done but the new ones. A man and a woman are the new ones, I know that. I know the list is in the safe."

"Where is the safe?"

Alpson tapped his left foot. "Just here, beneath my foot."

Doc turned to Jean-Pierre. "Call Eight-Finger Tom. I'm not going to put anyone less on a deviser's safe. Offer him whatever it takes to get out here right now."

Jean-Pierre rose and left.

Doc turned back to Alpson. "What else did they talk about?"

"Blackletter said *his* list was done. Taunted Angus with it. Good-spirited, like. 'I'm an old, old man and I finished my list first.' This afternoon they loaded up equipment and took it out to the airfield."

"What sort of equipment?"

"Don't know. Lots of it, though, all in big crates. Took eight slabside trucks to carry it. Loaded it onto two big airwings."

"This afternoon."

"Yes."

"Where were they going?"

The gangster shrugged. "Cretanis, somewhere. Some village. Adnum."

"Adennum?"

"That's it."

"What sort of airwings?"

"Big new Weissefrau Valks."

Doc sat back, looking distracted; his lips moved, but he didn't speak.

Harris said, "You mentioned big, dumb guys with him. Tell me about them."

"Stupid sodders. You can hardly understand their talk. They complain about everything. The cold. The heat. Us. One of them, name of Phipps, said something twisted his favorite firepiece all out of shape. Carried around a big lump of *iron* he tried to tell me used to be a gun. Stupid bugger."

"Phipps. Big guy, lots of muscle?"

"Huge, even more than you. Had a busted wing, but Blackletter sent him off to a doctor and he got that fixed right away. They were all big."

Doc said, "We'll talk again later. For now, show Lieu-tenant Athelstane their rooms. Angus', Darig's, Moon's, and Blackletter's."

The burly Novimagos guardsman seized Alpson by an ear and yanked him up from the chair. Alpson grunted but didn't complain and was led out.

Doc turned to Noriko. "We might be able to catch up to him in the *Frog Prince*."

She shook her head. "It's not much faster than Valkyries, Doc. Oh—you mean a straight flight."

He nodded.

Alastair smacked himself in the forehead. "Not again."

Noriko rose. "I'll have it ready by the time the rest of you get there." She limped out.

"Alastair?" Doc said. "Tell me what you make of this."

He knelt beside an upright cabinet in the plushly fur-nished room Alpson had identified as Darig MacDuncan's. The floor was covered with a colorful rug bearing an intri-cate geometric design; a four-poster bed surrounded by filmy curtains dominated the room.

Alastair and Harris moved over to look. Harris could hear Jean-Pierre, Gaby, and Alastair ransacking the room next door, the one Angus Powrie had lived in.

Doc knelt over a wooden strongbox. The lock had been forced and the lid was up. Harris could see a crumpled mass of gray cloth inside the box; there seemed to be wooden cubes beneath it. Doc held a curious object: a small, flexible brown disk with a loop attached to one side and an extrusion the size and shape of one finger-digit pro-truding from the other side. It seemed to be made of a translucent material and bent freely in Doc's fingers.

The context was wrong, and it took Harris a moment to realize that he was looking at something familiar. "Hey, that's a pacifier."

The other two looked at him, curious. "It's scarcely heavy enough to hurt a man when you hit him with it," Doc said.

"Huh?"

Doc mimed an overhand blow with a club. "A pacifier. A rubber or leather envelope filled with lead shot. Hoodlums use them to beat men unconscious."

"No, no, no. A pacifier is a nipple for babies. Pop it in their mouth and they suck on it. It's made of plastic." He took it from Doc, turned it over to look for a maker's mark. On one side, he found the almost invisible emboss reading "Made in Japan" and showed it to Doc. "Japan is the Wo of my world."

Harris stooped and rooted around in the box. The gray mass was a downy blanket with a maker's tag still attached to one seam. The cubes beneath it were alphabet blocks identical to ones Harris had had as a child. There was also a plastic rattle.

"Doc, this is all baby stuff from the grim world." Harris glanced at the two of them and found that each had one eye closed; Doc was looking at the objects with his left eye, Alastair with his right.

They looked at each other and opened their eyes. Alastair said, "It all has the aura of the man who lived in this room, but very, very strong. They're his baby goods, I'm sure."

Doc sat back, frowning. "Harris, you said the Changeling was young. How young?"

"Hard to say, especially here on the fair world. Not a teenager. Twenty, maybe twenty-five." He tried to remember the man's voice, tried to compare his face to what he'd since learned about the way the fair folk aged. "Closer to twenty."

"I think I have it," Doc said. "We know Duncan went to the grim world instead of dying twenty years ago. My guess, and these objects bear it out, is that he used old, old devisements to take the place and identity of a child of your world, Harris."

Harris snorted. "Whatever you say, Doc. I mean, I've seen weirder since I've been here. Just the prospect of that old guy crawling around in a crib and crying for milk is pretty strange."

"But that's precisely what he would have done. By his arts he would have made himself smaller and prevented the child's parents from recognizing the physical change. They would have noticed an alteration to his manner, of course. He would have been a screaming, shrieking tyrant."

"Like real babies, you mean."

"Worse. He would have leeched all joy from their lives and driven them to early death. But as little as your folk know about mine, they probably would not have realized what the change in him meant. They wouldn't have known the old ways to trick him, to get their baby back. So he would have used the identity he stole as a base for his activities on the grim world."

Alastair nodded. "And the child he stole, and sent back here, is Darig MacDuncan. Who calls himself the Changeling . . . even though it was *Duncan* who was actually the changeling."

"Raised by Angus," Doc said. "No wonder he's as twisted as he is. He'd no chance to be otherwise."

The captured gangsters were long gone and Doc's associates were gathering to leave when Eight-Finger Tom arrived. He was a short, slight man with quick mannerisms, a restless eye, and a gold tooth. He carried a small bag made of carpet. He had all ten fingers. He shook hands with Doc and said, "The usual?"

"Worse. It's a deviser's safe, an old one."

The other man grimaced. "Show me."

Doc took him into the office where they'd done the interrogation. Harris, waiting with the others in the hall, heard them pry up a panel from the wooden floor.

Tom's tone was curious: "What a strange design. And the handle—ouch! Who'd make a safe out of unsheathed steel? Bugger. Give me the gloves out of my pack, would you? The thin ones." There was a long wait. "Oh, yes. It's warded, all right. It's not enough to divine the combination; I'll need to mimic the timing, too." He raised his voice: "The rest of you stay out. We may be blowing up in here."

Doc chuckled.

Long, long moments of silence. Then, suddenly, Eight-Finger Tom appeared in the doorway, his bag in hand, his manner cheerful. "Not too bad," he told Jean-Pierre. "Blast would have sent the whole building front out into the street, but the thing was used enough that the combination and timing were imbedded all over the place. You know where to send my fee." He tipped his cap to the others. "Grace on you." And he jauntily marched out the door.

Gaby asked, "Why 'Eight-Finger'?"

Jean-Pierre said, "When he was a strongbox cracker, he robbed a gang boss. The gang came after him. He took a finger from every one of them he killed. Keeps them in a jar. The guard could never make a case against him, as they couldn't find the rest of the body. But Doc did, and gave him a choice: retire from his old life and do work for the Foundation, or . . . "

"Right."

Doc stepped out into the hall. Under his arm, he carried a sheaf of papers. "Time to go," he said.

CHAPTER SEVENTEEN

In his room at the Monarch Building, Harris found the carpetbag he'd seen at the bottom of his closet. He loaded it with the clothes and toilet articles he'd accumulated, the two big pistols from the truck, and the ammunition for them.

His entire collection of possessions from the fair world. It didn't seem like much.

He picked up Gaby's jeans and took them down the hall to her door. She opened it before he knocked; she looked on the verge of tears. "Harris, I'm *sorry*," she said.

"You should try them on before you say that." He handed her the jeans.

"Stop making jokes, you idiot. Tonight, you wouldn't have even gone if I hadn't backed you into it, would you?"

"Sure."

"Don't lie. Not to me."

"Okay." He took a deep breath, a delaying tactic, and sorted his thoughts. "No, I wouldn't. I would have stayed here."

"And you wouldn't have had to kill two men." Her voice shrank to a whisper. "It's my fault."

"No."

"Harris, you ought to go home to the grim world."

He leaned in close. "Gaby, the thing is, you were right.

When you said that about not just standing by while everybody else risked his life for you. I admire you for that, and it kills me, because I should have felt the same way and I didn't. *I'm* the one who screwed up. As usual."

"No, Harris—"

"We're going to England. Pack warm." He left her.

Jean-Pierre pulled open the rear doors of the slabside lorry and everyone piled out onto the tarmac of Gwaeddan Air Field.

Doc had parked outside a huge hangar set well away from the diminutive tower and commercial hangars. The hangar doors were closed; Doc led them through a side door and the small office beyond into the hangar proper.

There were five aircraft inside. One was a small, single-wing, single-engine propeller job that looked good for carrying popular musicians to their deaths. Two were two-seat biplanes, one gold, one blood-red, and Harris could see machine guns mounted on them. One was a larger black twin-engine job that looked as though it were raked for speed. These four planes were crowded into a third of the hangar.

The last plane . . . Harris gaped at it.

It had the wingspan of a 727. The wings extended across the top of the fuselage, with four huge engines spaced along them. Two stubby, vestigial wings were situated underneath the main wings, extending from the bottom of the fuselage. The fuselage itself was thicker than a 727's, and looked only two-thirds as long. Harris could see two banks of windows on the fuselage, one above, one below; Noriko was visible behind the top windshield. Below her, the windshield into the first lower compartment was an oversized bubble.

And the whole thing was made of wood.

It looked like a giant Dutch clog given wings and made glossy by a rubdown of wood polish. Harris thought it had to be about as maneuverable as the space shuttle.

"Tell me we're not flying in that," he said.

Jean-Pierre smiled. "The *Frog Prince*. Doc's creation. One of a kind, unless he can manage to sell the design."

"Why is it called that?"

"Kiss it and find out."

"I figured it was named after you."

Alastair said, "Because it lands on ground and water and is prettier on the inside than the outside."

"It would have to be." Harris hefted his bag and followed them to the rollaway steps positioned against the rear of the plane.

The steps led to a bare, wood-paneled compartment that had stairs to the upper level and a cabin door leading forward. As they came aboard, Doc gave the newcomers the penny tour. "The *Frog Prince* is forty paces long, fifty-two in span. The lower level is arranged in ten cabins. If there is ever a commercial version, it will accommodate forty passengers, or more if we install just seating, but the original is too full of equipment for that. Baggage goes up to the upper level with the stores, cockpit, and extra fuel tanks. Main fuel is in the wings."

Harris saw workmen drag the stairs away from the hull; Doc pulled the door closed and dogged it shut. He led them through a door in the center of the cabin's forward wall.

The next cabin up was a reproduction in miniature of Doc's laboratory. There was room for only two tables, and they were currently clear of equipment; the walls were heavily laden with racks of gear and cabinets, everything lashed down or locked in place. "The men we're chasing are flying Valkyries, which are very durable cargo planes that can be outfitted with guns and bomb racks. The Changeling's planes are probably armed." He pointed to the world map occupying a section of wall. He tapped Neckerdam. "But the Valks have limited range. To get to Cretanis, they'll have to put in somewhere north, probably Acadia, to refuel." He tapped Nova Scotia. "Then northeast, either to Hel or Nordland." He touched

Greenland and Iceland in turn. "Then they can reach Cretanis." He touched the British Isles. "The *Frog Prince* can take it in one hop."

"So to speak," Harris said.

Doc led them forward. The next door opened into what looked like a small bedroom, including a rug, two sofas, and windows to either side with pull-down window shades. "Joseph, none of the sleeper compartments is large enough to accommodate you, so you should take this cabin. The sofas fold out into beds, or you can use the deck."

Joseph tossed his duffel onto one of the sofas.

The next cabin was a narrow galley, including a stove, sink, closed pantries, and cabinets stacked with plates. Harris saw that the cabinets had slots instead of doors, with dishes inserted through the vertical slot and lowered into place via a horizontal slot, so they would not come spilling out in rough air. Doc and his audience breezed on through.

Next was something that looked to Harris like a train's sleeper car: right and left of the aisle were three rows of curtained bunks, above and below, a total of twelve bunks. The curtains varied in color, some red, some gold, all looking like velvet or velour.

"Sleeping cabin," Doc said. "The landing gear is hidden away behind the bunks." He pitched his bag into one of the lower starboard bunks. "Choose yourselves a place to sleep. There's another cabin like this one forward, if you prefer." Alastair took the bunk farthest forward.

Harris chose an upper bunk on the port side. He was surprised to see that his bunk had a little fan in a corner bracket and find that the mattress was actually comfortable. "First class," he said.

Doc said, "It's supposed to be a luxury craft."

The next cabin forward had several small sofas and tables, windows to either side, hull doors to either side, even a talk-box on one of the tables. "The main salon,"

Doc said. "And water debarkation. From the doors you step down on the water stabilization wings."

Next up was another sleeper-car cabin. Gaby picked a bunk and left her bag there. The door forward out of this cabin opened into a narrow hallway between small cabins right and left. "Jakes port, wash-stall starboard," Doc said. "I don't recommend you wash up in rough flying weather." He pointed to a tiny circular staircase leading up. "That goes up to the cockpit, and the door forward goes into another private sleeping cabin."

Jean-Pierre took his bag into that forward cabin.

"Pretty cool, Doc," Harris said helpfully. "I'd order one if I could save enough out of my allowance."

"I'll remember that. Everyone, prepare yourselves for takeoff." He climbed the stairs out of sight.

Jean-Pierre called, "Takeoff is best from in here. Come in."

Harris and the others filed on in. Jean-Pierre's was the cabin Harris had seen from the outside, with the over-sized window forward; it provided an unimpeded view of the tarmac in front of the plane, and the cabin's sofa and chairs were set up to provide the best view possible.

Jean-Pierre was fiddling with ice, glasses, and bottles from a corner cabinet. "Sit. What are you drinking?"

Harris took one of the chairs. "Nothing, thanks."

Alastair, Gaby, and Joseph took the couch; Alastair and Gaby accepted uisge. Jean-Pierre handed them the drinks. He switched out the cabin light and took the other chair just as the first starboard motor shuddered and coughed into life.

"No seatbelts?" Harris asked.

"It's supposed to be a luxury craft," Jean-Pierre said in deft mimicry of Doc's voice. "No crashing allowed."

"Ah. Comforting."

The other three engines sputtered into life, one after another. Harris was surprised at the noise they made. He'd flown in jets, but the shuddering roar of this prop plane was new to him. It vibrated his bones.

The *Frog Prince* lumbered into motion, bobbing a little,

moving slowly and awkwardly through a series of turns until it stood at one end of an airstrip.

The pitch of the engines became louder, more insistent. The plane picked up speed. Harris felt the ride get smooth as the front of the plane came up off the ground—and suddenly they were heading skyward at an angle that put Harris in mind of stalls and sudden, uncontrolled descents. He tried to keep his voice from squeaking: "Just how good a pilot is Doc?"

Jean-Pierre laughed. "Only fair, like me. Fortunately, Noriko's our pilot. She could fly a paper kite through a shotgun blast and bring it out unhurt." Harris heard ice clatter as the man took a drink. "In just a moment she'll give us the View."

On cue, the *Frog Prince* heeled over to port. Harris saw the lights of distant towns disappear to the right. Then Neckerdam moved into view from the left.

The island was a concentrated mass of light. Harris was surprised at the amount of red, green, and blue light scattered among the white-yellow glow he expected. He could make out the clusters of skyscrapers, fingers of light reaching optimistically for the sky.

"Damnation," Harris said.

"There's the Monarch Building," Gaby said.

Harris almost didn't spot it. It was a column of glowing windows with four broad white bands across it—the ledges filled with statues.

Then the plane's turn put the island out of sight to their right. They stared at more distant lights on the coastline stretching away south . . . and then they were pointed out over the water, nothing ahead but stars above and moonlight on the waves below.

Jean-Pierre sighed. He rose and turned the cabin light back on; Harris blinked at the sudden glare.

"I'll be up for a while, studying the papers from the Aremorcy safe," Jean-Pierre said. "If anyone is foolish enough to join me, I'll be in the lounge. To the rest of you, I say, warm dreams."

❀   ❀   ❀

"Thirty-five names," Harris said. "All of them with 'Eliminated' written out to the side, with a date. They go back about twenty years. Gaby's name is at the very bottom, in longhand instead of typed, and it says 'Transferred.' The date is right—it's the day we brought her back."

Jean-Pierre looked over a sheaf of papers at him. The two of them occupied the plane's lounge; they were alone. "I think I have more of that file here. The name above Gabriela's, was it a Carlo Salvanelli?"

"That's right."

"See what you make of this." Jean-Pierre shoved a stapled stack of papers at him. "It looks like it came off a printing press."

"No, a laser printer." Harris held it close and could see the faint rough edges to the printed letters. "That's like a printing press individual people can own. My friend Zeb has one."

The papers were miniature biographies. Each one corresponded to one of the names on Harris' list. Some were short, others ran several pages.

Gaby's record, the shortest one, listed her name, profession, birthplace, and interests. Harris skimmed through the others. "Weird people," he said.

"How so?"

"Most of them seemed to be mental cases. It looks like a third of them or so were in and out of mental hospitals at one time or another. Several ended up bums or were in VA hospitals when they were 'eliminated.' But a lot of them, including some of the ones I just mentioned, did a lot of stuff. This woman was a famous psychic in England. I remember her getting killed—bunch of snide people asking, why couldn't she predict her own death? And this other guy won a Silver Star at Okinawa—that's a big military decoration and a big war."

"I think I have the counterpoint of your list." Jean-Pierre held up another sheaf. "People killed here in the fair world in the last twenty years. Of course, this list was made on a proper typewriter.

"Here's one I've heard of. A woman doctor. Patented several processes, some of which didn't work. One that did, insulin from pigs, made her rich about ten years ago. I always wanted to know what sort of stupid name Stevens is."

"It's a very common name on my world."

"Well, you have stupid names—" Jean-Pierre shut up for a moment. "Is Salvanelli a common name on your world?"

"I don't think so. It sounds Italian, but I don't think I've heard it before."

"It's Isperian. Very common. There are thousands of Salvanellis, immigrants, in Neckerdam."

"Well, there's no mistake. This shows them eliminating him in New York City."

"And Stevens in Nyrax."

"Are you thinking what I'm thinking?"

"Yes. There were other people from the grim world on the fair world . . . and the Changeling has been systematically tracking them down and killing them."

"And Duncan doing the same on my world . . . to people from your world. Why?"

Jean-Pierre shrugged. "I don't know, but I wager Doc will be fascinated. By the way, your name and Gabriela's are the last additions at the bottom of this list."

"Oh, great."

Jean-Pierre yawned and stretched. "In case you haven't noticed, the sun is well up."

He was right. Round patches of sunlight wandered around the cabin floor with every movement of the airplane.

"Yeah. So?"

"So after I tell Doc about this, I'm to bed. How long have you been awake?"

"I don't know. I'm not sleepy."

"Get some sleep anyway." Jean-Pierre rose and went forward.

Harris continued looking through the papers.

The dead man on the concrete finally moved, lifting his head to stare at Harris. There was hurt sorrow in his eyes. He pointed at Harris. His expression didn't say "I hate you," even "I blame you." Harris read it as though it were newsprint: "You can never fix this."

Harris gasped and came fully awake. The light over his bunk was still on. The fan still drove air into his face. It smelled like sausage cooking; someone had to be back in the galley, rustling up breakfast.

He lay there and rubbed his eyes. He'd fallen asleep for a moment. He needed to sleep. He was so tired that sometimes he couldn't tell the engines throbbing from the waves of tiredness flowing through him. But the face was waiting for him. Whenever he closed his eyes he saw the dead man staring sightlessly upward.

Harris kept his own eyes open.

His thoughts floated around unconnected. *He might have shot them, wonder what a hot dog costs, if I drank a gallon of xioc I might not sleep for a week, blasting through the sky in the belly of a giant frog. Grow up Gaby doesn't want you anymore. He's waiting for you behind your eyelids. Transitions, he'll get you when you move in or out, in the transitions.*

He felt the idea click home like the last piece in a jigsaw puzzle. He sat up so fast he banged his head on the ceiling of the bunk. He cursed, hit the wood in anger, and swung out of the bunk. Almost falling, he landed on the slightly tilted floor.

Wearing only boxer shorts, he moved forward out of the darkened sleeper-cabin into the lounge. It was empty of people; the circles of light moving around on the floor were brighter than ever. He stayed well away from them, irrationally afraid that he'd crumble into dust if they fell on him. He flopped onto the sofa in front of the talk-box. "Gabrielle," he said.

The gray, lifeless screen of the talk-box stared

implacably back at him. Annoyed, he switched it on. The screen slowly brightened into static.

"Gabrielle, I hope you can hear me. I think you can." Harris licked suddenly dry lips. "I'm in the plane with Doc. This is Harris. I'm the one who knows something about you."

Nothing.

"Gabrielle, I don't care how stupid this looks. I think you can hear me. Please talk to me."

The screen wavered into focus and suddenly Gabrielle stared at him. She was her usual solemn self, and looked worried when she saw him. "You look bad," she said.

"No sleep."

"No one has ever called to me before."

"They always used the talk-box operator to reach one another. I bet the operator doesn't know where to find you."

She looked puzzled. "No."

"Gabrielle, can you tell me what you're seeing right now?"

"You."

He shook his head impatiently. He regretted it; his head swam. "I mean, around you. What you're looking into, what you're sitting behind, everything."

"My mirror."

"You're looking into a mirror. Who's the fairest of them all?" He giggled, then cut the laugh off when he realized how strange it sounded. "How did you know I wanted to talk to you?"

"I heard you call my name. I hear talking all the time. That's how I learned about Doc. I heard his name many times. People spoke of him in terms of praise. Excitement. Anger. Sometimes they made plans to hurt him. Finally I looked for him and found him."

"How do you do that?"

"I make eyes on the other side of the mirror open up. Just as I did a moment ago with you." Her expression was so vulnerable, so helplessly open that Harris wanted to crawl through the screen to comfort her.

"A while back, you started to ask me what I knew about you. I didn't understand that then. It's because you don't know anything about yourself, do you?"

She didn't answer, as if by waiting she could make him lose interest in the question.

"Gabrielle, would you show me your horse?"

Her expression went from worried to completely lost. "How do you know about my horse? I've never shown it to anyone."

"I know it has eight legs. Show it to me."

She didn't seem to be able to tear her gaze away from Harris. But she reached out of sight under the table and brought up a stuffed toy, a big, cuddly red pony with too many legs. She clutched it to her as though it could shield her from the world.

"What do you know about yourself?"

She flinched as though he'd raised a hand to strike her. "You're right. I don't know anything. I've been here a long time. I can't get out. No one comes to visit. Maybe I was born here. I never saw anyone until I made the eye behind the mirror open up the first time."

"Gabrielle, if I leave the room for a minute, will you wait here for me?"

"Maybe."

"*Please.* It's really important."

She crushed the doll to her and gave him a tentative nod.

He managed to get to his feet and stumble forward out of the lounge. A few steps more and he was beside the bunk where he'd seen Gaby toss her bag. He parted the curtain.

She was there, tousled, adorable, wearing a long-sleeved green shirt that came to her knees. Her mouth was slightly open and her eyes moved back and forth behind her eyelids. He knew it would take a sudden invasion by a marching band to wake her up from this state.

Softly, cautiously, he slipped his arms behind her back and behind her knees and lifted her out of the bunk.

She turned and pressed her face up against his chest. He whispered, "Don't wake up, baby. Just a few steps." And he cursed the exhaustion that made his legs tremble as he gently carried her back into the lounge.

He managed to sit back on the sofa without dropping or waking her.

Gabrielle was still on the screen. She looked at Gaby but couldn't see her face. "Who is this?"

"A friend." Gently, Harris shook Gaby. "Wake up, baby. Look at who's on TV."

She stirred. The talk-box picture broke up for a moment. Gabrielle looked surprised. "The eye blinked," she said.

Gaby murmured something incoherent.

"Wake up, Gaby. Look at the TV. It's Frank Langella and Kevin Kline. They're naked."

Gaby's eyes opened. She stared up at Harris, confused, then looked around.

She caught sight of the talk-box.

Her gasp and Gabrielle's were simultaneous.

The picture on the screen started to break up. The two women reached for one another. "Don't go," they said.

Then the picture faded to static.

Gaby collapsed back against Harris and burst out in tears. He held her while her shoulders shook.

CHAPTER EIGHTEEN

"It was transitions," Harris said, his voice slurred and dull. "Moving in and out. That's how I figured it out."

Doc sat on the other side of the lounge's table. "You're not making any sense."

"I know." Harris laughed. The sound was high-pitched and strained. He cut it off. "You couldn't make Gaby's magic go."

"Magic is a discredited term—"

"Oh, just pipe down. But obviously she had a lot of it. Your devices told you so." He chanted the last words to the tune of the old Sunday School song—"Jesus loves me, this I know . . . "

Doc scowled. "Yes."

"You see, the thing was, Gaby knew the fair world before she got here. It didn't freak her out the way it did me. But Gabrielle didn't even know herself. Tried to ask me about her once. You remember."

Gaby, wearing a robe over her nightshirt, was huddled in one of the chairs, her legs drawn up. She still looked upset.

"There's no mystic twin. Gaby and Gabrielle are the same person. When she sleeps, her mind goes running off into talk-box land. Transitions, in and out of sleep, get it? It's like the people who get radio waves on their braces and fillings. Except she's a lot better."

"She must be, if her mind can walk between worlds. She called to me even when she was living on the grim world."

Gaby stirred. "Don't talk about me as though I'm not here."

"I'm sorry, Gabriela." Doc looked apologetic. "It does make sense. I could never coax your ability out . . . because it only works when your mind wanders among the dreams. The conjurer's circle might actually have inhibited you."

"Then what good is it to me? Especially if I can't remember who the hell I am when I'm asleep?"

"There are techniques that might help. We'll explore them after I've slept." Doc fixed Harris with a stern look. "I'm having Alastair come from the cockpit to give you something. You need sleep worse than I."

"No need." Harris closed his eyes. There was nothing behind them but darkness. "Funny thing is, I think I can sleep now." He stood and looked at Gaby. "Are you going to be okay?"

"I don't know. Maybe it's irrational, but I feel like that long-lost sister just died."

"I'm sorry. I hope she didn't." He turned away.

He made it back to his bunk and crawled in. For the first time since he boarded the *Frog Prince*, he luxuriated and stretched as he settled in.

He savored the memory of holding her one more time, the way she'd unconsciously nestled against him when he picked her up. Then he slid away into a dark, comfortable place and was gone.

"I want you to listen for the voices," Doc said.

Gaby, eyes closed, sat facing the talk-box. Her expression did not change.

"Are you listening?"

"Yes." Her voice was subdued.

"What do you hear?"

"Talking. So much. I can't make out the words."

"Look around. What do you see?"

Gaby turned her head one way and then the other but did not open her eyes. "My room."

"What's in it?"

"My table. My bed. The walls. It's lonely."

"Go sit down by the table and pick up your horse. We'll give you someone to talk to."

"All right."

Doc picked up the leather helmet from the table and strapped it on. He pulled the mask portion over his face and snapped it in place. He knew the dangling tubes gave him the appearance of the offspring of an elephant and a human, something he'd heard of but never seen. He briefly wondered what sort of devisements would make such a conception possible, and whether either party enjoyed it.

His improvised gear also hung out of the nose of the mask. He turned on the talk-box, then moved around back and attached two wires from his nose gear to leads on the machine.

Harris, rubbing the stubble on his chin, appeared in the doorway to the aft sleeping cabin. He looked very grimworldish in his new jeans and old jeans jacket, and he seemed more rested. His eyes got big as he spotted Doc in this peculiar gear. Doc held up a finger to shush him and waved him to sit in one of the chairs positioned to the side. Harris complied, looking confused.

Doc flipped the switch at his neck. Now, with his mouth muffled, Gaby should not be able to hear his voice, while his words would go out over unused talk-box wireless frequencies. "Gabrielle," he said. "Gabrielle, this is Doc. If you can hear me, please look at me. Please open up the eye beyond the mirror."

He heard the high-pitched whine of the talk-box turning itself on. He pulled off the mask and moved around to the front.

The screen showed Gabrielle sitting, looking more like

a lost little girl than he'd ever seen her. She glanced between Gaby and him. "Grace, Doc."

"Grace. Gabrielle, you know why I've called you."

"Maybe. Because of her."

"She's another part of you, Gabrielle. I want you to meet her. Talk to her."

"I'm scared of her."

"Don't be. Please stay."

He turned to Gaby. She wasn't in the deep, eye-moving sleep; that was encouraging. But she was tense, perspiring. "Gaby, in a moment I'm going to ask you to open your eyes. You'll be able to hear voices other than mine. You must not become alarmed. You're safe, surrounded by friends. Do you understand?"

"Yes."

"Please open your eyes."

Gaby did so and stared straight at her doppleganger.

The talk-box screen faded and twisted, the horizontal and vertical controls both lost, but straightened out again. Gabrielle remained there. She looked ready to bolt.

"Gaby, can you see her?"

"Yes." There was strain in her voice.

"Greet her. You know her name."

"Hi, Gabrielle."

Gabrielle's voice was a whisper, almost inaudible over the engine roar. "Grace."

Gaby was still perspiring; she looked tired, tense.

"Gabrielle, I want you to think about your horse. Hold it to you, think about how it feels."

The woman on the screen was already holding the pitiful plush toy as though it were a life preserver; she clutched it tighter and rocked in her seat.

Gaby's hands came up as though she were holding something to her. Her pose was a mirror of Gabrielle's.

"Gaby, can you feel it?"

"Yes. It's velvet. It smells like cinnamon. Angus Powrie says they've grabbed Caster Roundcap."

"What?"

The talk-box screen went to static. Gaby jolted. She looked down at her empty arms. Her face twisted and she bowed her head. Doc realized she was trying not to cry.

He knelt before her. "Gabriela, I'm sorry. You're awake now, aren't you?"

Harris, looking tentative, moved behind her sofa and went to work massaging her shoulders.

"I'm awake. I'm fine. It's so stupid," she said. She wouldn't look up at him; her hair hung before her eyes. "It's not real. The horse. The room. But it's like remembering something I used to love, something I've forgotten about for years and years . . . "

"Why did you say that about Angus Powrie?"

She finally looked up at him. Her expression was an odd mix of hurt and defiance. "I *heard* it. I felt the doll. I could see you through this mirror. I heard this babble of voices, like the cocktail party from hell, and I got this headache. It's still with me." She rubbed her temple. "And then in the middle of it was this voice, this smooth, nasty voice. It said something like, 'Angus Powrie has reported in. He's acquired Caster Roundcap. We'll call to you if we have anything more . . . ' And then I lost it."

"Because I shouted." He took her hand and gave it a reassuring squeeze. "I'm sorry. We did well. Next time I'll try to keep myself under control. For now, you ought to get some rest."

"No, thanks. Noriko is going to give me my first piloting lesson." She reached up and patted one of Harris' hands. "Thanks, Harris. I think I'm all right." She stood, not looking at either one of them, and went forward.

Doc asked, "Does she ever follow anyone's advice?"

"Sure. When it happens to match what she plans to do anyway." Harris' gesture took in the talk-box set. "Was that good?"

"I think so. But it seemed to be a tremendous strain on her. I don't like that."

"Where do I know the name Caster Roundcap?"

"I called to him about you."

"Oh, yeah. The expert on the grim world."

"And now it seems I've dragged him into danger." He sighed. "Obviously the Valks have reached Cretanis already. But we land in less than a bell. Maybe we can get to Caster before anything worse happens to him."

"Can you call ahead and tell the police, the guard, to be on the lookout?"

Doc shook his head. "I could, but then they would be on the lookout for me, as well. I have a longstanding disagreement with Maeve the Tenth that makes it impractical for me to announce my arrival."

"Great. I'm helping a guy that everybody in the world either works for or wants to kill."

Doc nodded. "That about sums it up."

The *Frog Prince*, Noriko and Doc once more at the controls, made a sweet, smooth landing at the Suliston airstrip. The strip had its lights on, but those beacons winked to darkness almost as soon as the plane taxied to a halt inside the designated hangar.

Over his shoulder, Doc called, "Do you have the papers?"

Jean-Pierre's voice floated faintly back up to him. "Right here." Doc heard the man clinking coins through his hands. He smiled.

As he and Noriko went through their shutdown checklist, he felt a sudden stir of cold air as exterior hatches were opened. Moments later, he saw Jean-Pierre walk into view before the plane and approach the arriving officials. Jean-Pierre moved among them, talking comfortably, gesturing proudly at the plane, dropping coins into hands with slippery ease.

In just a few beats he was back, sauntering into the cockpit. "They're our very good friends," he said, "and anxious not to annoy our employer with irrelevant questions or paperwork. As long as the coin holds out, of course."

"Of course," Doc said. "Who's our employer?"

"Why, that famous construction magnate, Joseph of Neckerdam." Jean-Pierre gestured like a man stating a fact of nature. "He's biggest, he's boss."

"Stands to reason. Now go out and arrange to have us refueled and served. Hire Joseph a lorry or a car. And ask about any Valkyries landing."

"Perfection is never enough for you, Doc."

The road was a one-lane blacktop situated between towering ranks of trees—the biggest, most gnarled oaks Harris had ever seen. They leaned across the road and stretched limbs down as though waiting to swat unwary motorists off the road. There were no streetlights, no reflective signs on dangerous turns, no stripes down the middle to indicate lanes. In the car they'd hired—a huge convertible roadster, the personal property of one of the airfield owners—Jean-Pierre roared ahead with a singular indifference to the fate of the vehicle or its passengers.

Harris clutched his jacket tight around him; it was inadequate in the cold air whipping across them. "First thing we get back," he shouted, "I invent the seatbelt."

"Seat restraints aren't new," Doc shouted back. "They're just not necessary." He had Duncan Blackletter's tracer in his hand; its screen cast a green glow on his features. He frowned at it.

"Ask Jean-Pierre to drive smack into one of those big trees, then try to tell me that again."

Doc waved his objections away. "Shut off your screen device, would you? You too, Gaby. They're interfering with this."

"Sure."

Doc raised his voice even louder so Jean-Pierre, Noriko and Alastair, in the front seat, and Joseph in the rumble seat could also hear him. "Adennum is a village. I don't think we need worry too much with it. Near it is an ancient site of worship, the Adennum Complex. It has a great hill, circle stones, standing stones, radiating lines and paths;

it covers a lot of ground. It's sacred to the goddess Sull, Lady of the Dark World, Bringer of Death and Knowledge, and it's very old."

Gaby tried futilely to keep the wind from whipping her hair into a nightmarish tangle. "You think Duncan Blackletter will be at the complex."

"Yes. The village is just a village. The complex is a place of power."

"What does he want there?"

"We'll find out. We'll look at the site. If he hasn't arrived yet, we'll set up for him. A couple of us will go on to Beldon, the capital, and see whether we can find out anything about Caster Roundcap or the Valkyries.

"But if they're here now . . . we move against them." He looked back at the tracer. "I get a signal. There are men of the grim world within a few destads."

The village of Adennum was still at this hour of the night. Harris saw only glimpses of the houses as they roared along the village's winding streets, but he marveled at the strange architecture. The homes looked like small, round hills built of irregular stone. No two were alike in size or contours, but all doors opened to the east. Soft light emerged through the second-story shuttered windows. Harris thought that someone had erected tall, thin white columns all over the village, but realized he was looking at enormous beeches lining the roadways. Then the car was past the town and into the forest again.

After another mile, the trees fell away to the left and the travelers could look out over a large plain. Harris could see the silhouettes of standing stones, lone sentinels set up at intervals in a straight line. He saw small circles of stones laid into the earth.

Doc kept his attention on the tracer. "Not here," he said. "But getting closer."

The field of stones went on for hundreds of yards, then the trees encroached again and hid them from sight.

A few minutes more, then Alastair shouted, "Someone is conjuring nearby. I can see trails of overflow power."

"The great hill, probably. It's the correct direction." Doc leaned forward to tap Jean-Pierre's shoulder. He pointed to a turnoff marked by a standing stone. "Go past. The approach may be guarded."

Jean-Pierre passed the turnoff, but a few hundred feet further found a spot where he could pull off the road behind a screen of trees.

Doc said, "Noriko, you're vanguard."

She nodded. From the boot of the car she removed her scabbarded sword. She slung it over her shoulder by its cord, exchanged a quick look with Jean-Pierre, and loped off into the trees.

Doc gathered the rest and followed at a slower pace. Harris watched with interest as they fell without discussion into formation to pass through the trees: Doc was first and center, Alastair and Jean-Pierre yards out to either side. Joseph solemnly walked some distance back from Doc; Gaby and Harris trailed him. Gaby had her rifle slung by its strap. She kept her attention on the surrounding woods.

Jean-Pierre was first to notice a white scar cut into an oak branch off to his left. "Noriko's mark." He went to look at it, then waved the others over.

Harris took a quick look at the man slumped at the base of the tree. He was short, muscular, not bad looking. His gray suit was streaked with dirt and leaves. His face was familiar. "This is the guy who shot at me when I was driving," Harris said.

Jean-Pierre looked unhappy. "Blackletter probably has a lot of men here if he can spread them around guarding the approach."

Ahead they saw lights through the trees—stationary lights, very bright, very high—and became even more cautious, creeping along with teeth-grinding slowness. Soon enough the trees thinned and gave way to an open field. Jean-Pierre and the others crouched low and moved carefully forward from tree to tree.

Ahead of them was a treeless hill; it was a rounded cone, perfect and artificial. Wooden poles, more than a dozen, rose from the lower crest of the summit. At the top of each was a spotlight shining down on the hilltop.

There was a great deal of equipment set up on the summit. Harris saw dozens of wooden cabinets the width of a man and twice as tall. Each one was wired with flickering lights, green and red, that put him in mind of Christmas trees. More wooden cabinets were laid lengthwise across the tops of the upright ones. He could see silhouettes moving around in the center of the arrangement, but they were just silhouettes to him. There was a steady motor noise from the top of the hill.

The arrangement reminded Harris of something. It took him a moment to remember what.

Stonehenge. The cabinets were set up like a wooden Stonehenge, each one representing a monolithic stone. On this model, none of the stones was missing; even the massive lintel stones were represented.

Long yards of bare, hard ground separated the line of trees from the lower slope of the hill and the four lorries parked there.

Doc squatted and studied the situation. "Where's Noriko?"

Jean-Pierre nodded toward the trucks. "There first. Since there's been no noise, she'll either have eliminated the guards . . . or found that there are none. Now she'll be circling around to deal with as many perimeter guards as she may."

"That's the right idea. Very well. Priorities." Doc counted them off on his fingers. "One. Evaluate the situation. If it's just too much for us, retreat; we'll follow them. Two. Retrieve Caster Roundcap and any other prisoners. Three. Stop whatever they're doing. Four. Capture—or kill, if we must—Duncan, the Changeling, Angus Powrie. Any questions?"

There were none.

Doc looked them over. "Joseph, I hate to say it, but you move . . . "

"Like a dying steer in a glassworks," Joseph said.

"You've said it a little more pointedly than I would have. Get to the trucks. Take three of them out of commission and wait there." He turned to Gaby and regret crossed his face. "I must ask this. If worst comes to worst, will you kill to save me? Or Jean-Pierre, or any of us?"

Harris saw pain cross her face. She looked not at Doc but at him, Harris, for a long moment. "Yes."

"Go with Joseph. When trouble starts, the men in the woods will head back to the hill and the trucks. You have to support us and keep them off you. If you have to retreat, take the truck Joseph has spared."

She nodded.

"Alastair, Jean-Pierre, Harris and I will spread out around the hill and ascend. Gods grace us. Let's move out." He rose and immediately glided off clockwise around the hill.

For a moment, Harris felt a thrill of accomplishment. Doc had counted him in without asking. Maybe he had no more proving to do.

On the other hand, he'd just been included in something that would probably get him killed.

CHAPTER NINETEEN

Harris, creeping counter-clockwise around the hill, kept Gaby and Joseph in sight as they moved across open ground toward the trucks. The two of them were mostly concealed by shadows; he had little difficulty picking out their motion, but then he'd been watching them since they left him. Maybe Blackletter's men, occupied by other things, would miss them.

They reached the four trucks and disappeared among them. Still no noise from the top of the hill. Harris felt the coil of tension around his chest let go. He picked up his pace.

Alastair would be some yards behind him; ahead, nothing but forest verge and Blackletter's guards. He kept his revolver pointed high.

It took him long, tense minutes to pass to the other side of the hill. In spite of the cold air, he sweated his shirt and jacket through. But he encountered no one and decided that he'd gone far enough. He stared up the hill; the Cabinet-henge at the top of the hill looked the same from this side as the other.

How to climb—the gun in hand or in his jacket pocket? He decided on the latter approach. Even as regular and gentle a hill as that was, he felt certain he'd need both hands to climb it in the dark.

He took the lowest portion of the hill on two feet. But the first time his foot slipped beneath him, he deliberately went flat, quiet as he could manage, and began negotiating a deal with God—payable only if the men at the top of the hill hadn't heard him.

Doc lay prone and wondered how he might cross the last fifteen paces to the henge of cabinets . . . when Blackletter's men made it easy for him.

The green and red lights on the cabinets and the spots atop the poles flared into incandescence for a moment, then went black.

A column of swirling light shot skyward from the center of the wooden circle and the ground rumbled.

Doc felt a voice in the rumble. He knew it was the goddess of this place. He knew she felt pain. Then both the light and the noise faded.

Doc heard laughter, cheers, applause from the men inside the circle. But he took advantage of the sudden darkness, moving forward spiderlike to the outer ring of wooden blocks. He drew his automatic.

He edged around the cabinet and peered into the center of the arrangement. The overhead lights were out and there was no moon, but some of the men were carrying electrical torches.

Twenty men, he estimated. At the center of the layout was a wooden altar; smoke still rose from it, but all Doc smelled was burned wood. Doc saw a pile of ten large metal drums and, near them, a large piece of machinery Doc took to be a generator; two men were pulling at its starter and cursing.

He closed his right eye and looked with his good one.

The whole area blazed with the green-yellow light of a recent devisement. He was surprised by its intensity. And inconvenienced; it would be difficult to pick out any lesser glows in that wash of light. He opened his other eye and the glow faded.

As he waited for his eyes to adjust to the darkness, it happened.

Jean-Pierre's voice: "Angus Powrie!"

Gunshots, four in quick succession.

Men shouted. Some dropped to the ground. Others ran blindly.

Doc almost cursed. On the hilltop, his friends' few guns faced their twenty. This was not going to be good.

More gunshots. Doc heard an autogun open up. Maybe it was Alastair's. Regardless, he had to do something before Duncan's men realized just what an advantage they had.

He aimed at the pile of metal drums and fired three quick shots, then ducked back behind his cabinet.

More shouting: "This side, too! They're all around us!"

Another autogun began chattering. Doc felt blows as his cabinet was hammered.

He spun in place, dragging a toe, making the crudest possible circle to stand within. He concentrated and made the sound of gunfire fade away.

"Great Smith," he said. "I will give you lives in combat." The ancient, wicked promise made him quail inside, but he had nothing else to sacrifice. "Give me a spark from your anvil. Give me a wind from your bellows. Give me a blow from your hammer. I have faithfully served the gods. I will keep faith with you!"

He focused on the promise, imagined it as a living thing, a demon that must be stroked and fed, and felt his power grow within him.

More blows against his back. Shouting, dim and distant; he tried to keep it at bay.

A raging, roaring pride swelled inside him. It snapped him upright, stretched him to the limits of his limbs. He heard his own roar mingle with the shouts of his enemies. The pride within him longed to see those men smashed flat as by the broad head of a hammer, their bones crushed, their blood soaking the earth.

He stepped around the cabinet and flung the power he felt in his hand.

Fire leaped from his palm. It was no larger than his

fist, but it unerringly flew to the liquid leaking from the drums he'd fired upon.

The pool of fuel caught fire and began burning brightly. Now he heard the cries of the men, loud and close in his ears, and he exulted in their fear. There was more gunfire but he felt no pain.

He made a sweeping gesture, a circle in the air, and wind tore across the hilltop, rocking the cabinets. The fire flamed up into incandescence under the pile of drums.

The blow. He balled his hand into a fist and struck his left palm with it—and felt the last of the power leap from him.

The drums blew with a shattering roar of anger. Doc saw a new column of light leap up into the sky, but this was fire, violently propelling warped and ruined metal drums into the air before it. Light and heat washed over him, knocking men down where they stood or ran, sending some of the cabinets tumbling down the hill.

The explosion blew Doc off his feet. He felt the hard earth of the hill slap his back, driving the wind out of him. There was no pain.

Burning wood and metal rained down around him. He lay where he'd fallen, all the strength gone from him, and impatiently waited to regain control of his limbs.

He'd promised lives. He had to take them . . . or the god would be angry with him. He groped around, found the butt of his gun, and opened his mind to the flood of greed for life and blood he could feel waiting beyond it.

Harris saw the bright light from beyond the cabinet ahead, heard the blow of the explosion. The wooden block leaned over toward him, toppled, and began bouncing end-over-end at him.

He rolled sideways, sliding down the slope, scraping cloth and flesh off elbows, knees, ribs. The cabinet smashed to pieces behind him.

The towering column of flame illuminated the hilltop, the slope, the treetops dozens of yards away. He saw three men—Jean-Pierre, Angus Powrie, and a skeletally thin man he did not recognize—grappling together, Jean-Pierre on Powrie's back, the redcap reaching around for him, the third man bound and caught up among them. They rolled out of sight over the crest of the hill further ahead.

The flash illuminated the lorries; Gaby and Joseph, out of sight between the rearmost two, looked up to see the gold-and-orange mushroom cloud climbing skyward.

"Oh, God."

"They'll be coming, Gabriela." Joseph turned to look toward the forest verge. "Be ready. Wherever you watch, I will watch the other way."

She didn't answer. She stared up at the flaming hilltop a long moment more, then worked the rifle's bolt to chamber a round. She propped the rifle on the lorry's fender and aimed up the hill.

Alastair stood behind one of the cabinets that remained stubbornly upright. He leaned out to the left, fired off a blind burst, then moved over to lean out right. This time he aimed, targeting a man whose back burned as he ran; a quick burst and that target was down, burning but unmoving.

"Beldon Royal Guard!" he shouted, a deep, commanding bellow unlike his true voice. "You're all prisoners of the Crown! First Unit, move up! Sixth Unit, move up!" He changed to a shrill tone: "Aye aye! Marksmen, target and fire at will!" Another voice, thick with the accent of Neckerdam: "Royals! Let's get out of here! Run—!" He punctuated his last shout by leaning and firing again, and cut off his own command with a scream of pain.

He had no more vocal ability than any man on the street, but maybe, may it please the gods, with bullets whistling, fires burning, and men screaming, the enemy would believe it all. He leaned out again and swept a burst across the silhouettes he saw moving before him.

❧   ❧   ❧

Gaby saw the first two men running down the hill toward the trucks. She held her breath, aimed slow and sure as Jean-Pierre had taught her, put one man's chest in her sights, and squeezed the trigger.

The man's knee bent the wrong way when his weight came down on it. She heard his scream, saw him fall and roll a few yards, and suddenly she felt like puking into the grass.

Instead, she ejected the cartridge and chambered another one.

The second man continued down the hill. Him she missed; her bullet kicked up dirt a yard below him. He skidded to a halt, turned, and began racing back up the hill. His companion crawled slowly after him.

"Left," Joseph said. "Toward the roadway."

She shot the bolt, then aimed across the broad hood of the lorry and fired again.

Harris raced after Angus and Jean-Pierre, and was on them almost before he knew it.

Jean-Pierre lay in a pool of something white and revolting—his own vomit. The other man, old, thin, bespectacled, lay with his hands and feet bound; he stared imploringly at Harris.

Angus Powrie stood over the two of them. Blood ran down his left shoulder. He carried a double-barreled shotgun and pointed it at Jean-Pierre's face. His face, illuminated by fire from the hill, wore a smile so cold and hard Harris would have sworn it was cut from ice.

Harris skidded to a stop only half-a-dozen steps from them and took aim at Angus. "Drop it," he said. "Or I'll kill you." His words were punctuated by gunfire from the hilltop.

Angus didn't look at him. He continued to smile down at Jean-Pierre. "Smooth action on this trigger," he said. "Kill me, and the baby prince dies. Throw your own gun away and he won't."

Harris saw Jean-Pierre shaking his head. The prince was folded over like a piece of paper; Angus had to have hit him in the balls.

"I don't believe you," Harris said.

"Then he and I both die." Angus' gaze flicked up to Harris, then returned to Jean-Pierre. "Damned shame when it doesn't have to happen, boy. I can leave, he can leave, you can leave, we all meet later and kill each other. Or you can decide to be a hero and kill your friend."

Harris couldn't find it, the perfect solution. The only way everyone could be happy was if Angus was telling the truth . . . and if Harris did what he said. He could feel the eyes of the elderly man on him, too.

"I don't believe you."

Angus looked at him, though his gun remained aimed rock-steady at Jean-Pierre. His expression was solemn, open. "Son, I give you my word of honor. Throw your piece away and we all walk away from this."

Jean-Pierre shook his head and tried to get to his knees. He couldn't; he rocked in the pool of his vomit. His voice was a pained wheeze. "Don't. He has no honor. I'm dead, Harris. Kill him for me."

There was nothing but calm resolve in Angus' eyes.

Harris swore and tossed his gun down the hill. Jean-Pierre managed to get up to his knees.

"And the other one in your pocket. I'm not stupid, boy."

Harris complied.

Angus smiled, showing the points of his teeth. "But you are." He pulled both triggers.

The blast caught Jean-Pierre in the chest and face, blowing him over backwards.

Harris looked at his friend. Jean-Pierre's chest and half his head had been erased by a paintbrush dipped in dark, dark red. There was white noise, a scream of static, in Harris' head where his thoughts should be.

In slow motion, he turned to look at Angus Powrie.

The redcap was smiling at him. He had the shotgun broken open. He was pulling two new shells from his shirt pocket, moving them down to load them into the gun.

The static in Harris' head grew into a roar of hate. In slow motion, he forced his hand back to the holster over his kidney.

He got the pistol out, swung it in line, saw Angus' eyes widen with surprise.

He fired.

Darkness sprouted from Angus' gut.

He fired.

There was an explosion. The open shotgun went flying and Harris saw raw, red-black meat where Angus' left hand had been. Angus turned.

He fired. A dark circle appeared on Angus' back. Angus began running.

He fired. Angus lurched forward and rolled down the hill, arms and legs flailing. Then the redcap was up at the base of the hill and running toward the safety of the trees.

He fired.

He fired.

His gun began clicking, the noise of failure. Angus disappeared among the trees.

Harris looked at Jean-Pierre. The prince's one remaining eye was turned skyward.

And the white noise filling Harris' mind found expression in his voice, a roar of pain that stripped his throat raw.

Alastair saw motion in his peripheral vision. He dropped, aiming left as he fell, and fired. The burst caught the gangster in mid-aim. The man fell, a surprised look on his face. Alastair switched to single-shot and put a bullet between the man's eyes to make sure of him.

There was a thump from behind. He spun around.

A headless man stood there, arterial blood pumping up from his neck. His head was rolling away down the hill. He fell, revealing Noriko crouched behind. She held her blade in her right hand and an automatic pistol, doubtless picked up from one of the men, in her left.

Alastair nodded his thanks. He switched back on full auto, then scrambled around the left side of his cabinet.

A silhouette appeared before him, moving across his line of vision. Alastair aimed, then swung his barrel up as the firelight revealed the man's white, white hair.

It was Doc . . . and it wasn't. Alastair watched as his friend aimed without looking and put a bullet into the brain of a man directly behind him. Doc's arm swung around and the gun fired again, taking down a sniper Alastair hadn't even seen, but Doc never looked at the man he killed.

His face in the firelight was smiling, serene, perfect. His eyes did not blink.

Alastair shuddered. Doc was with the gods of blood and fire now.

Men ran down the hill. Gaby counted six of them. Two tripped, one after another, and rolled a good thirty yards. One got up and began limping; the other lay still.

She shot the one who ran toward the trucks. He, too, fell and did not move. She felt the knot in her stomach tighten again.

The other men were headed toward the trees. They waved and shouted at the men coming out of the forest, directing them to run.

There were two more gunshots from the top of the hill, then silence. Cabinets continued to burn. Gaby watched the last of the men move, reach the trees and disappear.

Joseph waited beside her. "It is a bad thing to be clumsy," he said. "I feel I have not helped much. Perhaps I should go up and see what has happened."

"Okay."

"Will you be—"

"Just go, dammit."

He began his long, lumbering walk up the hill.

❧   ❧   ❧

They descended the hill toward her in a slow, single line.

Joseph carried Doc like a baby. She could see Doc jerk and twitch.

Alastair was next. He was talking to Jean-Pierre. But as they got closer Gaby realized that the thin man wasn't Jean-Pierre, but an older gentleman with glasses.

Harris came next. He staggered under the weight of the tarpaulin-wrapped mass he carried, but his face was fixed, his eyes unseeing.

Noriko brought up the rear. She wouldn't look up.

Gaby tried to make sense of it as Joseph reached the trucks. Where was Jean-Pierre? Then she saw the expression on Harris' face, on the faces of the others, and she knew. Her vision blurred under tears.

The old man, handsome in spite of his leanness, animated in spite of his grimness, was talking. "I'm sorry about your friend. I know his family. Fine people. We can't wait."

"One bell of our time is so precious?" Alastair asked, anger in his voice. "One bell?"

"A bell might be death for us all."

They passed Gaby. Alastair got to the rear of the truck and lowered the tailgate. Joseph set Doc down in the truck bed.

Harris didn't look at Gaby as he passed. He walked to the back and gently placed his precious cargo down beside Doc.

Alastair said, "Joseph, can you drive this?"

"I can."

"Drive. Back to the airfield. Forget about the other car." Alastair swung up into the rear of the truck. Harris and Noriko followed suit and lifted the tailgate.

Gaby, numb, got into the passenger side of the cab. Joseph was already in the driver's seat. "What happened?" she asked.

He told her.

CHAPTER TWENTY

Alastair inserted the hypodermic into Doc's vein and drove the plunger home. He withdrew the needle and set it aside.

Doc gave one final twitch, then heaved a sigh and relaxed. His eyes closed. His breathing slowed and became more regular.

Alastair silently cursed the gods that had brought him here.

With the forests of Cretanis disappearing behind them, one of their number, a good friend, was dead. One had left his mind in the land of the gods and was now drugged into a stupor. The rest were numbed by grief. And if what their new ally had hinted at was true, they needed more strength for what lay ahead.

He drew shut the drapes over Doc's bunk on the *Frog Prince* and went forward. Turbulence made the footing unsteady.

The others were arrayed in the lounge—except for Noriko, who flew the plane on its westward course, and Jean-Pierre, whose body now lay in the cargo compartment under most of the ice from the galley.

Someone had thoughtfully set out Jean-Pierre's decanters of spirits and several glasses, most of which were now in use. Alastair took a clean one, poured it full of uisge, and sat down to glare at Caster Roundcap. "Now," he said. "Your story."

The solemn old man cleared his throat and, in a clear voice and lilting accent, began.

"Forty years ago, I met a man. His name was Theo MacAllister. An odd-looking fellow; he was bald. I asked him if it was from an accident and he said no, just a characteristic of his family. And he'd laugh as though it were a grim joke.

"He was an inventor. He made a pocket knife with a can-opener as one of the blades. Earned a fortune from it and some other devices. And he was a prophet."

Alastair stirred. "What did he prophesy?"

"He predicted the Colonial War between Castilia and the League of Ardree, a year before the first sign of trouble. He predicted the World Crisis decades before anyone else.

"And the most interesting thing was this: He was completely immune to iron poisoning." The old man waited for some show of surprise from the others; he saw none. That seemed to satisfy him. He nodded, patted down his pockets, and brought out a pipe and a pouch full of tobacco.

"Anyway . . . He was prone to fits of loneliness. One time when he was in his cups I helped him home. He told me where he was from. The grim world. Of course I did not believe him. I didn't believe there *was* a grim world, much less that he was one of her sons. But he was able to convince me. Such conviction in his stories, such truth in his predictions.

"I began to search for other signs of grimworlders. Theo's history gave me thoughts on what to look for. I found stories. I found living men and women, some of whom would admit to remembering the grim world. Some of them never did, but I could often see through their deceptions." He finished packing the bowl of his pipe, struck a match, puffed until he could draw smoke to his satisfaction.

"I am a historian, an arcanologist, by trade—my father's trade, and his mother's before him—and made the study of the grim world my hobby. From the clues I could draw from the grimworlders I met, I developed some theories about the two worlds."

"He's dead," Harris said.

Caster froze. The others did, too. The poor young man's mind wasn't even here. He had to be reliving the events on the hill, the death of the Acadian prince.

Harris continued, "Theo MacAllister. I remember him from the Changeling's lists. Angus Powrie killed him years ago."

"Oh, how sad." Caster shook his head. "I tried to track him down a few years ago and could not. His children said he'd vanished. I knew then something very bad was in the wind."

Alastair asked, "What theories?"

"I have little proof for any of this," Caster said. "A little evidence and a growing conviction based on things I've heard.

"First, I'm certain that there *is* a grim world. I think she is a sister to our fair world. Perhaps they were one world once, and developed into twins in their infancy.

"Second, I believe it is possible, though rare, to move from the grim world to here. By extension, it is likely that one can go the other way. I'd never heard of it being done . . . unless Angus Powrie's hints about Duncan Blackletter are true. I'd believe anything of Blackletter from the years I knew him."

Alastair gave him a hard look. "You're a friend of his?"

"Oh, no. Never that. When I knew him, he was just a quiet deviser, an old, retired student trying to reconstruct forgotten rituals, living in Novimagos. He saw my early papers on the grim world and wrote letters of praise. We corresponded, exchanged ideas . . . And then one day I heard he was dead, and learned that he deserved to be. A pity I find that the story of his death is erroneous."

"He was famous," Harris said. "How is it you didn't recognize his name?"

"He went by another one," Caster said. "He called himself Duncan MaqqRee."

Alastair swore. "Crass of him. To go by the name of his enemy."

Caster shrugged. "Where was I?"

"Moving from the grim world," Alastair said.

"Ah, yes. In my youth, when I could still travel most moons of the year and keep my health, I discovered that three sites resonated with the same devisement energy given off by the men and women of the grim world. After much study I concluded that these were actually the ends of bindings between the worlds—a sort of umbilical cord.

"Using globes and devisements of my own design, I set up similar links on a much smaller scale. Two worlds, represented by the globes, united by cords that let them share health, share strength, even share events."

Gabriela said, "Meaning that things happening on one globe might be duplicated on the other."

"Very good." Caster nodded approvingly. "Not an exact duplication, by any means. A dim reflection. The greater the event, the greater the likelihood that it would be reflected. I could dab a tiny bit of paint on one globe and nothing might happen to the other. But if I set a portion of one globe afire, a similar portion on the other would usually char.

"Over the years, I've done an immense amount of experimenting on my globes. Even today, they're still spinning in my town house, unless that Powrie person damaged them. By arduous trial and error, and examination of the three sites I've mentioned, I think I've discovered much about the relationships of the two worlds."

Alastair impatiently gestured for him to continue. Caster took a moment to formulate a perfect smoke ring; he puffed it up toward the ceiling. "I think these 'umbilical cords' determine the way things people and objects make the transition from one world to the other.

"I've heard enough from the men and women I've interviewed to suspect that the grim world ranges ahead of us in the development of science . . . and lags far behind in the sophistication, and especially acceptance, of its devisements. I believe the cords ensure this. Grimworlders told me of advanced devices they had with them when they made the transition. What do you suppose happened to them when they reached the fair world?"

Gaby spoke again. "Twisted until they're useless."

"You've seen it, then. Yes, they're ruined. I think this is a prophylactic effect—protection for the fair world. I believe our world protects herself from scientific advances that still bear rough edges; she won't allow the passage of anything that could do her harm. Likewise, I think the properties of devices and devisements taken hither-thither would be ruined or diminished. In one world, the old ways are manifest. In the other, the ways of cold, unfettered science dominate.

"But what does get through—the people, I mean—I believe they have a disproportionate effect on the world they've come to. The men and women I talked to from the grim world spoke of this world feasting on them like leeches. The fairworlders drank in and adopted their language, their manners, their ideas. I think that every grimworlder who has come here has added much to our language and store of knowledge.

"I think, in short, that the two world-sisters march together, but the grim world is the vanguard—the first to challenge the unknown, the first to suffer the beatings of change. The fair world hangs back, remains safe and strong, and grants the benefits of her health and wisdom to her sister."

Alastair looked thoughtful. "I won't say that this doesn't make some sense, from what we've already learned. But what were the events at Adennum Complex all about?"

"Adennum is one of the three sites, of course. The other

two are the Prophetess' Stone at Omphalia in Panelassion, and at Itzamnál, navel of the Sky Lizard and Earth Lizard in Aluxia. And the ritual you saw at the top of the hill at Adennum, enabled by that portable standing-stone circle made of wood, was nothing less than an effort to cut away the cord linking the two worlds."

"Was it successful?"

"Yes."

"What do you mean, yes?"

"Yes. It was successful." Caster sent another smoke ring at the ceiling. "The cord at Adennum went away. I could feel it. I'm sensitized to those specific emissions of power, after all.

"The goddesses bleed. And the other half of the expedition, led by Duncan Blackletter, was supposed to be doing the same exact thing at Omphalia at the same time. Their plan was to meet in Aluxia afterward and finish the ritual by cutting the third cord together."

Alastair looked among his companions. They seemed as troubled as he.

Caster continued, "Powrie said that these events could not be accomplished until all the men who'd made the transition from one world to the other were gone from at least one of the worlds. I assume that's been done." He saw Harris nod. "Well, then. I regret to say that my life's work has been correct and true. I have successfully identified some of the basic tenets that govern the way our world works. And I seem to have helped a very bad man use that knowledge to a very bad end."

Alastair said, "What end? With the cords cut, doesn't that mean travel between the two worlds will be impossible?"

The scholar shook his head. "Oh, no, Goodsir Kornbock. Travel was never dependent on the cords—else it could only be done from those three sites. No, only the constraints laid down by the goddesses are gone. Devisers who know how to move from one world to the other can carry whatever they wish with them. I can only assume that the fair world is unprepared for what the grim world can bring her . . . and vice versa."

Gaby looked even more glum. "Alastair, we've got things . . . guns, drugs, bombs you wouldn't believe. One bomb could destroy Neckerdam."

"The whole city?"

"All of it. One bomb could turn the whole island into burned slag and kill everybody there. Maybe Duncan can't get his hands on one; they're hard to get. But he can bring all sorts of things that will give us grief."

Alastair went white. He turned back to Caster. "If we stop Duncan in Aluxia, can we repair the cords?"

"If my model work is accurate—and so far, I must say, it has been absolutely correct—then you won't have to. Even if the third cord is cut, given time, all three will eventually regrow."

"So this only creates a brief period in which Duncan can act freely."

"No. The problem is this. In my experiments, once I'd cut the links between my globes, I was able to forge new ones. Links with different defining characteristics. Once they were in place, the old ones would not regrow. All I had to do first was make sure that neither globe was contaminated by a taint of the other."

Everyone turned to look at Harris and Gaby. Gaby glared back. "Boil that down into English. I mean Low Cretanis. You're saying that Duncan killed every fair-worlder on the grim world so he could cut the links. And if he manages to finish off the grimworlders on the fair world, he can set up new ones."

"New ones with different characteristics. If he has the skill, he could, for instance, decide that every grimworlder who comes to the fair world ever after becomes devoted to him. And vice versa. An army of slaves in each world . . . slaves that the natives are unprepared to defeat. He could become a god."

Alastair stood. "If there's anything I hate," he said, "it's being in charge. I'm going up to tell all this to Noriko and make some talk-box calls. One to Panelassion to confirm that the second ceremony took place. Another to a friend of Doc's in Aluxia so we can have some allies in place before Duncan gets there.

"Joseph, keep an eye on Doc. Tell me if there's any change in his manner. Goodsir Roundcap, find yourself a bunk; this will be a long flight. Gaby, Harris, get what sleep you can." He shook his head as if, by denying it, he could undo everything that had happened in the last few bells. He headed forward.

Harris went aft. Gaby started to follow him, but Caster intercepted her. "Goodlady?"

"What is it?"

"You *are* one of them, aren't you?" Up close, he tried to take in every detail of her, saw the subtle signs of wrongness about her. "A grimworlder."

"Well . . . yes."

"I'd like to speak with you. At length. About your world. Your history."

She looked away, staring after the vanished Harris. After a long moment she met his gaze again. "I think I'd better not."

"Why?"

"Why do you think?"

"You think I might misuse what I learned."

"I think you might *use* what you learned. That's just as bad."

"A telling shot. We'll talk later." He watched her hurry after Harris.

Gaby paused outside Harris' bunk and called his name.

There was no answer. She heard slow, regular breathing from beyond his curtains.

Asleep already. He usually wasn't able to sleep so fast. He must have been exhausted by what he'd gone through. She cursed Caster Roundcap for delaying her. She went forward to her own bunk.

❀   ❀   ❀

Harris heard her call his name. He waited, his eyes closed. *Just go*, he silently begged.

She did.

Now he knew, he finally understood, why she'd told him she didn't want him anymore.

Because he was a man of good intentions.

But good intentions didn't win fights. They didn't get things done. They didn't point toward the future. They didn't save Jean-Pierre's life. He'd let her down in every conceivable way.

He applauded her decision. Maybe she wouldn't take too long to find someone else. Someone who didn't screw up and get people killed. Someone like Alastair. Someone like Doc. It surprised him that he didn't want to smash the face of whomever she chose. He wished her well.

He heard Joseph set up a chair a few steps aft. Wood creaked, even over the roar of the engines, as the giant settled.

It was the last thing Harris heard before sleep claimed him.

He awoke feeling no different.

He climbed out of his bunk. Joseph, still sitting, looked at him. There was no censure in his expression.

But then, Joseph didn't have a whole lot of cause to be judgmental. Harris ignored him and went forward.

There was no one in the lounge. It was dark outside. He continued through the forward sleeping compartment and to the door into Jean-Pierre's cabin. He walked in and closed the door behind him, shutting the world away.

He found the sofa by touch and settled into it. Ahead, through the bubble of a window, there were stars above, gray nothingness beneath. The stars looked far too optimistic; he decided that the nothingness was right.

Someone settled onto the couch beside him. He jumped about a foot.

"It is I." Noriko's voice.

"Oh, Jesus. You scared me." He took a couple of deep

breaths. "I'm sorry, Noriko. I didn't know you were in here."

"I was not asleep. You have not disturbed me."

"I came in here . . . I don't know. I kind of half expected him to be here. Maybe his ghost. Pouring whiskey for everybody and smart-assing as usual." He looked into the void of the sea. "Noriko, I killed him."

"Angus Powrie killed him."

"Yeah, but I could have stopped him. I just couldn't figure out how in time."

She leaned against him, resting her head against his shoulder. He was surprised by the closeness. He put his arm around her.

Her voice, when it came, was quiet, barely audible over the engines. "Jean-Pierre hunted Angus Powrie since he was a youth. He spent a fortune on investigators, on newsmen. They hounded Powrie all over the world. Powrie had to stay in hiding because of Jean-Pierre. When they found each other, one of them had to die. Harris, Jean-Pierre killed *himself*. He broke cover, he leaped upon his enemy instead of shooting him. He forgot in his anger that Powrie always incapacitates his victim with a blow to the groin. Powrie is expert at that attack; it is his favorite. Nothing you did could have saved Jean-Pierre. Nothing.

"But I will not lie to you. You did fail, in a way. You failed to make the best of Jean-Pierre's death by avenging him. Perhaps he will not be too angry with you."

"I hope not. I'd hate to have him chewing me out through eternity."

She chuckled.

"How well did you know him?"

"He was my husband."

"What?"

"We were married three years ago." He heard her sigh. "It was not a good idea. He had lost the fiancée his father had picked for him. She was frail and prone to fits of despondency as pureblood princesses tend to be, and she leaped from a high cliff, though Jean-Pierre tried to catch her. He and I had been friends, sometimes lovers, and he turned to me in his grief . . . and stayed with me in his passion.

"But afterward, nothing changed. He chose not to make plans for the future. Not of life, nor home, nor children. After a year we decided to look different ways. But he would not let me divorce him yet."

"Why not?"

"His father did not favor me as a match for the prince. Jean-Pierre took offense. He told me that one day they would pay me an immense bribe to cast him aside. He insisted that I accept. That way, he said, the insult would be avenged, and yet everyone would have what he wanted."

"That sounds like Jean-Pierre."

They rode on in silence for a while.

He asked, "Do you know if he liked me?"

"You did not know? Yes. He did. He liked the way you could talk to everyone. Ignoring rank. Ignoring concerns of light and dark and dusky. He liked it that you taught me."

"I wish I could go back and just tell him, JayPee, I'm glad you're my friend. And good-bye."

"I, too. Harris?"

"Yes?"

"You should worry less about whether people like you."

"Maybe."

"Not maybe. Yes." She sighed. "Promise me you will remember what I have asked."

"Okay."

Doc heard three clangs, the notes of a hammer on an anvil. They trailed off into the distance. He opened his eyes.

Joseph sat a few feet away, studying him. His face was as grave as ever, but there was some deeper sorrow in his eyes.

"Tell me," Doc said.

Joseph told him. When he was done, Doc was silent a long moment. "Joseph, when you said that death followed in my wake, you were right."

"I am sorry I ever said that."

"Why?"

"Because it was wrong. Death does not follow you. It is ahead of you, Doc, like a line of enemies. Ahead of you because you aim yourself at it. You and your allies hurl yourselves at it to keep it at bay. You pass through it. Inevitably, one of you is caught. But I hate to think what things would be like if no one hurled himself at that line."

Gaby woke feeling rested but, for once, not grateful for it. She'd prefer to sleep until the heaviness inside her went away.

She dressed in her new jeans—a little baggy, in the fashion of fair world men's clothes, but a reasonable fit—and went back to the lounge. No one else was there. The sky outside the windows was just lightening with dawn; the eastern faces of high clouds were striped with orange sunlight.

She sat in her usual place and stared at the talk-box.

Time to stop relying on other people for everything. She closed her eyes. She tried to reach out for that familiar loneliness she'd felt twice before.

Slowly, the engines' roar dwindled to nothingness. She felt a pressure grow behind her eyes and heard a static in her ears.

The static became voices. They blended and blurred into a mass of words. "Can't authorize the when it sets sail not before the equinox operator help so there we were married your sister instead and came out soaking wet set aside some forest lands cost you eighty libs *mi espada se rompio* forty is the best you can when will you come . . . ." The pressure in her head grew greater but did not quite hurt.

She opened her eyes.

Her room. Walls of irregular stone, dark with age, no door or window allowing exit. An ornate rug, handwoven, on the floor. Her four-poster bed of dark wood with curtains of transparent silk in pastel blue. Her table. Her doll. The silvery mirror the height of a man on the far wall. The dress she wore, heavy but somehow not hot, not cumbersome. All hers.

Gabrielle's.

But she remembered Gaby, too. There was no conflict; the memories fit together like lovers' fingers intertwining. She smiled in sudden delight. She'd found her missing sister at last.

She listened for certain names, for specific voices. Eventually she found them.

"Goodsir Blackletter, we were attacked . . . -plete success. Goodsir Powrie has been to see a . . . left Siluston in that flying boat . . . dead, but Roundcap still lives . . . the storm cloud?"

She tried to make an eye open where she heard the voice, but there was no eye. They were speaking over a voice-only set. She could not hear any reply. She could not clear up the transmission; words went missing despite her best effort, and the pressure in her head increased. It distracted her, annoyed her.

"Gabrielle." Doc's voice. That eye she could open, and did. She saw the mirror brighten, her own reflection fade. Then, through it, she saw herself, dressed as Gaby; her eyes were closed. Doc was beside her, concern on his face.

"Gabrielle, you need to come out. I think you're hurting yourself."

"You can call me Gaby. I remember everything."

"Gaby, just come out *now*."

"I don't want to. I'm just getting it right."

"Do it."

"Not yet!" Anger flashed through her.

She heard a shattering noise. Doc disappeared.

She couldn't open that eye again. Uh-oh. She sighed, closed her eyes, and relaxed her hold on her surroundings. She felt them slip away. The floor rocked and she felt the sofa appear beneath her.

And the odd pressure inside her head resolved itself into pain, a solid steel spike of hurt driven deep into her brain. She cried out, clutched her head, tried to curl up into a ball. The pain wouldn't let go.

She felt Doc hold her and heard him speak her name, softly, insistently. Finally the spike of pain began to withdraw. "I'm all right, I'm all right," she said.

"You are not. You've dangerously extended yourself. I want you to promise me that you won't do that again unless I'm around."

She straightened in spite of the hurt. She looked him in the eye. "No."

His face registered surprise. "Well. Will you at least take it under advisement?"

In spite of the pain, she grinned. "That much I'll do."

Then she saw the talk-box.

It was ruined. The glass of the tube was scattered in tiny pieces on the floor before it; Gaby found pieces on her legs and in her lap. The electronic elements behind were blackened and melted. "What the hell happened to that?"

"I think *you* did."

CHAPTER TWENTY-ONE

They sighted Neckerdam after dawn the following day. Alastair reported that friends of the Sidhe Foundation had visited Omphalia in Panelassion, the second of Caster's three sites; Harris remembered Panelassion being the fair world's Greece. The Sidhe Foundation men found the same sort of Cabinet-henge arrangement there, abandoned; the ceremony was completed, the second link to the grim world cut.

Harris decided not to return to the forward cabin for the Neckerdam landing. The shade of Jean-Pierre might be waiting there for him. He stayed in the lounge and, through its windows, watched the landing, then the refueling and reprovisioning that followed.

Workmen of the Sidhe Foundation came with a coffin for Jean-Pierre. Harris saw Doc go outside and issue them orders. They brought the casket aboard. A few minutes later they left with it, carrying it like pallbearers.

The last of Jean-Pierre. Harris waved good-bye from behind a small round window.

Other men brought new stores, more weapons, additional ammunition, books requested by Doc and Caster Roundcap. Harris asked for a welding torch; Alastair told him the lab was already fitted with one.

Harris checked the map in the lab cabin and found

their destination: the nation of Aluxia. Alastair had pronounced it "Alushia." It sprawled across what on the grim world would have been Yucatan, Guatemala, and Belize.

Doc came back aboard with a man and woman. He introduced Harris to Ladislas and Welthow, pilots employed by the Foundation—"Aboard," Doc said, "so Noriko and the rest of the pilots can get some rest instead of being bound to the cockpit."

The new pilots both wore battered leather bomber-style jackets—his black, hers red.

Ladislas, whom Doc said was from faraway Dacisperia, was a head shorter than Harris but had a firm grip. His dark hair, pale complexion, and the point to his ears gave him a sinister aspect. He obviously enjoyed it, and cultivated a smile full of both charm and menace. He spoke with a heavy accent full of rolling R's: "I understand some of you are learning to fly. Perhaps we will find out if the *Frog Prince* is capable of an outside loop."

Alastair said, "Perhaps we will find out if you can pass through spinning propellers without being hurt."

Welthow, nicknamed Welthy, was a head shorter than Ladislas. Her hair was blond, twined into a waist-length braid. She had muscles like a cat and a grin that suggested she'd just been at the cream. Harris decided that she looked like pure sex in a compact frame. He was surprised that he felt like noticing. "Ignore Ladislas," she said. "He's crashed in every outside loop he's tried. Won't rest until he gets it right."

Doc got them and their gear squared away.

Through the windows, Harris saw the mechanics shake their heads over the engines, but by midmorning the *Frog Prince* was airborne.

When the others came back to the lounge or the bunks after seeing the takeoff show, Harris waved Joseph over. "Do you know how to use a welder?"

"I do."

"Would you help me put something together? I have a kind of a sick toy in mind. Something that will give one of Duncan's men fits."

"With such a goal, I would be happy to help."

Gaby sat with Doc in front of the replacement talk-box and learned everything she could about talk-boxes.

There were four types. Singles could only receive sound. Doubles could send and receive sound. Triples could receive sound and pictures. Quadruples, like most of the ones scattered through Doc's headquarters, could send and receive sound and pictures. Most of the triples and quadruples in existence, and most of the broadcasts for them, were black-and-white, but color was available— just very expensive.

Each talk-box could receive signals two ways, from the Ether or the Grid.

The Grid was a network of cables stretching to many parts of the world. It was used mostly for two-way communications, like the telephone system she was used to. But most parts of the Grid could handle full sound and picture transmissions. Two people with quadruples set up on the Grid could talk to one another's TV images.

The Ether seemed to be radio/TV broadcast transmissions. It was made up mostly of entertainment and news programming, but certain portions were set aside for communications between talk-boxes not set up on the Grid. These included the devices installed in the cockpit of the *Frog Prince* and the bridges of liftships— what the fairworlders called zeppelins and blimps—and ships at sea.

There was still a third arrangement, enjoyed by the talk-box in the lounge of the *Frog Prince*. That talk-box was set up to send and receive through the Ether, but could also broadcast to and receive from special relay stations attached to the Grid. Doc said he paid a fortune for the service. "But at critical times, the ability to call into the Grid from the plane can save your life."

"Pretty good, Doc." Gaby smiled and decided not to tell him that the grimworlders had such things in their cars.

Homes that could afford it tended to have one quadruple for entertainment and one double to act as a telephone. But if the double broke down, the owner could plug the quadruple into the Grid and use it for ordinary communications. Gaby found the arrangement handy.

"You," Doc said, "seem to have an affinity for the Grid. You say you've never seen any entertainment broadcasts as Gabrielle."

"Can't remember any, no."

"So the Grid may act as some enormous antenna for your Gift. Even across the gulf between worlds. I wonder if you could tap into the Grid of the grim world, too."

"That would be something. But I don't think I ever have."

"We'll try another time. For now, we'll try a couple of tests. I want you to see if you can find and talk to a central Grid operator in Neckerdam. And then—well, I had Brian Banwite deliver a handful of talk-boxes for this craft, because I want you to try to blow some of them up."

"Oh, good."

"It wouldn't bother me at all if some of the pieces broke off and stuck on impact," Harris said.

Joseph nodded. "That simplifies matters. Instead of welding, we will solder."

They started with a smallish bronze bowl. They assembled small pieces of iron or steel, each from one-half to one inch in length, and sharpened each one to a razory point or edge. Harris thought about sacrificing his lockback hunting knife from the grim world, letting Joseph cut it into shards, but decided that they had enough raw material from the bits of ferrous metal in the lab's scrap drawer.

Joseph meticulously soldered all those blades to the convex surface of the bowl. The sharp edges pointed up; some were angled. When it was done, Harris decided that it looked like a cheese grater designed by a serial killer.

Joseph looked at it. "This will hurt someone very badly."

"That bothers you, doesn't it?"

"Yes."

"But you made it anyway."

The giant was slow in answering. "All I want is for the world to leave me alone, and never again to hear bones cracking under my hands. But if the world must drag me back into its affairs, if it insists that I hurt anyone, I will hurt those who seem to find such joy in inflicting pain. Men like Duncan and those who serve him."

With a hammer and ream, Harris punched three holes at regular intervals around the bowl's rim and used a file to sand them smooth. He tied a long cord to each hole, then spent a while tying the whole arrangement on over his clothes.

He'd have to practice while wearing the thing. Otherwise he might carve himself when doing kicks.

Joseph looked at him. "You were right," he said. "That is the product of a disturbed mind."

Harris beamed at him. "Just the effect I was looking for."

Gaby scowled at Doc's face in the mirror of Gabrielle's room. "Are you ready?"

"A moment." She saw him pull on a pair of aviator-style goggles. "Now I am. Are you angry?"

"No, but I'll force it." She put all the heat and anger she could into her words: "I think you *suck!*"

Doc winked out. Gaby looked at her own, or rather Gabrielle's, surprised expression.

She relaxed and came to in her own body, seated beside the talk-box. The device's electronic guts, smashed and smoking, lay all over the lounge floor. "Cool."

Doc pulled his goggles off. "Headache?"

"A little one. Not as bad as last time. But then, I wasn't in as long." She rubbed her temples. "How was it?"

"More violent than before. I think you're improving. What is it that I suck?"

"Uhhh . . ."

In the hours it took to make the toy, Harris took the occasional trip to the galley for food, to the water closet forward, and to the lounge to take a look out the windows.

The terrain graduated to low, mist-covered mountains, dramatic and beautiful as the Appalachians of his own world; much later, the land grew flatter and covered with the lush springtime growth of the southeastern United States.

He saw cities, but the land wasn't crowded with them, and the infrequent roads looked like roads rather than a tight webwork of scars. There was wilderness down there, not crowded out by farmlands, and Harris abruptly wished he were in the heart of it, sitting with his back to an aromatic evergreen and wondering what sort of fair folk lived among the trees.

Well after dark, they landed at the airstrip serving the city of Lackderry on what would have been the Gulf of Mexico. "A good city for soirées," Alastair said, beaming. "One of Jean-Pierre's favorite places. On our way back perhaps I'll go on the town and drink my own weight in his honor."

They were flying again by midnight, south over the water, Noriko and Doc back at the controls.

Shortly after dawn, they crossed over the northernmost coastline of Aluxia and put down in an airfield— just a flat field with no pavement, no lights, and a tower that deserved to be called such only because it was two stories instead of one and featured a wind sock on a pole. Doc and Gaby went out to deal with the field officials— he because he'd been here before and knew the drill, she because her Spanish was recognizably the same as the Castilian spoken by half the people of Aluxia. Noriko, Ladislas, and Welthy went over the engines.

Hot, wet, heavy air flooded the *Frog Prince* and Harris decided that he didn't feel like taking a walk outside. He stayed in the lounge.

"You're looking haggard," Alastair told him.

"Speak for yourself." Alastair could have; he had dark rings under his eyes.

"Too much air travel. Trains are much better for the constitution. And for lovemaking."

Half a bell later, with Welthy and Ladislas back at the controls, they were flying south over forest-covered flatland, the darkest living green Harris had ever seen, almost never broken by the path of a'river.

Harris climbed the stairs to the upper deck.

One of the cargo holds was mostly empty. Harris dragged what cargo was there against the forward bulkhead and used the rest of the compartment for training. After an hour, he got pretty good at tying the new toy securely and was sure that he'd be able to move naturally while wearing the thing. Of course, he'd have to switch back to baggy fair world clothes for a while.

The aroma of meat and onions drew him back down. Alastair, singing to himself, cooked steaks with onions and mushrooms in the little galley. The doctor brought a huge platter of meat into the lounge and carried a smaller platter up to the cockpit. The others swooped down on the plate he'd left behind.

Harris briefly considered being mad at himself for enjoying the meal. Maybe, after the events in Cretanis, nobody should ever have an appetite again.

Nah.

Not long after noon, he heard a call floating down from the cockpit, Welthy's voice: "She's in sight, prepare to land." But it was Gaby's cry of "Oh, how *beautiful*!" that brought him forward to Jean-Pierre's cabin.

It was standing room only; the sofas and chairs were already full. The view through the bubble-window showed him why.

The *Frog Prince* angled down toward a great sheet of blue water, a miles-long lake surrounded by green mountain peaks. To port, Harris saw three great mountains on the south side of the lake; to starboard, there was some sort of community built on the north slopes. Every moment of travel presented Harris with a new, glorious, picture-postcard view.

The lake grew larger and larger. The pilots obviously meant to land there.

The *Frog Prince* set down with a noise like a washing machine set on overdrive. Water sheeted up over the bubble-window and the plane shuddered with the friction of landing. Harris gripped the doorframe for balance.

Then the water drained away from the window and the *Frog Prince* heeled very slightly starboard, swinging slowly around to face the village on the slope. Harris could see terraces where small houses were built from wooden poles and thatch. As more of the village came into view, he gaped at the blood-red pyramid that dominated the other buildings. Below it, at water's edge, was a dock protruding into the water; people, tiny forms barely visible at this distance, stood on it.

As the plane completed its turn, the castle came into view to the extreme right, set above and well back from the village. It was a ruin of some antiquity, its stones dark with more than age—it looked like it had been burned, much of the course of its walls toppled. But frameworks of metal and wood surrounded the old structure, some unfinished project of repair.

Welthy and Ladislas brought the *Frog Prince* alongside the dock as delicately as though they were returning a borrowed Rolls-Royce to its owner's garage. The plane's port wing hung over the dock. The men and women gathered there retreated until the propellers stopped spinning.

Doc stepped out onto the port landing wing. Through

the window, Harris saw a flash of movement outside, a brown-and-yellow blur hurling itself at Doc . . . and then the man staggered back inside, his attacker wrapped around him.

She was a woman with milk-and-coffee skin and hair that was a lustrous black. She wore what Harris thought of as Hollywood safari gear—shorts and short-sleeved shirt with many pockets, knee-high socks and sturdy shoes—but instead of khaki or tan, her clothes were a fading yellow. The scarf tied around her neck was gold with jaguar spots. She had her legs wrapped around Doc's waist and was kissing him with such enthusiasm that Harris found himself impressed and envious.

Finally she broke the clinch. "Welcome to Aluxia," she said.

"With welcomes like that, I must leave many times."

She smiled and released him, dropping to her feet. Harris saw she was tiny, not more than four and a half feet tall. Her eyes matched her hair and her mouth was a handsome curve just a little too wide for her face. She was both beautiful and built, and Harris thought she made quite a reception committee.

She finally turned to look at the others. "Alastair, a thousand blessings." Her smile faded. "Noriko, I heard about Jean-Pierre. I am so sorry." The smile returned, no less luminous than before. "Doc, introduce me to my new friends."

"Ish, this is Joseph, who builds things of steel. Gaby Donohue, who may someday be remembered as the discoverer and first priestess of the talk-box god. Harris Greene, who knows how to box with his feet. And Caster Roundcap, arcanologist. Everyone, I present you Ixyail del Valle, princess and rebel—called Ish by her friends."

Doc and friends debarked and the villagers crowded around them. These men and women were no taller than Harris' sternum, but the young ones looked very strong and fit. They seemed dressed for visitors. Though some of the men wore nothing more than white cloth tied around their middles, many wore calf-length breeches and jackets that were a crimson dark enough to be nearly black; each jacket was embroidered with brilliantly colored geometric designs Harris could not decipher. The women were in dark ankle-length skirts, undecorated, beneath sleeveless blouses, like ponchos bound at the sides, embroidered with the same sorts of designs.

They stared openly at the northerners, especially at Doc and the late-arriving Welthy, whose fair hair seemed to draw their eyes.

Ish dragged Doc before one of the villagers, a middle-aged man whose clothes were the darkest and whose embroidery was the brightest. "This is Balam, the *ahau*, or lord, of the villages around the lake. Don't call him the lord of the lake—that is a title reserved for one of their local gods."

Doc bowed. The village lord, seemingly unable to tear his gaze away from Doc's hair, bowed back. Ish gestured for the man to accompany her and Doc up to the village, and the whole mass of people drifted in their wake. "I spent a lot of Foundation money bringing very expensive dyes to these people. A rich bribe, much appreciated. Too, they are a peaceful folk. I think they will stay friendly."

There was a stir at the back of the crowd. They turned to see two older villagers, a man and a woman, pressing Caster Roundcap from both sides, smiling, talking at him in excited tones. He answered them briefly in their own language.

Caster saw Doc watching. He looked up and shrugged. "I told you I'd been here before. It appears some are old enough to remember me."

Ish said, "Now I *know* they will stay friendly."

In the village plaza, east of the blood-red pyramid and in its shadow, the villagers of Itzamnál hosted them in a feast. They served fish and small steamed crabs, something like a mild tamale the size of an orange and wrapped in banana leaves, papaya the size of watermelons, coarse, tasty corn tortillas that were more gray than brown, roast turkey, roast pig, honey and bitter chocolate sauce for flavor . . . Harris decided that Jean-Pierre would have approved; he ate heartily, without guilt.

Caster nodded over at the grim bulk of the fortress a hundred yards away. "They've begun repairs since last I was here."

Ish spat. "Another project of the blood-drinking, sons-of-Castilian-pigs government. I think they plan to put everything in shape so they can build a hotel and bring up wealthy Castilians to take the waters and stare at the volcanoes. This place is sacred. It should not be a play-ground. When I hear they have done this, I will use bombs and throw the first carloads of wealthy visitors off the mountain road. That will discourage them."

Harris, alarmed, looked at Alastair, but the doctor shook his head and gave him a "pay no mind" expression.

"I don't see anyone working on it now," Caster said mildly.

"I sent them away! All workmen from the city. Any of them could be spies for Blackletter."

Harris asked, "Why is it ruined when everything else is in good repair? I'm used to seeing pictures where the pyramids are overgrown and the more modern stuff is kept up."

Caster gestured, a broad sweep that took in the lake and its surroundings. "During the Castilian conquest, the whole area of Itzamnál was a retreat for Aluxian kings who continued to fight. It was eventually conquered and the Castilians built that hulk. A few years later, the Aluxians came back, burned it, and kicked the Castilians out." He shrugged. "Of course, the Aluxians kept fight-ing among themselves once the Castilians were at bay, and effectively destroyed themselves as a military power. The new government is not so easy to shake off."

The village lord exchanged a few words with Caster.

Alastair asked, "What does he say?"

Caster and Ish smiled. Caster said, "He tells us it's time. Half a bell since the last one. Look at the lake."

They did. Nothing was different: the water was so still that the *Frog Prince* barely moved.

Then, in patches, the surface began to roil, as though the entire lake were heated to the point of boiling. The patches spread out to join one another. In less than a minute, the lake's surface as far as they could see was a frothing mass. Steam rose from the water.

"Jesus," Harris said. "How hot is that?"

Caster shook his head. "Not very. It's usually warm; now it's just a bit warmer, not even uncomfortable. It's brought on by volcanic activity deep under the water."

"Volcanoes!" Ish glared at him. "It's the breath of the lizard in the earth. The trouble with you arcanologists is that you dissect and analyze your devisements until you forget to believe in them."

They watched as the roiling finally settled down. The steam, a solid layer, lifted clear of the lake's surface and slowly, gracefully rose until it was lost into the sky.

In a wood-pole hut given over to her use, Ish spread out a hand-drawn map of the kidney-shaped lake and its surroundings. Doc held down two of the corners for her.

Ish tapped a point not far from the village, two places along the southeast curve of the lake, and one on the southwest. "These are the passes out of Itzamnál. I have a man at each one. Scouts of the Hu'unal, my people, trustworthy. And another here," she tapped the land portion between the two southward curves of the lake, "on the tallest mountain. No lorries full of cabinets can get in without our knowing. None is here now. We've even searched the castle, top to bottom, to make sure nothing is left there. All that's there is wood, stone, and cement for the repairs."

Harris asked, "What if they come in a seaplane like we did?"

"What if they do? They land, they taxi toward shore, and we shoot them." She shrugged as though it were a small concern.

Doc frowned over the map. "Caster, which part is the sacred area?"

"It's all sacred. But the link with the other world is strongest in the vicinity of the village, centering on the pyramid. You'd have to perform the ceremony here, anywhere within a few hundred paces."

"That's encouraging. I'd hate to have to protect fifty square destads of lake and mountain."

Ish rolled up the map. "So. All questions answered? Good. Everybody go away. Now I can finally get some sleep."

As Doc turned away to follow the others, she caught him by the collar. "Not you." She smiled up at him. "I insist on company."

Harris took a walk around the village, followed everywhere by two children and an old woman who seemed fascinated by his every move but too shy to talk to him.

Though the pyramid and the other buildings on the plaza around it were stone, he saw that the houses of the villagers were not just made of wood—they seemed constructed of living trees. New branches budded from the wall poles driven into the earth. Vines and ferns sprouted out of the thatch roofs. He saw women at work pruning their houses.

Near the village and all around the lake, he could see fields of what looked like tall grass; wind would stir the plants in great rolling waves. These weren't the sort of fields he was used to from Iowa. They grew up the slopes of the mountains, some at angles of forty-five degrees or more. He saw men working them, pulling waist-high bushes and weeds free and hurling them downslope. He walked alongside the field nearest the village and saw that the tall grass was actually corn—or maize, most likely.

The ground was so warm he felt it through his leather

soles, and though the air was thin and cold, the water in the lake stayed comfortable—he dipped his hand into it and decided that it was somewhere around eighty degrees.

All through his walk, he heard the screeching from the forest he'd thought must be birds—big, ugly ones from the sound of them. But when he returned to the *Frog Prince,* Caster told him they were howler monkeys. "Best get used to their noise," the arcanologist said. "You don't have much choice."

Half a bell after the display of roiling water, it happened again. This time Harris sat cross-legged on the dock and watched the whole event, from the first boiling patch to the disappearance of the steam cloud far overhead.

Alastair stepped out of the plane onto the port water wing. "Ladislas is taking first watch, at four bells. I relieve him at five bells."

"I'll take the watch at six bells, then." Harris frowned. "Ixyail is a weird one. What was all that talk about bombs?"

The doctor smiled. "It was just talk; she's very excitable. She actually is a rebel, an enemy of the Aluxian government, and they would arrest and execute her if they knew she were here. But she confines herself to spying and sabotage. No attacks on the innocent."

"Good. Is Doc serious about her?"

Alastair shrugged. "It's complicated. But they've been friends and lovers for some time."

"Oh. I just sort of thought, the way he jumps into every bad situation that comes along, that he'd have sworn off relationships until he was retired or something."

"What sort of idiot would punish himself that way?" The doctor looked offended.

"Just a thought. Never mind. I'll see you at six bells." Harris rose and breezed past the doctor to return to his bunk.

Three days passed.
Gaby spent some time each day before the talk-box.

With each attempt, the use of her ability became easier
. . . and more difficult.

It was easier to project herself into the mind and room
of Gabrielle. She could do that almost effortlessly. Each
time, it took longer for her to feel the pressure that promised pain.

But on the second day, lying in her bunk, she put herself
in Gabrielle's room . . . and could not hear the hiss of
voices. The room was peaceful. She never felt pressure
behind her eyes. She could not find the Grid.

The next morning, she began experimenting. Her practice went as usual from the lounge of the *Frog Prince*.
But from any other cabin, from outside the plane, she
failed to reach the Grid.

"I don't get it," she complained to Doc.

He considered for a moment before answering. "Gaby,
in uniting you with Gabrielle, it may be that I have fatally
compromised your Gift. It may be a thing that belongs
to dreaming. Giving your waking mind access to it may
have damaged it. May continue to do so. It could be a
delicate machine, and it may be burning out from over-
use or unaccustomed wear."

"Damn." She turned her thoughts away from the loss
she might be facing. "I heard Duncan a few minutes ago."

"What was he saying?"

"I only heard a snatch of conversation, very faint. Something about the lake being effectively sealed off, and then a
few words about something being in place." She gave him
an apologetic look. "I couldn't get any more. I'm sorry."

"Don't be. We're now sure his people are in the vicinity. Things could happen anytime now. If you can, keep
listening . . . but don't tire yourself to excess."

"I won't," she lied.

In the darkness of the dock, Harris shivered. He
wouldn't have believed that the air could turn so cold
after dark. Every morning when he'd awakened, bowls
of standing water had been frozen over the top.

A distant buzz, like an insistent insect, intruded on his thoughts. He stood at the edge of the dock and tried to spot the source of the noise, but all he did see was the sudden flaring of a signal fire atop the mountain peak on the other side of the lake.

A plane, it had to be a plane. He stuck his head through the hatch into the *Frog Prince*. "Up and at 'em!" he shouted. "There's a plane coming in!" Then he trotted up the slope to the village and hammered the frame of the curtained doorway to Ish's hut. "Doc! Incoming!"

By the time he got back to the plane, Doc's associates were stumbling out of it, some half-dressed, all clutching weapons. They turned in the direction of the noise. The buzzing increased slowly in volume, but still there was nothing to see.

"It's a Hammerling engine," Noriko said. "Hear the way it misses? It's not in good repair." Harris wondered where Welthow and Ladislas were, but not for long; one engine on the *Frog Prince* coughed into life, its propeller spinning. A second engine followed.

Alastair cast off the lines lashing the plane to the dock and joined the others. "Get moving," he said, though the pilots could not hear him. Then something caught his attention and he pointed. "There. Low, at eight bells."

Everyone looked slightly left of straight ahead.

A triplane—something Harris had never seen outside of pictures in a book. Almost invisible in the faint light cast by the crescent moon, it came at them just feet above the water. Harris winced. The *Frog Prince* was moving, but couldn't possibly get clear before—

It opened fire. Angry gouts of flame erupted from the plane. Twin lines of water-spray erupted from the lake's surface and converged on the *Frog Prince*.

CHAPTER TWENTY-TWO

People scattered, Caster and Noriko leaping into the water. Bullets tore into the *Frog Prince* and sent wood chips flying. One engine coughed and died immediately. The triplane roared past, a mere six feet above the plane it had just strafed, climbing to keep from slamming into the mountain slope ahead.

Alastair stood and opened up with his autogun. His long burst didn't seem to affect the attacker. Doc, hopping on one foot as he struggled to pull a boot onto the other, joined his associates.

Harris helped Caster and Noriko out of the water. He took an anxious look at the *Frog Prince*; only one engine was running, and it was sputtering, but in dim light from the cockpit he could see Welthy and Ladislas moving, and they didn't appear to be hurt.

Villagers emerged from their huts. Many more, Harris saw, merely peeked from curtained doorways.

The attacking plane continued to climb, then wheeled around in a counterclockwise circle and headed toward the Castilian fort. It passed over the ruined structure . . . and Harris saw a flash of rocket trail as something fired out of the cockpit into the center of the old fortress.

The plane passed over the castle and began a gentle

turn. There was a flash of light from the interior of the structure; it illuminated the mountain slope behind.

Doc struck his forehead. "Damn me for an idiot. I forgot about Duncan's paint-spraying missile. They didn't *need* to bring the equipment in by lorry!" He charged toward the fort.

The others followed, spreading out. But the triplane angled toward them, firing again, its bullets plowing indiscriminately through the huts of the people of Itzamnál.

This time everyone returned fire, sending lead into the aging triplane's flanks and belly. Alastair put a good burst into its side; Harris saw its cockpit riddled with holes. When the plane was past, they rose and began running again.

The triplane waggled its wings. It didn't look to Harris like a celebration of victory; it seemed to be slewing out of control. It turned to pass once more over the castle. Then it climbed at an ever-increasing angle, as if the pilot sought to reach the silvery arc of the moon.

The plane continued its arc until it stood on its tail. Harris heard the engine catch and fail. Then the plane heeled over and dropped, spinning, an unaerodynamic fall, to smash into the far wall of the castle.

Doc was almost to the castle gate when automatic gunfire erupted from the entrance into the fortress.

Harris saw him go down. Doc continued into a controlled tumble, getting clear of the trail, finishing up behind a gentle rise in the earth; apparently unhurt, he returned fire with his pistol. Alastair joined him, went prone, and opened fire with his Klapper.

Harris left the trail and scrambled upslope. In a few seconds he was at right angles to the castle entrance, out of sight of its defenders. He cut across toward the fortress' western wall. This wall stood tall and unbroken, portions of it lighter and in better repair than others; its upper reaches were overgrown with the wooden framework the repairmen had been working from. Perhaps he could find a dangling rope or a rough patch of original wall to climb.

Below, he saw Doc's other associates spreading out from the trail, returning fire against Blackletter's men.

There was a brief whoosh and the sky above the castle lit up. It didn't look like the pyrotechnics that had erupted from Adennum Complex. Harris guessed that the crashed plane was on fire.

Above the gunfire, he heard the rattling of a generator and the faint suggestion of chanting. But he trotted the entire length of the west wall and found no way up.

"Harris!"

He spun. Joseph stood at the bottom of the wall toward the castle's front face. Harris ran downslope to join him.

Joseph pointed. "You want to go up?"

"It's a hell of a good idea."

"Get on my back."

Harris did. He wrapped his arms around Joseph's neck. On account of the "cheese-grater" he was wearing, he wasn't willing to settle in against Joseph; he had to keep his knees pressed to the giant's back.

Joseph didn't seem to mind. He started climbing.

His hands seemed to find every crack between the stones of the wall. To Harris, it seemed as though his fingers settled, even oozed, into the gaps. Joseph hauled himself up with great speed and utter confidence. Harris took a look at the ground below and waited for fear of heights to claim him as it had at the construction site, but it didn't.

In moments, he was able to step off onto the highest of the wooden repair walkways. There was a coil of rope on the walkway. He quickly tied it off and then kicked it over the side; it unrolled as it fell. Then he stepped up between the battlements and joined Joseph atop the wall. He had an excellent view of the castle's interior.

On the far wall hung the smashed triplane, burning

furiously. The fire had already spread to wooden walkways and support beams.

Below, occupying most of the castle's courtyard, was another Cabinet-henge. At the center was a small fire surrounded by men; red smoke rose from the fire.

The castle didn't seem to have any sort of gatehouse, just a gate and drawbridge flanked by round towers. He could see men clustered to either side of the opening, spraying gunfire out at Harris' friends.

Harris saw what they were firing. Klapper autoguns and what looked like machine guns, against the pistols and occasional autoguns of his friends.

"Get under cover," he said. He didn't wait to look. He drew both pistols and lay down at the interior edge of the wall. He sighted in on one of the groups of gunmen and opened fire.

He'd emptied one gun before there was a reaction. One of the silhouettes by the gate slumped to the ground. Others turned and opened fire on Harris.

He heard something whistle near him. A little piece of the stone wall beneath him exploded, sending a shard of stone into his chin. It hurt, but it was a dull pain.

There was a wet, meaty noise above him. Harris glanced up.

Joseph still stood there. A small crater had appeared on the exposed flesh of his chest. The giant looked a trifle puzzled. As Harris watched, his chest began to resume its normal shape.

Joseph walked back to the battlements. He reached past them and yanked. There was a cracking noise. He came up with a wooden beam, something like a four-by-six, at least ten feet long. He began walking along the wall toward its southern face.

Harris switched to his second gun and continued to fire. Some of the men below had quit the gate and were sheltering behind the cabinets. They fired at him. Harris saw another man at the gate fall down; it wasn't one he was aiming at. Maybe his friends were making headway.

He paused to reload. Joseph got to the corner where the walls met and turned toward the gate.

The plane on the far wall exploded. Burning wreckage dropped into the courtyard. A sheet of fire blew out over the castle, raining flaming debris everywhere. Something lit on Harris' cheek and bit him; he swatted the ember off his flesh and began firing again.

Joseph reached the west tower flanking the gate. He stepped off the wall. Harris froze, arrested by the sight of his friend attempting to kill himself.

Joseph fell forty feet to the ground. He flattened just a little when he hit. He stood up immediately and swung his improvised club. Even at this distance, Harris could hear the crack as it met the head of one of the gunmen at the gate. The blow swatted that man aside. Joseph stepped forward and drove his beam into the chest of the next gunman.

The men around the gate turned their fire on Joseph. Harris saw the giant shudder and jerk as he was hit, perhaps dozens of times. But Joseph waded into his enemies, swinging his club, smashing men to the ground.

Harris kept firing until his second gun was empty again. He thought he saw two men fell under his gunfire. He began to reload.

A hard, cold piece of metal pressed up against his temple. His stomach seized up and he froze.

A man's voice, hard and cold: "Drop those pieces of shit over the edge."

Harris complied. Below, he saw one of the gate defenders fall backwards, hit by fire from outside.

"Your other gun, too, dickhead. Angus told us about you."

Harris carefully, slowly drew out the revolver from his belt holster and dropped it off the wall.

The man stepped back. "Stand up and turn around."

Harris did. He turned to face Phipps. The man wore a dirt-streaked grimworld suit and burgundy-and-yellow power tie that seemed doubly incongruous in this setting.

Phipps smiled. "Here it comes, punk." Then he froze.

A woman's brown arm snaked from behind Phipps and relieved him of his pistol. Ixyail stepped back and away from the grimworlder. She carried another gun in her left hand. She, too, was smiling. "Two big steers fighting," she said. "I must see this. That will be worth all the climbing."

Phipps looked at her, confused, taking a moment to realize that he'd just been given permission to beat Harris to death. "All right," he said. "Just as good."

He stepped forward.

Harris knuckle-punched him in the throat. Phipps clutched at the injury, surprise in his eyes.

Harris grabbed him by the tie and yanked. Phipps sailed off the wall, his arms flailing. He got out one strangled cry before he smashed into the flagstones four stories below.

"Give me that." Harris, exasperated, took Phipps' revolver from Ixyail.

"That was no fight." She looked disappointed.

"Give Joseph some support. I'm going down."

He found temporary wooden stairs leading to the ground. As he descended, he saw Joseph, one of his legs near-useless and dragging, smashing one of the gunmen against a wooden cabinet. The last defender still at the gate fell over backwards and Alastair charged in, still firing at him, nearly stumbling over his body. Men were regrouping among the cabinets; some opened fire on the doctor, who dove behind a pile of masonry rubble.

Many of the wooden cabinets were on fire, as was the entire east wall of the castle. Flame and smoke rose into the sky.

Harris saw the squat shape of Angus Powrie moving among the cabinets, red-gold from reflected flame. Harris hurried down the steps, firing at targets of opportunity as he descended.

✤   ✤   ✤

Noriko ran in behind Alastair and Doc, keeping as low as she could. One of the bleeding men on the ground raised a handgun. She lashed out with her blade, dispassionately watched as the gun and the hand that held it went flying.

Joseph, his face and body riddled with small craters, spun on them and raised the six-foot remnant of his club, but recognized them and stayed his hand.

Gunfire from the cabinets ahead. Doc angled right, diving, rolling behind bags of cement. Noriko headed left, hoping her dark clothes would make her tough to pick out in this light.

The lights decorating the cabinets abruptly brightened and burned out. The shaft of light Noriko remembered from Adennum launched itself toward the stars. The ground rumbled. She heard Doc groan. She knew it was from pain at having failed a second time. She felt it herself.

All the incoming fire seemed to be aimed at Doc and Alastair; maybe she hadn't been seen. She moved between two of the cabinets, headed toward the center, her senses alert.

Not alert enough. A loop settled around her neck and drew tight; a cold barrel pressed against the flesh of her neck. A gruff voice with a lowlander accent said, "Drop that toy, girl."

Harris moved into the circle of burning cabinets. In the center, the fire still issued a little red smoke, but no one stood near it.

That last shot had been his fifth. He swung out the cylinder of Phipps' pistol and dumped out its load of brass, then tried to reload.

No such luck. The ammunition in his pockets was a different type. He cursed, replaced the unspent cartridge and snapped the weapon shut, rotating the cylinder so that the one live round was ready to fire.

There was motion in his peripheral vision.

Angus Powrie stood four steps away. He held a Wexstan shotgun pistol in both hands, aimed upward. The cord at its end held its barrel to Noriko's neck. Noriko's face betrayed no emotion.

Angus caught sight of Harris in almost the same instant. "Drop your gun," said the redcap, "or she's dead."

Noriko shook her head, a mere suggestion of motion.

Harris took careful aim at him. "You need to come up with a new dialogue coach."

Powrie looked confused. "Maybe you didn't understand me, boy."

"Who was it who said that experience consists of recognizing it when you make the same mistake again?"

They waited there for long seconds, while the fire on the east wall blazed up brighter and gunfire blasted from the south arc of the ring of cabinets.

Harris kept his aim true. "Noriko?"

Her voice was faint. "Yes?"

"You're my friend, and I love you."

"I know."

"If it comes to it . . . good-bye."

"Good-bye."

He waited. Noriko slowly brought her hands up. Harris cleared his throat, held Powrie's attention. "Angus, listen. I'm willing to forgive and forget the thing with Jean-Pierre if you'll do something for me."

"Which is?"

"Kill yourself."

Noriko clapped her hands on either side of the Wexstan's cylinder.

Angus yanked the trigger. The cylinder, trapped between Noriko's hands, could not rotate; the hammer could not draw back or fall.

Harris fired. The bullet took Angus high in the chest. It didn't stagger the redcap.

Angus wound up and struck Noriko, a punishing blow to her cheek; her legs gave way but she kept the grip on the gun.

Harris ran forward and side-kicked, catching Powrie

in the chest, throwing him to the ground. Harris dropped the empty pistol. Noriko crawled away.

Powrie was up in a split-second, charging. Harris sidestepped, grabbed the man's sleeve and added some momentum to the charge. The redcap flew past and slammed into the burning side of a cabinet. It didn't slow him; he bounced off and stepped away from the wood, fast enough that the fire didn't even char his shirt.

The redcap's pointed teeth gleamed in the firelight. He held up his undamaged left hand. "You ruined this," he said. "Now it's all better. I'm going to break your neck with it." He came at Harris, grabbing.

Harris leaned left, blocked right-handed, and as Angus reached him he spun into a backfist. The blow smashed the dwarf's nose into a flat, bloody mess of gristle. Angus staggered past a couple of steps.

Harris backed away, dancing, his hands at chin level to guard.

Angus turned, unslowed. Blood poured across his mouth but his smile mocked Harris. He charged again.

Suddenly Harris was in Sonny Walters' position, fighting the long-range battle against an enemy who had to close constantly. He fought it the way Sonny did, nailing Angus at the moments of transition, dancing away, throwing baffling combinations. He didn't forget the crucial difference between the two fights—he couldn't allow Angus ever to get a grip on him. He threw hard blocks against every grab and boxing-style punch Angus tried against him. He hammered the redcap's ribs, ears, stomach, knee. He kicked Angus full in the mouth and watched him spit out a half dozen teeth.

Then Angus took Harris' best cross to his jaw. He stumbled forward to his knees . . . and brought an uppercut straight from the ground, slamming it into Harris' crotch.

The thin cloth of the pants was no protection. Angus' fist crunched into the spike-laden bowl Harris wore as an athletic cup. Razory points and edges of cold iron and steel gouged Angus' fist, shredding flesh, ripping tendons and cartilage.

Angus staggered back, horror on his face as he stared at the new ruin of his left hand. Pieces of iron protruded from it.

Harris bent over, the pain from the blow making it hard for him to stand straight. He found his voice; it emerged as a wheeze. "Hurts, doesn't it?"

Angus didn't answer. The flesh on his hand not covered with blood was already blistering; he frantically plucked at it, pulling iron bits free. His eyes were wide.

Noriko stepped up beside Harris and fired the Wexstan. The shotgun discharge tore Angus' tormented expression away as though it were a paper mask, leaving behind only blood and bone. Angus' head rocked and he fell. He slapped onto the stone of the courtyard.

Harris stood over him and got his breathing back under control. He glanced over at Noriko and was amazed to see her cheeks wet with tears. Her words were barely audible over the crackle of burning wood: "I am sorry, Harris. He was yours, but I had to. Family honor demanded."

He took her in his arms and held her. "It's all right."

They collected in the center of the henge. Doc, unhurt, was first on the scene. Then Harris and Noriko.

Welthow, lately arrived, knelt beside Joseph. The giant's face did not express concern or hurt. His body was riddled with bullet-holes, but one by one they slowly began to contract to nothingness. Bits of dark metal worked their way free of his flesh and dropped to the stones.

Alastair moved from one fallen form to the next. With most, he did little more than check pulse and then close the victim's eyes.

The others trickled in. Gaby pushed a couple of gunmen before her, keeping them at riflepoint; both were fairworlders. Gaby looked in alarm at the blood streaking

Harris' crotch. "Not mine," he said, but did not elaborate.

Ish moved to Doc, touched his cheek, stayed beside
him.

"They finished the ritual," Doc said. "We've failed."

CHAPTER TWENTY-THREE

Angus Powrie and fourteen of Duncan's men were dead. Another dozen, most of them injured, were dragged off one by one into Harris' workout cargo hold, now pressed into duty as a temporary gaol.

Ladislas had a leg injury, a twisted ankle sustained as he left the *Frog Prince*. Joseph was almost recovered from the craters and divots that had marked him a few minutes before. And two of the villagers, one of them a child, were dead, killed during the triplane's strafing run; another was hurt.

The villagers added wood to the fire raging in the fortress. The lake's last remnant of Castilian rule would never be rebuilt.

Doc's associates retreated to the *Frog Prince* dock to watch the structure burn down. Noriko and Welthy worked to repair the damage done the plane during the strafing run.

One of the prisoners talked freely when pressed. "We were set up in some wretched hole of a town," he said. "The old man called it Lady of the Birds."

"Ixquetzal," said Ish. "Territorial capital of the blood-drinking sons of Castilians."

"He rented a warehouse, had us set everything up in a chalk circle. Said when we got here, all we had to do was hold the fort. When the ceremony was done, he'd bring us back. He was *supposed* to bring us back."

Doc dragged the man off to the cargo hold, then returned to the dock. Alastair said, "Ixquetzal next, I assume. Duncan will be working up the strength to bring them back."

Doc shook his head. "It took a tremendous amount of energy for Duncan to send them here at all. To bring them back would probably have killed him. Powrie probably had a return arrangement; the rest were sacrificed. He'll have packed up and taken off already. We need to get back to Neckerdam. Noriko, how long on the repairs?"

"We could take off now, but I don't want to fly all the way home on three engines. By dawn, I think, for the port inboard engine."

"Dawn." Doc balled up his fists, pressed them to his eyes. "All right. Keep at them. We need to get Harris and Gaby to where we can protect them."

Harris, dressed once more in his grimworld jeans, sat with his back to one of the dock's wooden support poles. "Let me get something straight, Doc. Duncan has to kill us if he's going to forge a new link between the worlds. He can't do that while we're alive because we have the wrong whatchamacallit valences."

"Firbolg. Yes. You could go back to the grim world and he would not need to kill you. But Gaby he would still need to kill. Remember, her Firbolg Valence lights up their registers on either world."

"Right. So we have to wait around until he makes a move on us. We can set up the Army, Air Force, Navy, and Marines around us, but it all boils down to when he decides to attack."

"Correct. Or until Caster's 'umbilical cords' recover. Which could be months or years."

"So rather than wait, I think we need to force his hand."

"I'd considered that. The best way would be to begin the very ceremony he wants to initiate. Threaten to define the new links ourselves." He smiled apologetically at Gaby.

"Of course, we'd have to send Harris home and kill you first."

"Let's not," she said.

"But even if we pretended to be planning it, Duncan has a few grimworlders of his own on the fair world. We got one tonight, but we'd have to capture the other two and send them home first."

Harris shook his head. "So let's take a different approach. Bring in more grimworlders of our own. Or make him think that we're about to, so he has to act right away to stop us. It's better than waiting around."

Doc considered that. "You're right, and I'm an idiot." He rose. "Ish, I need you to translate for me with the village leader. I have to apologize, make restitution to him somehow for the unhappiness I've brought to Itzamnál. Everyone, we leave when Noriko pronounces the engine ready."

By the time the sun rose they'd been in the air for half a bell.

Harris stared at the wooden ceiling above his bunk. Angus Powrie's beret was tucked away in the storage drawer beneath him. Noriko had been too numbed by events to think about it, but he knew that the royal family of Acadia would want to have it—tangible evidence of the death of their enemy. But it felt strange to take a trophy from a man he'd helped to kill.

A hand parted the curtain. It was Gaby, dressed in her yellow nightshirt. Her expression was grave.

"Hi," he said.

"I want to make a deal with you."

"Shoot."

"As soon as we get back to Neckerdam, you go home to New York."

"And?"

"And once everything is done here, I join you." She blinked. "We give it another try. Us."

He thought about it. "You want me to leave you behind? Why?"

"So you'll be safe. So you'll get away from all this craziness. It's doing something very bad to you, Harris. That whole thing with that athletic cup was just too weird. You have to go home."

He studied her face, the features that he held in so many corners of his memory. He wondered what she would have looked like in a bridal gown. "No."

"*Yes*, Harris. It's what I want you to do."

"Sorry."

"Why not?"

He stirred, restless. "Gaby, it's kind of hard to explain."

"Do it anyway."

"Okay. For years and years now, I've kind of defined myself by fighting. Harris Greene, Great Fighter. People would look at me and that's what they'd say. I really was, you know. So you want to know why it was I lost so much?"

"Why?"

"Because they expected it. They wanted it. I could see the other guy's eyes, and he wanted me to lose. The crowds wanted me to lose. It's taken me all this time to figure out that I was just giving them what they wanted. Maybe just so they'd like me better."

"What does this have to do with what I was talking about?"

"I'm not going back to New York just so you'll like me better. Turn my back on Doc and all the rest? Maybe cost him the little bit of an edge I could give him? What would that make me?" He paused to consider his next words. "Gaby, I've decided that I really love this place. I'm not going to let Duncan Blackletter wreck it. I'm not going to throw the one fight that ever mattered. And when it's done, I'm going to stay here."

"I'm not. I'm going home."

He closed his eyes. He felt one more little piece of his heart break away and go drifting into the void. "Funny. I've said this once tonight already."

"What's that?"

"I love you. And good-bye."

He waited for her to leave.

She didn't. He looked at her again.

She was smiling at him, the gentle smile she would save for him in the moments they were closest. He hadn't seen it in a long time. It made his chest ache.

She bent down to give him a kiss like warm silk. It sent an electric charge to his fingertips and toes. He took her head in his hands and sustained the kiss.

Gaby drew back, still smiling, then climbed into the bunk with him. She reached up to draw the curtains closed.

"Gaby—what the hell's going on?"

She brushed her cheek along his. "Do you remember my uncle Pete?"

"Another one of your dizzying non sequiturs. Pedro, right? The cop? Yeah. I met him when he came up from Mazatlán to visit you. He told funny stories about his job."

"My favorite uncle. When he was young, he went to the university. He was going to be a poet. I read some of his poems. They were wonderful."

Harris put his arms around her and pulled her close—gently, afraid that she might evaporate. No, she was real; he could feel the warmth of her through the nightshirt. He felt himself grow hard beneath his boxer shorts. He didn't adjust himself to conceal it from her. "Baby, I don't understand."

"They talked him out of it. His brothers and his father. They said it wasn't manly. Poetry, I mean. So he became a cop like the rest of them. Sits on his lawn furniture and drinks beer and watches the clouds go by, and wishes he were flying up there with them. When I met you, you were so much like him, always dreaming. You could always make me laugh."

"Leave our sex life out of it, okay?"

She chuckled and kissed him again. "The problem was, there was never a direction I could point at and say, 'That's the way Harris is going. That's who he is.' You always just did whatever I wanted. Whatever *anybody* wanted. I waited and waited for you to become you, and you never did. After a while you were part me, part Uncle Pete. There was no such person as Harris."

"So you dumped me because I was putty in your hands."

"Uh-huh. I don't want putty, Harris. I push all the time. How am I supposed to respect someone who doesn't push back? And now you do." She ran her hand through the hair on his chest.

"Gaby, what would you have done if I had taken you up on your deal just now?"

"I would have watched you go home and then cried a lot. Because I decided I wasn't going back. I'm staying here, too."

"You lied to me."

She smiled down at him. "Damned right I did. I reserve the right to do that. Now, why don't you shut up for a minute?" She tugged down the waistband of his shorts.

He arched to make that easier, pulled the shorts the rest of the way down, kicked them free. He ran his hand up the smooth curve of her leg, carrying the hem of her nightshirt up with it. She wore nothing beneath it. She helped him pull the garment off and discarded it to the side.

Skin to skin, for the first time in forever. She leaned down to brush her lips across his; he stroked her from the nape of her neck to the swell of her behind, luxuriating in the feel of her. She reached down to take a hold of him and moved down to guide him into her.

"Gaby, I don't want to spoil this—"

"So don't talk, dummy."

"— but we're lying in an open compartment."

"Oh, yeah." She smiled at him. "Harris, this is the fair world. If anybody's listening, they can stuff cotton in their ears, or cheer, or sing along if they want. I can take it if you can." She began to move atop him.

✦   ✦   ✦

A few steps away, Alastair listened until he identified the noises faintly audible over the engine growl. He rolled over, pulling the pillow around his head. "Well, it's about time," he grumbled.

CHAPTER TWENTY-FOUR

Gaby continued to work on her Gift. She was able to spend more time each day in Gabrielle's room without developing headaches. But each day she found she needed to be closer to the talk-box for her Gift to work. Finally, she found she had to keep her hands on it.

Yet even as the range of her Gift dwindled, she learned how to do something Gabrielle had long known—to force open the "eyes" of talk-boxes at specific addresses rather than just wait for voices to alert her to their presence. She could call direct to Doc's talk-box whether or not he was there, or to any other talk-box she'd already visited; she could explore, sensing unknown talk-boxes as eyes, and force them open. Her growing versatility pleased her.

That, and Harris. Things were finally working out. The recent change between them kept her happily distracted.

Doc put her in charge of the private grid of talk-box cameras set up throughout his headquarters—his version of a closed-circuit security camera network. With the turn of a tuning dial, she could change her talk-box viewpoint to throughout Doc's floors, including the basement levels, the exterior of the Monarch Building, even the distant Gwaeddan Air Field hangar.

And when she was *within* the Sidhe Foundation grid,

working from Gabrielle's little room, she was able to flit from view to view with the speed of thought.

She also continued her research into Duncan Blackletter . . . and, for that matter, into Dr. Desmond MaqqRee, and the feud that had erupted between the two men more than thirty years before.

Doc wouldn't help; as always, he just shook his head and told her it wasn't relevant. "I've made him my responsibility. That's all you need worry about. Stop prying."

But she didn't. She pored through old newspapers from Novimagos and other nations. She consulted birth records, sometimes calling civic halls as far away as Cretanis. She sought homelords who had owned properties rented by either man.

She could find no birth record for Duncan Blackletter. That was hardly surprising; it was commonly believed that his name was a false one. But neither could she find a birth record for Doc. Though the fair world was not as crazy for paperwork as the grim world, she was already learning that it was unusual for someone to be given as important a task as building bridges for the throne of Cretanis without having a lengthy paper trail pointing to his family and education. She couldn't even find out where Dr. Desmond MaqqRee had received his degree.

Doc arranged for the painting of conjurer's circles throughout the four stories that served him as headquarters. By the time he was done, every room was decorated with four or five of the things, none quite touching another, arranged to occupy the maximum possible floor space. Harris spent days carefully stepping between freshly painted lines and symbols, then helped lay concealing rugs over the circles, brown wrapping paper over the ones in the hangar.

"Your cleanup bill is going to be amazing," he told Doc. "Even if they don't attack."

"Yes. But in the likely event Duncan uses another of

his rockets to launch a conjurer's circle into our mist, this should spoil some of his plans." Doc sighed and rubbed his eyes. "Assuming, that is, that I find enough time to study, correct, and activate every one of these damned things."

"There's no need to curse, Doc."

A false gas-line scare engineered by Doc allowed him to evacuate the ten floors beneath his. The Sidhe Foundation provided the inconvenienced businesses with temporary accommodations in an unfinished skyscraper. Meanwhile, Lieutenant Galt Athelstane and a unit of his Novimagos Guard took possession of the topmost of the abandoned floors, the same floor from which the Changeling's men had fired their rocket many days before.

Caster accepted Doc's thanks and the offer of a boat trip back to Cretanis—accompanied by Foundation bodyguards. "I would be delighted to help you at any time," he said. "But next time, let's keep it to something I can solve over the talk-box, shall we?"

At the end of the third day, Doc announced, "We move to step two."

The room cost four pennies a day and was almost worth it. The floor sagged. So did the bed and exhausted-looking chair. Even the radiator was bowed in the middle. Fergus Bootblack, sitting on the bed, looked at the bottle of potato liquor in his hand and decided that it was the only thing with straight lines in the entire room. He took another drink. It even burned a straight line down his throat.

"I was surprised to learn—"

Fergus jerked in surprise, banging his head on the wall behind. He almost dropped the bottle.

Doc stood in front of him. Harris Greene closed the door to the hall and leaned back against it.

Doc waited for Fergus to regain his composure. He started over. "I was surprised to learn that you were living in a place like this."

Fergus stared at his visitors. They had to be here to shoot him, finally.

He said, "Can't afford anything better. No one will hire me because you fired me." He offered the bottle to Doc.

Doc shook his head. He sat in the chair—and sat farther down than he apparently expected to; his rear nearly met the floorboards. "No one will hire Fergus Bootblack, no. You could have left and changed your name. You didn't."

"I'm used to my name."

"And it seems to me that Blackletter would want you. You're good at what you do and have served him satisfactorily in the past. He'd pay you enough to live better than this."

Fergus carefully capped the bottle and set it aside. It wouldn't do to have something bad happen to it when he was shot. That would be unfair to a decent bottle of liquor. "His men offered."

"And you refused. Checked in here under your true name. A stupid thing to do if you've recently disappointed someone like Duncan Blackletter. Why did you do it?"

He mumbled something inaudible.

"Why, Fergus?"

"Because I'm sorry." Fergus covered his eyes. That way the sudden tears wouldn't show. His drunkenness and weakness revolted him. "I'm *sorry*. Enough? Will you go now? Or at least shoot me?"

"I could do that. Or I could give you a chance to make it up to me."

Fergus looked up without meaning to. Doc's expression was calm, serious. Compromised, Fergus just wiped his eyes. "I don't understand."

"I want you to do something for me, Fergus. You might die doing it. But if you don't—well, you'll never work for me again, but I'll give you a letter of recommendation from the Foundation. Worth gold in any profession. You'd be able to keep your name, maybe make it worth something again."

Fergus licked dry lips. "What do you want me to do?"

"Go to Blackletter's people. Tell them you've reconsidered. Tell them I denied you the last pay I owed you, so you broke into my floors to take what you were owed. And you saw some things you're sure they'll want to know about. Things that have driven up your asking price." He considered. "Of course, they'll want you to prove yourself. Harris had some ideas about that."

It was the quietest bell of the night, the time when the milkmen begin their rounds, and the three men sitting in the car fidgeted in the third hour of their surveillance.

Then one came alert and pointed. "Here he is."

Fergus looked up. Alastair Kornbock walked the final steps to the stoop of his building. The man's step was brisk, his face merry. The bottle in his hand was still half-full.

He was to the top of the stairs and reaching for the front door handle when Fergus called his name.

He turned and saw Fergus and the other man as they emerged from the parked car. The driver remained in his seat and started the vehicle.

Alastair smiled drunkenly. "Grace, Fergus. Who is your friend?" Then his expression changed. "Wait, you're—"

"Do it," said the tall man.

Fergus gulped and brought up a short-barrelled revolver, aiming the iron sights at the center of Alastair's stomach.

Alastair dropped his bottle and reached under his coat. He had his pistol in his hand before the bottle shattered.

Fergus squeezed the trigger. The gun kicked. Alastair staggered back, slamming into the doorway, breaking glass. Redness appeared over his heart. He slid down to sit against the door. His expression was shocked, pleading.

Fergus fired at Alastair's heart. More redness erupted from the downed man's stomach.

Alastair slumped to the side and his eyes closed.

"Not bad," the tall man told Fergus. He took the gun out of Fergus' hand. "Let's go."

Fergus stood there and shook. Idiot. He'd gotten the order wrong.

Clouds gathered before dawn and stayed to block the sun. Doc opened the hangar landing door to look up at them through his good eye.

Traces of green Gift-energy shot through them like lightning. He closed the landing door.

Alastair, beside him, asked, "Was I correct?"

"With your depressing regularity, yes. It's a summoning. I don't know what harm it can do, though. The building is shielded from lightning strikes."

Alastair brought out his pocket watch and consulted it. "I hope they don't wait too long. My stomach's a bit twitchy."

"It's simply sore. Wearing the vest just makes being shot akin to being hit with a sledgehammer. Plus the explosives you had packed on it—what did Harris call them? Squibs."

"Next time, you get to be shot."

By noon, two bells, the sky was almost as black as night. The clouds hung heavy with rain. But not one drop fell on Neckerdam.

Doc's windowless communications center was one floor up from the laboratories. A big room, it was nonetheless cramped with talk-boxes of every variety, shelves of partially disassembled electrical devices, tables, chairs, coils of copper wire. It smelled to Gaby of dust and ozone.

Gaby and Alastair sat side by side at the main table. She stared into her talk-box while he indifferently watched a panel of unlit lightbulbs.

"It would've been nice to have a few more days," he said.

"Why?"

"We'd have to keep the deception up. Announce my

death in the notices. I want to know who'd show up for my funeral."

"Oh, you'd just want to pop out of your casket and scare everyone. How's your chest?"

"Not bad. And I think I'm trimmer for hauling that monster of a vest around all those hours."

The talk-box beeped, signal of an incoming call. Gaby frowned; the pitch of the beep said that it had not come through the Monarch Building switchboard, but was a direct call to one of the Foundation's private numbers. She switched over to it.

A woman she vaguely recognized—middle-aged, rather faded-looking, friendly. "Goodlady Donohue?"

"Yes?"

"Grace. It's Essyllt Tathlumwright."

"Oh, yes. From the Beldon Hall of Records." Gaby looked aside at Alastair. She wished he weren't here to take this call, but she was on duty; she shouldn't leave to take it on another talk-box. "What can I do for you?"

"Quite the reverse. I found the information you were looking for. All very public, just not where I expected it."

"Wonderful." Gaby dug out her notebook, ignored Alastair's puzzled glance. "Please, go ahead."

"Desmond MaqqRee, born One Sixteen M.X.R. Father unknown, mother Rowena Redcliff. Wed Dierdriu Legarra One Forty-Five M.X.R. They had a—"

"Father *unknown*?" Gaby tensed. She'd half-expected that answer but had hoped to be wrong.

"Well . . . technically, yes. Practically speaking, no."

"What does that mean?"

"I did a little reading on Rowena Redcliff. She was the mistress of Prince Correus, Queen Maeve's husband and consort. And 'MaqqRee' is a dialectal variant of High Cretanis; it means 'son of the king.' I think Goodsir MaqqRee's paternity is probably well established . . . in the court of Cretanis, at any rate."

"You mean he's the son of this Correus." She relaxed.

"Yes. As far as anyone can tell, Goodlady Redcliff remained true to the prince until her death. But it's not uncommon to cut down on the numbers of eligible claimants to a throne by not recognizing the issue of affairs.

"Where was I? Oh, yes, education. Took his doctorate in engineering in One Thirty-Eight M.X.R." She looked apologetic. "That's all I have for now. But it gives us a place to start."

Gaby lay her pencil down. "It certainly does. I really appreciate it, uh, Goodlady Tathlumwright."

"Essyllt."

"Gaby. Thanks a lot. I'm kind of in the middle of things right now, but I'll call back soon."

The older woman smiled and faded from the screen.

Gaby turned and winced when she saw Alastair's disapproving expression.

"Checking up on Doc?"

"Well . . . Yes. I've been trying to figure out this whole Doc-Duncan thing. I'd been wondering around if Doc were maybe Duncan's son." She saw Alastair's guarded look and felt a little satisfaction. "You wondered about that, too, didn't you?"

"Once or twice."

"I mean, it would help explain why their paths seemed to keep crossing. Why Doc claims some sort of personal responsibility for Duncan. But if Doc's father was the King of Cretanis—"

"Prince Consort. Yes, that probably rules your theory out. But not necessarily. We'd have to look into Goodlady Redcliff's history."

"Did you know any of what she was telling me?"

"No, Doc's always been close-mouthed about this sort of thing. I knew that he didn't get along with Maeve the Tenth, but not why. This would explain it, if she considered him a pretender to the throne, a threat to her children. His half-brothers and half-sisters, that is." Alastair shut up as a green bulb lit on the console. He glanced at the handwritten tag beneath it. "Garage. King's Road entrance."

Gaby physically dialed her talk-box to the viewer that watched the garage. The screen remained full of static. "That's odd." She dialed it a notch further. A ceiling-corner view of the garage swam into focus.

A new panel truck was parked in the mechanic's bay. Men poured out of it—fairworlders, plus a couple of men large enough to be grimworlders. Most carried grim world assault rifles and bags of gear; the fairworlders all wore gloves. Fergus Bootblack, not armed, was the last man out and immediately moved over to the elevator door.

Gaby dialed up to the hangar, where Doc had said he and Alastair would be for a chime or two. The rotorkite swam into view. "Doc."

He wasn't visible, but she heard his voice: "I'm here, Gaby."

"They've arrived. In the garage. I count fourteen of them. Fergus is with them. They seem to have screwed up the old camera, I mean viewer, but they missed the new one you put in."

"I'm coming down. Alert the others."

She dialed the room up eighty-nine and informed Lieutenant Athelstane.

Then Harris, in the laboratory. She felt a stab of worry as she repeated her message to him, and added, "Don't you *dare* get hurt."

"I promise."

"I mean it. I love you."

"I love you." He forced a smile for her.

She switched off and returned the view to the garage. The men were clustered around the elevator.

Alastair said, "If Fergus is as good as he always thought he was, getting around the blocks on the elevator should pose no—ah." On a different board, another green light, near the top of a long column of them, blinked off; the one beneath it immediately blinked on. The glow descended, mirroring the progress of the elevator. "There it goes."

"Alastair, why do you carry an autogun?" She switched

to the view of the elevator interior. It showed nothing but empty car, floors gliding by outside the cage.

"To shoot people."

"I mean, doesn't that get in the way of the Hippocratic Oath? Or whatever you have on the fair world?" She began switching back and forth between garage and elevator views.

"You mean the Oath of Diancecht? Not technically." He shrugged. "I can't intentionally harm my patients. But the sort of men I point the gun at can't even *be* my patients until I shoot them. Not so?"

"Alastair, you're weird."

The elevator glided to a stop in the garage. The men waited as Fergus entered. Gaby watched as Fergus reached up for the elevator viewer. After a moment, that view winked out. She returned to the garage view and saw the men board the elevator car.

Gaby switched the set over to the laboratory view and took another look at Harris. "I want to listen," she told Alastair. "I have to go in."

"Gods' luck to you. I'm going to join Doc in the stairwell." He rose.

She closed her eyes and opened them almost immediately. Gabrielle's face stared solemnly back at her from the mirror.

She opened an eye beyond it and looked down on the hallway outside the laboratories. She saw the elevator rise into view of her camera and stop. The men inside drew open the cage and spilled out. Their faces were now covered in gear that gave them an insectile look.

Gaby hissed and opened another eye. The laboratory swam into view. Harris was there. "Harris, they're here—"

"Right. Masks on, everybody. Thanks, Gaby—"

"Harris, they've got gas masks, too."

"Shit!" He turned to look out of frame. "Welthy, forget the gas bomb. Everybody, get behind the barricades." Gaby saw him pull the bulky tan-colored mask and breathing unit into place.

It wrenched her to do it, but Gaby left him and opened another eye. Lieutenant Athelstane was already looking at her. "They're there," she told him.

She didn't wait for a reply. She knew his job as well as her own; he was to lead his men in a charge up the stairs to hit the laboratory intruders from behind while Doc led the other pincer above.

She reopened the laboratory eye. Or, rather, she tried to; but it wouldn't open. And the eye felt strange—not absent, as a destroyed talk-box would feel, but as though it were resisting her.

The men with Fergus followed him out of the elevator.

"Main laboratory," Fergus said. His voice wasn't muffled by a grimworld gas mask; they hadn't given him one. He nodded toward two of the doors. "At this hour, they'll probably be there. That's where I saw the new grimworlders and the devices Doc was building to shield them." He gestured toward another door, farther down the hall. "Valence laboratory. Doc might be there instead."

Costigan, the taller of the grimworlders, waved his men into place. They flanked the three doors, ready with the miraculous rifles that shot explosives like mortars and bullets like autoguns. Costigan pulled out one of the tracer devices and turned it on. "That's a big signal," he said. "They're in there, all right." He raised his hand, a 'stand by' signal for his men.

Fergus glanced at Dominguez, his guard. The dusky grimworlder's eyes narrowed. Dominguez said, "Almost over, little boy. Behave yourself and I don't get to kill you."

Costigan shouted "Go go go!" His men kicked the doors open, threw in the special grenades.

Fergus heard noises like big cans crumpling and saw smoke spreading through the laboratory. Costigan's men charged in, firing.

The resistance abruptly vanished and Gaby opened the eye into the laboratory.

She saw the smoke canisters fly into the lab and detonate. Harris and the others were already behind the reinforced barricades Doc had set up behind several of the tables. Smoke obscured Gaby's vision as men poured into the room, shooting as they came. She saw return fire erupt from behind the barricades.

The scene riveted her. She couldn't afford that. She opened another eye. The stairwell. Doc, Ish, and Noriko were there; incongruously, Ish was the one of the three carrying an autogun. "Doc, they're in the lab."

"We're on our way."

Gaby switched away from him. She flickered as fast as she could among all the viewers of Doc's system, channel-surfing. Smoke, rotorkite, two garage views, Athelstane's men racing up the stairs, elevator interior, ropes swinging by in the cloud-dark skies outside the Monarch Building—

She froze in sudden confusion. Something was very wrong.

Harris fired a long burst into the smoke. His Klapper autogun seized up. Alastair had warned him that the complex weapons were prone to do that. He cursed and yanked the bolt back. A deformed brass casing resisted him, then popped free of the chamber. He pulled the bolt the rest of the way back and released it, racking another cartridge into place, then raised the gun and fired again, blindly. No friends were set up ahead of him— he could only hit enemies.

Gunfire hit the front of his table. He crouched down and waited for the lethal rain to end.

The fear was there again, but it didn't cripple or slow him. It no longer embarrassed him.

He heard a sudden whirring and felt the air pressure change. Welthy had activated the air-blowers from her position.

There was a sudden crackle of electricity. Harris faintly heard something—bootheels, he thought—banging the wood floor. He smiled. One of the intruders had to have charged up to a table in the first row and touched it . . . and been felled by the electrical current coursing through it. The outermost of the traps Doc had arranged for the lab.

Gaby flicked back to the last of the confusing views. Ropes dangling outside one of the ledge cameras. The south—she could tell by the buildings in the distance. The same facing as the laboratory.

She switched to the lab view. It was all smoke and gunfire. She shouted Harris' name but there was no answer.

Stairwell views. Nobody was visible in the east; Athelstane's force must be beyond the viewer, perhaps already to the doors leading into the hallway. But in the west view she saw Ixyail and then Alastair flit by and out of frame. "Alastair!"

She waited a long, breathless moment, then Alastair came back into view. "Gaby, there's no time—"

"Tell Doc there are ropes outside the building. From above. Something's going on out there."

Alastair turned. Doc came back into view. "I hear you," he said. "Tell Athelstane he's on his own. We're going back up to the hangar. We'll go up on the roof to have a look."

She switched back to the east stairwell—or tried to. The eye there stubbornly resisted her. Why?

Back to the elevator interior, then the main garage view. She'd seen Fergus disable both cameras. Now they worked again. Why?

Either they fixed themselves, not likely, or Duncan had arranged for them to come back on. Meaning that he needed them.

He had to be using them. Maybe just the way Gaby was. Exposed to the grim world's uses of communications gear and surveillance equipment, Duncan must have figured out how to do artificially what she did naturally. That probably accounted for the viewers she couldn't peer through; he had to be using them just then.

So it was up to her to stop him.

Time to die.

Fergus lashed out with his elbow and took Dominguez in the throat, under the mask.

Dominguez fell back against the wall. Fergus wrenched the magical rifle out of his hands and shot him with it, a short burst to the face, where his grimworld armor would not protect him. The rifle kicked less than an autogun.

Costigan and the others looked at him in slow-motion surprise.

Fergus held the trigger down and traversed the weapon left to right, firing low, at thighs and knees. Costigan shrieked and fell backwards, his legs ruined. On the floor, he kept yelling as he bled. Another man joined him. Four men left.

Barrels swung in Fergus' direction, so slow, so slow. He traversed the weapon right to left and continued firing. Two more collapsed. Two got behind cover, one behind the stairwell door, one leaping to take cover behind a hallway bench.

The man at the stairway leaned into view and brought his rifle up. Fergus aimed the roaring weapon at him. Bullets took the man in the chest, where the armor protected him, but sheer impact was enough; he fell back anyway.

The magical rifle ran dry. Fergus dropped it. It took forever to fall.

The man behind the bench brought his own weapon up. Fergus spread his arms wide as if to embrace him, as if to welcome the bullets.

Something dark appeared on the gunman's forehead and his head jerked back. His rifle fired a short burst into the ceiling. He fell forward onto the bench.

Someone behind Fergus was shouting, "Hold your fire,

it's Fergus." Lieutenant Athelstane, an automatic pistol in hand, moved past Fergus, not glancing at him. He waved men past. They charged forward to flank the lab doors just as Costigan's men had done. "Fergus, are you hit?"

Fergus only understood that his name had been spoken. That no more bullets were coming.

He looked down at himself. There was no blood. He felt a vague sense of disappointment.

He fainted, following his rifle to the floor.

Joseph batted the table. It took no more effort than swatting a fly. More than a manweight of hardwood and lab equipment flew out of his way, leaving nothing between him and the grimworld mercenary.

The man fired at him with another of those hurtful rifles. Joseph felt the bullets tear into him. Enough damage and he knew that he might die.

But they had done nowhere near enough.

He grabbed the barrel and yanked. The man, trying hard to hold on, came off his feet, then fell to his knees as the weapon was wrenched from his grip.

The air was starting to clear. He liked that. Seeing the enemy was much better than groping around blindly for him. He tossed the gun aside.

Joseph picked the man up around the torso. He squeezed—carefully, carefully. The man's air emerged in a helpless gasp. When Joseph felt the ribs begin to give, he let go. The man hit the lab floor and lay still.

Beyond, Joseph saw Novimagos guardsmen appear in the doorway. They pointed rifles and autoguns at the intruders. Lieutenant Athelstane shouted, "Surrender or we open fire!"

The three men not already felled by bullets, electrical traps, or Joseph's bear hugs looked back at the guns aimed their way. They carefully set their assault rifles aside and raised their hands.

Gaby opened the eye into the hangar.

There was nothing going on there. She prepared to switch views again.

But she saw the ceiling shudder and a hole open in it. A trail of fire stretched to the floor, leaving a silvery missile driven into the concrete.

Black paint issued from the missile, spraying out in a sloppy circle.

Gaby smiled. The missile had landed on the brown paper covering one of the conjurer's circles. Doc had explained their purpose to her and the others: the circles waited to be struck with energies unique to displacement, summoning. Such power would fuel their counter-devisements, which would exert power over whatever appeared within them, damaging the sturdy, twisting the living. Meaning that anything that appeared within them would be racked with pain, helpless and useless.

The paint circle sprayed by the missile overlapped two of Doc's defensive conjurer's circles. Gaby watched as the missile's second tier of sprayers laid down the crude symbols just within the ring.

There was a crackle of energy and men appeared— four fair world gunmen and Adonis. They stood in a circle, facing out, just as the attackers disguised as musicians had done.

The men brought their guns up. Then, as one, they doubled over as pain from Doc's defensive devisement hit them. Most of them were throwing up by the time they hit the floor.

Adonis lost height and gained girth as if it were a putty man squashed by a child. Its face registered surprise. Then it stretched up to its accustomed height, shook itself, and looked impassively at the fallen men.

One of them, his face twisted with pain, tried to talk to him, words that were so low Gaby couldn't hear them.

Adonis looked around, scanning the hangar. It focused a moment on the talk-box, looking straight at Gaby, then turned away. It spotted what it wanted on the wall near the rotorkite and headed that way.

A switch on the wall. Adonis threw it, and in the top of the picture frame Gaby saw the hangar roof shudder as the overhead door began to lift.

Uncoiling ropes snaked down in to the hangar, and dark-armored men rappelled down beside the rotorkite.

Gaby grimaced. If men just came physically through the roof hatch, the conjurer's circles would do no good.

She went looking for Doc.

The voice buzzed through the speaker in Duncan's ear. "Sir? This is Greencoat." The man sounded uncertain; he'd been uncomfortable with the new grimworld equipment.

"I'm here."

"The missile team isn't answering because they're all sick. But Adonis did find the switch. We are in and we have the hangar."

"Sick. Some trick of Doc's." Duncan hissed his frustration. "Very well. The laboratory team has stopped answering. We have to assume they've been beaten. Don't send any men down the building exterior; we need to concentrate our forces. Send the entire force in through the hangar and kill everyone."

"Yes, sir."

Duncan leaned back, irritably drumming his fingers on the arms of his chair. The signal still showed a large number of grimworlders alive on one of Doc's floors. Whoever these men were, they had managed to break the first wave of Duncan's attack.

But only the first. He had more in store for them. The thought made him smile.

Gaby first tried the topmost viewer in the west stairwell, only a floor or two below the hangar—and there Doc was, Ixyail beside him, racing up the stairs, in sight only for a moment.

That was only a viewer; Gaby couldn't talk through it, couldn't warn him.

Wait. Maybe she could.

She lashed out at the viewer in anger.

Alastair flinched as the viewer above his head burst and rained sparks down on him. "Gods!"

Above, at the landing, Doc skidded to a stop and looked back. Ixyail and Noriko barely slowed in time to keep from running into him. Doc said, "I wonder what it did to make her mad at it."

But with the four of them stopped, their clattering footsteps no longer obscured the noises from above—cries of orders over the cries of pain and sound of men being sick.

There were men up there, and they were active, not brought low by Doc's conjurer's circles.

Gaby reopened the eye into the laboratory. Athelstane's men were shackling captured gunmen; most of the attackers, though badly hurt, appeared to have survived, saved by their grimworld armor. Harris was in view, talking rapidly with Athelstane. Gaby heaved a sigh of relief. "Athelstane."

The lieutenant and Harris turned to look at her.

"There's a problem in the hangar. Doc's going there. I think you and your men should join him."

She heard one of the guards, a woman, say, "Gods, not more stairs."

Athelstane shot a dirty look at the woman. "Quiet, you. Very well, goodlady, we're on our way." He waved a hand at his guards and trotted out of frame.

Harris moved to follow.

"Harris, don't!"

"Gaby, if there are problems—"

"Listen . . . " He'd survived one encounter already. There had to be some way she could convince him to stay behind now, not to charge into another dangerous situation. The answer came to her in a burst of enlightenment. "I think Duncan's in the talk-boxes. Using them to track our movements. I want you to make like Mister Actor Guy. Stay in front of this one and talk to Doc and everybody else as if they're still in the room with you. It might screw him up."

Harris looked after Athelstane and grimaced. "Dammit. All right. But wait a second. Let's see if we can do to him what he's doing to us." He ran out of frame.

He was back in a moment with a radio headset. "This was on one of the grimworlders. Check it out." He put it on, fiddled with it. "Testing, one, two, three . . . "

Gaby switched away from the laboratory talk-box and listened. Then she heard Harris again, two voices; one was crisp and clear, the other distant and fuzzy. She went looking for the fainter signal.

The first of the soldiers descending the stairs rounded the turn, coming into view on the landing. Alastair and Ixyail opened up with their autoguns. The attack caught the first two men by surprise. They fell; those behind brought up their guns to fire. Alastair and Ish ducked behind the cover of the banister and backed down the stairs.

"This will not work," Doc shouted over the gunfire. "We can't hold here long against those weapons. And if they have any sense, they're covering the other stairways and elevators."

"We could perhaps lure some of them ahead of the others," Noriko shouted back. "Take their weapons and use them against the rest. When the enemy is stronger, you must use his strength against him."

Doc nodded. "That's partly correct." He clapped Alastair on the back. "Fighting retreat," he told the healer.

Alastair nodded without looking back. Doc gestured for Noriko to follow him. Together, they trotted down three stories, past a set of armored doors that normally kept people from lower floors from reaching Doc's floors. Then Doc sat cross-legged in the center of the landing. Above, the gunfire went on and on.

Doc used his bronze penknife to prick his wrist. He drew a conjurer's circle around him in his own blood, took a moment to assure himself that it was unbroken. "I may be gone for a few beats," he told Noriko. "If I can't defend myself—"

"Don't worry," she assured him.

He closed his eyes and sank within himself.

And spoke. To a god. To the worst of them, the war-bringer, the conqueror.

"Hear me," he pleaded. "Weapons beg to be wielded. Grant me knowledge of them. Power over them. I will use them, and entertain you with noise and pain and blood."

It was a loathsome bargain. But he sent it out into the void like an outstretched hand, and when mad laughter began bubbling up within him he knew that it had been accepted.

The mirror remained a reflection, but suddenly Harris' second voice was much clearer: "—two, three. Test-ing—"

She switched back to the lab for a brief moment. "Got it." Then she returned to the new eye she'd found.

She extended her perceptions. She could feel other eyes not far away, a direction she'd never felt before.

She opened one of them and heard: "— heavy resis-tance in both stairwells, and they have the elevators locked off. But it should not take more than part of a chime."

Duncan's voice: "Very well."

But she couldn't see anything; this was a sound-only place.

A moment later, she found an eye that provided sight as well as sound. It looked out on a huge room. It was a vast metal framework crowded with what looked like rigid, upright bags attached to metal cross-braces. It all looked like steel, a shocking amount of bare steel for the fair world.

She opened another eye—and did not have enough time to see what lay beyond. She was suddenly swept away in a tidal wave of words and thoughts: dry, emotionless knowledge that tore through her with such force that it left her no strength to think.

She yelled in sudden fright, unable for the moment even to remember her name or purpose, and tried to extend herself around the vastness that carried her along.

Names, hundreds of names, grimworld dates and grimworld money transactions, personal details, embarrassing facts that could twist men to the will of another, crimes of the past, evaluations of the psyche, technical specifications, techniques of industry, construction, history of the fair world, history of the grim world, comparisons and contrasts, projected trends, structure of the stock market, mountains of knowledge on physics and chemistry, biology and geology— She couldn't see anything; the knowledge was without form. Its cold impersonality numbed her. Its immensity crushed her. She gave one final cry and winked out of existence, conquered by the force she had encountered.

The mind-wisp that was Doc floated up to the first of the attackers in the stairwell. The man looked through him, could not see him.

Doc looked at the man, seeing not a human being but a machine made of meat and blood, carrying more machines and devices designed to make him more powerful, more lethal.

With just a glance, he understood all there was to know about the man's long gun, the M16, with its monstrous rate of fire and grenade launcher. More grenades in the man's belt pouch, tear gas and smoke. Ammunition. Body armor. Gas mask hanging unused in its case. Satchel charge in the backpack.

And they all cried to him, begging to be used.

He smiled benignly at them and began granting wishes.

He reached out to the smoke and tear-gas devices, imparting a bit of his strength to them. Then he moved on to the next man up the stairs and granted his blessing again. A third man, more wishes granted—

Behind him, there was a sharp bang as the devices in the first man's belt went off, flooding him and his immediate surroundings with black smoke and stinging fog. Doc laughed and flew on, touching another half-dozen men before he reached the top of the stairs.

Adonis he left alone. Adonis carried nothing that called to him, no weapon that begged for his attention.

More grenades went off behind him. Men cried out. Doc swept across the hangar, touching the men writhing on the floor; he reached the men standing at the elevators and granted his loving touch to their grenades. Then he floated on to the far stairwell, smiling at the music made by the men behind as their weapons erupted in smoke and pain.

More men on those far stairs, firing down at someone else.

It was getting harder to grant the wishes of the implements of war. Each one he touched took a little out of him. He could barely see his surroundings and knew there was not much more of him to give. Still he swept down the stairs, speaking approving words to the tools of destruction, giving them the power to act. Behind, there were more explosions and cries.

He travelled down a long stretch in which no weapons clamored for his attention. Then he met a new group of men.

He recognized the first of them. Athelstane of the Novimagos Guard. The lieutenant's weapons, too, begged for his attention, but Doc looked in vain for grenades. It was hard to think, so hard—and then his vision swam and he could see no more.

"Doc, Gaby, is there any word on those additional troops?" Harris felt like an idiot, talking to an unoccupied corner of the room. Not that he hadn't done it before, dozens of time, in college stage productions and rehearsals—but Ladislas and Welthy, guarding the door, kept smirking at him.

Harris reached into his coat pocket and pulled out the device there. Doc's device, the new one. Until this morning he'd been carrying a device that masked his signal, the telltale energies that marked him as a grimworlder. This recent replacement did just the opposite: magnified those signals so that anyone with a tracer would read him not as a single grimworlder but as a whole pack of them.

He left it on. Until Doc pronounced the building clear of enemies, Harris got to be the decoy for Duncan Blackletter.

An interesting role. He wondered if he'd get to see the old man again. He wondered what he'd do to the sick son of a bitch.

Then Ladislas' expression changed to one of surprise. Harris followed the man's gaze.

There, on the talk-box, Duncan Blackletter smiled benignly out at him.

'Harris set the device down. "I don't have time for you, Duncan."

"Nor I for you. But I'm delighted to find you are all together." Duncan turned to the clay man. "Joseph, I really have to insist that you kill Doc and Goodsir Greene here, and any other grimworlders you find. Except Goodlady Donohue. I do need to study her before I have you kill her, too. Oh, yes, and smash everyone who tries to stop you."

Joseph flexed his fingers. "I will smash you instead."

"Oh, I forgot. By your making, by your name, I command you to remember your master!"

Joseph shouted and staggered back. Letters of the old script of Cretanis appeared on his forehead. Smoke rose from him as the letters seared themselves into his flesh.

Harris scrambled across bodies and grabbed up his

autogun. He fired at Duncan's face, taking the talk-box to pieces with a stream of lead.

He looked at Joseph.

The clay man was upright again. The letters were charred black on his forehead. He looked stricken. He turned to Harris, his eyes full of dismay.

"Oh, Harris," he said. "I am so very sorry."

He advanced, his hands outstretched.

CHAPTER TWENTY-FIVE

Harris backed away from Joseph. "Please don't do this."

"I have no choice." Joseph's voice was full of pain. "Kill me, Harris, *please*. Because I have to kill you."

Harris bumped up against a table and was suddenly halted. He scrambled sideways to elude Joseph's grab. He brought up the barrel of his autogun but couldn't bring himself to fire.

He heard a familiar jackhammer roar and the flesh of Joseph's side erupted with craters.

Joseph nodded and turned toward his attacker. "Yes, Welthy. Do that again. Only much, much more." His face twisted with sadness. "Forgive me. I have to smash you now." He grabbed the corner of a lab table and hefted it as easily as if it were a cardboard box; a fortune in scientific equipment slid off to crash on the floor.

He spun the table through the air. Welthy tried to jump aside, but the corner of the tabletop caught her in the gut. It smashed her into the wall behind. A moment's agony crossed her features and she fell like a broken thing.

"Ladislas, get out of here!" Harris shouted. "Don't attack him! Joseph, I'm going to run now."

"Then I will go to Gaby and take her. I have to, and I know where she is. Stay instead and kill me."

Harris aimed and fired. He struggled to keep the gun

in line as he poured ammunition into the body of his friend.

Joseph staggered. His chest deformed with the damage he took. He kept coming.

Harris heard the higher-pitched crack of a pistol shot. A crater sprouted in Joseph's forehead. But the flesh there reformed instantly, the burned letters unchanged.

Joseph grabbed another table and flung it at Ladislas. The table took the man in the chest, hurling him back into the wall. Harris saw Ladislas' brief look of surprise give way to blankness.

Harris fired again. Joseph's shoulder flowed like wax under the impacts. Then Harris' autogun ran dry.

Joseph's face twisted in sympathy. "You did very well," he said.

Alastair and Ish jumped as the stairwell above them erupted in smoke and shouts. Suddenly there were continuous muffled explosions above them, but no gunfire being directed against them. They held their position, peering into the thickening cloud above, then began to retreat as it started to flow down the stairs toward them.

They descended two stories and reached Doc's conjurer's circle. Doc sat slumped, and Noriko, half-frantic, slapped his cheeks, pried an eye open to peer at it. "He is unconscious," she told Alastair. "Help him."

He joined her. "You help Ish." Noriko rose, wordless, and left him.

Alastair gave Doc a quick look. He didn't need to; he knew the problem from many times before. Devisement-induced exhaustion and collapse. He reached in his pocket for the small kit of medical essentials he carried when his bag was inconvenient.

Noriko saw Adonis emerge from the wall of smoke above. The creature descended toward them, carefully navigating each step with absurd delicacy dictated by its great size and awkward build.

Ixyail swore loudly in Castilian, words Noriko didn't understand, and opened fire with the Klapper. Her long, continuous burst tore through Adonis, meeting little resistance, tearing away bloody hunks of red-black meat. Adonis, not inconvenienced, kept coming.

Noriko drew her blade and sailed up past Ish. She stopped just short of Adonis and, lightning-fast, slashed at the arm it reached toward her. A section of cloth and meat fell away and hit the stairs with a disgusting plop.

No, not meat. In her peripheral vision, Noriko saw the stuff separate into a hundred distinct worms that crawled off in different directions.

Adonis' counterstrike was slow, clumsy, inviting her to step in and gut him. She stepped in.

It was a feint. Its off-hand slashed at her face. Warned by Harris' experience with the creature, she went under the blow, stepped past Adonis so close that she brushed against its side, and spun against its unprotected back.

Her blade took Adonis in the side of the neck. It bit through flesh the consistency of rotted grapes, snapped something harder within, and emerged from the far side.

Adonis clutched its head . . . and lifted it clear of its body. It collapsed in a puddle of clothes and squirming sludge.

Noriko stepped daintily back and watched as the mess that had been Adonis spread across the stairs. Soon there was nothing but three manweights of worms crawling away from empty clothes and oversized human bones.

Ish stared up at her. "Thank you," she said. "Next time I will know always to bring a sword to a gunfight."

Down at the landing, Doc shook off Alastair's restraining hand and got unsteadily to his feet. Ish turned to look. "Are you well? What now?"

Doc leaned against the wall. "We cover these stairs and wait for Athelstane's men to get to us with gas masks." His voice was weary; it looked as though he were having trouble focusing. "Then I want to see where those men came from."

❊   ❊   ❊

Gunfire woke Fergus. He looked around.

Blackletter's gunmen lay in the corridor, dead or unconscious. The gunfire came from the laboratory. Fergus rose
and looked in through the laboratory door.

Joseph, the clay man, looked liked a pincushion of the
gods, so mottled was his skin with the craters and divots of gunfire. No longer could he be mistaken for a man
even at this range. He chased Harris around the ruined
lab, inconsiderately stepping on bound men as his path
took him across them.

He carried a four-foot club, the leg of a lab table. He
swung it, a fast, brutal attack. Harris struck the table leg
with his hand, snapping it in the middle, sending half
its length spinning across the room, but he continued
to back away from his attacker.

Fergus forced his mind into some sort of working order.
The old man had said Joseph was still his. This proved
it. And with the evidence before him, Fergus doubted
that any amount of gunfire would be enough to stop
Joseph.

He turned to one of the grimworlders he'd killed and
opened the man's backpack. Inside were several of the
items and weapons he'd seen during his long night of
questioning. And there was the one he wanted, the bomb-
in-a-bag they called a satchel charge.

He pulled out the haversack full of explosives and drew
the man's knife from its sheath. His fingertips tingled.
It had to be made of steel. Stupid grimworlders.

He flipped open the sack and stared at the loops of
cord fastened to its side. His mind was suddenly a blank.
All night he'd surreptitiously watched as Costigan and
Dominguez instructed Blackletter's men on the use of
this equipment, and now he couldn't remember what they
did to light the fuse.

Joseph tried to keep himself from thinking as he backed
Harris up into one of the heavy metal barricades. If he

thought, he might come up with tactics to use against his enemy. He didn't want to do that. He wanted to be stupid. To give Harris whatever advantage he could. Harris rolled back over the barricade and came up to his feet before Joseph could take advantage of his moment of awkwardness.

But Joseph kicked the barricade, throwing it and Harris to the floor with brutal force. He wished he hadn't thought of doing that.

He felt a sting in his back. He turned.

Fergus Bootblack stood there. His hands were empty. So was his face; there was no emotion there to prick at Joseph's guilt, to increase his sorrow.

"I have to smash you now, Fergus."

The mechanic just shrugged.

Joseph swatted him. He felt Fergus' upper arm break under the blow. The mechanic flew sideways, landing beside the door to the hall.

Joseph turned again. He pulled the metal barricade off Harris. The man's eyes were open but unfocused. Joseph picked him up and held him nearly at arm's length, as if the man were a steering wheel.

Joseph could feel the knife still protruding from his back. It felt heavier than it should. Something hung from it. No matter. "Harris," he said. "Wake up. I have to kill you now."

Harris came awake with the sickening realization that these would be his last moments on Earth.

Joseph held him almost gently. "I am going to break your neck," the giant said. "That way it will be over fast."

Harris kicked him in the head. Joseph's features deformed and then stretched back to normal.

Harris had the sudden impression of fire blooming behind Joseph. Then he was traveling backwards, the giant still clutching him. He saw clouds overhead and knew that he was falling.

He felt a sudden blow and the world spun away from him.

❦   ❦   ❦

Duncan hissed in sudden vexation. Now his hangar unit was no longer answering him—unless cursing and moaning counted.

He'd failed. In part, at least; he'd wasted men. But it would still be a success if Joseph were able to kill Harris Greene, Gaby Donohue and the other grimworlders present.

He switched the talk-box dial. Captain Walbert's lean, bearded face came into view. "Captain!"

"Sir?"

"We're done. Take us away."

"Yes, sir."

Duncan saw relief in the captain's face. He switched off and frowned. The captain just did not show the proper enthusiasm. He'd actually had the nerve to protest hovering here and inviting retaliation from the Monarch Building. Of course it was dangerous—the *Storm Cloud* was a flying bomb. So was any hydrogen-filled liftship. But this job required nerve and toughness, which Walbert did not appear to possess. He'd have to be replaced.

Doc loosed the cables holding the rotorkite rotors in place while Noriko climbed into the cockpit. Ish gathered the rappelling ropes and drew them out of the way, but they were already beginning to withdraw from the hangar. Rain fell on them all through the open roof door.

Overhead was a vast gray expanse hovering below the cloud layer. It was a liftship—a huge vessel, easily two hundred paces from end to end, with the name *Storm Cloud* painted along its side. The ship slowly drifted eastward; in a few moments it would be clear enough for the rotorkite to lift off. Not far above the liftship was the solid mass of clouds Doc had studied earlier.

Doc understood the clouds now. They were not an attack; they'd been a screen for the liftship's approach. He chided himself; he'd been prepared for another airplane fly-by and rocket launch, but not for a liftship invasion.

He popped open one of the rotorkite's gullwing doors and climbed in, then dogged his door shut. Noriko spun up the rotors. Doc ignored the noise as Ish pounded on his door from outside.

"Checklist?" Noriko asked.

"No. Just take her up."

Harris became aware of a dull roar as his hearing and consciousness returned. His chest felt constricted. He opened his eyes.

He dangled in the wind, the collar of his jeans jacket in Joseph's grip. The giant, with his other hand, held onto the lowest wingtip of one of the ledge gargoyles.

There was a crater in Joseph's back a foot deep and three feet in diameter. Opaque gray fluid poured out of it, something like clay barely diluted with water. The giant's eyes were dull, nearly unseeing.

Far above him was the skyscraper-sized zeppelin-liftship.

Harris looked down. There was nothing between his feet and the sidewalk but a thousand feet of air.

"Harris."

"Yes, Joseph." He reached up and tried to get a grip on the clay man's arm. It was slick with the fluid from his back. Joseph shook him and easily broke his grasp.

"I'm going to die, Harris. When I do, I will fall, and you will fall, and you will die too. But I want you to understand that I do not do this myself. I cannot stop myself."

"I understand." Harris tried to reach up for the ledge with the statues. His arm was a yard too short. He touched the face of the wall and could find no purchase. "Are you sure you can't just tell Duncan to stuff himself? I'd really appreciate it."

"No. My limbs do not move in a direction that disobeys him. Can you forgive me? *Please*, Harris."

"Yes, Joseph. It's not your fault." He felt his throat tighten with grief for the pain Joseph was feeling.

"The explosion was propitious. It allows me to give you

a few extra moments of life without disobeying Duncan. And it means I will not be able to harm Gaby."

Harris heard a scrape from behind Joseph; he turned his head back to look.

A rope dangled behind Joseph, ten feet away. It brushed the statuary, stretching from the liftship above to somewhere below Harris. And it was moving, swaying toward him. "Just hold on as long as you can, Joseph."

The rope swayed a yard closer. Harris looked up and saw the liftship's propellers turning. The ship was moving, dragging the rope along with it.

Joseph began to droop. Harris saw that the damage to his back was worse than before—made deeper and rougher by water erosion, Joseph's "bleeding." Harris grimaced.

"I am losing strength, Harris."

"How do you want to be remembered?" The rope edged closer. It almost touched Joseph. Another yard and it would be within Harris' reach.

"It will do no good for me to tell you."

"Tell me anyway."

"I would like to be remembered for having hurt no one. But that would be a lie."

The rope slid to within inches of Harris' hand. Joseph finally saw it. He looked puzzled.

Harris stretched, grabbed it, and dragged it to his right hand. With all his strength, he kicked away from the building face. The move pulled him free of Joseph's grasp.

Harris swung out from the building, then back toward it, hitting the wall two full yards away from the giant. He managed to get his feet up and took the impact with his legs.

Joseph's face twisted into a faint smile. "No, I was wrong. It will please me to be remembered for having failed in my last duty."

He fell, leaving a stain of gray clay on the wall.

Harris watched him disappear. Something hard and bitter swelled in his throat, closing it.

He felt his feet lose contact with the wall; they were now half a foot away from the stone. He looked up.

The liftship was picking up speed, carrying its trailing ropes and Harris away from the Monarch Building.

Gaby woke up feeling tired but peaceful, as though the blast of knowledge through her had washed her clean.

She was in Gabrielle's room. She tried to slide out and back into her body, but couldn't.

That was surprising. It hadn't happened since she'd first put the two halves of herself together. She felt a tug of fear and opened the eye in the communications room.

She saw herself slumped in her chair, her head lolled back, mouth slightly opened. Her eyes moved rapidly under closed lids. She didn't look hurt.

She tried to switch to the eye into the laboratory, but it was gone.

Then memory returned of her unexpected swim in knowledge. She must have fallen into a veritable sea of information.

Data. Duncan must have brought a computer from the grim world. Hooked it into his communication grid here. She hadn't been prepared to handle that amount of information.

Information—something about information she'd recently received was nagging at her. Names, dates . . . then she had it.

Essyllt Tathlumwright had said that Doc was born in 116 M.X.R. Gaby translated numbers in her head. That would have been Scholars' Year 1303. More than a *hundred and thirty* years ago. Doc was older than even she had thought. She'd read accounts of purebloods who achieved incredible age.

That made him old enough—

She looked into her mirror, sought out a specific eye, and opened it. The face of Essyllt Tathlumwright appeared, looking startled. "Goodness," the older woman said. "I don't think I even had it switched on."

"You must have," Gaby said. "Pardon me for calling back so soon—"

"You've changed."

"What?"

"Your clothes. You've changed. It's very becoming."

Gaby looked down at Gabrielle's dress and smiled. "Thank you. There's something I forgot to ask before. Did Desmond MaqqRee and his wife have any children?"

"Oh, yes." Essyllt looked at a sheaf of notes on the table before her. "One, a son. Named—"

"Duncan?"

"That's right." Essyllt beamed approvingly. "Born One Thirty-Eight M.X.R. You've been doing your research, too."

"Yes." Gaby felt cold sickness crawl through her. She tried to keep it from showing. "I have to run, Essyllt."

"Until later, then. Grace." Essyllt faded away again.

What had it done to Doc to believe that he'd killed his own son twenty years ago? What would it do to him to have to kill him now?

Dangerous as Duncan was, she had to prevent that, for Doc's sake. Gaby frantically looked for another eye.

His arms trembled from exhaustion, but Harris kept climbing. The gaping doors in the bottom of the gondola were not much farther above.

He had seen no one peering through that hole at him. He looked down and saw the skyscrapers of Neckerdam moving sedately below. This time there was no vertigo to bother him. So far, so good.

The rotorkite approached the liftship from astern, rising above it. "We can't stand off and trade fire with it," Doc said. He thought about it for a bare second. "So drop me on top."

"You're insane," Noriko said. "Do you remember being so exhausted you could barely stand, less than a chime ago? You're drained."

"It wasn't as bad as the time in Cretanis. I promised less, it took less. And Duncan is tired, too. He had to have put everything he had into holding that cloud together for so long."

"But his men, his soldiers, aren't. They're fresh and have better guns than you. No."

Doc gave her a surprised look. "When did you become so contrary?"

She looked flustered, also unusual. "I'm simply not going to let you kill yourself so that you will think of me as a good, obedient associate."

"I won't kill myself," he said, keeping confidence in his voice. "Noriko, I *have* to deal with Duncan. No one else can; he's a Deviser. No one else has to. Get me to him. If we don't stop him now, he will be back."

He saw her expression of resignation. She kept the rotorkite on course and said nothing more.

Duncan heard the distant *thup-thup-thup* of a rotorkite. He switched to the cockpit view again.

Captain Walbert turned from the wheel to look at him. "Yes, sir."

"We have more trouble. Doc or some of his men have taken to the air."

"Yes, sir. I've already sent the men to the gun platform."

The liftship's gun opened up before Noriko anticipated it, when the rotorkite was still half a stad away. Doc winced as he heard and felt bullets rap against the fuselage. Immediately the pitch of the engines changed, climbed. Noriko veered, lost some altitude, then gained a little back. She began evasive maneuvers, making the aircraft a more difficult target.

She brought the rotorkite in from astern, so close beside the liftship's great vertical fin that Doc feared a sudden breeze would hurl them into it, so close to the liftship's skin that the man at the ship's tail lookout position ducked down into his niche as the rotorkite passed over.

She was so low, in fact, that the men on the armament platform, toward the bow, couldn't depress their guns far enough to hit her without endangering the liftship. Doc actually felt the rotorkite's landing gear hit the liftship's skin; the kite bounced a little higher and continued forward, just above the curve of the ship's skin, until they were halfway or more to the bow.

"Best do it now," Noriko said. "Hear the engine? We will not get another pass; I have to land."

Doc didn't dare open the gullwing door. He'd be fighting rotor wash and affecting the rotorkite's flight characteristics. He kicked the window out instead. He leaned out.

Five paces below was the skin of the liftship; the rotorkite's window, still in its frame, hit it and began bouncing down its curving slope. "A little closer, Noriko."

The rotorkite's talk-box popped. Gaby's voice: "Is anyone there?"

While Noriko slowly brought the rotorkite down, Doc leaned out further, drew out his clasp-knife, and pulled it open. He'd need to use it to anchor himself against falling, then cut his way through the skin. He pulled on a pair of gloves; liftship skeletons were made of steel, uncoated for reasons of weight, their crews wearing heavy uniforms and gloves as protection.

Noriko finally felt steady enough to thumb the button on the talk-box. "I'm here, Gaby. With Doc."

"Don't let him get anywhere near Duncan. Duncan's his son—"

Doc grimaced and leaped free. He hit the rubber-cloth surface of the liftship and bounced, rolling down the slope. On his second impact, he managed to drive the knife into the ship's skin. He slid further downslope, cutting a rent three paces long in the skin; then he got his free hand into the tear and stopped sliding.

Wash from the rotors pushed at him as the rotorkite banked away. Noriko must have begun the maneuver as soon as she understood Gaby's statement. But it was too late. He was within striking distance of Duncan at long last.

As Harris got his hands on the lip of the bomb bay, his strength failed him. He hung there, legs wrapped around the trailing rope, and waited for his energy to come back.

It didn't.

He cursed. He'd just have to do the job without it.

Then Darig MacDuncan, the Changeling, stepped into view above and kicked him full in the head.

Sudden, shocking pain in his temple—Harris' right hand slipped and he rotated a half-turn, gripping the lip of the bomb bay floor with only his left. He frantically grabbed the rope with his right.

Just in time. Darig, smiling, stepped on the fingers of his left hand. The pain cost him his grip.

The sudden adrenaline was what he needed. He hauled on the rope for all he was worth, popped up over the lip of the floor, and grabbed Darig's ankle. He yanked. The Changeling fell, scrambling frantically as his legs stretched out over more than a thousand feet of air.

Harris grabbed the Changeling's belt and hauled. The Changeling, teeth bared, grabbed the sturdy base of a winch and didn't budge, so Harris used him for purchase. He pulled himself up atop the blond man and onto the metal floor beyond.

He put his back to the wall of this small metal cabin, next to a doorway hatch. "Give up, Darig." His words came out in gasps as he struggled to gain control of his breath. "Or I'll kick the hell out of you and you'll end up a big red smear on a Neckerdam street."

The Changeling glared. "I am not afraid of death, bug. But I will make it worth something." He grabbed Harris' leg and pushed off, rolling out through the hole.

Harris frantically gripped the lip of the hatch beside him. The Changeling's weight yanked at him, threatened to tear him free; the impact stretched him taut. Another second and he'd slide out the hole, paired with Darig in a skydive to death.

With his free leg, he kicked Darig. He felt the kick land . . . and suddenly there was no more weight on his leg. Harris lay exhausted, gasping, and pulled himself back into the relative safety of the bomb bay.

Duncan flipped his talk-box from empty room to empty room. The only scene that told him anything was that of the hangar, where members of the Novimagos Guard collected his men. He knew his radio transmissions were compromised; he'd heard someone call a testing pattern over his radio on the laboratory squad's frequency.

The grimworlder signal on his tracer was much reduced. Joseph had to have killed most of the grimworlders. Still, two signals remained, one back at the Monarch Building and one . . .

Here. He scowled at the little screen. One of the grimworlders had to be keeping up with the liftship, either on the ground or in the rotorkite he'd heard.

The view on his talk-box flickered and was suddenly gone, replaced by the face of Gaby Donohue. She was dressed in archaic fashion and her hair was much longer than the last time he'd seen her.

"Goodlady Donohue. What an unexpected surprise. I see Joseph hasn't gotten to you yet."

"Joseph's my friend, Duncan."

"Not anymore. He's already killed Harris Greene. He'll be coming for you and Doc soon."

He saw her turn pale. He enjoyed giving people bad news. Their reactions were usually memorable.

Her voice was faint. "You're lying."

"I have no reason to lie."

Her breathing became shallow. He thought he could see hatred struggling with despair within her.

One of them won, but he wasn't sure which. She leaned forward. Her voice was a whisper: "Duncan, there's something I've got to know."

He leaned forward to catch her words. "What's that?"

"Are you Doc's son? Duncan MaqqRee?"

He smiled. "I'm afraid so. A word of advice that will do *you* no good: Some fathers think they can dictate their children's lives forever. Why do you ask?"

"Just curious," she said; her voice was even quieter; he leaned still closer.

Then she opened her mouth and screamed.

Gaby Donohue's image exploded out at Duncan. He felt something sharp tear at his face. Then pain, worse than any he'd known in twice ten years. He reeled away from it and went off balance. His toppling chair carried him to the floor. "Gods!"

He couldn't open his eyes. Things tore when he tried to do that. He raised his hands to them, encountered flesh and blood and sharp edges. "Captain!"

No answer. There were distant cries, a faraway roaring that began to grow louder.

Captain Walbert stood alone at the wheel; with all his men assigned to other tasks or left behind in the Monarch Building, he had to fly his ship practically single-handed. But that wasn't why his back and shoulders were locked with tension. No, that was the fault of Duncan Blackletter, with his unreasonable orders and anger spewing across the talk-box every few beats. It could only be moments before some new offense would issue from the screen—

He was right, after a fashion. He heard a scream from the talk-box behind him and it burst, raining sparks and debris all over his back.

The crewman at the bow gun fired again, trying to put his stream of tracers onto the rotorkite sinking away from the liftship. The rotorkite was a difficult target, in spite of the plume of smoke that was already billowing from its engine compartment.

He heard a shriek beside him, an odd noise to come from the talk-box the old sodder had had installed so the liftship would be "modern." Then the talk-box exploded. He saw glass and fire rain down through the hatch into the liftship interior.

Fire—

The talk-box in the rotorkite's cockpit panel burst, raining hot bits of glass and wire all over Noriko. She jerked in surprise. The rotorkite veered, but she kept control, getting far enough away that the liftship's guns would no longer pose a threat to her.

She looked back at *Storm Cloud* and saw it. A glow, golden-yellow, shone through the liftship's skin toward the bow, illuminating the ship's metal skeleton from within. The skin there began to char black.

Doc paused on the catwalk running down the center of the *Storm Cloud*'s interior. He took his bearings. Directly above, crewmen descended toward him along access ladders, their feet in felt boots. Below, blue-uniformed officers ascended toward him. None would shoot at him, nor he at them, with giant envelopes of hydrogen surrounding them. Forty feet below was the access shaft down to the liftship's gondola.

Then he saw fire blossom above, toward the bow.

He leaped over the catwalk rail and dropped past the men below, catching one crossbeam twenty feet down, stopping his plummet through sheer grace and strength; the impact wrenched his shoulder and he felt the flesh of his arm sear where it came into contact with steel. Then he dropped again, slowed himself by grabbing a beam ten feet above the shaft, and hit the catwalk beside the access shaft. He could already feel the heat from the wave of fire advancing toward him, and the men above were yelling. He swung into the shaft and slid down the length of the metal ladder into the gondola.

Above were the roar of fire and the screams of the men caught in it. His arms trembled from iron poisoning.

He stood in the vehicle's bomb bay. He saw the hatch leading into a room forward, another leading aft, open doors showing the buildings of Neckerdam below. And Harris Greene, panting, stood in the forward doorway.

"Fancy meeting you here," said Harris.

"I'll look aft, you look forward," Doc said. "Don't waste time. We're on fire."

"Good to see you, too." Harris went forward.

The third door Doc opened belonged to Duncan.

His withered, ancient son lay bleeding on the floor. Doc saw the ruin of the man's eyes and winced in sympathy.

For a moment he was awash in memories. Dierdriu smiling at their baby boy as she nursed him. Finding the body of the child Duncan strangled the morning he left home forever. The guardsman of Beldon telling him his wife had been found in the river. The body of Siobhan Damvert with her head twisted around nearly backwards and her eyes staring sightlessly.

Doc tried to harden himself against what had to happen now. And, just as it had been twenty years ago, he could not.

Duncan moved feebly, hearing him. "Captain?"

"No."

"Desmond." Duncan shrank away from him, drawing back against the wall of his cabin. "Father. Don't kill me."

Doc felt something break in his heart. "I'm sorry, Duncan. Gaols cannot hold you. If you do not die now, someone else will die because of you." He crossed the cabin, knelt before his boy, and drew his pistol. He saw his hand shake. His head felt light as once more the decision to do what he had to do threatened to overwhelm him.

Duncan brushed his leg against Doc's.

Doc saw a flare of brightness as lightning leaped between them. He heard the unaimed gun fire in his hand, felt his muscles jerk as the electrical jolt coursed through him.

Then he knew nothing more.

Duncan heard Doc fly across the cabin, hurled by the force of the old devisement. Doc hit the wall with a shuddering impact. Duncan heard him slide to the floor and go still. Smelled the odor of charred flesh rising from him.

Imbecile, Duncan thought. *You didn't think I'd prepared myself after our last meeting? For years I've renewed that devisement each morning . . . and finally it has proved worth the effort.*

He straightened up, ignoring the pain in his eyes— the hurt and blindness would be gone once he passed some gold to very expensive doctors he knew. He groped around on his tabletop. *Now, where did I leave that knife?*

The gondola narrowed as Harris continued forward. The passageway passed between a small washroom starboard and a larger radio room port.

The next chamber was some sort of map room with windows to either side. Two long tables were laid out with maps and charts Harris didn't bother to look at. The hatch forward was open.

Harris stepped through into the control room, the forward end of the gondola. Windows all around provided a panoramic view of Neckerdam and the river immediately ahead. A large, impressively carved wooden wheel, a ship's wheel, was situated at the very front.

A uniformed man stood there, impassively guiding the airship on its course. He turned a little as Harris entered. He was bearded, looked sober and intelligent.

"Where's Duncan?" Harris asked.

"Aft," the captain replied. "Cabin Four."

"We're on fire."

"You think I don't know?" The man sagged just a little. "I'll be putting her into the river. I won't let her fall on the city. You have nothing to fear from me." He turned away.

Knife in hand, Duncan crawled up his father's body. Three cuts, he decided. A grimworld smiley-face. One blow each into Doc's eyes, then a sweet curve across his throat. It would be a charming way to remember the man; a pity he couldn't photograph the moment. Then, he'd make his way to the pilot room and find out just what was going on—

For the second time, someone entered his cabin without permission. "Captain?" he asked.

Harris stepped through the doorway and sidekicked. The blow caught Duncan in the sternum and threw him off Doc's body. Harris felt frail bones break under the blow.

Duncan, twisting in pain but not unconscious, crawled away from his enemy. There was hate as well as pain in his voice this time: "Who's there?"

Harris stared at the shriveled, bloody-faced thing in the corner. Every bit of him wanted to take another two steps and kick the life from Duncan Blackletter.

But Duncan had caught Doc in a trap. He might have others waiting. Harris wouldn't let Duncan win through a mistake. Even the delay it took to kill him might prove fatal.

He grabbed Doc beneath the arms, pulled him out into the passageway. Doc looked bad, with burns on his arm, smoke rising from his hair and clothes.

"Who is it?" Duncan asked, voice harsh yet quavering. "Talk to me, you wretch—"

Harris let go of Doc. He stepped back into the cabin and swung the door away from the wall. He struck an open-palm blow at the inside knob. The blow knocked it free. "Enjoy your ride," he said, his voice cold. Then he stepped out again and closed the door.

As he dragged Doc forward, he could feel the liftship tilting down at the bow; the angle increased, became troublesome even before he got into the bomb bay.

Smoke poured down from the access hatch; the air was hot and getting hotter. In a bare minute, he'd be burning. He heard pounding from the direction of Duncan's cabin. Pounding and shouting.

The gondola was only two or three hundred feet above the ground. Even as he watched, the liftship moved out over the river.

The gear in the bomb bay included a winch. But it was wound with cable and not rope—nothing he could tie around Doc.

With his knife, he cut free a piece of the rappelling line he'd climbed. He tied one end to a loop at the end of the winch cable, the other end to Doc. He hoped the decidedly non-Boy Scouts knots would hold. The skin on his back was blistering from heat before he was done.

"Captain?" he called.

"Not done yet," the man replied.

Harris shook his head. He gently levered Doc over the lip of the hole in the floor, keeping his grip on the rope, playing it out as carefully as he could; it still tore flesh of his palms as Doc descended.

A moment later, he threw the main lever on the winch, watched the motor turn and cable unspool; he grabbed the cable with both bloody hands, swung out over open space, and rode the cable down, Doc dangling a dozen feet below him.

The heat was scarcely better here. He glanced up, saw the entire surface of the liftship glowing gold and white, a cleansing fire that would burn the last of Duncan Blackletter's stain from this world.

Witnesses along Neckerdam's eastern shore and Pataqqsit's western saw the slate-gray airship sail majestically over the river. The golden glow brightened in the ship's bow, then swept toward the stern, making an oblong sun of the ship, eating through its rubberized cloth skin, twisting its metal skeleton with unimaginable heat.

Two men made it out of the liftship, descending by cable from the gondola; one towed the other away from the descending wreckage. When the gondola was a dozen yards from the water's surface, a third man, his back afire, leaped out through the forward windows.

The ship was completely consumed with fire as it touched down on the water. It rested there a long moment, burning, dying, then began its final descent to the bottom of the river.

Tugboats and Novimagos Guard rescue craft approached as close as they dared and picked up the survivors.

Gaby opened her eyes.

The room was dark, but not so dark that she couldn't recognize Harris' face above her own. Recognize the feel of him as he crushed her to him. She held on to him with fierce strength.

She was in her own room in the Monarch Building, more tired than she thought it was possible to feel, but not too tired to remember. "Doc?"

"He's a little burned, a little stiff. He'll be okay."

"The others?"

"Everybody's banged up some. Except Joseph. Joseph . . . didn't make it."

"Dammit." She was silent a long moment. "What about Duncan? And the Changeling?"

"Dead. Really, truly, dental-records-prove-it dead. They scraped Darig off a rooftop the day it happened, fished what's left of Duncan out of the river yesterday."

"*Yesterday*—"

"You've been asleep for a couple of days, baby. You wiped yourself out."

"Did Doc . . . " She forced herself to ask the question. "Did Doc have to kill him?"

"No. If anybody did . . . I did. And you did, with that marvelous stunt with the exploding talk-boxes. You blew out talk-boxes in the liftship, in the Monarch Building, and all over this part of Neckerdam." He smiled. "It sort of makes sense. Gaby Donohue, Programming Director. You beat him with TV."

EPILOGUE

The stoneware urn held a shovelful of clay. That was all of Joseph anyone had been able to recover.

As the priestess spoke about death and rebirth, summer and spring, crops and trees, Gaby placed a loaf of bread in the urn. Doc, leaning on the cane he'd be using for a few weeks, added a leather pouch of salt.

Alastair contemplated a glass flask of fine uisge before placing it down in the clay. Noriko followed suit with a cup and a plate of fine copper, a fork and a knife of silver. Ixyail added the pouch packed with clothes and coin.

Last in the ceremony, Harris placed the tiny jeweled axe, symbol of warriors and warrior-kings, into the urn. He stepped away and linked arms with Gaby.

The six of them drew away from the graveside. Workers of the cemetery capped the urn, then carefully lifted it and lowered it into the grave.

Harris looked out over the people attending the graveside ceremony. Associates of the Sidhe Foundation. Sturdy construction workers, Joseph's fellow workers, uncomfortable in dress clothes. A detachment of Novimagos Guard in full uniform, ready to fire the salute for a man who had briefly been, by association with Doc, a guardsman. An interesting gathering.

"Harris," Gaby said.

He smiled at her. She was resplendent in a shimmering gown of red. He admired the funerary garb of the fair world. He felt foolish in his matching dress suit, but she'd said he was gorgeous and he didn't mind her lie. "What?"

"This is an interment, not a stakeout."

"Oh, that's right."

"So stop giving everybody the eye."

The priestess carefully poured a handful of grain into the grave. She withdrew. The guardsmen fired their volley. The men and women in attendance rose, freed from the obligation of ritual, and began talking to one another. Workmen shoveled dirt into the grave.

Harris drank in the details. Ladislas and Welthy, too hurt to attend, even after being tended by Alastair, would want to know everything. And Fergus, who was not so badly hurt but who felt unwanted around the associates—and, for the most part, was correct. "Doc."

"Yes?"

"What are you going to do about Fergus?"

"Just what I promised him. He did very well during Duncan's assault . . . but I cannot forget that he betrayed us."

"Oh, well." He didn't press Doc. The man had buried his son earlier today. He looked so glum, so inconsolable, it seemed unlikely that a smile would ever cross his face again.

Ixyail asked what Harris never would have dared to. "Doc, how did it happen?" Her voice was soft, full of sympathy; even her Castilian accent was fainter than usual.

Doc didn't pretend to misunderstand. "I'm not sure. I've never been sure. It might have been inheritance. I was pureblood, and pureblood Daoine Sidhe and their children are often tainted with madness. One of the prices we pay for being long-lived." He shook his head, a sorrowful gesture. "Dierdriu wasn't touched, just melancholy, a sadness I always thought I could end. But when Duncan began to make his name, she killed herself from grief. From shame.

"Duncan always said it was my fault he became what he was. Restrictions he abhorred. Rules he could not abide. His hatred of guidance became hatred of any restriction, any limit. Understanding his mother's sadness taught him to manipulate others through their weaknesses."

Ish asked, "Are you ever going to try again?"

He didn't answer.

Gaby said, "You didn't kill him, you know."

He managed a bare smile. "You went to some considerable effort to make sure of that. I appreciate your intent. Have you two thought about my offer?"

"To stay on as associates?" Harris looked speculatively at Gaby. She smiled back. "We want to," he said. "But we don't know if we'll have time. There are a lot of things we want to do."

"Study my Gift," Gaby said.

"Invent martial arts movies for the fair world."

"Learn to fly."

"Teach tae kwon do."

"Get married."

"Have kids, God help us."

"Go back to the grim world every so often."

"Think we can do all that and still be Foundation associates?" Harris asked.

Doc blinked owlishly at them. "Please try. And if you succeed—" he turned his gaze on Ish "—tell me how you do it. I might need to know."

Both women turned their smiles on him. "It's a deal," they said.

ANNOUNCING:
THE ARCANA

A GROUNDBREAKING NEW SERIES FROM THE BESTSELLING AUTHOR OF *LION OF IRELAND*!

They are **The Arcana.** Collectively, they are the ultimate symbols of cosmic power. Millennia ago they were the treasures of the gods of creation, honored and cherished in four great cities since swept away by the rivers of time. The Spear of Light came from Gorias. The city of Falias contained The Stone of Destiny. From Murias came The Cup of Blood. The Sword of Flame was enshrined within Findias.

Properly used by an adept, these four together have the power to create worlds—or to destroy them. The three volumes of The Arcana by Morgan Llywelyn and Michael Scott tell of the desperate quest to rediscover the ancient tools of creation and restore a world that lives only in memory. A world everyone longs to return to, in their most secret dreams. The lost world at the outermost limit of human desire.

Book One tells the story of Silverhand, he who was foretold, he who is destined to save the world from Chaos and begin the long climb back to the world that lives within us all.

Silverhand is the first novel in an extraordinary ground-breaking fantasy world created by a multiple New York Times bestselling author. *Silverhand*, **Book I of** *The Arcana*, represents her first foray into pure fantasy, and in it Llywelyn makes it obvious that she needed a larger framework than that provided by the Celtic fantasy genre, even though her contributions to that genre have made her one of the two or three most successful fantasy authors that we have ever seen.

———————————

"One of my all-time favorite authors."
—**Jude Devereaux**

"[*Red Branch*:] One of the most powerful stories I have ever read....The result is a total captivation of the reader into a landscape that is vivid, vital and victorious even in tragedy...."
—**Anne McCaffrey**

WATCH FOR VOLUME ONE OF

THE ARCANA:

SILVERHAND

COMING IN HARDCOVER
APRIL 1995
FROM BAEN BOOKS

0-671-87652-X ◆ 480 pages ◆ $22.00

GRAND ADVENTURE

IN GAME-BASED UNIVERSES

With these exciting novels set
in bestselling game universes,
Baen brings you synchronicity at its
best. We believe that familiarity with
either the novel or the game will
intensify enjoyment of the other.
All novels are the only authorized
fiction based on these games and
are published by permission.

THE BARD'S TALE™

(continued)

WING COMMANDER™

The computer game which supplies the background world for these novels is a current all-time bestseller. Fly with the best the Confederation of Earth has to offer against the ferocious catlike alien Kilrathi!

Freedom Flight   0-671-72145-3 ◆ $4.99 ☐
Mercedes Lackey & Ellen Guon

End Run   0-671-72200-X ◆ $4.99 ☐
Christopher Stasheff & William R. Forstchen

Fleet Action   0-671-72211-5 ◆ $4.99 ☐
William R. Forstchen

Heart of the Tiger   0-671-87653-8 ◆ $5.99 ☐
William R. Forstchen & Andrew Keith

STARFIRE™

See this strategy game come to explosive life in these grand space adventures!

Insurrection   0-671-72024-4 ◆ $5.99 ☐
David Weber & Steve White

Crusade   0-671-72111-9 ◆ $4.99 ☐
David Weber & Steve White

- -

If not available through your local bookstore, send this coupon and a check or money order for the cover price(s) to Baen Books, Dept. BA, P.O. Box 1403, Riverdale, NY 10471. Delivery can take up to ten weeks.

NAME: _____

ADDRESS: _____

_____

_____

I have enclosed a check or money order for $ _____

To Read About Great Characters Having Incredible Adventures You Should Try 🖋 🖋 🖋

BAEN

IF YOU LIKE...	YOU SHOULD TRY...
Anne McCaffrey . . .	Elizabeth Moon Mercedes Lackey Margaret Ball
Marion Zimmer Bradley . . .	Mercedes Lackey Holly Lisle
Mercedes Lackey . . .	Holly Lisle Josepha Sherman Ellen Guon Mark Shepherd
J.R.R. Tolkien . . .	Elizabeth Moon
David Drake . . .	David Weber S.M. Stirling
Robert A. Heinlein . . .	Jerry Pournelle Lois McMaster Bujold